Khushwant Singh was born in 1915 in [...], [...]jab. Today he is India's best-known columnist and journalist. Among the works he has published are a classic two-volume history of the Sikhs, several novels (the best known of which are *Delhi, Train to Pakistan* and *The Company of Women)* and a number of translated works and non-fiction books on Delhi, nature and current affairs. His autobiography, *Truth, Love and a Little Malice* was published in 2002.

*

Bhisham Sahni was born in 1915 in Rawalpindi (now in Pakistan). His first collection of short stories, *Bhagya Rekha* (Line of Fate) was published in 1953. Since then he has published five novels, eight collections of short stories, three plays and a biography of his late brother, the actor and writer Balraj Sahni. Many of his books have been translated into various languages. His most famous novel, *Tamas*, was awarded the Sahitya Akademi Award in 1975.

*

Saadat Hasan Manto widely regarded as the world's greatest short story writer in Urdu was born on 11 May 1912 at Samrala in Punjab's Ludhiana district. In a literary, journalistic, radio-scripting and film-writing career spread over more than two decades, he produced around 250 stories, scores of plays and a large number of essays, many of them, controversial. He was tried for obscenity half a dozen times, thrice before and thrice after Independence. Two of his greatest stories—'Colder than Ice' and 'The Return'—were among works considered 'obscene' by the Pakistani censors. He also wrote over a dozen films, including *Eight Days, Chal Chal Re Naujawan* and *Mirza Ghalib*. The last one was shot after Manto moved to Pakistan in January 1948. Manto's greatest work was produced in the last seven years of his life, a time of great financial and emotional hardship for him. He died several months short of his forty-third birthday in January 1955 in Lahore.

MEMORIES OF MADNESS

Train to Pakistan
Khushwant Singh

Tamas
Bhisham Sahni

Stories
Saadat Hasan Manto

PENGUIN BOOKS

Penguin Books India (P) Ltd., 11 Community Centre, Panchsheel Park, New Delhi 110 017, India
Penguin Books Ltd., 80 Strand, London WC2R 0RL, UK
Penguin Putnam Inc., 375 Hudson Street, New York, NY 10014, USA
Penguin Books Australia Ltd., 250 Camberwell Road, Camberwell, Victoria 3124, Australia
Penguin Books Canada Ltd., 10 Alcorn Avenue, Suite 300, Toronto, Ontario M4V 3B2, Canada
Penguin Books (NZ) Ltd., Cnr Rosedale and Airborne Roads, Albany, Auckland, New Zealand

First published by Penguin Books India 2002
This anthology copyright © Penguin Books India 2002

Train to Pakistan copyright © Ravi Dayal publisher

Tamas copyright © Bhisham Sahni

'Colder than Ice', 'The Return', 'Mozail', 'The Assignment', 'The Last Salute', 'Toba Tek Singh' first published in *Kingdom's End and Other Stories* by Saadat Hasan Manto (translated by Khalid Hasan) copyright © Verso Books 1987

'Mishtake', 'A Tale of 1947', 'Bitter Harvest', 'A Believer's Version', 'Wages' first published in *Partition: Sketches and Stories* by Saadat Hasan Manto (translated by Khalid Hasan) copyright © Penguin Books India 1991

10 9 8 7 6 5 4 3 2 1

Typeset in Sabon by Mantra Virtual Services, New Delhi
Printed at Repro India Ltd., Navi Mumbai

'He is not dead, there is still some life left in him.'
'I can't. I am really exhausted.'
— Saadat Hasan Manto

Contents

TRAIN TO PAKISTAN

KHUSHWANT SINGH

Dacoity

The summer of 1947 was not like other Indian summers. Even the weather had a different feel in India that year. It was hotter than usual, and drier and dustier. And the summer was longer. No one could remember when the monsoon had been so late. For weeks, the sparse clouds cast only shadows. There was no rain. People began to say that God was punishing them for their sins.

Some of them had good reason to feel that they had sinned. The summer before, communal riots, precipitated by reports of the proposed division of the country into a Hindu India and a Muslim Pakistan, had broken out in Calcutta, and within a few months the death toll had mounted to several thousand. Muslims said the Hindus had planned and started the killing. According to the Hindus, the Muslims were to blame. The fact is, both sides killed. Both shot and stabbed and speared and clubbed. Both tortured. Both raped. From Calcutta, the riots spread north and east and west: to Noakhali in East Bengal, where Muslims massacred Hindus; to Bihar, where Hindus massacred Muslims. Mullahs roamed the Punjab and the Frontier Province with boxes of human skulls said to be those of Muslims killed in Bihar. Hundreds of thousands of Hindus and Sikhs who had lived for centuries on the Northwest Frontier abandoned their homes and fled towards the protection of the predominantly Sikh and Hindu communities in the east. They travelled on foot, in bullock carts, crammed into lorries, clinging to the sides and roofs of trains. Along the way—at fords, at crossroads, at railroad stations—

they collided with panicky swarms of Muslims fleeing to safety in the west. The riots had become a rout. By the summer of 1947, when the creation of the new state of Pakistan was formally announced, ten million people—Muslims and Hindus and Sikhs—were in flight. By the time the monsoon broke, almost a million of them were dead, and all of northern India was in arms, in terror, or in hiding. The only remaining oases of peace were a scatter of little villages lost in the remote reaches of the frontier. One of these villages was Mano Majra.

Mano Majra is a tiny place. It has only three brick buildings, one of which is the home of the moneylender Lala Ram Lal. The other two are the Sikh temple and the mosque. The three brick buildings enclose a triangular common with a large peepul tree in the middle. The rest of the village is a cluster of flat-roofed mud huts and low-walled courtyards, which front on narrow lanes that radiate from the centre. Soon the lanes dwindle into footpaths and get lost in the surrounding fields. At the western end of the village there is a pond ringed round by keekar trees. There are only about seventy families in Mano Majra, and Lala Ram Lal's is the only Hindu family. The others are Sikhs or Muslims, about equal in number. The Sikhs own all the land around the village; the Muslims are tenants and share the tilling with the owners. There are a few families of sweepers whose religion is uncertain. The Muslims claim them as their own, yet when American missionaries visit Mano Majra the sweepers wear khaki sola topees and join their womenfolk in singing hymns to the accompaniment of a harmonium. Sometimes they visit the Sikh temple, too. But there is one object that all Mano Majrans—even Lala Ram Lal—venerate. This is a three-foot slab of sandstone that stands upright under a keekar tree beside the pond. It is the local deity, the *deo* to which all the villagers—Hindu, Sikh, Muslim or pseudo-Christian— repair secretly whenever they are in a special need of blessing.

Although Mano Majra is said to be on the banks of the Sutlej River, it is actually half a mile away from it. In India villages cannot afford to be too close to the banks of rivers. Rivers change their moods with the seasons and alter their courses without warning. The Sutlej is the largest river in the Punjab. After the monsoon its waters rise and spread across its vast sandy bed, lapping high up the mud embankments on either side. It becomes an expanse of muddy turbulence more than a mile in breadth. When the flood subsides, the river breaks up into a thousand shallow streams that wind sluggishly between little marshy islands. About a mile north of Mano Majra the Sutlej is spanned by a railroad bridge. It is a magnificent bridge—its eighteen enormous spans sweep like waves from one pier to another, and at each end of it there is a stone embankment to buttress the railway line. On the eastern end the embankment extends all the way to the village railroad station.

Mano Majra has always been known for its railway station. Since the bridge has only one track, the station has several sidings where less important trains can wait, to make way for the more important.

A small colony of shopkeepers and hawkers has grown up around the station to supply travellers with food, betel leaves, cigarettes, tea, biscuits and sweetmeats. This gives the station an appearance of constant activity and its staff a somewhat exaggerated sense of importance. Actually the stationmaster himself sells tickets through the pigeonhole in his office, collects them at the exit beside the door, and sends and receives messages over the telegraph ticker on the table. When there are people to notice him, he comes out on the platform and waves a green flag for trains which do not stop. His only assistant manipulates the levers in the glass cabin on the platform which control the signals on either side, and helps shunting engines by changing hand points on the tracks to get them onto the sidings. In the evenings, he lights the long line of lamps on the platform. He takes heavy aluminum lamps to the signals and sticks them in the clamps behind the red and green glass. In the mornings, he brings them back and puts out the lights on the platform.

Not many trains stop at Mano Majra. Express trains do not stop at all. Of the many slow passenger trains, only two, one

from Delhi to Lahore in the mornings and the other from Lahore
to Delhi in the evenings, are scheduled to stop for a few minutes.
The others stop only when they are held up. The only regular
customers are the goods trains. Although Mano Majra seldom
has any goods to send or receive, its station sidings are usually
occupied by long rows of wagons. Each passing goods train
spends hours shedding wagons and collecting others. After dark,
when the countryside is steeped in silence, the whistling and
puffing of engines, the banging of buffers, and the clanking of
iron couplings can be heard all through the night.

All this has made Mano Majra very conscious of trains. Before
daybreak, the mail train rushes through on its way to Lahore,
and as it approaches the bridge, the driver invariably blows two
long blasts on the whistle. In an instant, all Mano Majra comes
awake. Crows begin to caw in the keekar trees. Bats fly back in
long silent relays and begin to quarrel for their perches in the
peepul. The mullah at the mosque knows that it is time for the
morning prayer. He has a quick wash, stands facing west towards
Mecca and with his fingers in his ears cries in long sonorous
notes, '*Allah-o-Akbar*'. The priest at the Sikh temple lies in bed
till the mullah has called. Then he too gets up, draws a bucket of
water from the well in the temple courtyard, pours it over himself,
and intones his prayer in monotonous singsong to the sound of
splashing water.

By the time the 10:30 morning passenger train from Delhi
comes in, life in Mano Majra has settled down to its dull daily
routine. Men are in the fields. Women are busy with their daily
chores. Children are out grazing cattle by the river. Persian wheels
squeak and groan as bullocks go round and round, prodded on
by curses and the jabs of goads in their hindquarters. Sparrows
fly about the roofs, trailing straw in their beaks. Pye-dogs seek
the shade of the long mud walls. Bats settle their arguments, fold
their wings, and suspend themselves in sleep.

As the midday express goes by, Mano Majra stops to rest.
Men and children come home for dinner and the siesta hour.
When they have eaten, the men gather in the shade of the peepul

tree and sit on the wooden platforms and talk and doze. Boys ride their buffaloes into the pond, jump off their backs, and splash about in the muddy water. Girls play under the trees. Women rub clarified butter into each other's hair, pick lice from their children's heads, and discuss births, marriages and deaths.

When the evening passenger from Lahore comes in, everyone gets to work again. The cattle are rounded up and driven back home to be milked and locked in for the night. The women cook the evening meal. Then the families foregather on their rooftops where most of them sleep during the summer. Sitting on their charpais, they eat their supper of vegetables and chapattis and sip hot creamy milk out of large copper tumblers and idle away the time until the signal for sleep. When the goods train steams in, they say to each other, 'There is the goods train.' It is like saying goodnight. The mullah again calls the faithful to prayer by shouting at the top of his voice, 'God is great.' The faithful nod their amens from their rooftops. The Sikh priest murmurs the evening prayer to a semicircle of drowsy old men and women. Crows caw softly from the keekar trees. Little bats go flitting about in the dusk and large ones soar with slow graceful sweeps. The goods train takes a long time at the station, with the engine running up and down the sidings exchanging wagons. By the time it leaves, the children are asleep. The older people wait for its rumble over the bridge to lull them to slumber. Then life in Mano Majra is stilled, save for the dogs barking at the trains that pass in the night.

It had always been so, until the summer of 1947.

One heavy night in August of that year, five men emerged from a keekar grove not far from Mano Majra, and moved silently towards the river. They were dacoits, or professional robbers, and all but one of them were armed. Two of the armed men carried spears. The others had carbines slung over their shoulders. The fifth man carried a chromium-plated electric torch. When they came to the embankment, he flicked the torch alight. Then he grunted and snapped it off.

'We will wait here,' he said.

He dropped down on the sand. The others crouched around him, leaning on their weapons. The man with the torch looked at one of the spearmen.

'You have the bangles for Jugga?'

'Yes. A dozen of red and blue glass. They would please any village wench.'

'They will not please Jugga,' one of the gunmen said.

The leader laughed. He tossed the torch in the air and caught it. He laughed again and raised the torch to his mouth and touched the switch. His cheeks glowed pink from the light inside.

'Jugga could give the bangles to that weaver's daughter of his,' the other spearman said. 'They would look well with those large gazelle eyes and the little mango breasts. What is her name?'

The leader turned off the torch and took it from his mouth. 'Nooran,' he said.

'Aho,' the spearman said. 'Nooran. Did you see her at the spring fair? Did you see that tight shirt showing off her breasts and the bells tinkling in her plaits and the swish-swish of silk? Hai!'

'Hai!' the spearman with the bangles cried. 'Hai! Hai!'

'She must give Jugga a good time,' said the gunman who had not yet spoken. 'During the day, she looks so innocent you would think she had not shed her milk teeth.' He sighed. 'But at night, she puts black antimony in her eyes.'

'Antimony is good for the eyes,' one of the others said. 'It is cooling.'

'It is good for other people's eyes as well,' the gunman said.

'And cooling to their passions, too.'

'Jugga?' the leader said.

The others laughed. One of them suddenly sat erect.

'Listen!' he said. 'There is the goods train.'

The others stopped laughing. They all listened in silence to the approaching train. It came to a halt with a rumble, and the wagons groaned and creaked. After a time, the engine could be heard moving up and down, releasing wagons. There were loud explosions as the released wagons collided with the ones on the sidings. The engine chuffed back to the train.

'It is time to call on Ram Lal,' the leader said, and got to his feet.

His companions rose and brushed the sand off their clothes. They formed a line with their hands joined in prayer. One of the gunmen stepped in front and began to mumble. When he stopped, they all went down on their knees and rubbed their foreheads on the ground. Then they stood up and drew the loose ends of their turbans across their faces. Only their eyes were uncovered. The engine gave two long whistle blasts, and the train moved off towards the bridge.

'Now,' the leader said.

The others followed him up the embankment and across the fields. By the time the train had reached the bridge, the men had skirted the pond and were walking up a lane that led to the centre of the village. They came to the house of Lala Ram Lal. The leader nodded to one of the gunmen. He stepped forward and began to pound on the door with the butt of his gun.

'Oi!' he shouted. 'Lala!'

There was no reply. Village dogs gathered round the visitors and began to bark. One of the men hit a dog with the flat side of his spear blade. Another fired his gun into the air. The dogs ran away whimpering and started to bark louder from a safer distance.

The men began to hammer at the door with their weapons. One struck it with his spear which went through to the other side.

'Open, you son of fornication, or we will kill the lot of you,' he shouted.

A woman's voice answered. 'Who is it who calls at this hour? Lalaji has gone to the city.'

'Open and we will tell you who we are or we will smash the door,' the leader said.

'I tell you Lalaji is not in. He has taken the keys with him. We have nothing in the house.'

The men put their shoulders to the door, pressed, pulled back and butted into it like battering-rams. The wooden bolt on the other side cracked and the doors flew open. One of the men with a gun waited at the door; the other four went in. In one corner of the room two women sat crouching. A boy of seven with large black eyes clung to the older of the two.

'In the name of God, take what we have, all our jewellery, everything,' implored the older woman. She held out a handful of gold and silver bracelets, anklets and earrings.

One of the men snatched them from her hands.

'Where is the Lala?'

'I swear by the Guru he is out. You have taken all we have. Lalaji has nothing more to give.'

In the courtyard four beds were laid out in a row.

The man with the carbine tore the little boy from his grandmother's lap and held the muzzle of the gun to the child's face. The women fell at his feet imploring.

'Do not kill, brother. In the name of the Guru—don't.'

The gunman kicked the women away.

'Where is you father?'

The boy shook with fear and stuttered, 'Upstairs.'

The gunman thrust the boy back into the woman's lap, and the men went out into the courtyard and climbed the staircase. There was only one room on the roof. Without pausing they put their shoulders to the door and pushed it in, tearing it off its hinges. The room was cluttered with steel trunks piled one on top of the other. There were two charpais with several quilts rolled up on them. The white beam of the torch searched the room and caught the moneylender crouching under one of the charpais.

'In the name of the Guru, the Lalaji is out,' one of the men said, mimicking the woman's voice. He dragged Ram Lal out by his legs.

The leader slapped the moneylender with the back of his hand. 'Is this the way you treat your guests? We come and you hide under a charpai.'

Ram Lal covered his face with his arms and began to whimper.

'Where are the keys of the safe?' asked the leader, kicking him on the behind.

'You can take all—jewellery, cash, account books. Don't kill anyone,' implored the moneylender, grasping the leader's feet with both his hands.

'Where are the keys of your safe?' repeated the leader. He knocked the moneylender sprawling on the floor. Ram Lal sat up, shaking with fear.

He produced a wad of notes from his pocket. 'Take these,' he said, distributing the money to the five men. 'It is all I have in the house. All is yours.'

'Where are the keys of your safe?'

'There is nothing left in the safe; only my account books. I have given you all I have. All I have is yours. In the name of the Guru, let me be.' Ram Lal clasped the leader's legs above the knees and began to sob. 'In the name of the Guru! In the name of the Guru!'

One of the men tore the moneylender away from the leader and hit him full in the face with the butt of his gun.

'Hai!' yelled Ram Lal at the top of his voice, and spat out blood.

The women in the courtyard heard the cry and started shrieking, *'Dakoo! Dakoo!'*

The dogs barked all round. But not a villager stirred from his house.

On the roof of his house, the moneylender was beaten with butts of guns and spear handles and kicked and punched. He sat on his haunches, crying and spitting blood. Two of his teeth were smashed. But he would not hand over the keys of his safe. In sheer exasperation, one of the men lunged at the crouching figure with his spear. Ram Lal uttered a loud yell and collapsed on the floor with blood spurting from his belly. The men came out. One of them fired two shots in the air. Women stopped wailing. Dogs stopped barking. The village was silenced.

The dacoits jumped off the roof to the lane below. They yelled defiance to the world as they went out towards the river.

'Come!' they yelled. 'Come out, if you have the courage! Come out, if you want your mothers and sisters raped! Come out, brave men!'

No one answered them. There was not a sound in Mano Majra. The men continued along the lane, shouting and laughing, until they came to a small hut on the edge of the village. The leader halted and motioned to one of the spearmen.

'This is the house of the great Jugga,' he said. 'Do not forget our gift. Give him his bangles.'

The spearman dug a package from his clothes and tossed it over the wall. There was a muffled sound of breaking glass in the courtyard.

'O Juggia,' he called in a falsetto voice, 'Juggia!' He winked at his companions. 'Wear these bangles, Juggia. Wear these bangles and put henna on your palms.'

'Or give them to the weaver's daughter,' one of the gunmen yelled.

'Hai,' the others shouted. They smacked their lips, making the sound of long, lecherous kisses. 'Hai! Hai!'

They moved on down the lane, still laughing and blowing kisses, towards the river. Juggut Singh did not answer them. He didn't hear them. He was not at home.

Juggut Singh had been gone from his home about an hour. He had only left when the sound of the night goods train told him that it would now be safe to go. For him, as for the dacoits, the arrival of the train that night was a signal. At the first distant rumble, he slipped quietly off his charpai and picked up his turban and wrapped it round his head. Then he tiptoed across the courtyard to the haystack and fished out a spear. He tiptoed back to his bed, picked up his shoes, and crept towards the door.

'Where are you going?'

Juggut Singh stopped. It was his mother.

'To the fields,' he said. 'Last night wild pigs did a lot of damage.'

'Pigs!' his mother said. 'Don't try to be clever. Have you forgotten already that you are on probation—that it is forbidden for you to leave the village after sunset? And with a spear! Enemies will see you. They will report you. They will send you back to jail.' Her voice rose to a wail. 'Then who will look after the crops and the cattle?'

'I will be back soon,' Juggut Singh said. 'There is nothing to worry about. Everyone in the village is asleep.'

'No,' his mother said. She wailed again.

'Shut up,' he said. 'It is you who will wake the neighbours. Be quiet and there will be no trouble.'

'Go! Go wherever you want to go. If you want to jump in a well, jump. If you want to hang like your father, go and hang. It is my lot to weep. My kismet,' she added, slapping her forehead, 'it is all written there.'

Juggut Singh opened the door and looked on both sides. There was no one about. He walked along the walls till he got to the end of the lane near the pond. He could see the grey forms of a couple of adjutant storks slowly pacing up and down in the mud looking for frogs. They paused in their search. Juggut Singh stood still against the wall till the storks were reassured, then went off the footpath across the fields towards the river. He crossed the dry sand bed till he got to the stream. He stuck his spear in the ground with the blade pointing upward, then stretched out on the sand. He lay on his back and gazed at the stars. A meteor shot across the Milky Way, trailing a silver path down the blue-black sky. Suddenly a hand was on his eyes.

'Guess who?'

Juggut Singh stretched out his hands over his head and behind him, groping; the girl dodged them. Juggut Singh started with the hand on his eyes and felt his way up from the arm to the shoulder and then on to the face. He caressed her cheeks, eyes and nose that his hands knew so well. He tried to play with her lips to induce them to kiss his fingers. The girl opened her mouth and bit him fiercely. Juggut Singh jerked his hand away. With a quick movement he caught the girl's head in both his hands and brought her face over to his. Then he slipped his arms under her waist and hoisted her into the air above him with her arms and legs kicking about like a crab. He turned her about till his arms ached. He brought her down flat upon him limb to limb.

The girl slapped him on the face.

'You put your hands on the person of a strange woman. Have you no mother or sister in your home? Have you no shame? No wonder the police have got you on their register as a bad character. I will also tell the Inspector sahib that you are a badmash.'

'I am only badmash with you, Nooro. We should both be locked up in the same cell.'

'You have learned to talk too much. I will have to look for another man.'

Juggut Singh crossed his arms behind the girl's back and crushed her till she could not talk or breathe. Every time she started to speak he tightened his arms round her and her words got stuck in her throat. She gave up and put her exhausted face against his. He laid her beside him with her head nestling in the hollow of his left arm. With his right hand he stroked her hair and face.

The goods train engine whistled twice and with a lot of groaning and creaking began to puff its way towards the bridge. The storks flew up from the pond with shrill cries of 'kraak, kraak' and came towards the river. From the river they flew back to the pond, calling alternately long after the train had gone over the bridge and its puff-puffs had died into silence.

Juggut Singh's caresses became lustful. His hand strayed from the girl's face to her breasts and her waist. She caught it and put it back on her face. His breathing became slow and sensuous. His hand wandered again and brushed against her breasts as if by mistake. The girl slapped it and put it away. Juggut Singh stretched his left arm that lay under the girl's head and caught her reproving hand. Her other arm was already under him. She was defenceless.

'No! No! No! Let go my hand! No! I will never speak to you

again.' She shook her head violently from side to side, trying to avoid his hungry mouth.

Juggut Singh slipped his hand inside her shirt and felt the contours of her unguarded breasts. They became taut. The nipples became hard and leathery. His rough hands gently moved up and down from her breasts to her navel. The skin on her belly came up in goose flesh.

The girl continued to wriggle and protest.

'No! No! No! Please. May Allah's curse fall on you. Let go my hand. I will never meet you again if you behave like this.'

Juggut Singh's searching hand found one end of the cord of her trousers. He pulled it with a jerk.

'No,' cried the girl hoarsely.

A shot rang through the night. The storks flew up from the pond calling to each other. Crows started cawing in the keekar trees. Juggut Singh paused and looked up into the darkness towards the village. The girl quietly extricated herself from his hold and adjusted her dress. The crows settled back on the trees. The storks flew away across the river. Only the dogs barked.

'It sounded like a gunshot,' she said nervously, trying to keep Juggut Singh from renewing his love-making. 'Wasn't it from the village?'

'I don't know. Why are you trying to run away? It is all quiet now.' Juggut Singh pulled her down beside him.

'This is no time for jesting. There is murder in the village. My father will get up and want to know where I have gone. I must get back at once.'

'No, you will not. I won't let you. You can say you were with a girl friend.'

'Don't talk like a stupid peasant. How . . .' Juggut Singh shut her mouth with his. He bore upon her with his enormous weight. Before she could free her arms he ripped open the cord of her trousers once again.

'Let me go. Let me . . .'

She could not struggle against Juggut Singh's brute force. She did not particularly want to. Her world was narrowed to the rhythmic sound of breathing and the warm smell of dusky skins raised to fever heat. His lips slubbered over her eyes and cheeks. His tongue sought the inside of her ears. In a state of frenzy she dug her nails into his thinly bearded cheeks and bit his nose. The stars above her went into a mad whirl and then came back to their places like a merry-go-round slowly coming to a stop. Life came back to its cooler, lower level. She felt the dead weight of the lifeless man; the sand gritting in her hair; the breeze trespassing on her naked limbs; the censorious stare of the myriads of stars. She pushed Juggut Singh away. He lay down beside her.

'That is all you want. And you get it. You are just a peasant. Always wanting to sow your seed. Even if the world were going to hell you would want to do that. Even when guns are being fired in the village. Wouldn't you?' she nagged.

'Nobody is firing any guns. Just your imagination,' answered Juggut Singh wearily, without looking at her.

Faint cries of wailing wafted across to the riverside. The couple sat up to listen. Two shots rang out in quick succession. The crows flew out of the keekars, cawing furiously.

The girl began to cry.

'Something is happening in the village. My father will wake up and know I have gone out. He will kill me.'

Juggut Singh was not listening to her. He did not know what to do. If his absence from the village was discovered, he would be in trouble with the police. That did not bother him as much as the trouble the girl would be in. She might not come again. She was saying so: 'I will never come to see you again. If Allah forgives me this time, I will never do it again.'

'Will you shut up or do I have to smack your face?'

The girl began to sob. She found it hard to believe this was the same man who had been making love to her a moment ago.

'Quiet! There is someone coming,' whispered Juggut Singh, putting his heavy hand on her mouth.

The couple lay still, peering into the dark. The five men carrying guns and spears passed within a few yards of them. They had uncovered their faces and were talking.

'Dakoo! Do you know them?' the girl asked in a whisper.

'Yes,' Juggut said, 'The one with the torch is Malli.' His face went tight. 'That incestuous lover of his sister! I've told him a thousand times this was no time for dacoities. And now he has brought his gang to my village! I will settle this with him.'

The dacoits went up to the river and then downstream towards the ford a couple of miles to the south. A pair of lapwings pierced the still night with startled cries: Teet-tittee-tittee-whoot, tee-tee-whoot, tee-tee-whoot, tit-tit-tee-whoot.

'Will you report them to the police?'

Juggut Singh sniggered. 'Let us get back before they miss me in the village.'

The pair walked back towards Mano Majra, the man in front, the girl a few paces behind him. They could hear the sound of wailing and the barking of dogs. Women were shouting to each other across the roofs. The whole village seemed to be awake. Juggut Singh stopped near the pond and turned round to speak to the girl.

'Nooro, will you come tomorrow?' he asked, pleading.

'You think of tomorrow and I am bothered about my life. You have your good time even if I am murdered.'

'No one can harm you while I live. No one in Mano Majra can raise his eyebrows at you and get away from Jugga. I am not a badmash for nothing,' he said haughtily. 'You tell me tomorrow what happens or the day after tomorrow when all this—whatever it is—is over. After the goods train?'

'No! No! No!' answered the girl. 'What will I say to my father now? This noise is bound to have woken him up.'

'Just say you had gone out. Your stomach was upset or something like that. You heard the firing and were hiding till the dacoits had left. Will you come the day after tomorrow then?'

'No,' she repeated, this time a little less emphatically. The excuse might work. Just as well her father was almost blind. He would not see her silk shirt, nor the antimony in her eyes. Nooran walked away into the darkness, swearing she would never come again.

Juggut Singh went up the lane to his house. The door was open. Several villagers were in the courtyard talking to his mother. He turned around quietly and made his way back to the river.

In bureaucratic circles Mano Majra has some importance because of an officers' rest house just north of the railway bridge. It is a flat-roofed bungalow made of khaki bricks with a veranda in front facing the river. It stands in the middle of a squarish plot enclosed by a low wall. From the gate to the veranda runs a road with a row of bricks to deckle edge each side and mark it off from the garden. The garden is a pancake of plastered mud without a blade of grass to break its flat, even surface, but a few scraggy bushes of jasmine grow beside the columns of the veranda and near the row of servants' quarters at the rear of the house. The rest house was originally built for the engineer in charge of the construction of the bridge. After the completion of the bridge, it became the common property of all senior officers. Its popularity is due to its proximity to the river. All about it are wild wastes of pampas grass and *dhak*, or flame of the forest, and here partridges call to their mates from sunrise to sundown. When the river has receded to its winter channel, bulrushes grow in the marshes and ponds left behind. Geese, mallard, widgeon, teal and many other kinds of waterfowl frequent these places, and the larger pools abound with rahu and malli and mahseer.

Throughout the winter months, officers arrange tours that involve a short halt at the Mano Majra rest house. They go for waterfowl at sunrise, for partridges during the day, fish in the afternoons, and once more for ducks when they come back in their evening flight. In spring the romantic come to ruminate— to sip their whisky and see the bright orange of the dhak shame the rich red hues of the sun setting over the river; to hear the soothing snore of frogs in the marshes and the rumble of trains that go by; to watch fireflies flitting among the reeds as the moon comes up from under the arches of the bridge. During the early months of summer, only those who are looking for solitude come to the Mano Majra rest house. But once the monsoon breaks, the visitors multiply, for the swollen waters of the Sutlej are a grand and terrifying sight.

On the morning before the dacoity in Mano Majra, the rest house had been done up to receive an important guest. The sweeper had washed the bathrooms, swept the rooms, and sprinkled water on the road. The bearer and his wife had dusted and rearranged the furniture. The sweeper's boy had unwound the rope on the punkah which hung from the ceiling and put it through the hole in the wall so that he could pull it from the veranda. He had put on a new red loincloth and was sitting on the veranda tying and untying knots in the punkah rope. From the kitchen came the smell of currying chicken.

At eleven o'clock a subinspector of police and two constables turned up on bicycles to inspect the arrangements. Then two orderlies arrived. They wore white uniforms with red sashes round their waists and white turbans with broad bands in front. On the bands were pinned brass emblems of the government of the Punjab—the sun rising over five wavy lines representing the rivers of the province. With them were several villagers who carried the baggage and the glossy black official dispatch cases.

An hour later a large grey American car rolled in. An orderly stepped out of the front seat and opened the rear door for his master. The subinspector and the policemen came to attention and saluted. The villagers moved away to a respectful distance. The bearer opened the wire-gauze door leading to the main bed-sitting room. Mr Hukum Chand, magistrate and deputy commissioner of the district, heaved his corpulent frame out of the car. He had been travelling all morning and was somewhat tired and stiff. A cigarette perched on his lower lip sent a thin stream of smoke into his eyes. In his right hand he held a cigarette tin and a box of matches. He ambled up to the subinspector and gave him a friendly slap on the back while the other still stood at attention.

'Come along, Inspector Sahib, come in,' said Hukum Chand. He took the inspector's right hand and led him into the room. The bearer and the deputy commissioner's personal servant followed. The constables helped the chauffeur to take the luggage out of the car.

Hukum Chand went straight into the bathroom and washed the dust off his face. He came back still wiping his face with a towel. The subinspector stood up again.

'Sit down, sit down,' he commanded.

He flung the towel on his bed and sank into an armchair. The punkah began to flap forward and backward to the grating sound of the rope moving in the hole in the wall. One of the orderlies undid the magistrate's shoes and took off his socks and began to rub his feet. Hukum Chand opened the cigarette tin and held it out to the subinspector. The subinspector lit the magistrate's cigarette and then his own. Hukum Chand's style of smoking betrayed his lower-middle-class origin. He sucked noisily, his mouth glued to his clenched fist. He dropped cigarette ash by snapping his fingers with a flourish. The subinspector, who was a younger man, had a more sophisticated manner.

'Well, Inspector Sahib, how are things?'

The subinspector joined his hands. 'God is merciful. We only pray for your kindness.'

'No communal trouble in this area?'

'We have escaped it so far, sir. Convoys of Sikh and Hindu refugees from Pakistan have come through and some Muslims have gone out, but we have had no incidents.'

'You haven't had convoys of dead Sikhs this side of the frontier. They have been coming through at Amritsar. Not one person living! There has been killing over there.' Hukum Chand held up both his hands and let them drop heavily on his thighs in a gesture of resignation. Sparks flew off his cigarette and fell on his trousers. The subinspector slapped them to extinction with obsequious haste.

'Do you know,' continued the magistrate, 'the Sikhs retaliated by attacking a Muslim refugee train and sending it across the border with over a thousand corpses? They wrote on the engine "Gift to Pakistan!"'

The subinspector looked down thoughtfully and answered:

'They say that is the only way to stop killings on the other side. Man for man, woman for woman, child for child. But we Hindus are not like that. We cannot really play this stabbing game. When it comes to an open fight, we can be a match for any people. I believe our R.S.S. boys beat up Muslim gangs in all the cities. The Sikhs are not doing their share. They have lost their manliness. They just talk big. Here we are on the border with Muslims living in Sikh villages as if nothing had happened. Every morning and evening the muezzin calls for prayer in the heart of a village like Mano Majra. You ask the Sikhs why they allow it and they answer that the Muslims are their brothers. I am sure they are getting money from them.'

Hukum Chand ran his fingers across his receding forehead into his hair.

'Any of the Muslims in this area well-to-do?'

'Not many, sir. Most of them are weavers or potters.'

'But Chundunnugger is said to be a good police station. There are so many murders, so much illicit distilling, and the Sikh peasants are prosperous. Your predecessors have built themselves houses in the city.'

'Your honour is making fun of me.'

'I don't mind your taking whatever you do take, within reason of course—everyone does that—only, be careful. This new government is talking very loudly of stamping out all this. After a few months in office their enthusiasm will cool and things will go on as before. It is no use trying to change things overnight.'

'They are not the ones to talk. Ask anyone coming from Delhi and he will tell you that all these Gandhi disciples are minting money. They are as good saints as the crane. They shut their eyes piously and stand on one leg like a yogi doing penance; as soon as a fish comes near—hurrup.'

Hukum Chand ordered the servant rubbing his feet to get some beer. As soon as they were alone, he put a friendly hand on the subinspector's knee.

'You talk rashly like a child. It will get you into trouble one day. Your principle should be to see everything and say nothing.

The world changes so rapidly that if you want to get on you cannot afford to align yourself with any person or point of view. Even if you feel strongly about something, learn to keep silent.'

The subinspector's heart warmed with gratitude. He wanted to provoke more paternal advice by irresponsible criticism. He knew that Hukum Chand agreed with him.

'Sometimes, sir, one cannot restrain oneself. What do the Gandhi-caps in Delhi know about the Punjab? What is happening on the other side in Pakistan does not matter to them. They have not lost their homes and belongings; they haven't had their mothers, wives, sisters and daughters raped and murdered in the streets. Did your honour hear what the Muslim mobs did to Hindu and Sikh refugees in the marketplaces at Sheikhupura and Gujranwala? Pakistan police and the army took part in the killings. Not a soul was left alive. Women killed their own children and jumped into wells that filled to the brim with corpses.'

'Harey Ram, Harey Ram,' rejoined Hukum Chand with a deep sigh. 'I know it all. Our Hindu women are like that: so pure that they would rather commit suicide than let a stranger touch them. We Hindus never raise our hands to strike women, but these Muslims have no respect for the weaker sex. But what are we to do about it? How long will it be before it starts here?'

'I hope we do not get trains with corpses coming through Mano Majra. It will be impossible to prevent retaliation. We have hundreds of small Muslim villages all around, and there are some Muslim families in every Sikh village like Mano Majra,' said the subinspector, throwing a feeler.

Hukum Chand sucked his cigarette noisily and snapped his fingers.

'We must maintain law and order,' he answered after a pause. 'If possible, get the Muslims to go out peacefully. Nobody really benefits by bloodshed. Bad characters will get all the loot and the government will blame us for the killing. No, Inspector Sahib, whatever our views—and God alone knows what I would have done to these Pakistanis if I were not a government servant—we must not let there be any killing or destruction of property. Let them get out, but be careful they do not take too much with them. Hindus from Pakistan were stripped of all their belongings before they were allowed to leave. Pakistani magistrates have become millionaires overnight. Some on our side have not done too badly either. Only where there was killing or burning the government suspended or transferred them. There must be no killing. Just peaceful evacuation.'

The bearer brought a bottle of beer and put two glasses before Hukum Chand and the subinspector. The subinspector picked up his glass and put his hand over it, protesting, 'No, sir, I could not be impertinent and drink in your presence.'

The magistrate dismissed the protest peremptorily. 'You will have to join me. It is an order. Bearer, fill the Inspector sahib's glass and lay out lunch for him.'

The subinspector held out his glass for the bearer to fill. 'If you order me to, I cannot disobey.' He began to relax. He took off his turban and put it on the table. It was not like a Sikh turban which needed re-tying each time it was taken off; it was just three yards of starched khaki muslin wrapped round a blue skullcap which could be put on and off like a hat.

'What is the situation in Mano Majra?'

'All is well so far. The *lambardar* reports regularly. No refugees have come through the village yet. I am sure no one in Mano Majra even knows that the British have left and the country is divided into Pakistan and Hindustan. Some of them know about Gandhi but I doubt if anyone has ever heard of Jinnah.'

'That is good. You must keep an eye on Mano Majra. It is the most important village on the border here. It is so close to the bridge. Are there any bad characters in the village?'

'Only one, sir. His name is Jugga. Your honour confined him to the village. He reports himself to the lambardar every day and comes to the police station once every week.'

'Jugga? Which one is he?'

'You must remember Juggut Singh, son of the dacoit Alam Singh who was hanged two years ago. He is that very big fellow.

He is the tallest man in this area. He must be six foot four—and broad. He is like a stud bull.'

'Oh yes, I remember. What does he do to keep himself out of mischief? He used to come up before me in some case or other every month.'

The subinspector smiled broadly. 'Sir, what the police of the Punjab has failed to do, the magic of the eyes of a girl of sixteen has done.'

Hukum Chand's interest was aroused.

'He has a liaison?' he asked.

'With a Muslim weaver's daughter. She is dark, but her eyes are darker. She certainly keeps Jugga in the village. And no one dares say a word against the Muslims. Her blind father is the mullah of the mosque.'

The two drank their beer and smoked till the bearer brought in lunch. They continued drinking and eating and discussing the situation in the district till late in the afternoon. Beer and rich food made Hukum Chand heavy with sleep. *Chicks* on the veranda had been lowered to keep out the glare of the noonday sun. The punkah flapped gently to and fro with a weary plaintive creak. A feeling of numb drowsiness came over Hukum Chand. He got out his silver toothpick, picked his teeth and rubbed the toothpick on the tablecloth. Even that did not help him ward off sleep. The subinspector noticed the magistrate nodding and stood up to take leave.

'Have I your permission to leave, sir?'

'If you want to rest, you can find a bed here.'

'You are very kind, sir, but I have a few things to attend to at the station. I will leave two constables here. If your honour desires my presence, they will inform me.'

'Well,' said the magistrate hesitantly, 'have you made any arrangements for the evening?'

'Is it possible for me to have overlooked that? If she does not please you, you can have me dismissed from service. I will tell the driver where to go and collect the party.'

The subinspector saluted and left. The magistrate stretched

himself on the bed for a late afternoon siesta.

The sound of the car leaving the bungalow woke Hukum Chand from his sleep. Pampas-stalk chicks which hung on the veranda had been folded into large Swiss rolls and tied between the columns. The stark white of the veranda was mellowed in the soft amber of the setting sun. The sweeper boy lay curled on the brick floor clutching the punkah rope in his hand. His father was sprinkling water all around the rest house. The damp smell of earth mixed with the sweet odour of jasmines came through the wire-gauze door. In front of the house, the servants had spread a large coir mat with a carpet on it. At one end of the carpet was a big cane chair, a table with a bottle of whisky, a couple of tumblers and plates of savouries. Several bottles of soda water stood in a row beneath the table.

Hukum Chand shouted for his servant to get his bath ready and bring in hot water for shaving. He lit a cigarette and lay in bed staring at the ceiling. Just above his head two geckos were getting ready for a fight. They crawled towards each other emitting little rasping noises. They paused with half an inch between them and moved their tails with slow, menacing deliberation, then came to a head-on collision. Before Hukum Chand could move away they fell with a loud plop just beside his pillow. A cold clammy feeling came over him. He jumped out of bed and stared at the geckos. The geckos stared back at him, still holding onto each other by the teeth as if they were kissing. The bearer's footsteps broke the hypnotic stare with which the magistrate and the geckos had been regarding each other. The geckos ran down the bed and up the wall back to the ceiling. Hukum Chand felt as if he had touched the lizards and they had made his hands dirty. He rubbed his hands on the hem of his shirt. It was not the sort of dirt which could be wiped off or washed clean.

The bearer brought a mug of hot water and laid out the shaving gear on the dressing table. He put on a chair his master's clothes— a thin muslin shirt, a pair of baggy trousers strung with a peacock-blue silken cord interwoven with silver thread. He brushed the magistrate's black pumps till they shone and put them beside the chair.

Hukum Chand shaved and bathed with great care. After bathing he rubbed skin-lotion on his face and arms and dusted himself with perfumed talcum powder. He dabbed his fingers with eau de cologne. Brilliantine made his hair smooth and soggy and showed the white at the roots of it. He had not dyed it for a fortnight. He waxed his thick moustache and twirled it till the ends stiffly pointed to his eyes; the roots of his moustache also showed purple and white. He put on his thin muslin shirt through which his aertex vest showed clearly. The trousers fell in ordered starchy folds. He dabbed his clothes with a swab of cotton dipped in scent of musk rose. When he was ready he looked up at the ceiling. The geckos were there staring at him with their bright, black, pin-point eyes.

The American car drove back into the driveway. Hukum Chand went up to the wire-gauze door still waxing his moustache. Two men and two women stepped out. One of the men carried a harmonium and the other a pair of drums. One of the women was old, with white hair dyed a rich henna-orange. The other was a young girl whose mouth was bloated with betel leaf and who wore a diamond glistening on one side of her flat nose. She carried a small bundle which jingled as she stepped out of the car. The party went and squatted on the carpet.

Hukum Chand carefully examined himself in the mirror. He noticed the white at the roots of his hair and smoothed it back again. He lit a cigarette and in his customary manner carried the tin of cigarettes with a matchbox on it. He half opened the wire-gauze door and shouted for his bearer to bring the whisky, which he knew had already been put on the table. It was to warn the people outside of his coming. As he came out he let the door slam noisily. With slow deliberate steps punctuated by the creaking of his glossy pumps he walked up to the cane chair.

The party stood up to greet the magistrate. The two musicians salaamed, bowing their heads low. The old toothless woman broke into a sonorous singsong of praise: 'May your fame and honour increase. May your pen write figures of thousands and hundreds of thousands.' The young girl just stared at him with her large eyes lined with antimony and lampblack. The magistrate made a gesture with his hand ordering them to sit down. The old woman's voice came down to a whimper. All four sat down on the carpet.

The bearer poured out the whisky and soda for his master. Hukum Chand took a large gulp and wiped his moustache with the back of his hand. He twirled the pointed ends nervously. The girl opened her bundle and tied the ankle-bells round her ankles. The harmonium player played a single note. His companion beat the drums all round the edges with a tiny mallet and tightened and loosened the leather thongs by hammering the ring of wooden blocks wedged between them. He beat the taut white skin with his fingers till the drums were in key with the harmonium. The accompaniment was ready.

The young girl spat out the betel saliva and cleared her throat with a series of deep chesty coughs that brought up phlegm. The old woman spoke:

'Cherisher of the poor. What does your honour fancy? Something classical—pukka—or a love song?'

'No, nothing pukka. Something from the films. Some good film song—preferably Punjabi.'

The young girl salaamed. 'As you order.'

The musicians put their heads together and after a brief consultation with the girl they began to play. The drums beat a preliminary tattoo and then softened down for the harmonium to join in. The two played for some time while the girl sat silently, looking bored and indifferent. When they finished the introductory piece, she blew her nose and cleared her throat again. She put her left hand on her ear and stretched the other towards the magistrate, addressing him in a shrill falsetto:

O lover mine, O lover that art gone,
I live but would rather die,
I see not for the tears that flow,

I breathe not, for I sigh.
As a moth that loves the flame,
By that flame is done to death,
Within myself have I lit a fire
That now robs me of my breath.
The nights I spend in counting stars,
The days in dreams of days to be
When homewards thou thy reins shall turn
Thy moon-fair face I again shall see.

The girl paused. The musicians started to play again for her to sing the refrain:

O letter, let my lover learn
How the fires of separation burn.

When the girl had finished her song, Hukum Chand flung a five-rupee note on the carpet. The girl and the musicians bowed their heads. The hag picked up the money and put it in her wallet, proclaiming: 'May you ever rule. May your pen write hundreds of thousands. May . . .'

The singing began again. Hukum Chand poured himself a stiff whisky and drank it in one gulp. He wiped his moustache with his hand. He did not have the nerve to take a good look at the girl. She was singing a song he knew well; he had heard his daughter humming it:

In the breeze is flying
My veil of red muslin
    Ho Sir, Ho Sir.

Hukum Chand felt uneasy. He took another whisky and dismissed his conscience. Life was too short for people to have consciences. He started to beat time to the song by snapping his fingers and slapping his thighs to each 'Ho Sir. Ho Sir.'

Twilight gave way to the dark of a moonless night. In the

swamps by the river, frogs croaked. Cicadas chirped in the reeds. The bearer brought out a hissing paraffin lamp which cast a bright bluish light. The frame of the lamp threw a shadow over Hukum Chand. He stared at the girl who sat sheltered from the light. She was only a child and not very pretty, just young and unexploited. Her breasts barely filled her bodice. They could not have known the touch of a male hand. The thought that she was perhaps younger than his own daughter flashed across his mind. He drowned it quickly with another whisky. Life was like that. You took it as it came, shorn of silly conventions and values which deserved only lip worship. She wanted his money, and he . . . well. When all was said and done she was a prostitute and looked it. The silver sequins on her black sari sparkled. The diamond in her nose glittered like a star. Hukum Chand took another drink to dispel his remaining doubts. This time he wiped his moustache with his silk handkerchief. He began to hum louder and snapped his fingers with a flourish.

One film song followed another till all the Indian songs set to tunes of tangos and sambas that Hukum Chand knew were exhausted.

'Sing anything else you know,' ordered the magistrate with lordly condescension. 'Something new and gay.'

The girl started to sing a song which had several English words in it:

Sunday after Sunday, O my life.

Hukum Chand exploded with an appreciative 'wah, wah.' When the girl finished her song, he did not throw the five-rupee note at her but asked her to come and take it from his hand. The old woman pushed the girl ahead.

'Go, the Government sends for you.'

The girl got up and went to the table. She stretched out her hand to take the money; Hukum Chand withdrew his and put the note on his heart. He grinned lecherously. The girl looked at her companions for help. Hukum Chand put the note on the table. Before she could reach it he picked it up and again put it on his chest. The grin on his face became broader. The girl turned back to join the others. Hukum Chand held out the note for the third time.

'Go to the Government,' pleaded the old woman. The girl turned round obediently and went to the magistrate. Hukum Chand put his arm round her waist.

'You sing well.'

The girl gaped wide-eyed at her companions.

'The Government is talking to you. Why don't you answer him?' scolded the old woman. 'Government, the girl is young and very shy. She will learn,' she exclaimed.

Hukum Chand put a glass of whisky to the girl's lips. 'Drink a little. Just a sip for my sake,' he pleaded.

The girl stood impassively without opening her mouth. The old woman spoke again.

'Government, she knows nothing about drink. She is hardly sixteen and completely innocent. She has never been near a man before. I have reared her for your honour's pleasure.'

'Then she will eat something even if she does not drink,' said Hukum Chand. He preferred to ignore the rest of the woman's speech. He picked up a meatball from a plate and tried to put it in the girl's mouth. She took it from him and ate it.

Hukum Chand pulled her onto his lap and began to play with her hair. It was heavily oiled and fixed in waves by gaudy celluloid hair-clips. He took out a couple of hairpins and loosened the bun at the back. The hair fell about her shoulders. The musicians and the old woman got up.

'Have we permission to leave?'

'Yes, go. The driver will take you home.'

The old woman again set up a loud singsong: 'May your fame and honour increase. May your pen write figures of thousands—nay, hundreds of thousands.'

Hukum Chand produced a wad of notes and put it on the table for her. Then the party went to the car, leaving the magistrate with the girl in his lap and the bearer waiting for orders.

'Shall I serve dinner, sir?'

'No, just leave the food on the table. We will serve ourselves. You can go.' The bearer laid out the dinner and retired to his quarters.

Hukum Chand stretched out his hand and put out the paraffin lamp. It went out with a loud hiss, leaving the two in utter darkness save for a pale yellow light that flickered from the bedroom. Hukum Chand decided to stay out of doors.

The goods train had dropped the Mano Majra wagons and was leaving the station for the bridge. It came up noisily, its progress marked by the embers which flew out of the funnel of the engine. They were stoking coal in the firebox. A bright red-and-yellow light travelled through the spans of the bridge and was lost behind the jungle on the other side. The train's rumble got fainter and fainter. Its passing brought a feeling of privacy.

Hukum Chand helped himself to another whisky. The girl in his lap sat stiff and frigid.

'Are you angry with me? You don't want to talk to me?' asked Hukum Chand, pressing her closer to him. The girl did not answer or look back at him.

The magistrate was not particularly concerned with her reactions. He had paid for all that. He brought the girl's face nearer his own and began kissing her on the back of her neck and on her ears. He could not hear the goods train any more. It had left the countryside in utter solitude. Hukum Chand could hear his breathing quicken. He undid the strap of the girl's bodice.

The sound of a shot shattered the stillness of the night. The girl broke loose and stood up.

'Did you hear a shot?'

The girl nodded. 'May be a shikari,' she answered, speaking to him for the first time. She refastened her bodice.

'There can't be any shikar on a dark night.'

The two stood in silence for some time—the man a little apprehensive; the girl relieved of the attentions of a lover whose breath smelled of whisky, tobacco and pyorrhea. But the silence told Hukum Chand that all was well. He took another whisky to make assurance doubly sure. The girl realized that there was no escape.

'Must be a cracker. Somebody getting married or something,' said Hukum Chand, putting his arms round the girl. He kissed her on the nose. 'Let us get married too,' he added with a leer.

The girl did not answer. She allowed herself to be dragged onto the table amongst plates covered with stale meatballs and cigarette ash. Hukum Chand swept them off the table with his hand and went on with his love-making. The girl suffered his pawing without a protest. He picked her up from the table and laid her on the carpet amongst the litter of tumblers, plates and bottles. She covered her face with the loose end of her sari and turned it sideways to avoid his breath. Hukum Chand began fumbling with her dress.

From Mano Majra came sounds of people shouting and the agitated barking of dogs. Hukum Chand looked up. Two shots rang out and silenced the barking and shouting. With a loud oath Hukum Chand left the girl. She got up, brushing and adjusting her sari. From the servants' quarters the bearer and the sweeper came out carrying lanterns and talking excitedly. A little later the chauffeur drove the car into the driveway, its headlights lighting up the front of the bungalow.

The morning after the dacoity the railway station was more crowded than usual. Some Mano Majrans made a habit of being there to watch the 10:30 slow passenger train from Delhi to Lahore come in. They liked to see the few passengers who might get on or off at Mano Majra, and they also enjoyed endless arguments about how late the train was on a given day and when it had last been on time. Since the partition of the country there had been an additional interest. Now the trains were often four or five hours late and sometimes as many as twenty. When they came, they were crowded with Sikh and Hindu refugees from Pakistan or with Muslims from India. People perched on the roofs with their legs dangling, or on bedsteads wedged in between the bogies. Some of them rode precariously on the buffers.

The train this morning was only an hour late—almost like pre-War days. When it steamed in, the crying of hawkers on the platform and the passengers rushing about and shouting to each other gave the impression that many people would be getting off. But when the guard blew his whistle for departure, most of them were back on the train. Only a solitary Sikh peasant carrying an ironshod bamboo staff and followed by his wife with an infant resting on her hip remained with the hawkers on the platform. The man hoisted their rolled bedding onto his head and held it there with one hand. In the other he carried a large tin of clarified butter. The bamboo staff he held in his armpit, with one end trailing on the ground. Two green tickets stuck out beneath his moustache, which billowed from his upper lip onto his beard. The woman saw the line of faces peering through the iron railing of the station and drew her veil across her face. She followed her husband, her slippers sloshing on the gravel and her silver ornaments all ajingle. The stationmaster plucked the tickets from the peasant's mouth and let the couple out of the gate, where they were lost in a tumult of greetings and embraces.

The guard blew his whistle a second time and waved the green flag. Then, from the compartment just behind the engine, armed policemen emerged. There were twelve of them, and a subinspector. They carried rifles and their Sam Browne belts were charged with bullets. Two carried chains and handcuffs. From the other end of the train, near the guard's van, a young man stepped down. He wore a long white shirt, a brown waistcoat of coarse cotton, and loose pyjamas, and he carried a holdall. He stepped gingerly off the train, pressing his tousled hair and looking all round. He was a small slight man, somewhat effeminate in appearance. The sight of the policemen emboldened him. He hoisted the holdall onto his left shoulder and moved jauntily towards the exit. The villagers watched the young man and the police party move from opposite directions towards the stationmaster who stood beside the gate. He had opened it wide for the police and was bowing obsequiously to the subinspector. The young man reached the gate first and stopped between the stationmaster and the police. The stationmaster quickly took the ticket from him, but the young man did not move on or make way for the subinspector.

'Can you tell me, Stationmaster Sahib, if there is a place I can stay in this village?'

The stationmaster was irritated. The visitor's urban accent, his appearance, dress and holdall had the stationmaster holding back his temper.

'There are no hotels or inns in Mano Majra,' he answered with polite sarcasm. 'There is only the Sikh temple. You will see the yellow flag-mast in the centre of the village.'

'Thank you, sir.'

The police party and the stationmaster scrutinized the youth with a little diffidence. Not many people said 'thank you' in these parts. Most of the 'thank you' crowd were foreign-educated. They had heard of several well-to-do young men, educated in England, donning peasant garb to do rural uplift work. Some were known to be Communist agents. Some were sons of millionaires, some sons of high government officials. All were looking for trouble, and capable of making a lot of noise. One had to be careful.

The young man went out of the station towards the village. He walked with a consciously erect gait, a few yards in front of the policemen. He was uneasily aware of their attention. The itch on the back of his neck told him that they were looking at him and talking about him. He did not scratch or look back—he just walked on like a soldier. He saw the flag-mast draped in yellow cloth with a triangular flag above the conglomeration of mud huts. On the flag was the Sikh symbol in black, a quoit with a dagger running through and two swords crossed beneath. He went along the dusty path lined on either side by scraggy bushes of prickly pear which fenced it off from the fields. The path wound its narrow way past the mud huts to the opening in the centre where the moneylender's house, the mosque and the temple faced each other. Underneath the peepul tree half a dozen villagers were sitting on a low wooden platform talking to each other. They got up as soon as they saw the policemen and followed them into Ram Lal's house. No one took any notice of the stranger.

He stepped into the open door of the temple courtyard. At the end opposite the entrance was a large hall in which the scripture, the Granth, lay wrapped in gaudy silks under a velvet awning. On one side were two rooms. A brick stairway ran along the wall to the roof of the rooms. Across the courtyard was a well with a high parapet. Beside the well stood a four-foot brick column supporting the long flag-mast with the yellow cloth covering it like a stocking.

The young man did not see anyone about. He could hear the sound of wet clothes being beaten on a slab of stone. He walked timidly to the other side of the well. An old Sikh got up with water dripping from his beard and white shorts.

'Sat Sri Akal.'

'Sat Sri Akal.'

'Can I stay for two or three days?'

'This is a gurdwara, the Guru's house—anyone may stay here. But you must have your head covered and you must not bring in any cigarettes or tobacco, nor smoke.'

'I do not smoke,' said the young man putting the holdall on the ground and spreading his handkerchief on his head.

'No, Babu Sahib, only when you go in near the Book, the Granth Sahib, you take your shoes off and cover your head. Put your luggage in that room and make yourself comfortable. Will you have something to eat?'

'That is very kind of you. But I have brought my own food.'

The old man showed the visitor to the spare room and then went back to the well. The young man went into the room. Its only furniture was a charpai lying in the middle. There was a large coloured calendar on one wall. It had a picture of the Guru on horseback with a hawk on one hand. Alongside the calendar were nails to hang clothes.

The visitor emptied his holdall. He took out his air mattress and blew it up on the charpai. He laid out pyjamas and a silk dressing gown on the mattress. He got out a tin of sardines, a tin of Australian butter and a packet of dry biscuits. He shook his water bottle. It was empty.

The old Sikh came to him, combing his long beard with his fingers.

'What is your name?' he asked, sitting down on the threshold.

'Iqbal. What is yours?'

'Iqbal Singh?' queried the old man. Without waiting for an answer, he continued. 'I am the bhai of the temple. Bhai Meet Singh. What is your business in Mano Majra, Iqbal Singhji?'

The young man was relieved that the other had not gone on with his first question. He did not have to say what Iqbal he was. He could be a Muslim, Iqbal Mohammed. He could be a Hindu, Iqbal Chand, or a Sikh, Iqbal Singh. It was one of the few names common to the three communities. In a Sikh village, an Iqbal Singh would no doubt get a better deal, even if his hair was shorn and his beard shaved, than an Iqbal Mohammed or an Iqbal Chand. He himself had few religious feelings.

'I am a social worker, Bhaiji. There is much to be done in our villages. Now with this partition there is so much bloodshed going on, someone must do something to stop it. My party has sent me here, since this place is a vital point for refugee movements. Trouble here would be disastrous.'

The bhai did not seem interested in Iqbal's occupation.

'Where are you from, Iqbal Singhji?'

Iqbal knew that meant his ancestors and not himself.

'I belong to district Jhelum—now in Pakistan—but I have been in foreign countries a long time. It is after seeing the world that one feels how backward we are and one wants to do things about it. So I do social work.'

'How much do they pay you?'

Iqbal had learned not to resent these questions.

'I don't get paid very much. Just my expenses.'

'Do they pay the expenses of your wife and children also?'

'No, Bhaiji. I am not married. I really . . .'

'How old are you?'

'Twenty-seven. Tell me, do other social workers come to this village?' Iqbal decided to ask questions to stop Meet Singh's interrogation.

'Sometimes the American padres come.'

'Do you like their preaching Christianity in your village?'

'Everyone is welcome to his religion. Here next door is a Muslim mosque. When I pray to my Guru, Uncle Imam Baksh calls to Allah. How many religions do they have in Europe?'

'They are all Christians of one kind or other. They do not quarrel about their religions as we do here. They do not really bother very much about religion.'

'So I have heard,' said Meet Singh ponderously. 'That is why they have no morals. The sahibs and their wives go about with other sahibs and their wives. That is not good, is it?'

'But they do not tell lies like we do and they are not corrupt and dishonest as so many of us are,' answered Iqbal.

He got out his tin opener and opened the tin of sardines. He spread the fish on a biscuit and continued to talk while he ate.

'Morality, Meet Singhji, is a matter of money. Poor people cannot afford to have morals. So they have religion. Our first problem is to get people more food, clothing, comfort. That can only be done by stopping exploitation by the rich, and abolishing landlords. And that can only be done by changing the government.'

Meet Singh, with disgusted fascination, watched the young man eating fish complete with head, eyes and tail. He did not pay much attention to the lecture on rural indebtedness, the average national income, and capitalist exploitation which the other poured forth with flakes of dry biscuits. When Iqbal had finished eating Meet Singh got up and brought him a tumbler of water from his pitcher. Iqbal did not stop talking. He only raised his voice when the bhai went out.

Iqbal produced a little packet of cellophane paper from his pocket, took a white pill from it and dropped it in the tumbler.

He had seen Meet Singh's thumb, with its black crescent of dirt under the nail, dipping into the water. In any case it was out of a well which could never have been chlorinated.

'Are you ill?' asked the old man, seeing the other wait for the pill to dissolve.

'No, it helps me to digest my food. We city-dwellers need this sort of thing after meals.'

Iqbal resumed his speech. 'To add to it all,' he continued, 'there is the police system which, instead of safeguarding the citizen, maltreats him and lives on corruption and bribery. You know all about that, I am sure.'

The old man nodded his head in agreement. Before he could comment, the young man spoke again. 'A party of policemen with an inspector came over on the same train with me. They will no doubt eat up all the chickens, the inspector will make a little money in bribes, and they will move on to the next village. One would think they had nothing else to do but fleece people.'

Reference to the police awakened the old man from his absent-minded listening. 'So the police have come after all. I must go and see what they are doing. They must be at the moneylender's house. He was murdered last night, just across from the gurdwara. The dacoits took a lot of cash and they say over five thousand rupees in silver and gold ornaments from his women.'

Meet Singh realized the interest he had created and slowly got up, repeating, 'I should be going. All the village will be there. They will be taking the corpse for medical examination. If a man is killed he cannot be cremated till the doctor certifies him dead.' The old man gave a wry smile.

'A murder! Why, why was he murdered?' stammered Iqbal, somewhat bewildered. He was surprised that Meet Singh had not mentioned the murder of a next-door neighbour all this time. 'Was it communal? Is it all right for me to be here? I do not suppose I can do much if the village is all excited about a murder.'

'Why, Babu Sahib, you have come to stop killing and you are upset by one murder?' asked Meet Singh, smiling. 'I thought you had come to stop such things, Babu Sahib. But you are quite safe in Mano Majra,' he added. 'Dacoits do not come to the same village more than once a year. There will be another dacoity in another village in a few days and people will forget about this one. We can have a meeting here one night after the evening prayer and you can tell them all you want. You had better rest. I will come back and tell you what happens.'

The old man hobbled out of the courtyard. Iqbal collected the empty tin, his knife and fork and tin plate, and took them to the well to wash.

In the afternoon, Iqbal stretched himself on the coarse string charpai and tried to get some sleep. He had spent the night sitting on his bedroll in a crowded third-class compartment. Every time he had dozed off, the train had come to a halt at some wayside station and the door was forced open and more peasants poured in with their wives, bedding and tin trunks. Some child sleeping in its mother's lap would start howling till its wails were smothered by a breast thrust into its mouth. The shouting and clamour would continue until long after the train had left the station. The same thing was repeated again and again, till the compartment meant for fifty had almost two hundred people in it, sitting on the floor, on seats, on luggage racks, on trunks, on bedrolls, and on each other, or standing in the corners. There were dozens outside perched precariously on footboards, holding onto the door handles. There were several people on the roof. The heat and smell were oppressive. Tempers were frayed and every few minutes an argument would start because someone had spread himself out too much or had trod on another's foot on his way to the lavatory. The argument would be joined on either side by friends or relatives and then by all the others trying to patch it up. Iqbal had tried to read in the dim light speckled with shadows of moths that fluttered round the globe. He had hardly read a paragraph before his neighbour had observed:

'You are reading.'

'Yes, I am reading.'

'What are you reading?'

'A book.'

It had not worked. The man had simply taken the book out of Iqbal's hand and turned over its pages.

'English.'

'You must be educated.'

Iqbal did not comment.

The book had gone round the compartment for scrutiny. They had all looked at him. He was educated, therefore belonged to a different class. He was a babu.

'What honourable noun does your honour bear?'

'My name is Iqbal.'

'May your Iqbal [fame] ever increase.'

The man had obviously taken him to be a Muslim. Just as well. All the passengers appeared to be Muslims on their way to Pakistan.

'Where does your wealth reside, Babu Sahib?'

'My poor home is in Jhelum district,' Iqbal had answered without irritation. The answer confirmed the likelihood of his being Muslim: Jhelum was in Pakistan.

Thereafter other passengers had joined in the cross-examination. Iqbal had to tell them what he did, what his source of income was, how much he was worth, where he had studied, why he had not married, all the illnesses he had ever suffered from. They had discussed their own domestic problems and diseases and had sought his advice. Did Iqbal know of any secret prescriptions or herbs that the English used when they were 'run down'? Iqbal had given up the attempt to sleep or read. They had kept up the conversation till the early hours of the morning. He would have described the journey as insufferable except that the limits to which human endurance could be stretched in India made the word meaningless. He got off at Mano Majra with a sigh of relief. He could breathe the fresh air. He was looking forward to a long siesta.

But sleep would not come to Iqbal. There was no ventilation in the room. It had a musty earthy smell. A pile of clothes in the corner stank of stale clarified butter, and there were flies buzzing all round. Iqbal spread a handkerchief on his face. He could hardly breathe. With all that, just as he had managed to doze off, Meet Singh came in exclaiming philosophically:

'Robbing a fellow villager is like stealing from one's mother. Iqbal Singhji, this is Kalyug—the dark age. Have you ever heard of dacoits looting their neighbour's homes? Now all morality has left the world.'

Iqbal removed the handkerchief from his face.

'What has happened?'

'What has happened?' repeated Meet Singh, feigning surprise. 'Ask me what has not happened! The police sent for Jugga—Jugga is a badmash number ten [from the number of the police register in which names of bad characters are listed]. But Jugga had run away, absconded. Also, some of the loot—a bag of bangles—was found in his courtyard. So we know who did it. This is not the first murder he has committed—he has it in his blood. His father and grandfather were also dacoits and were hanged for murder. But they never robbed their own village folk. As a matter of fact, when they were at home, no dacoit dared come to Mano Majra. Juggut Singh has disgraced his family.'

Iqbal sat up rubbing his forehead. His countrymen's code of morals had always puzzled him, with his anglicized way of looking at things. The Punjabi's code was even more baffling. For them truth, honour, financial integrity were 'all right', but these were placed lower down the scale of values than being true to one's salt, to one's friends and fellow villagers. For friends you could lie in court or cheat, and no one would blame you. On the contrary, you became a *nar admi*—a he-man who had defied authority (magistrates and police) and religion (oath on the scripture) but proved true to friendship. It was the projection of rural society where everyone in the village was a relation and loyalty to the village was the supreme test. What bothered Meet Singh, a priest, was not that Jugga had committed murder but that his hands were soiled with the blood of a fellow villager. If Jugga had done the same thing in the neighbouring village, Meet Singh would gladly have appeared in his defence and sworn on the holy Granth that Jugga had been praying in the gurdwara at the time of the murder. Iqbal had wearied of talking to people like Meet Singh. They did not understand. He had come to the conclusion that he did not belong.

Meet Singh was disappointed that he had failed to arouse Iqbal's interest.

'You have seen the world and read many books, but take it from me that a snake can cast its slough but not its poison. This saying is worth a hundred thousand rupees.'

Iqbal did not register appreciation of the valuable saying. Meet Singh explained: 'Jugga had been going straight for some time. He ploughed his land and looked after his cattle. He never left the village, and reported himself to the lambardar every day. But how long can a snake keep straight? There is crime in his blood.'

'There is no crime in anyone's blood any more than there is goodness in the blood of others,' answered Iqbal waking up. This was one of his pet theories. 'Does anyone ever bother to find out why people steal and rob and kill? No! They put them in jail or hang them. It is easier. If the fear of the gallows or the cell had stopped people from killing or stealing, there would be no murdering or stealing. It does not. They hang a man every day in this province. Yet ten get murdered every twenty-four hours. No, Bhaiji, criminals are not born. They are made by hunger, want and injustice.'

Iqbal felt a little silly for coming out with these platitudes. He must check this habit of turning a conversation into a sermon. He returned to the subject.

'I suppose they will get Jugga easily if he is such a well-known character.'

'Jugga cannot go very far. He can be recognized from a kos. He is an arm's length taller than anyone else. The Deputy sahib has already sent orders to all police stations to keep a lookout for Jugga.'

'Who is the Deputy sahib?' asked Iqbal.

'You do not know the Deputy?' Meet Singh was surprised.

'It's Hukum Chand. He is staying at the dak bungalow north of the bridge. Now Hukum Chand is a nar admi. He started as a foot-constable and see where he is now! He always kept the sahibs pleased and they gave him one promotion after another. The last one gave him his own place and made him Deputy. Yes, Iqbal Singhji, Hukum Chand is a nar admi—and clever. He is true to his friends and always gets things done for them. He has had dozens of relatives given good jobs. He is one of a hundred. Nothing counterfeit about Hukum Chand.'

'Is he a friend of yours?'

'Friend? No,no,' protested Meet Singh. 'I am a humble bhai of the gurdwara and he is an emperor. He is the government and we are his subjects. If he comes to Mano Majra, you will see him.'

There was a pause in the conversation. Iqbal slipped his feet into his sandals and stood up.

'I must take a walk. Which way do you suggest I should go?'

'Go in any direction you like. It is all the same open country. Go to the river. You will see the trains coming and going. If you cross the railroad track you will see the dak bungalow. Don't be too late. These are bad times and it is best to be indoors before dark. Besides, I have told the lambardar and Uncle Imam Baksh— he is mullah of the mosque—that you are here. They may be coming in to talk to you.'

'No, I won't be late.'

Iqbal stepped out of the gurdwara. There was no sign of activity now. The police had apparently finished investigating. Half a dozen constables lay sprawled on charpais under the peepul tree. The door of Ram Lal's house was open. Some villagers sat on the floor in the courtyard. A woman wailed in a singsong which ended up in convulsions of crying in which other women joined. It was hot and still. The sun blazed on the mud walls.

Iqbal walked in the shade of the wall of the gurdwara. Children had relieved themselves all along it. Men had used it as a urinal. A mangy bitch lay on her side with a litter of eight skinny pups yapping and tugging at her sagging udders.

The lane ended abruptly at the village pond—a small patch of muddy water full of buffaloes with their heads sticking out.

A footpath skirted the pond and went along a dry watercourse through the wheat fields towards the river. Iqbal went along the watercourse watching his steps carefully. He reached the riverside just as the express from Lahore came up on the bridge. He watched its progress through the criss-cross of steel. Like all the trains, it was full. From the roof, legs dangled down the sides onto the doors and windows. The doors and windows were jammed with heads and arms. There were people on buffers between the bogies. The two on the buffers on the tail end of the train were merrily kicking their legs and gesticulating. The train picked up speed after crossing the bridge. The engine driver started blowing the whistle and continued blowing till he had passed Mano Majra station. It was an expression of relief that they were out of Pakistan and into India.

Iqbal went up the riverbank towards the bridge. He was planning to go under it towards the dak bungalow when he noticed a Sikh soldier watching him from the sentry box at the end of the bridge. Iqbal changed his mind and walked boldly up to the rail embankment and turned towards Mano Majra station. The manoeuvre allayed the sentry's suspicion. Iqbal went a hundred yards up and then casually sat down on the railway line.

The passing express had woken Mano Majra from its late siesta. Boys threw stones at the buffaloes in the pond and drove them home. Groups of women went out in the fields and scattered themselves behind the bushes. A bullock cart carrying Ram Lal's corpse left the village and went towards the station. It was guarded by policemen. Several villagers went a little distance with it and then returned along with the relatives.

Iqbal stood up and looked all round. From the railway station to the roof of the rest house showing above the plumes of pampas, from the bridge to the village and back to the railway station, the whole place was littered with men, women, children, cattle, and dogs. There were kites wheeling high up in the sky, long lines of crows were flying from somewhere to somewhere, and millions of sparrows twittered about the trees. Where in India could one find a place which did not teem with life? Iqbal thought of his first reaction on reaching Bombay. Milling crowds—millions of them—on the quayside, in the streets, on railway platforms; even at night the pavements were full of people. The whole country was like an overcrowded room. What could you expect when the population went up by six every minute—five millions every year! It made all planning in industry or agriculture a mockery. Why not spend the same amount of effort in checking the increase in population? But how could you, in the land of the *Kama Sutra*, the home of phallic worship and the son cult?

Iqbal was woken from his angry daydreaming by a shimmering sound along the steel wires which ran parallel to the railway lines. The signal above the sentry's box near the bridge came down. Iqbal stood up and brushed his clothes. The sun had gone down beyond the river. The russet sky turned grey as shades of twilight spread across the plain. A new moon looking like a finely pared fingernail appeared beside the evening star. The muezzin's call to prayer rose above the rumble of the approaching train.

Iqbal found his way back easily. All lanes met in the temple–mosque–moneylender's house triangle with the peepul tree in the centre. Sounds of wailing still came from Ram Lal's house. In the mosque, a dozen men stood in two rows silently going through their genuflections. In the gurdwara, Meet Singh, sitting beside the Book which was folded up in muslin on a cot, was reciting the evening prayer. Five or six men and women sat in a semicircle around a hurricane lantern and listened to him.

Iqbal went straight to his room and lay down on his charpai in the dark. He had barely shut his eyes when the worshippers began to chant. The chanting stopped for a couple of minutes, only to start again. The ceremony ended with shouts of 'Sat Sri Akal' and the beating of a drum. The men and women came out. Meet Singh held the lantern and helped them find their shoes. They started talking loudly. In the babel the only word Iqbal could make out was 'babu'. Somebody who had noticed Iqbal come in, had told the others. There was some whispering and shuffling of feet and then silence.

Iqbal shut his eyes once more. A minute later Meet Singh stood on the threshold, holding the lantern.

'Iqbal Singhji, have you gone to bed without food? Would you like some spinach? I have also curd and buttermilk.'

'No, thank you, Bhaiji. I have the food I want.'

'Our poor food . . .' started Meet Singh.

'No, no, it is not that,' interrupted Iqbal sitting up, 'it is just that I have it and it may be wasted if I don't eat it. I am a little tired and would like to sleep.'

'Then you must have some milk. Banta Singh, the lambardar, is bringing you some. I will tell him to hurry up if you want to sleep early. I have another charpai for you on the roof. It is too hot to sleep in here.' Meet Singh left the hurricane lantern in the room and disappeared in the dark.

The prospect of having to talk to the lambardar was not very exciting. Iqbal fished out his silver hip flask from underneath the pillow and took a long swig of whisky. He ate a few dry biscuits that were in the paper packet. He took his mattress and pillow to the roof where a charpai had been laid for him. Meet Singh apparently slept in the courtyard to guard the gurdwara.

Iqbal lay on his charpai and watched the stars in the teeming sky until he heard several voices entering the gurdwara and coming up the stairs. Then he got up to greet the visitors.

'Sat Sri Akal, Babu Sahib.'

'Salaam to you, Babu Sahib.'

They shook hands. Meet Singh did not bother to introduce them. Iqbal pushed the air mattress aside to make room on the charpai for the visitors. He sat down on the floor himself.

'I am ashamed for not having presented myself earlier,'said the Sikh. 'Please forgive me. I have brought some milk for you.'

'Yes, Sahib, we are ashamed of ourselves. You are our guest and we have not rendered you any service. Drink the milk before it gets cold,' added the other visitor. He was a tall lean man with a clipped beard.

'It is very kind of you . . . I know you have been busy with the police . . . I don't drink milk. Really I do not. We city-dwellers . . .'

The lambardar ignored Iqbal's well-mannered protests. He removed his dirty handkerchief from a large brass tumbler and began to stir the milk with his forefinger. 'It is fresh. I milked the buffalo only an hour back and got the wife to boil it. I know you educated people only drink boiled milk. There is quite a lot of sugar in it; it has settled at the bottom,' he added with a final stir. To emphasize the quality of the milk, he picked up a slab of clotted cream on his forefinger and slapped it back in the milk.

'Here, Babuji, drink it before it gets cold.'

'No! No! No, thank you, no!' protested Iqbal. He did not know how to get out of his predicament without offending the visitors. 'I don't ever drink milk. But if you insist, I will drink it later. I like it cold.'

'Yes, you drink it as you like, Babuji,' said the Muslim, coming to his rescue. 'Banta Singh, leave the tumbler here. Bhai will bring it back in the morning.'

The lambardar covered the tumbler with his handkerchief and put it under Iqbal's charpai. There was a long pause. Iqbal had pleasant visions of pouring the milk with all its clotted cream down the drain.

'Well, Babuji,' began the Muslim. 'Tell us something. What is happening in the world? What is all this about Pakistan and Hindustan?'

'We live in this little village and know nothing,' the lambardar put in. 'Babuji, tell us, why did the English leave?'

Iqbal did not know how to answer simple questions like these. Independence meant little or nothing to these people. They did not even realize that it was a step forward and that all they needed to do was to take the next step and turn the make-believe political freedom into a real economic one.

'They left because they had to. We had hundreds of thousands of young men trained to fight in the war. This time they had the arms too. Haven't you heard of the mutiny of the Indian sailors?

The soldiers would have done the same thing. The English were frightened. They did not shoot any of the Indians who joined the Indian National Army set up by the Japanese, because they thought the whole country would turn against them.'

Iqbal's thesis did not cut much ice.

'Babuji, what you say may be right,' said the lambardar hesitantly. 'But I was in the last war and fought in Mesopotamia and Gallipoli. We liked English officers. They were better than the Indian.'

'Yes,' added Meet Singh, 'my brother who is a havildar says all sepoys are happier with English officers than with Indian. My brother's colonel's memsahib still sends my niece things from London. You know, Lambardar Sahib, she even sent money at her wedding. What Indian officers' wives will do that?'

Iqbal tried to take the offensive. 'Why, don't you people want to be free? Do you want to remain slaves all your lives?'

After a long silence the lambardar answered: 'Freedom must be a good thing. But what will we get out of it? Educated people like you, Babu Sahib, will get the jobs the English had. Will we get more lands or more buffaloes?'

'No,' the Muslim said. 'Freedom is for the educated people who fought for it. We were slaves of the English, now we will be slaves of the educated Indians—or the Pakistanis.'

Iqbal was startled at the analysis.

'What you say is absolutely right,' he agreed warmly. 'If you want freedom to mean something for you—the peasants and workers—you have to get together and fight. Get the bania Congress government out. Get rid of the princes and the landlords and freedom will mean for you just what you think it should. More land, more buffaloes, no debts.'

'That is what that fellow told us,' interrupted Meet Singh, 'that fellow . . . Lambardara, what was his name? Comrade Something-or-other. Are you a comrade, Babu Sahib?'

'No.'

'I am glad. That comrade did not believe in God. He said when his party came into power they would drain the sacred pool round the temple at Tarn Taran and plant rice in it. He said it would be more useful.'

'That is foolish talk,' protested Iqbal. He wished Meet Singh had remembered the comrade's name. The man should be reported to headquarters and taken to task.

'If we have no faith in God then we are like animals,' said the Muslim gravely. 'All the world respects a religious man. Look at Gandhi! I hear he reads the Koran Sharif and the Unjeel along with his Vedas and Shastras. People sing his praise in the four corners of the earth. I have seen a picture in a newspaper of Gandhi's prayer meeting. It showed a lot of white men and women sitting cross-legged. One white girl had her eyes shut. They said she was the Big Lord's daughter. You see, Meet Singh, even the English respect a man of religion.'

'Of course, Chacha. Whatever you say is right to the sixteenth anna of the rupee,' agreed Meet Singh, rubbing his belly.

Iqbal felt his temper rise. 'They are a race of four-twenties,' he said vehemently. [Section 420 of the Indian Penal Code defines the offence of cheating.] 'Do not believe what they say.'

Once again he felt his venom had missed its mark. But the Big Lord's daughter sitting cross-legged with her eyes shut for the benefit of press photographers, and the Big Lord himself—the handsome, Hindustani-speaking cousin of the King, who loved India like the missionaries—was always too much for Iqbal.

'I have lived in their country many years. They are nice as human beings. Politically they are the world's biggest four-twenties. They would not have spread their domain all over the world if they had been honest. That, however, is irrelevant,' added Iqbal. It was time to change the subject. 'What is important is: what is going to happen now?'

'We know what is happening,' the lambardar answered with some heat. 'The winds of destruction are blowing across the land. All we hear is kill, kill. The only ones who enjoy freedom are thieves, robbers and cutthroats.' Then he added calmly: 'We were better off under the British. At least there was security.'

There was an uneasy silence. An engine was shunting up and

down the railway line rearranging its load of goods wagons. The Muslim changed the subject.

'That is the goods train. It must be late. Babu Sahib, you are tired; we must let you rest. If you need us, we will be always at your service.'

They all got up. Iqbal shook hands with his visitors without showing any trace of anger. Meet Singh conducted the lambardar and the Muslim down to the courtyard. He then retired to his charpai there.

Iqbal lay down once more and gazed at the stars. The wail of the engine in the still vast plain made him feel lonely and depressed. What could he—one little man—do in this enormous impersonal land of four hundred million? Could he stop the killing? Obviously not. Everyone—Hindu, Muslim, Sikh, Congressite, Leaguer, Akali, or Communist—was deep in it. It was fatuous to suggest that the bourgeois revolution could be turned into a proletarian one. The stage had not arrived. The proletariat was indifferent to political freedom for Hindustan or Pakistan, except when it could be given an economic significance like grabbing land by killing an owner who was of a different religious denomination. All that could be done was to divert the kill-and-grab instinct from communal channels and turn it against the propertied class. That was the proletarian revolution the easy way. His party bosses would not see it.

Iqbal wished they had sent someone else to Mano Majra. He would be so much more useful directing policy and clearing the cobwebs from their minds. But he was not a leader. He lacked the qualifications. He had not fasted. He had never been in jail. He had made none of the necessary 'sacrifices'. So, naturally, nobody would listen to him. He should have started his political career by finding an excuse to court imprisonment. But there was still time. He would do that as soon as he got back to Delhi. By then, the massacres would be over. It would be quite safe.

The goods train had left the station and was rumbling over the bridge. Iqbal fell asleep, dreaming of a peaceful life in jail.

Early next morning, Iqbal was arrested.

Meet Singh had gone out to the fields carrying his brass mug of water and chewing a keekar twig he used as a toothbrush. Iqbal had slept through the rumble of passing trains, the muezzin's call, and the other village noises. Two constables came into the gurdwara, looking in his room, examined his celluloid cups and saucers, shining aluminum spoons, forks and knives, his thermos, and then came up onto the roof. They shook Iqbal rudely. He sat up rubbing his eyes, somewhat bewildered. Before he could size up the situation and formulate the curt replies he would like to have given, he had told the policemen his name and occupation. One of them filled in the blank spaces on a yellow piece of printed paper and held it in front of Iqbal's blinking eyes.

'Here is warrant for your arrest. Get up.'

The other slipped the ring at one end of a pair of handcuffs in his belt and unlocked the links to put round Iqbal's wrists. The sight of the handcuffs brought Iqbal wide awake. He jumped out of bed and faced the policemen.

'You have no right to arrest me like this,' he shouted. 'You made up the warrant in front of me. This is not going to end here. The days of police rule are over. If you dare put your hands on me, the world will hear about it. I will see that the papers tell the people how you chaps do your duty.'

The policemen were taken aback. The young man's accent, the rubber pillows and mattress and all the other things they had seen in the room, and above all, his aggressive attitude, made them uneasy. They felt that perhaps they had made a mistake.

'Babu Sahib, we are only doing our duty. You settle this with the magistrate,' one of them answered politely. The other fumbled uneasily with the handcuffs.

'I will settle it with the whole lot of you—police and magistrates! Come and disturb people in sleep! You will regret this mistake.' Iqbal waited for the policemen to say something so that he could go on with his tirade against law and order. But they had been subdued.

'You will have to wait. I have to wash and change and leave

my things in somebody's care,' said Iqbal aggressively, giving them another chance to say something.

'All right, Babu Sahib. Take as long as you like.'

The policemen's civil attitude deflated Iqbal's anger. He collected his things and went down the stairs to his room. He went to the well, pulled up a bucket of water and began to wash. He was in no hurry.

Bhai Meet Singh came back vigorously brushing his teeth with the end of the keekar twig which he had chewed into a fibrous brush. The presence of policemen in the gurdwara did not surprise him. Whenever they came to the village and could not find accommodation at the lambardar's house they came to the temple. He had been expecting them after the moneylender's murder.

'Sat Sri Akal,' said Meet Singh, throwing away his keekar toothbrush.

'Sat Sri Akal,' replied the policemen.

'Would you like some tea or something? Some buttermilk?'

'We are waiting for the Babu Sahib,' the policemen said. 'If you can give us something while he is getting ready, it will be very kind.'

Meet Singh maintained a casual indifference. It was not up to him to argue with the police or be nosy about their business. Iqbal Singh was probably a 'comrade'. He certainly talked like one.

'I will make some tea for him, too,' replied Meet Singh. He looked at Iqbal. 'Or will you have your own out of the big bottle?'

'Thank you very much,' answered Iqbal through the tooth paste froth in his mouth. He spat it out. 'The tea in the bottle must be cold by now. I would be grateful for a hot cup. And would you mind looking after my things while I am away? They are arresting me for something. They do not know themselves for what.'

Meet Singh pretended he had not heard. The policemen looked a little sheepish.

'It is not our fault, Babu Sahib,' one of them said. 'Why are you getting angry with us? Get angry with the magistrate.'

Iqbal ignored their protest by more brushing of his teeth. He washed his face and came back to the room rubbing himself with a towel. He let the air out of the mattress and the pillow and rolled them up. He emptied the holdall of its contents: books, clothes, torch, a large silver hip flask. He made a list of his things and put them back. When Meet Singh brought tea, Iqbal handed him the holdall.

'Bhaiji, I have put all my things in the holdall. I hope it will not be too much trouble looking after them. I would rather trust you than the police in this free country of ours.'

The policemen looked away. Meet Singh was embarrassed.

'Certainly, Babu Sahib,' he said meekly. 'I am your servant as well as that of the police. Here everyone is welcome. You like tea in your own cup?'

Iqbal got out his celluloid teacup and spoon. The constables took brass tumblers from Meet Singh. They wrapped the loose ends of their turbans round the tumblers to protect their hands from the hot brass. To reassure themselves they sipped noisily. But Iqbal was in complete possession of the situation. He sat on the string cot while they sat on the threshold and Meet Singh on the floor outside. They did not dare to speak to him for fear of rudeness. The constable with the handcuffs had quietly taken them off his belt and thrust them in his pocket. They finished their tea and looked up uneasily. Iqbal sat sullenly staring over their heads with an intensity charged with importance. He glared vacantly into space, occasionally taking a spinsterish sip of his tea. When he had finished, he stood up abruptly.

'I am ready,' he announced, dramatically holding out his hands. 'Put on the handcuffs.'

'There is no need for handcuffs, Babuji,' answered one of the constables. 'You had better cover your face or you will be recognized at the identification parade.'

Iqbal pounced on the opportunity. 'Is this how you do your duty? If the rule is that I have to be handcuffed, then handcuffed I shall be. I am not afraid of being recognized. I am not a thief or a dacoit. I am a political worker. I will go through the village as I am so that people can see what the police do to people they do not like.'

This outburst was too much for one of the constables. He spoke sharply:

'Babuji, we are being polite to you. We keep saying "ji", "ji" to you all the time, but you want to sit on our heads. We have told you a hundred times we are doing our duty, but you insist on believing that we have a personal grudge.' He turned to his colleague. 'Put the handcuffs on the fellow. He can do what he likes with his face. If I had a face like his, I would want to hide it. We will report that he refused to cover it.'

Iqbal did not have a ready answer to the sarcasm. He had a Semitic consciousness of his hooked nose. Quite involuntarily he brushed it with the back of his hand. Reference to his physical appearance always put him off. The handcuffs were fastened round his wrists and chained onto the policeman's belt.

'Sat Sri Akal, Bhaiji. I will be back soon.'

'Sat Sri Akal, Iqbal Singhji, and may the Guru protect you. Sat Sri Akal, Sentryji.'

'Sat Sri Akal.'

The party marched out of the temple courtyard, leaving Meet Singh standing with the kettle of tea in his hand.

At the time the two constables were sent to arrest Iqbal, a posse of ten men was sent to arrest Juggut Singh. Policemen surrounded his house at all points. Constables armed with rifles were posted on neighbouring roofs and in the front and rear of the house. Then six others armed with revolvers rushed into the courtyard. Juggut Singh lay on his charpai, wrapped from head to foot in a dirty white sheet and snoring lustily. He had spent two nights and a day in the jungle without food or shelter. He had come home in the early hours of the morning when he believed everyone in the village would be asleep. The neighbours had been vigilant and the police were informed immediately. They waited till he had filled himself with food and was sound asleep. His mother had gone out, bolting the door from the outside.

Juggut Singh's feet were put in fetters and handcuffs were fastened on his right wrist while he slept. Policemen put their revolvers in their holsters. Men with rifles joined them in the courtyard. They prodded Juggut Singh with the butt ends of their guns.

'O Jugga, get up, it is almost afternoon.'

'See how he sleeps like a pig without a care in the world.'

Jugga sat up wearily, blinking his eyes. He gazed at the handcuffs and the fetters with philosophic detachment, then stretched his arms wide and yawned loudly. Sleep came on him again and he began to nod.

Juggut Singh's mother came in and saw her courtyard full of armed policemen. Her son sat on the charpai with his head resting on his manacled hands. His eyes were shut. She ran up to him and clasped him by the knees. She put her head in his lap and started to cry.

Juggut Singh woke up from his reverie. He pushed his mother back rudely.

'Why are you crying?' he said. 'You know I had nothing to do with the dacoity.'

She began to wail. 'He did not do it. He did nothing. In the name of God, I swear he did nothing.'

'Then where was he on the night of the murder?' the head constable said.

'He was out in his fields. He was not with the dacoits. I swear he was not.'

'He is a badmash under orders not to go out of the village after sunset. We have to arrest him for that in any case.' He motioned to his men. 'Search the rooms and the barn.' The head constable had his doubts about Juggut Singh partaking in a dacoity in his own village. It was most unusual.

Four constables busied themselves looking around the house, emptying steel trunks and tin cans. The haystack was pulled down and the hay scattered in the yard. The spear was found without difficulty.

'I suppose this has been put here by your uncle?' said the head constable addressing the mother sourly. 'Wrap the blade in a piece of cloth, it may have blood stains on it.'

'There is nothing on it,' cried the mother, 'nothing. He keeps it to kill wild pigs that come to destroy the crops. I swear he is innocent.'

'We will see. We will see,' the head constable dismissed her. 'You better get proof of his innocence ready for the magistrate.'

The old woman stopped moaning. She did have proof—the packet of broken bangles. She had not told Jugga about it. If she had, he would certainly have gone mad at the insult and been violent to someone. Now he was in fetters and handcuffs, he could only lose his temper.

'Wait, brother policemen. I have the evidence.'

The policemen watched the woman go in and bring out a packet from the bottom of her steel trunk. She unwrapped the brown paper. There were broken pieces of blue and red glass bangles with tiny gold spots. Two of them were intact. The head constable took them.

'What sort of proofs are these?'

'The dacoits threw them in the courtyard after the murder. They wanted to insult Jugga for not coming with them. Look!' She held out her hands. 'I am too old to wear glass bangles and they are too small for my wrists.'

'Then Jugga must know who the dacoits were. What did they say when they threw them?' asked the head constable.

'Nothing, they said nothing. They abused Jugga . . .'

'Can't you keep your mouth shut?' interrupted Jugga angrily. 'I do not know who the dacoits were. All I know is that I was not with them.'

'Who leaves you bangles?' asked the head constable. He smiled and held up the bits of glass in his hands.

Jugga lost his temper. He raised his manacled fists and brought them heavily down on the head constable's palms. 'What seducer of his mother can throw bangles at me? What . . .'

The constables closed round Juggut Singh and started slapping him and kicking him with their thick boots. Jugga sat down on his haunches, covering his head with his arms. His mother began to beat her forehead and started crying again. She broke into the cordon of policemen and threw herself on her son.

'Don't hit him. The Guru's curse be on you. He is innocent. It is all my fault. You can beat me.'

The beating stopped. The head constable picked pieces of glass out of his palm, pressed out blood, and wiped it with his handkerchief.

'You keep the evidence of your son's innocence,' he said bitterly. 'We will get the story out of this son of a bitch of yours in our own way. When he gets a few lashes on his buttocks, he will talk. Take him out.'

Juggut Singh was led out of the house in handcuffs and fetters. He left without showing a trace of emotion for his mother, who continued to wail and beat her forehead and breasts. His parting words were:

'I will be back soon. They cannot give me more than a few months for having a spear and going out of the village. Sat Sri Akal.'

Jugga recovered his temper as quickly as he had lost it. He forgot the incident of the bangles and the beating as soon as he stepped across his threshold. He had no malice or ill will towards the policemen: they were not human like other human beings. They had no affections, no loyalties or enmities. They were just men in uniform you tried to avoid.

There was not much point in Juggut Singh covering his face. The whole village knew him. He went past the villagers, smiling and raising his manacled hands in a greeting to everyone. The fetters around his feet forced him to walk slowly with his legs apart. He had a devil-may-care jauntiness in his step. He showed his unconcern by twirling his thin brown moustache and cracking obscene jokes with the policemen.

Iqbal and the two constables joined Juggut Singh's party by the river. They all proceeded upstream towards the bridge. The head constable walked in front. Armed policemen marched on the sides and at the rear of the prisoners. Iqbal was lost in the khaki and red of their uniforms. Juggut Singh's head and shoulders showed above the turbans of the policemen. It was like a procession of horses with an elephant in their midst—taller, broader, slower, with his chains clanking like ceremonial trappings.

No one seemed to be in the mood to talk. The policemen were uneasy. They knew that they had made a mistake, or rather, two mistakes. Arresting the social worker was a blunder and a likely source of trouble. His belligerent attitude confirmed his innocence. Some sort of case would have to be made up against him. That was always a tricky thing to do to educated people. Juggut Singh was too obvious a victim to be the correct one. He had undoubtedly broken the law in leaving the village at night, but he was not likely to have joined in a dacoity in his own village. He would be too easily recognized by his enormous size. Also, it was quite clear that these two had met for the first time.

Iqbal's pride had been injured. Up to the time he met Juggut Singh, he was under the impression that he had been arrested for his politics. He had insisted on being handcuffed so that the villagers could see with what dignity he bore himself. They would be angered at such an outrage to civil liberties. But the men had gaped stupidly and the women peered through their veils and asked each other in whispers, 'Who is this?' When he joined the group that escorted Juggut Singh, the point of the policeman's advice, 'Cover your face, otherwise you may be recognized at the identification parade,' came home to him. He was under arrest in connection with the murder of Ram Lal. It was so stupid he could hardly believe it. Everyone knew that he had come to Mano Majra after the murder. On the same train as the policemen, in fact. They could be witness of his alibi. The situation was too ludicrous for words. But Punjabi policemen were not the sort who admitted making mistakes. They would trump up some sort of charge: vagrancy, obstructing officers in doing their duty, or some such thing. He would fight them tooth and nail.

The only one in the party who did not seem to mind was

Juggut Singh. He had been arrested before. He had spent quite as much time in jail as at home. His association with the police was an inheritance. Register number ten at the police station, which gave the record of the activities of the bad characters of the locality, had carried his father Alam Singh's name while he lived. Alam Singh had been convicted of dacoity with murder, and hanged. Juggut Singh's mother had to mortgage all their land to pay lawyers. Juggut Singh had to find money to redeem the land, and he had done that within the year. No one could prove how he had raised the money, but at the end of the year the police had taken him. His name was entered in register number ten and he was officially declared a man of bad character. Behind his back everyone referred to him as a 'number ten'.

Juggut Singh looked at the prisoner beside him several times. He wanted to start a conversation. Iqbal had his eyes fixed in front of him and walked with the camera-consciousness of an actor facing the lens. Juggut Singh lost patience.

'Listen. What village are you from?' he asked and grinned, baring a set of even teeth studded with gold points in the centres.

Iqbal looked up, but did not return the smile.

'I am not a villager. I come from Delhi. I was sent to organize peasants, but the government does not like the people to be organized.'

Juggut Singh became polite. He gave up the tone of familiarity. 'I hear we have our own rule now,' he said. 'It is Mahatma Gandhi's government in Delhi, isn't it? They say so in our village.'

'Yes, the Englishmen have gone but the rich Indians have taken their place. What have you or your fellow villagers got out of Independence? More bread or more clothes? You are in the same handcuffs and fetters which the English put on you. We have to get together and rise. We have nothing to lose but these chains.' Iqbal emphasized the last sentence by raising his hands up to his face and jerking them as if the movement would break the handcuffs.

The policemen looked at each other.

Juggut Singh looked down at the fetters round his ankles and the iron bars which linked them to the handcuffs.

'I am a badmash. All governments put me in jail.'

'But,' interrupted Iqbal angrily, 'what makes you a badmash? The government! It makes regulations and keeps registers, policemen and jailers to enforce them. For anyone they do not like, they have a rule which makes him a bad character and a criminal. What have I . . .'

'No, Babu Sahib,' broke in Juggut Singh good-humouredly, 'it is our fate. It is written on our foreheads and on the lines of our hands. I am always wanting to do something. When there is ploughing to be done or the harvest to be gathered, then I am busy. When there is no work, my hands still itch to do something. So I do something, and it is always wrong.'

The party passed under the bridge and approached the rest house. Juggut Singh's complacency had put Iqbal off. He did not want to waste his breath arguing with a village bad character. He wanted to save his words for the magistrate. He would let him have it in English—the accent would make him squirm.

When the police brought in the prisoners the subinspector ordered them to be taken to the servants' quarters. The magistrate was in his room dressing. The head constable left the prisoners with his men and came back to the bungalow.

'Who is this small chap you have brought?' asked the subinspector, looking a little worried.

'I arrested him on your orders. He was the stranger staying at the Sikh temple.'

The answer irritated the subinspector. 'I do not suppose you have any brains of your own! I leave a little job to you and you go and make a fool of yourself. You should have seen him before arresting him. Isn't he the same man who got off the train with us yesterday?'

'The train?' queried the head constable, feigning ignorance. 'I did not see him on the train, cherisher of the poor. I only carried out your orders and arrested the stranger loitering about the village under suspicious circumstances.'

The subinspector's temper shot up.

'Ass!'

The head constable avoided his officer's gaze.

'You are an ass of some place,' he repeated with greater vehemence. 'Have you no brains at all?'

'Cherisher of the poor, what fault have I . . .'

'Shut up!'

The head constable started looking at his feet. The subinspector let his temper cool. He had to face Hukum Chand, who relied on him and did not expect to be let down. After some thought, the subinspector peered through the wire-gauze door.

'Have I permission to enter?'

'Come in. Come in, Inspector Sahib,' Hukum Chand replied. 'Do not wait on formalities.'

The subinspector went in, and saluted.

'Well, what have you been doing?' asked the magistrate. He was rubbing cream on his freshly shaven chin. In a tumbler on the dressing table a flat white tablet danced about the bottom, sending up a stream of bubbles.

'Sir, we have made two arrests this morning. One is Jugga badmash. He was out of his house on the night of the dacoity. We are bound to get some information out of him. The other is the stranger whose presence had been reported by the headman and you ordered him to be arrested.'

Hukum Chand stopped rubbing his chin. He detected the attempt to pass off the second arrest onto him.

'Who is he?'

The inspector shouted to the head constable outside.

'What is the name of the fellow you arrested at the Sikh temple?'

'Iqbal.'

'Iqbal what?' questioned the magistrate loudly.

'I will just find out, sir.' The head constable ran across to the servants' quarters before the magistrate could let fly at him. Hukum Chand felt his temper rising. He took a sip out of his glass. The subinspector shuffled uneasily. The head constable came back a few minutes later and coughed to announce his return.

'Sir,' he coughed again. 'Sir, he can read and write. He is educated.'

The magistrate turned to the door angrily.

'Has he a father and mother, a faith, or not? Educated!'

'Sir,' faltered the head constable, 'he refuses to tell us his father's name and says he has no religion. He says he will speak to you himself.'

'Go and find out,' roared the magistrate. 'Whip him on his buttocks till he talks. Go . . . no, wait, the Subinspector Sahib will handle this.'

Hukum Chand was in a rage. He gulped down the fizzing water in the tumbler and mopped his head with the shaving towel. A belch relieved him of his mounting wrath.

'Nice fellows, you and your policemen! You go and arrest people without finding out their names, parentage or caste. You make me sign blank warrants of arrest. Some day you will arrest the Governor and say Hukum Chand ordered you to do so. You will have me dismissed.'

'Cherisher of the poor, I will go and look into this. This man came to Mano Majra yesterday. I will find out his antecedents and business.'

'Well, then, go and find out, and do not just stand and stare,' barked Hukum Chand. He was not in the habit of losing his temper or of being rude. After the subinspector had left, he examined his tongue in the mirror and put another tablet of seltzer in the tumbler.

The subinspector went out and stopped on the veranda to take a few deep breaths. The magistrate's wrath decided his attitude. He would have to take a strong line and finish the shilly-shallying. He went to the servants' quarters. Iqbal and his escort stood apart from Juggut Singh's crowd. The young man had a look of injured dignity. The subinspector thought it best not to speak to him.

'Search this man's clothes. Take him inside one of the quarters and strip him. I will examine them myself.'

Iqbal's planned speech remained undelivered. The constable almost dragged him by the handcuffs into a room. His resistance had gone. He took off his shirt and handed it to the policeman. The subinspector came in and without bothering to examine the shirt ordered:

'Take off your pyjamas!'

Iqbal felt humiliated. There was no fight left in him. 'There are no pockets to the pyjamas. I cannot hide anything in them.'

'Take them off and do not argue.' The subinspector slapped his khaki trousers with his swagger stick to emphasize the order.

Iqbal loosened the knot in the cord. The pyjamas fell in a heap around his ankles. He was naked save for the handcuffs on his wrists. He stepped out of the pyjamas to let the policemen examine them.

'No, that is not necessary,' broke in the subinspector. 'I have seen all I wanted to see. You can put on your clothes. You say you are a social worker. What was your business in Mano Majra?'

'I was sent by my party,' answered Iqbal, re-tying the knot in the cord of his pyjamas.

'What party?'

'People's Party of India.'

The subinspector looked at Iqbal with a sinister smile. 'The People's Party of India,' he repeated slowly, pronouncing each word distinctly. 'You are sure it was not the Muslim League?'

Iqbal did not catch the significance of the question.

'No, why should I be a member of the Muslim League? I . . .'

The subinspector walked out of the room before Iqbal had finished his sentence. He ordered the constables to take the prisoners to the police station. He went back to the rest house to report his discovery to the magistrate. There was an obsequious smile on his face.

'Cherisher of the poor, it is all right. He says he has been sent by the People's Party. But I am sure he is a Muslim Leaguer. They are much the same. We would have had to arrest him in any case if he was up to mischief so near the border. We can charge him with something or other later.'

'How do you know he is a Muslim Leaguer?'

The subinspector smiled confidently. 'I had him stripped.'

Hukum Chand shook his glass to churn the dregs of chalk at the bottom, and slowly drank up the remaining portion of the seltzer. He looked thoughtfully into the empty tumbler and added:

'Fill in the warrant of arrest correctly. Name: Mohammed Iqbal, son of Mohammed Something-or-other, or just father unknown. Caste: Mussulman. Occupation: Muslim League worker.'

The subinspector saluted dramatically.

'Wait, wait. Do not leave things half done. Enter in your police diary words to the effect that Ram Lal's murderers have not yet been traced but that information about them is expected soon. Didn't you say Jugga has something to do with it?'

'Yes, sir. The dacoits threw glass bangles in his courtyard before leaving. Apparently he had refused to join them in their venture.'

'Well, get the names out of him quickly. Beat him if necessary.'

The subinspector smiled. 'I will get the names of the dacoits out of him in twenty-four hours and without any beating.'

'Yes, yes, get them in any way you like,' answered Hukum Chand impatiently. 'Also, enter today's two arrests on separate pages of the police station diary with other items in between. Do not let there be any more bungling.'

The subinspector saluted again.

'I will take good care, sir.'

Iqbal and Jugga were taken to Chundunnugger police station in a tonga. Iqbal was given the place of honour in the middle of the front seat. The driver perched himself on the wooden shaft alongside the horse's flank, leaving his seat empty. Juggut Singh sat on the rear seat between two policemen. It was a long and dusty drive on an unmetalled road which ran parallel to the railway track. The only person at ease was Jugga. He knew the policemen and they knew him. Nor was the situation unfamiliar to him.

'You must have many prisoners in the police station these

days,' he stated.

'No, not one,' answered one of the constables. 'We do not arrest rioters. We only disperse them. And there is no time to deal with other crimes. Yours are the first arrests we have made in the last seven days. Both cells are vacant. You can have one all to yourself.'

'Babuji will like that,' Jugga said. 'Won't you, Babuji?'

Iqbal did not answer. Jugga felt slightly snubbed, and tried to change the subject quickly.

'You must have a lot of work to do with this Hindustan-Pakistan business going on,' he remarked to the constable.

'Yes. There is all this killing and the police force has been reduced to less than half.'

'Why, have they joined up with Pakistan?'

'We do not know whether they have joined up on the other side—they kept protesting that they did not want to go at all. On the day of Independence, the Superintendent sahib disarmed all Muslim policemen and they fled. Their intentions were evil. Muslims are like that. You can never trust them.'

'Yes,' added another policeman, 'it was the Muslim police taking sides which made the difference in the riots. Hindu boys of Lahore would have given the Muslims hell if it had not been for their police. They did a lot of *zulum*.'

'Their army is like that, too. Baluch soldiers have been shooting people whenever they were sure there was no chance of running into Sikh or Gurkha troops.'

'They cannot escape from God. No one can escape from God,' said Juggut Singh vehemently. Everyone looked a little surprised. Even Iqbal tuned round to make sure that the voice was Juggut Singh's.

'Isn't that right, Babuji? You are a clever man, you tell me, can one escape the wrath of God?'

Iqbal said nothing.

'No, of course not,' Jugga answered himself. 'I tell you something which Bhai Meet Singh told me. It is worth listening to, Babuji. It is absolutely sixteen annas' worth in the rupee.'

Every rupee is worth sixteen annas, thought Iqbal. He refused to take interest. Jugga went on.

'The Bhai told me of a truckful of Baluch soldiers who were going from Amritsar to Lahore. When they were getting near the Pakistan border, the soldiers began to stick bayonets into Sikhs going along the road. The driver would slow down near a cyclist or a pedestrian, the soldiers on the footboard would stab him in the back and then the driver would accelerate away fast. They killed many people like this and were feeling happier and happier as they got nearer Pakistan. They were within a mile of the border and were travelling at great speed. What do you think happened then?'

'What?' asked an obliging policeman. They all listened intently—all except Iqbal. Even the driver stopped flogging the horse and looked back.

'Listen, Babuji, this is worth listening to. A pariah dog ran across the road. The very same driver of the truck who had been responsible for killing so many people swerved sharply to the right to avoid the dog, a mangy pariah dog. He crashed into a tree. The driver and two of the soldiers were killed. All the others seriously wounded. What do you say to that?'

Policemen murmured approval. Iqbal felt irritated.

'Who caused the crash, the dog or God?' he asked cynically.

'God, of course,' answered one of the policemen. 'Why should one who enjoyed killing human beings be bothered by a stray dog getting under his wheels?'

'You tell me,' said Iqbal coldly. He squashed everyone except Jugga, who was irrepressible. Jugga turned to the tonga driver. The man had started whipping his horse again.

'Bhola, have you no fear of God that you beat your animal so mercilessly?'

Bhola stopped beating the horse. The expression on his face was resentful: it was his horse and he could do what he liked to it.

'Bholeya, how is business these days?' asked Jugga, trying to make up.

'God is merciful,' answered the driver pointing to the sky with his whip, then added quickly, 'Inspector sahib is also merciful. We are alive and manage to fill our bellies.'

'Don't you make money off these refugees who are wanting to go to Pakistan?'

'And lose my life for money?' asked Bhola angrily. 'No, thank you, brother, you keep your advice to yourself. When the mobs attack they do not wait to find out who you are, Hindu or Muslim; they kill. The other day four Sikh Sardars in a jeep drove alongside a mile-long column of Muslim refugees walking on the road. Without warning they opened fire with their sten guns. Four sten guns! God alone knows how many they killed. What would happen if a mob got hold of my tonga full of Muslims? They would kill me first and ask afterwards.'

'Why didn't a dog get under the jeep and upset it?' asked Iqbal sarcastically.

There was an awkward pause. No one knew what to say to this sour-tempered babu. Jugga asked naïvely:

'Babuji, don't you believe that bad acts yield a bitter harvest? It is the law of karma. So the bhai is always saying. The Guru has also said the same in the Book.'

'Yes, absolutely, sixteen annas in the rupee,' sneered Iqbal.

'Achhaji, have it your own way,' said Jugga, still smiling. 'You will never agree with ordinary people.' He turned to the driver again.

'Bholeya, I hear a lot of women are being abducted and sold cheap. You could find a wife for yourself.'

'Why, Sardara, if you can find a Mussulmanni without paying for her, am I impotent that I should have to buy an abducted woman?' replied Bhola.

Jugga was taken aback. His temper began to rise. The policemen, who had started to snigger, looked nervously at Juggut Singh. Bhola regretted his mistake.

'Why, Juggia,' he said, changing his tone. 'You make fun of others, but get angry when someone retorts.'

'If these handcuffs and fetters had not been on me, I would

have broken every bone in your body,' said Jugga fiercely. 'You are lucky to have escaped today, but if I hear you repeat this thing again I will tear your tongue out of your mouth.' Jugga spat loudly.

Bhola was thoroughly frightened. 'Do not lose your temper. What have I . . .'

'Bastard.'

That was the end of the conversations. The uneasy silence in the tonga was broken only by Bhola swearing at his horse. Jugga was lost in angry thoughts. He was surprised that his clandestine meetings were public knowledge. Somebody had probably seen him and Nooran talking to each other. That must have started the gossip. If a tonga driver from Chundunnugger knew, everyone in Mano Majra would have been talking about if for some time. The last to learn of gossip are the parties concerned. Perhaps Imam Baksh and his daughter Nooran were the only ones in the village who knew nothing of what was being said.

The party reached Chundunnugger after noon. The tonga came to a halt outside the police station, which was a couple of furlongs distant from the town. The prisoners were escorted through an arched gateway which had WELCOME painted on it in large letters. They were first taken to the reporting room. The head constable opened a large register and made the entries of the day's events on separate pages. Just above the table was an old framed picture of King George VI with a placard stating in Urdu, BRIBERY IS A CRIME. On another wall was pasted a coloured portrait of Gandhi torn from a calendar. Beneath it was a motto written in English, HONESTY IS THE BEST POLICY. Other portraits in the room were those of absconders, bad characters, and missing persons.

After the daily diary entries had been made, the prisoners were taken across the courtyard to their cells. There were only two cells in the police station. These were on one side of the courtyard facing the policemen's barracks. The wall of the farther end of the square was covered by a railway creeper.

Jugga's arrival was the subject of much hilarity.

'Oye, you are back again. You think it is your father-in-law's house,' shouted one of the constables from his barrack.

'It is, seeing the number of policemen's daughters I have seduced,' answered Juggut Singh at the top of his voice. He had forgotten the unpleasantness in the tonga.

'Oye, Badmasha, you will not desist from your badmashi. Wait till the Inspector sahib hears of what you said and he will put hot chillies up your bottom.'

'You cannot do that to your son-in-law!'

With Iqbal it was different. His handcuffs were removed with apologies. A chair, a table, and a charpai were put in his cell. The head constable collected all the daily newspapers and magazines, English and Urdu, that he could find and left them in the cell. Iqbal's food was served on a brass plate and a small pitcher and a glass tumbler were put on the table beside his charpai. Jugga was given no furniture in his cell. His food was literally flung at him and he ate his chapattis out of his hand. A constable poured water onto his cupped palm through the iron bars. Jugga's bed was the hard cement floor.

The difference in treatment did not surprise Iqbal. In a country which had accepted caste distinctions for many centuries, inequality had become an inborn mental concept. If caste was abolished by legislation, it came up in other forms of class distinction. In thoroughly westernized circles like that of the civil servants in the government secretariat in Delhi, places for parking cars were marked according to seniority, and certain entrances to offices were reserved for higher officials. Lavatories were graded according to rank and labelled SENIOR OFFICERS, JUNIOR OFFICERS, CLERKS AND STENOGRAPHERS and OTHER RANKS. With a mental make-up so thoroughly sectionalized, grading according to their social status people who were charged or convicted of the same offence did not appear incongruous. Iqbal was A-class. Jugga was the rock-bottom C.

After his midday meal, Iqbal lay down on the charpai. He heard snoring from Jugga's cell. But he himself was far too disturbed to sleep. His mind was like the delicate spring of a watch, which quivers for several hours after it has been touched. He sat up and began to turn over the pile of newspapers the head constable had left him. They were all alike: the same news, the same statements, the same editorials. Except for the wording of the headlines, they might all have been written by the same hand. Even the photographs were the same. In disgust, he turned to the matrimonial ads. There was sometimes entertainment there. But the youth of the Punjab were as alike as the news. The qualities they required in a wife were identical. All wanted virgins. A few, more broad-minded than the rest, were willing to consider widows, but only if they had not been deflowered. All demanded women who were good at h. h. a., or household affairs. To the advanced and charitable, c. & d. [caste and dowry] were no bar. Not many asked for photographs of their prospective wives. Beauty, they recognized, was only skin-deep. Most wanted to 'correspond with horoscopes'. Astronomical harmony was the one guarantee of happiness. Iqbal threw the papers away, and rummaged through the magazines. If anything, they were worse than the newspapers. There was the inevitable article on the Ajanta cave frescoes. There was the article on Indian ballet. There was the article on Tagore. There was the article on the stories of Prem Chand. There were the articles on the private lives of film stars. Iqbal gave up, and lay down again. He felt depressed about everything. It occurred to him that he had hardly slept for three days. He wondered if this would be considered a 'sacrifice'. It was possible. He must find some way of sending word to the party. Then, perhaps . . . He fell asleep with visions of banner headlines announcing his arrest, his release, his triumphant emergence as a leader.

In the evening a policeman came to Iqbal's cell, carrying another chair.

'Is somebody going to share my cell?' asked Iqbal a little apprehensively.

'No, Babuji. Only the Inspector sahib. He wishes to have a word with you. He is coming now.'

Iqbal did not answer. The policeman studied the position of the chair for a moment. Then he withdrew. There was a sound of voices in the corridor, and the subinspector appeared.

'Have I your permission to enter?'

Iqbal nodded. 'What can I do for you, Inspector Sahib?'

'We are your slaves, Mr Iqbal. You should command us and we will serve you,' the subinspector answered with a smile. He was proud of his ability to change his tone and manner as the circumstances required. That was diplomacy.

'I did not know you were so kind to people you arrested for murder. It is on a charge of murder that you have brought me here, isn't it? I do not suppose your policemen told you I came to Mano Majra yesterday on the same train as they did.'

'We have framed no charge. That is for the court. We are only detaining you on suspicion. We cannot allow political agitators in the border areas.' The subinspector continued to smile. 'Why don't you go and do your propaganda in Pakistan where you belong?'

Iqbal was stung to fury, but he tried to suppress any sign of his anger.

'What exactly do you mean by "belonging to Pakistan", Inspector Sahib?'

'You are a Muslim. You go to Pakistan.'

'That is a bloody lie,' exploded Iqbal. 'What is more, you know it is a bloody lie. You just want to cover up your stupidity by trumping up a false case.'

The Inspector spoke back sourly.

'You should use your tongue with some discrimination, Mr Iqbal. I am not in your father's pay to have to put up with your "bloodys". Your name is Iqbal and you are circumcised. I have examined you myself. Also, you cannot give any explanation for your presence in Mano Majra. That is enough.'

'It will not be enough when it comes up in court, and in the newspapers. I am not a Muslim—not that that matters—and what I came to Mano Majra for is none of your business. If you do not release me within twenty-four hours I will move a habeas corpus petition and tell the court the way you go about your duties.'

'Habeas corpus petition?' The subinspector roared with laughter. 'It seems you have been living in foreign lands too long, Mr Iqbal. Even now you live in a fool's paradise. You will live and learn.'

The subinspector left the cell abruptly, and locked the steel bar gate. He opened the adjoining one behind which Jugga was locked.

'Sat Sri Akal, Inspector Sahib.'

The subinspector did not acknowledge the greeting.

'Will you ever give up being a badmash?'

'King of pearls, you can say what you like, but this time I am innocent. I swear by the Guru I am innocent.'

Jugga remained seated on the floor. The subinspector stood leaning against the wall.

'Where were you on the night of the dacoity?'

'I had nothing to do with the dacoity,' answered Jugga evasively.

'Where were you on the night of the dacoity?' repeated the subinspector.

Jugga looked down at the floor. 'I had gone to my fields. It was my turn of water.'

The subinspector knew he was lying. 'I can check up the turn of water with the canal man. Did you inform the lambardar that you were going out of the village?'

Jugga only shuffled his feet and kept on looking at the floor.

'Your mother said you had gone to drive away wild pigs.'

Jugga continued to shuffle his feet. After a long pause he said again, 'I had nothing to do with the dacoity. I am innocent.'

'Who were the dacoits?'

'King of pearls, how should I know who the dacoits were? I was out of the village at the time, otherwise you think anyone would have dared to rob and kill in Mano Majra?'

'Who were the dacoits?' repeated the subinspector menacingly. 'I know you know them. They certainly know you. They left a gift of glass bangles for you.'

Jugga did not reply.

'You want to be whipped on your buttocks or have red chillies put up your rectum before you talk?'

Jugga winced. He knew what the subinspector meant. He had been through it—once. Hands and feet pinned under legs of charpais with half a dozen policemen sitting on them. Testicles twisted and squeezed till one became senseless with pain. Powdered red chillies thrust up the rectum by rough hands, and the sensation of having the tail on fire for several days. All this, and no food or water, or hot spicy food with a bowl of shimmering cool water put outside the cell just beyond one's reach. The memory shook him.

'No,' he said. 'For God's sake, no.' He flung himself on the floor and clasped the subinspector's shoes with both his hands. 'Please, O king of pearls.' He was ashamed of himself, but he knew he could never endure such torture again. 'I am innocent. By the name of the Guru, I had nothing to do with the dacoity.'

Seeing six foot four of muscle cringing at his feet gave the subinspector a feeling of elation. He had never known anyone to hold out against physical pain, not one. The pattern of torture had to be carefully chosen. Some succumbed to hunger, others—of the Iqbal type—to the inconvenience of having to defecate in front of the policemen. Some to flies sitting on their faces smeared with treacle, with their hands tied behind them. Some to lack of sleep. In the end they all gave in.

'I will give you two days to tell me the names of the dacoits,' he said. 'Otherwise, I will beat your behind till it looks like the tail of a ram.'

The subinspector freed his feet from Jugga's hands and walked out. His visits had been a failure. He would have to change his tactics. It was frustrating to deal with two people so utterly different.

KALYUG

Early in September the time schedule in Mano Majra started going wrong. Trains became less punctual than ever before and many more started to run through at night. Some days it seemed as though the alarm clock had been set for the wrong hour. On others, it was as if no one had remembered to wind it. Imam Baksh waited for Meet Singh to make the first start. Meet Singh waited for the mullah's call to prayer before getting up. People stayed in bed late without realizing that times had changed and the mail train might not run through at all. Children did not know when to be hungry, and clamoured for food all the time. In the evenings, everyone was indoors before sunset and in bed before the express came by—if it did come by. Goods trains had stopped running altogether, so there was no lullaby to lull them to sleep. Instead, ghost trains went past at odd hours between midnight and dawn, disturbing the dreams of Mano Majra.

This was not all that changed the life of the village. A unit of Sikh soldiers arrived and put up tents near the railway station. They built a six-foot-high square of sandbags about the base of the signal near the bridge, and mounted a machine gun in each face. Armed sentries began to patrol the platform and no villagers were allowed near the railings. All trains coming from Delhi stopped and changed their drivers and guards before moving on to Pakistan. Those coming from Pakistan ran through with their engines screaming with release and relief.

One morning, a train from Pakistan halted at Mano Majra railway station. At first glance, it had the look of the trains in the days of peace. No one sat on the roof. No one clung between the bogies. No one was balanced on the footboards. But somehow it was different. There was something uneasy about it. It had a ghostly quality. As soon as it pulled up to the platform, the guard emerged from the tail end of the train and went into the stationmaster's office. Then the two went to the soldiers' tents and spoke to the officer in charge. The soldiers were called out and the villagers loitering about were ordered back to Mano Majra. One man was sent off on a motorcycle to Chundunnugger. An hour later, the subinspector with about fifty armed policemen turned up at the station. Immediately after them, Mr Hukum Chand drove up in his American car.

The arrival of the ghost train in broad daylight created a commotion in Mano Majra. People stood on their roofs to see what was happening at the station. All they could see was the black top of the train stretching from one end of the platform to the other. The station building and the railings blocked the rest of the train from view. Occasionally a soldier or a policeman came out of the station and then went back again.

In the afternoon, men gathered in little groups, discussing the train. The groups merged with each other under the peepul tree, and then everyone went into the gurdwara. Women, who had gone from door to door collecting and dropping bits of gossip, assembled in the headman's house and waited for their menfolk to come home and tell them what they had learned about the train.

This was the pattern of things at Mano Majra when anything of consequence happened. The women went to the headman's house, the men to the temple. There was no recognized leader of the village. Banta Singh, the headman, was really only a collector of revenue—a lambardar. The post had been in his family for several generations. He did not own any more land than the others. Nor was he a head in any other way. He had no airs about him: he was a modest hard-working peasant like the rest of his fellow villagers. But since government officials and the police dealt with him, he had an official status. Nobody called him by his name. He was 'O Lambardara', as his father, his father's father, and his father's father's father had been before him.

The only men who voiced their opinions at village meetings were Imam Baksh, the mullah of the mosque, and Bhai Meet Singh. Imam Baksh was a weaver, and weavers are traditionally the butts of jokes in the Punjab. They are considered effeminate and cowardly—a race of cuckolds whose women are always having liaisons with others. A series of tragedies in his family had made him an object of pity, and then of affection. The Punjabis love people they can pity. His wife and only son had died within a few days of each other. His eyes, which had never been very good, suddenly became worse and he could not work his looms any more. He was reduced to beggary, with a baby girl, Nooran, to look after. He began living in the mosque and teaching Muslim children the Quran. He wrote out verses from the Quran for the village folk to wear as charms or for the sick to swallow as medicine. Small offerings of flour, vegetables, food, and castoff clothes kept him and his daughter alive. He had an amazing fund of anecdotes and proverbs which the peasants loved to hear. His appearance commanded respect. He was a tall, lean man, bald save for a line of white hair which ran round the back of his head from ear to ear, and he had a neatly trimmed silky white beard that he occasionally dyed with henna to a deep orange-red. The cataract in his eyes gave them a misty philosophical look. Despite his sixty years, he held himself erect. All this gave his bearing a dignity and an aura of righteousness. He was known to the villagers not as Imam Baksh or the mullah but a chacha, or 'Uncle'.

Meet Singh inspired no such affection and respect. He was only a peasant who had taken to religion as an escape from work. He had a little land of his own which he had leased out, and this, with the offerings at the temple, gave him a comfortable living. He had no wife or children. He was not learned in the scriptures, nor had he any faculty for conversation. Even his appearance was against him. He was short, fat, and hairy. He was the same age as Imam Baksh, but his beard had none of the serenity of the other's. It was black, with streaks of grey. And he was untidy. He wore his turban only when reading the scripture. Otherwise, he went about with his long hair tied in a loose knot held by a little wooden comb. Almost half of the hair was scattered on the nape of his neck. He seldom wore a shirt and his only garment— a pair of shorts—was always greasy with dirt. But Meet Singh was a man of peace. Envy had never poisoned his affection for Imam Baksh. He only felt that he owed it to his own community to say something when Imam Baksh made any suggestions. Their conversation always had an undercurrent of friendly rivalry.

The meeting in the gurdwara had a melancholic atmosphere. People had little to say, and those who did spoke slowly, like prophets.

Imam Baksh opened the discussion. 'May Allah be merciful. We are living in bad times.'

A few people sighed solemnly, 'Yes, bad days.'

Meet Singh added, 'Yes, Chacha—this is Kalyug, the dark age.'

There was a long silence and people shuffled uneasily on their haunches. Some yawned, closing their mouths with loud invocations to God: 'Ya Allah. Wah Guru, wah Guru.'

'Lambardara,' started Imam Baksh again, 'you should know what is happening. Why has not the Deputy sahib sent for you?'

'How am I to know, Chacha? When he sends for me I will go. He is also at the station and no one is allowed near it.'

A young villager interjected in a loud cheery voice: 'We are not going to die just yet. We will soon know what is going on. It is a train after all. It may be carrying government treasures or arms. So they guard it. Haven't you heard, many have been looted?'

'Shut up,' rebuked his bearded father angrily. 'Where there are elders, what need have you to talk?'

'I only . . .'

'That is all,' said the father sternly. No one spoke for some time.

'I have heard,' said Imam Baksh, slowly combing his beard with his fingers, 'that there have been many incidents with trains.'

The word 'incident' aroused an uneasy feeling in the audience. 'Yes, lots of incidents have been heard of,' Meet Singh agreed after a while.

'We only ask for Allah's mercy,' said Imam Baksh, closing the subject he had himself opened.

Meet Singh, not meaning to be outdone in the invocation to God, added, 'Wah Guru, wah Guru.'

They sat on in silence punctuated by yawns and murmurs of 'Ya Allah' and 'Hey wah Guru'. Several people, on the outer fringe of the assembly, stretched themselves on the floor and went to sleep.

Suddenly a policeman appeared in the doorway of the gurdwara. The lambardar and three or four villagers stood up. People who were asleep were prodded into getting up. Those who had been dozing sat up in a daze, exclaiming, 'What is it? What's up?', then hurriedly wrapped their turbans round their heads.

'Who is the lambardar of the village?'

Banta Singh walked up to the door. The policeman took him aside and whispered something. Then as Banta Singh turned back, he said loudly: 'Quickly, within half an hour. There are two military trucks waiting on the station side. I will be there.'

The policeman walked away briskly.

The villagers crowded round Banta Singh. The possession of a secret had lent him an air of importance. His voice had a tone of authority.

'Everyone get all the wood there is in his house and all the kerosene oil he can spare and bring these to the motor trucks on the station side. You will be paid.'

The villagers waited for him to tell them why. He ordered them off brusquely. 'Are you deaf? Haven't you heard? Or do you want the police to whip your buttocks before you move? Come along quickly.'

People dispersed into the village lanes whispering to each other.

The lambardar went to his own house.

A few minutes later, villagers with bundles of wood and bottles of oil started assembling outside the village on the station side. Two large mud-green army trucks were parked alongside each other. A row of empty petrol cans stood against a mud wall. A Sikh soldier with a sten gun stood on guard. Another Sikh, an officer with his beard neatly rolled in a hair net, sat on the back of one of the trucks with his feet dangling. He watched the wood being stacked in the other truck and nodded his head in reply to the villagers' greetings. The lambardar stood beside him, taking down the names of the villagers and the quantities they brought. After dumping their bundles of wood on the truck and emptying bottles of kerosene into the petrol cans, the villagers collected in a little group at a respectful distance from the officer.

Imam Baksh put down on the truck the wood he had carried on his head and handed his bottle of oil to the lambardar. He re-tied his turban, then greeted the officer loudly, 'Salaam, Sardar Sahib.'

The officer looked away.

Iman Baksh started again, 'Everything is all right, isn't it, Sardar Sahib?'

The officer turned around abruptly and snapped, 'Get along. Don't you see I am busy?'

Imam Baksh, still adjusting his turban, meekly joined the villagers.

When both the trucks were loaded, the officer told Banta Singh to come to the camp next morning for the money. The trucks rumbled off towards the station.

Banta Singh was surrounded by eager villagers. He felt that he was somehow responsible for the insult to Imam Baksh. The villagers were impatient with him.

'O Lambardara, why don't you tell us something? What is all this big secret you are carrying about? You seem to think you have become someone very important and don't need to talk to us any more,' said Meet Singh angrily.

'No, Bhai, no. If I knew, why would I not tell you? You talk like children. How can I argue with soldiers and policemen? They told me nothing. And didn't you see how that pig's penis spoke to Chacha? One's self-respect is in one's own hands. Why should I have myself insulted by having my turban taken off?'

Imam Baksh acknowledged the gesture gracefully. 'Lambardar is right. It somebody barks when you speak to him, it is best to keep quiet. Let us all go to our homes. You can see what they are doing from the tops of your roofs.'

The villagers dispersed to their rooftops. From there the trucks could be seen at the camp near the station. They started off again and went east along the railway track till they were beyond the signal. Then they turned sharp left and bumped across the rails. They turned left again, came back along the line towards the station, and disappeared behind the train.

All afternoon, the villagers stood on their roofs shouting to each other, asking whether anyone had seen anything. In their excitement they had forgotten to prepare the midday meal. Mothers fed their children on stale leftovers from the day before. They did not have time to light their hearths. The men did not give fodder to their cattle nor remember to milk them as evening drew near. When the sun was already under the arches of the bridge everyone became conscious of having overlooked the daily chores. It would be dark soon and the children would clamour for food, but still the women watched, their eyes glued to the station. The cows and buffaloes lowed in the barns, but still the men stayed on the roofs looking towards the station. Everyone expected something to happen.

The sun sank behind the bridge, lighting the white clouds which had appeared in the sky with hues of russet, copper, and orange. Then shades of grey blended with the glow as evening gave way to twilight and twilight sank into darkness. The station became a black wall. Wearily, the men and women went down to their courtyards, beckoning the others to do the same. They did not want to be alone in missing anything.

The northern horizon, which had turned a bluish grey, showed orange again. The orange turned into copper and then into a

luminous russet. Red tongues of flame leaped into the black sky.
A soft breeze began to blow towards the village. It brought the
smell of burning kerosene, then of wood. And then—a faint acrid
smell of searing flesh.

The village was stilled in a deathly silence. No one asked
anyone else what the odour was. They all knew. They had known
it all the time. The answer was implicit in the fact that the train
had come from Pakistan.

That evening, for the first time in the memory of Mano Majra,
Imam Baksh's sonorous cry did not rise to the heavens to proclaim
the glory of God.

The day's happenings cast their gloom on the rest house. Hukum
Chand had been out since the morning. When his orderly came
from the station at midday for a thermos flask of tea and
sandwiches, he told the bearer and the sweeper about the train.
In the evening, the servants and their families saw the flames
shooting up above the line of trees. The fire cast a melancholy
amber light on the khaki walls of the bungalow.

The day's work had taken a lot out of Hukum Chand. His
fatigue was not physical. The sight of so many dead had at first
produced a cold numbness. Within a couple of hours, all his
emotions were dead, and he watched corpses of men and women
and children being dragged out, with as little interest as if they
had been trunks or bedding. But by evening, he began to feel
forlorn and sorry for himself. He looked weary and haggard
when he stepped out of the car. The bearer, the sweeper, and
their families were on the roof looking at the flames. He had to
wait for them to come down and open the doors. His bath had
not been drawn. Hukum Chand felt neglected and more
depressed. He lay on his bed, ignoring the servants' attentions.
One unlaced and took off his shoes and began to rub his feet.
The other brought in buckets of water and filled the bathtub.
The magistrate got up abruptly, almost kicking the servant, and
went into the bathroom.

After a bath and a change of clothes, Hukum Chand felt

somewhat refreshed. The punkah breeze was cool and soothing. He lay down again with his hands over his eyes. Within the dark chambers of his closed eyes, scenes of the day started coming back in panoramic succession. He tried to squash them by pressing his fingers into his eyes. The images only went blacker and redder and then came back. There was a man holding his intestines, with an expression in his eyes which said: 'Look what I have got!' There were women and children huddled in a corner, their eyes dilated with horror, their mouths still open as if their shrieks had just then become voiceless. Some of them did not have a scratch on their bodies. There were bodies crammed against the far end wall of the compartment, looking in terror at the empty windows through which must have come shots, spears and spikes. There were lavatories, jammed with corpses of young men who had muscled their way to comparative safety. And all the nauseating smell of putrefying flesh, faeces and urine. The very thought brought vomit to Hukum Chand's mouth. The most vivid picture was that of an old peasant with a long white beard; he did not look dead at all. He sat jammed between rolls of bedding on the upper rack meant for luggage, looking pensively at the scene below him. A thin crimson line of coagulated blood ran from his ear onto his heard. Hukum Chand had shaken him by the shoulder, saying 'Baba, Baba!' believing he was alive. He was alive. His cold hand stretched itself grotesquely and gripped the magistrate's right foot. Cold sweat came out all over Hukum Chand's body. He tried to shout but could only open his mouth. The hand moved up slowly from the ankle to the calf, from the calf to the knee, gripping its way all along. Hukum Chand tried to shout again. His voice stuck in his throat. The hand kept moving upwards. As it touched the fleshy part of his thigh, its grip loosened. Hukum Chand began to moan and then with a final effort broke out of the nightmare with an agonized shriek. He sat up with a look of terror in his eyes.

The bearer was standing beside him looking equally frightened. 'I thought the Sahib was tired and would like his feet pressed.' Hukum Chand could not speak. He wiped the sweat off his forehead and sank back on the pillow, exclaiming 'Hai Ram, hai Ram.' The nervous outburst purged him of fear. He felt weak and foolish. After some time a sense of calm descended on him.

'Get me some whisky.'

The bearer brought him a tray with whisky, soda, and a tumbler. Hukum Chand filled a quarter of the glass with the honey-coloured liquid. The bearer filled the rest with soda. The magistrate drank half of the glass in a gulp and lay back. The alcohol poured into his system, warming his jaded nerves to life. The servant started pressing his feet again. He looked up at the ceiling, feeling relaxed and just pleasantly tired. The sweeper started lighting lamps in the rooms. He put one on the table beside Hukum Chand's bed. A moth fluttered round the chimney and flew up in spirals to the ceiling. The geckos darted across from the wall. The moth hit the ceiling well out of the geckos' reach and spiralled back to the lamp. The lizards watched with their shining black eyes. The moth flew up again and down again. Hukum Chand knew that if it alighted on the ceiling for a second, one of the geckos would get it fluttering between its little crocodile jaws. Perhaps that was its destiny. It was everyone's destiny. Whether it was in hospitals, trains, or in the jaws of reptiles, it was all the same. One could even die in bed alone and no one would discover until the stench spread all round and maggots moved in and out of the sockets of the eyes and geckos ran over the face with their slimy clammy bellies. Hukum Chand wiped his face with his hands. How could one escape one's own mind! He gulped the rest of the whisky and poured himself another.

Death had always been an obsession with Hukum Chand. As a child, he had seen his aunt die after the birth of a dead child. Her whole system had been poisoned. For days she had had hallucinations and had waved her arms about frantically to ward off the spirit of death which stood at the foot of her bed. She had died shrieking with terror, staring and pointing at the wall. The scene had never left Hukum Chand's mind. Later in his youth, he had fought the fear of death by spending many hours at a cremation ground near the university. He had watched young and old brought on crude bamboo stretchers, lamented for, and then burned. Visits to the cremation ground left him with a sense of tranquillity. He had got over the immediate terror of death, but the idea of ultimate dissolution was always present in his mind. It made him kind, charitable and tolerant. It even made him cheerful in adversity. He had taken the loss of his children with phlegmatic resignation. He had borne with an illiterate, unattractive wife, without complaint. It all came from his belief that the only absolute truth was death. The rest—love, ambition, pride, values of all kinds—was to be taken with a pinch of salt. He did so with a clear conscience. Although he accepted gifts and obliged friends when they got into trouble, he was not corrupt. He occasionally joined in parties, arranged for singing and dancing—and sometimes sex—but he was not immoral. What did it really matter in the end? That was the core of Hukum Chand's philosophy of life, and he lived well.

But a trainload of dead was too much for even Hukum Chand's fatalism. He could not square a massacre with a philosophical belief in the inevitability of death. It bewildered and frightened him by its violence and its magnitude. The picture of his aunt biting her tongue and bleeding at the mouth, her eyes staring at space, came back to him in all its vivid horror. Whisky did not help to take it away.

The room was lit by the headlights of the car and then left darker than before; the car had probably been put into the garage. Hukum Chand grew conscious of the coming night. The servants would soon be retiring to their quarters to sleep snugly surrounded by their women and children. He would be left alone in the bungalow with its empty rooms peopled by phantoms of his own creation. No! No! He must get the orderlies to sleep somewhere nearby. On the veranda perhaps? Or would they suspect he was scared? He would tell them that he might be wanted during the night and must have them at hand; that would pass unnoticed.

'Bairah.'

'Sahib.' The bearer came in through the wire-gauze door.

'Where have you put my charpai for the night?'

'Sahib's bed has not been laid yet. It is clouded and there might be rain. Would Huzoor like to sleep on the veranda?'

'No, I will stay in my room. The boy can pull the punkah for an hour or two till it gets cool. Tell the orderlies to sleep on the veranda. I may want them for urgent work tonight,' he added, without looking up at the man.

'Yes, Sahib. I will tell them straightaway before they go to bed. Should I bring the Sahib's dinner?'

Hukum Chand had forgotten about dinner.

'No, I do not want any dinner. Just tell the orderlies to put their beds on the veranda. Tell the driver to be there too. If there is not enough space on the veranda, tell him to sleep in the next room.'

The bearer went out. Hukum Chand felt relieved. He had saved face. He could sleep peacefully with all these people about him. He listened to the reassuring sounds of human activity—the servants arguing about places on the veranda, beds being laid just outside his door, a lamp being brought in the next room, and furniture being moved to make place for charpais.

The headlights of the car coming in, lit the room once more. The car stopped outside the veranda. Hukum Chand heard voices of men and women, then the jingle of bells. He sat up and looked through the wire-gauze door. It was the party of musicians, the old woman and the girl prostitute. He had forgotten about them.

'Bairah.'

'Huzoor.'

'Tell the driver to take the musicians and the old woman back. And . . . let the servants sleep in their quarters. If I need them, I will send for them.'

Hukum Chand felt a little stupid being caught like that. The servants would certainly laugh about it. But he did not care. He poured himself another whisky.

The servants started moving out before the bearer came to speak to them. The lamp in the next room was removed. The driver started the car again. He switched on the headlights and switched them off again. The old woman would not get in the car and began to argue with the bearer. Her voice rose higher and higher till it passed the bounds of argument and addressed itself to the magistrate inside the room.

'May your government go on forever. May your pen inscribe figures of thousands—nay, hundreds of thousands.'

Hukum Chand lost his temper. 'Go!' he shouted. 'You have to pay my debt of the other day. Go! Bearer, send her away!'

The woman's voice came down. She was quickly hustled into the car. The car went out, leaving only the flickering yellow light of the oil lamp beside Hukum Chand's bed. He rose, picked up the lamp and the table, and put them in the corner by the door. The moth circled round the glass chimney, hitting the wall on either side. the geckos crawled down from the ceiling to the wall near the lamp. As the moth alighted on the wall, one of the geckos crept up stealthily behind it, pounced, and caught it fluttering in its jaws. Hukum Chand watched the whole thing with bland indifference.

The door opened and shut gently. A small dark figure slid into the room. The silver sequins on the girl's sari twinkled in the lamplight and sent a hundred spots of light playing on the walls and the ceiling. Hukum Chand turned around. The girl stood staring at him with her large black eyes. The diamond in her nose glittered brightly. She looked thoroughly frightened.

'Come,' said the magistrate, making room for her beside him and holding out his hand.

The girl came and sat down on the edge of the bed, looking away. Hukum Chand put his arm round her waist. He stroked her thighs and belly and played with her little unformed breasts. She sat impassive and rigid. Hukum Chand shuffled further away and mumbled drowsily, 'Come and lie down.' The girl stretched herself beside the magistrate. The sequins on her sari tickled his face. She wore perfume made of khas; it had the fresh odour of dry earth when water has been sprinkled on it. Her breath smelled of cardamom, her bosom of honey. Hukum Chand snuggled against her like a child and fell fast asleep.

Monsoon is not another word for rain. As its original Arabic name indicates, it is a season. There is a summer monsoon as well as a winter monsoon, but it is only the nimbused southwest winds of summer that make a *mausem*—the season of the rains. The winter monsoon is simply rain in winter. It is like a cold shower on a frosty morning. It leaves one chilled and shivering. Although it is good for the crops, people pray for it to end. Fortunately, it does not last very long.

The summer monsoon is quite another affair. It is preceded by several months of working up a thirst so that when the waters come they are drunk deep and with relish. From the end of February, the sun starts getting hotter and spring gives way to summer. Flowers wither. Then flowering trees take their place. First come the orange showers of the flame of the forest, the vermilion of the coral tree, and the virginal white of the champak. They are followed by the mauve Jacaranda, the flamboyant gul mohur, and the soft gold cascades of the laburnum. Then the trees also lose their flowers. Their leaves fall. Their bare branches stretch up to the sky begging for water, but there is no water. The sun comes up earlier than before and licks up the drops of dew before the fevered earth can moisten its lips. It blazes away all day long in a cloudless grey sky, drying up wells, streams and lakes. It sears the grass and thorny scrub till they catch fire. The fires spread and dry jungles burn like matchwood.

The sun goes on, day after day, from east to west, scorching relentlessly. The earth cracks up and deep fissures open their gaping mouths asking for water; but there is no water—only the shimmering haze at noon making mirage lakes of quicksilver. Poor villagers take their thirsty cattle out to drink and are struck dead. The rich wear sunglasses and hide behind chicks of khus fibre on which their servants pour water.

The sun makes an ally of the breeze. It heats the air till it becomes the loo and then sends it on its errand. Even in the intense heat, the loo's warm caresses are sensuous and pleasant. It brings up the prickly heat. It produces a numbness which makes the head nod and the eyes heavy with sleep. It brings on a stroke which takes its victim as gently as breeze bears a fluff of thistledown.

Then comes a period of false hopes. The loo drops. The air becomes still. From the southern horizon a black wall begins to advance. Hundreds of kites and crows fly ahead. Can it be . . . ? No, it is a dust storm. A fine powder begins to fall. A solid mass of locusts covers the sun. They devour whatever is left on the trees and in the fields. Then comes the storm itself. In furious sweeps it smacks open doors and windows, banging them forward and backward, smashing their glass panes. Thatched roofs and corrugated iron sheets are borne aloft into the sky like bits of paper. Trees are torn up by the roots and fall across power lines. The tangled wires electrocute people and start fires in houses. The storm carries the flames to other houses till there is a conflagration. All this happens in a few seconds. Before you can say *Chakravartyrajagopalachari*, the gale is gone. The dust hanging in the air settles on your books, furniture and food; it gets in your eyes and ears and throat and nose.

This happens over and over again until the people have lost all hope. They are disillusioned, dejected, thirsty and sweating. The prickly heat on the back of their necks is like emery paper. There is another lull. A hot petrified silence prevails. Then comes the shrill, strange call of a bird. Why has it left its cool bosky shade and come out in the sun? People look up wearily at the lifeless sky. Yes, there it is with its mate! They are like large black-and-white bulbuls with perky crests and long tails. They are pie-crested cuckoos who have flown all the way from Africa ahead of the monsoon. Isn't there a gentle breeze blowing? And hasn't it a damp smell? And wasn't the rumble which drowned the birds' anguished cry the sound of thunder? The people hurry to the roofs to see. The same ebony wall is coming up from the east. A flock of herons fly across. There is a flash of lightning which outlines the daylight. The wind fills the black sails of the clouds and they billow out across the sun. A profound shadow falls on the earth. There is another clap of thunder. Big drops of rain fall and dry up in the dust. A fragrant smell rises from the earth. Another flash of lightning and another crack of thunder like the roar of a hungry tiger. It has come! Sheets of water, wave after wave. The people lift their faces to the clouds and let the abundance of water cover them. Schools and offices close. All work stops. Men, women, and children run madly about the streets, waving their arms and shouting 'Ho, Ho,'—hosannas to the miracle of the monsoon.

The monsoon is not like ordinary rain which comes and goes. Once it is on, it stays for two months or more. Its advent is greeted with joy. Parties set out for picnics and litter the countryside with the skins and stones of mangoes. Women and children make swings on branches of trees and spend the day in sport and song. Peacocks spread their tails and strut about with their mates; the woods echo with their shrill cries.

But after a few days the flush of enthusiasm is gone. The earth becomes a big stretch of swamp and mud. Wells and lakes fill up and burst their bounds. In towns, gutters get clogged and streets become turbid streams. In villages, mud walls of huts melt in the water and thatched roofs sag and descend on the inmates. Rivers which keep rising steadily from the time the summer's heat starts melting the snows, suddenly turn to floods as the monsoon spends itself on the mountains. Roads, railway tracks and bridges go under water. Houses near the riverbanks are swept down to the sea.

With the monsoon, the tempo of life and death increases. Almost overnight, grass begins to grow and leafless trees turn green. Snakes, centipedes and scorpions are born out of nothing. The ground is strewn with earthworms, ladybirds and tiny frogs. At night, myriads of moths flutter around the lamps. They fall in everybody's food and water. Geckos dart about filling themselves with insects till they get heavy and fall off ceilings. Inside rooms, the hum of mosquitoes is maddening. People spray clouds of insecticide, and the floor becomes a layer of wriggling bodies and wings. Next evening, there are many more fluttering around the lamp shades and burning themselves in the flames.

While the monsoon lasts, the showers start and stop without warning. The clouds fly across, dropping their rain on the plains as it pleases them, till they reach the Himalayas. They climb up the mountainsides. Then the cold squeezes the last drops of water out of them. Lightning and thunder never cease. All this happens in late August or early September. Then the season of the rains gives way to autumn.

A roll of the thunder woke Hukum Chand. He opened his eyes. There was a grey light in the room. In the corner, a weary yellow flame flickered through the soot of the lamp chimney. There was a flash of lightning followed by another peal of thunder. A gust of cool, damp breeze blew across the room. The lamp fluttered and went out. Raindrops began to fall in a gentle patter.

Rain! At long last the rain, thought the magistrate. The monsoon had been a poor one. Clouds had come, but they were high and fleecy and floated by, leaving the land thirstier than before. September was very late for the rain, but that only made it more welcome. It smelled good, it sounded good, it looked good—and above all, it did good. Ah, but did it? Hukum Chand felt feverish. The corpses! A thousand charred corpses sizzling and smoking while the rain put out the fire. A hundred yards of charred corpses! Beads of sweat broke out on his temples. He felt cold and frightened. He reached across the bed. The girl had left. He was all alone in the bungalow. He got his wrist watch from under the pillow and cupped his hands round the dial. The glow-worn green of the radium hands pointed to 6:30. He felt comforted. It was fairly late in the morning. The sky must be heavily overcast. Then he heard the sound of coughing on the veranda, and felt reassured. He sat up with a jerk.

A dull pain rocked his forehead. He shut his eyes and held his head between his hands. The throbbing ebbed away. After a few minutes, he opened his eyes, looked around the room—and saw the girl. She hadn't left. She was asleep on the big cane armchair, wrapped in her black sequined sari. Hukum Chand felt a little foolish. The girl had been there two nights, and there she was sleeping all by herself in a chair. She was still, save for the gentle heaving of her bosom. He felt old and unclean. How could he have done anything to this child? If his daughter had lived, she would have been about the same age. He felt a pang of remorse. He also knew that his remorse and good resolutions went with the hangover. They always did. He would probably drink again and get the same girl over and sleep with her—and feel badly about it. That was life, and it was depressing.

He got up slowly and opened the attaché case that lay on the table. He looked at himself in the mirror on the inside of the lid. There was a yellow rheum in the corners of his eyes. The roots of his hair were showing white and purple. There were several folds of flesh under his unshaven jaw. He was old and ugly. He stuck out his tongue. It was coated with a smooth pale yellow from the middle to the back. Dribble ran down the tip onto the table. He could smell his own breath. It must have been nauseating for the girl! No wonder she spent the night in an uncomfortable chair. Hukum Chand took out a bottle of liver salts and put several large teaspoonfuls into a glass. He unscrewed the thermos flask and poured in the water. The effervescence bubbled over from all sides of the tumbler onto the table. He stirred the water till the fizz died down, then drank it quickly. For some time he stood with his head bent and his hands resting on the table.

The dose of salts gurgled down pleasantly. An airy fullness rose from the pit of his stomach up to his throat and burped out in a long satisfying belch. The throbbing ebbed away and the ache receded into the back of his head. A few cups of strong hot tea and he would be himself again. Hukum Chand went to the bathroom. From the door opening out towards the servants' quarters he shouted for his bearer.

'Bring shaving water and bring my tea. Bring it here. I will take it in myself.'

When the bearer came, Hukum Chand took the tea tray and the mug of hot shaving water into the bedroom and put them on the table. He poured himself a cup of tea and laid out his shaving things. He lathered his chin and shaved and sipped his tea. The tinkle of the china and silver did not disturb the girl. She slept with her mouth slightly open. She looked dead except for the periodic upward movement of her breasts vainly trying to fill her bodice. Her hair was scattered all over her face. A pink celluloid clip made in the shape of a butterfly dangled by the leg of the chair. Her sari was crushed and creased, and bits of sequins glistened on the floor. Hukum Chand could not take his eyes off her while he sipped his tea and shaved. He could not analyse his feelings except that he wanted to make up to her. If she wanted to be slept with, he would sleep with her. The thought made him uneasy. He would have to drink hard to do that to her now.

The noise of shuffling feet and coughing on the veranda disturbed Hukum Chand's thoughts. It was a cough intended to draw attention. That meant the subinspector. Hukum Chand finished his tea and took his clothes into the bathroom to change. Afterwards, he went out of the door which opened towards the quarters and stepped onto the veranda. The subinspector was reading a newspaper. He jumped up from his chair and saluted.

'Has your honour been out walking in the rain?'

'No, no. I just went round the servants' quarters. You are early. I hope all is well.'

'These days one should be grateful for being alive. There is no peace anywhere. One trouble after another . . .'

The magistrate suddenly thought of the corpses. 'Did it rain in the night? How is it going near the railway station?'

'I went by this morning when the rain had just started. There wasn't very much left—just a big heap of ashes and bones. There are many skulls lying about. I do not know what we can do about them. I have sent word to the lambardar that no one is to be allowed near the bridge or the railway station.'

'How many were there? Did you count?'

'No, sir. The Sikh officer said there were more than a thousand. I think he just calculated how many people could get into a bogie and multiplied it by the number of bogies. He said that another four or five hundred must have been killed on the roofs, on footboards and between buffers. They must have fallen off when they were attacked. The roof was certainly covered with dried-up blood.'

'Harey Ram, Harey Ram. Fifteen hundred innocent people! What else is a Kalyug? There is darkness over the land. This is only one spot on the frontier. I suppose similar things are happening at other places. And now I believe our people are doing the same. What about the Muslims in these villages?'

'That is what I came to report, sir. Muslims of some villages have started leaving for the refugee camps. Chundunnugger has been partly evacuated. Pakistan army lorries with Baluchi and Pathan soldiers have been picking them up whenever information has been brought. But the Mano Majra Muslims are still there and this morning the lambardar reported the arrival of forty or fifty Sikh refugees who had crossed the river by the ford at dawn. They are putting up at the temple.'

'Why were they allowed to stop?' asked Hukum Chand sharply. 'You know very well the orders are that all incoming refugees must proceed to the camp at Jullundur. This is serious. They may start the killing in Mano Majra.'

'No, sir, the situation is well in hand up till now. These refugees have not lost much in Pakistan and apparently no one molested them on the way. The Muslims of Mano Majra have been bringing them food at the temple. If others turn up who have been through massacres and have lost relations, then it will be a different matter. I had not thought of the river crossings. Usually, after the rains the river is a mile in breadth and there are no fords till November or December. We have hardly had any rain this year. There are several points where people can cross and I have not got enough policemen to patrol the riverside.'

Hukum Chand looked across the rest-house grounds. The rain was falling steadily. Little pools had begun to form in the ditches. The sky was a flat stretch of slate grey.

'Of course, if it keeps raining, the river will rise and there will not be many fords to cross. One will be able to control refugee movements over the bridges.'

A crash of lightning and thunder emphasized the tempo of the rain. The wind blew a thin spray onto the veranda.

'But we must get the Muslims out of this area whether they like it or not. The sooner the better.'

There was a long pause in the conversation. Both men sat staring into the rain. Hukum Chand began to speak again.

'One should bow before the storm till it passes. See the pampas grass! Its leaves bend before the breeze. The stem stands stiff in its plumed pride. When the storm comes it cracks and its white plume is scattered by the winds like fluffs of thistledown.' After a pause he added, 'A wise man swims with the current and still gets across.'

The subinspector heard the platitudes with polite attention. He did not see their significance to his immediate problem. Hukum Chand noticed the blank expression on the police officer's face. He had to make things more plain.

'What have you done about Ram Lal's murder? Have you made any further arrests?'

'Yes, sir, Jugga badmash gave us the names yesterday. They are men who were at one time in his own gang: Malli and four others from village Kapura two miles down the river. But Jugga was not with them. I have sent some constables to arrest them this morning.'

Hukum Chand did not seem to be interested. He had his eyes fixed somewhere far away.

'We were wrong about both Jugga and the other fellow.' The Inspector went on: 'I told you about Jugga's liaison with a Muslim weaver's girl. That kept him busy most nights. Malli threw bangles into Jugga's courtyard after the dacoity.'

Hukum Chand still seemed far away.

'If your honour agrees, we might release Jugga and Iqbal after we have got Malli and his companions.'

'Who are Malli and his companions, Sikh or Muslim?' asked Hukum Chand abruptly.

'All Sikhs.'

The magistrate relapsed into his thoughts once more. After

some time he began to talk to himself. 'It would have been more convenient if they had been Mussulman. The knowledge of that and the agitator fellow being a Leaguer would have persuaded Mano Majra Sikhs to let their Muslims go.'

There was another long pause. The plan slowly pieced itself together in the subinspector's mind. He got up without making any comment. Hukum Chand did not want to take any chances.

'Listen,' he said. 'Let Malli and his gang off without making any entry anywhere. But keep an eye on their movements. We will arrest them when we want to . . . And do not release the badmash or the other chap yet. We may need them.'

The subinspector saluted.

'Wait. I haven't finished.' Hukum Chand raised his hand. 'After you have done the needful, send word to the commander of the Muslim refugee camp asking for trucks to evacuate Mano Majra Muslims.'

The subinspector saluted once more. He was conscious of the honour Hukum Chand had conferred by trusting him with the execution of a delicate and complicated plan. He put on his raincoat.

'I should not let you go in this rain, but the matter is so vital that you should not lose any time,' said Hukum Chand, still looking down at the ground.

'I know, sir.' The subinspector saluted again. 'I shall take action at once.' He mounted his bicycle and rode away from the rest house onto the muddy road.

Hukum Chand sat on the veranda staring vacantly at the rain falling in sheets. The right and wrong of his instructions did not weigh too heavily on him. He was a magistrate, not a missionary. It was the day-to-day problems to which he had to find answers. He had no need to equate them to some unknown absolute standard. There were not many 'oughts' in his life. There were just the 'is' s. He took life as it was. He did not want to recast it or rebel against it. There were processes of history to which human beings contributed willy-nilly. He believed that an individual's conscious effort should be directed to immediate ends like saving life when endangered, preserving the social structure and honouring its conventions. His immediate problem was to save Muslim lives. He would do that in any way he could. Two men who had been arrested on the strength of warrants signed by him should have been arrested in any case. One was an agitator, the other a bad character. In troubled times, it would be necessary to detain them. If he could make a minor error into a major investment, it would really be a mistake to call it a mistake. Hukum Chand felt elated. If his plan could be carried out efficiently! If only he could himself direct the details, there would be no slips! His subordinates frequently did not understand his mind and landed him in complicated situations.

From inside the rest house came the sound of the bathroom door shutting and opening. Hukum Chand got up and shouted at the bearer to bring in breakfast.

The girl sat on the edge of the bed with her chin in her hands. She stood up and covered her head with the loose end of the sari. When Hukum Chand sat down in the chair, she sat down on the bed again with her eyes fixed on the floor. There was an awkward silence. After some time Hukum Chand mustered his courage, cleared his throat and said, 'You must be hungry. I have sent for some tea.'

The girl turned her large sad eyes on him. 'I want to go home.'

'Have something to eat and I will tell the driver to take you home. Where do you live?'

'Chundunnugger. Where the Inspector Sahib has his police station.'

There was another long pause. Hukum Chand cleared his throat again. 'What is your name?'

'Haseena. Haseena Begum.'

'Haseena. You are *haseen*. Your mother has chosen your name well. Is that old woman your mother?'

The girl smiled for the first time. No one had paid her a compliment before. Now the Government itself had called her beautiful and was interested in her family.

'No, sir, she is my grandmother. My mother died soon after I was born.'

'How old are you?'

'I don't know. Sixteen or seventeen. Maybe eighteen. I was not born literate. I could not record my date of birth.'

She smiled at her own little joke. The magistrate smiled too. The bearer brought in a tray of tea, toast and eggs.

The girl got up to arrange the teacups and buttered a piece of toast. She put it on a saucer and placed it on the table in front of Hukum Chand.

'I will not eat anything. I have had my tea.'

The girl pretended to be cross.

'If you do not eat, then I won't eat either,' she said coquettishly. She put away the knife with which she was buttering the toast, and sat down on the bed.

The magistrate was pleased. 'Now, do not get angry with me,' he said. He walked up to her and put his arms round her shoulders. 'You must eat. You had nothing last night.'

The girl wriggled in his arms. 'If you eat, I will eat. If you do not, I will not either.'

'All right, if you insist.' Hukum Chand helped the girl up with his arm around her waist and brought her to his side of the table. 'We will both eat. Come and sit with me.'

The girl got over her nervousness and sat in his lap. She put thickly buttered toast in his mouth and laughed when he said 'Enough, enough,' through his stuffed mouth. She wiped the butter off his moustache.

'How long have you been in this profession?'

'What a silly question to ask! Why, ever since I was born. My mother was a singer and her mother was a singer till as long back as we know.'

'I do not mean singing. Other things,' explained Hukum Chand, looking away.

'What do you mean, other things?' asked the girl haughtily. 'We do not go about doing other things for money. I am a singer and I dance. I do not suppose you know what dancing and singing are. You just know about other things. A bottle of whisky and other things. That is all!'

Hukum Chand cleared his throat with a nervous cough. 'Well . . . I did not do anything.'

The girl laughed and pressed her hand on the magistrate's face. 'Poor Magistrate Sahib. You had evil intentions, but you were tired. You snored like a railway engine.' The girl drew her breath in noisily and imitated his snoring. She laughed more loudly.

Hukum Chand stroked the girl's hair. His daughter would have been sixteen, seventeen, or eighteen, if she had lived. But he had no feeling of guilt, only a vague sense of fulfilment. He did not want to sleep with the girl, or make love to her, or even to kiss her on the lips and feel her body. He simply wanted her to sleep in his lap with her head resting on his chest.

'There you go again with your deep thoughts,' said the girl, scratching his head with her finger. She poured out a cup of tea and then poured it into the saucer. 'Have some tea. It will stop you thinking.' She thrust the saucerful of tea at him.

'No, no. I have had tea. You have it.'

'All right. I will have tea and you have your thoughts.'

The girl began to sip the tea noisily.

'Haseena.' He liked repeating the name. 'Haseena,' he started again.

'Yes. But Haseena is only my name. Why don't you say something?'

Hukum Chand took the empty saucer from her hand and put it on the table. He drew the girl closer and pressed her head against his. He ran his fingers through her hair.

'You are Muslim?'

'Yes, I am Muslim. What else could Haseena Begum be? A bearded Sikh?'

'I thought Muslims from Chundunnugger had been evacuated. How have you managed to stay on?'

'Many have gone away, but the Inspector Sahib said we could stay till he told us to go. Singers are neither Hindu nor Muslim in that way. All communities come to hear me.'

'Are there any other Muslims in Chundunnugger?'

'Well . . . yes,' she faltered. 'You can call them Muslim, Hindu or Sikh or anything, male or female. A party of *hijras* (hermaphrodites) are still there.' She blushed.

Hukum Chand put his hand across her eyes.

'Poor Haseena is embarrassed. I promise I won't laugh. You are not Hindu or Muslim, but not in the same way as a hijra is not a Hindu or Muslim.'

'Do not tease me.'

'I won't tease you,' he said removing his hand. She was still blushing. 'Tell me why the hijras were spared.'

'I will if you promise not to laugh at me.'

'I promise.'

The girl became animated.

'There was a child born to someone living in the Hindu locality. Without even thinking about communal troubles the hijras were there to sing. Hindus and Sikhs—I do not like Sikhs—got hold of them and wanted to kill them because they were Muslim.' She stopped deliberately.

'What happened?' asked Hukum Chand eagerly.

The girl laughed and clapped her hands the way hijras do, stretching her fingers wide. 'They started to beat their drums and sing in their raucous male voices. They whirled round so fast that their skirts flew in the air. Then they stopped and asked the leaders of the mob, "Now you have seen us, tell us, are we Hindus or Muslims?" and the whole crowd started laughing— the whole crowd except the Sikhs.'

Hukum Chand also laughed.

'That is not all. The Sikhs came with their kirpans and threatened them saying, "We will let you go this time, but you must get out of Chundennugger or we will kill you." One of the hijras again clapped his hands and ran his fingers in a Sikh's beard and asked, "Why? Will all of you become like us and stop having children?" Even the Sikhs started laughing.'

'That is a good one,' said Hukum Chand. 'But you should be

careful while all this disturbance is going on. Stay at home for a few days.'

'I am not frightened. We know so many people so well and then I have a big powerful Magistrate to protect me. As long as he is there no one can harm a single hair of my head.'

Hukum Chand continued to run his hands through the girl's hair without saying anything. The girl looked up at him smiling mischievously. 'You want me to go to Pakistan?'

Hukum Chand pressed her closer. A hot feverish feeling came over him. 'Haseena.' He cleared his throat again. 'Haseena.' Words would not come out of his mouth.

'Haseena, Haseena, Haseena. I am not deaf. Why don't you say something?'

'You will stay here today, won't you? You do not want to go away just yet?'

'Is that all you wanted to say? If you do not give me your car, I cannot go five miles in the rain. But if you make me sing or spend another night here you will have to give me a big bundle of notes.'

Hukum Chand felt relieved.

'What is money?' he said with mock gallantry. 'I am ready to lay down my life for you.'

For a week, Iqbal was left alone in his cell. His only companions were the piles of newspapers and magazines. There was no light in his cell, nor was he provided with a lamp. He had to lie in the stifling heat listening to night noises—snores, occasional gunshots, and then more snoring. When it started to rain, the police station became more dismal than ever. There was nothing to see except rain falling incessantly, or sometimes a constable running across between the reporting rooms and the barracks. There was nothing to hear except the monotonous patter of raindrops, an occasional peal of thunder, and then more rain. He saw little of Jugga in the neighbouring cell. On the first two evenings, some constables had taken Jugga out of his cell. They brought him back after an hour. Iqbal did not know what they had done to him. He didn't ask and Jugga said nothing. But his repartee with the policemen became more vulgar and more familiar than before.

One morning a party of five men were brought to the station in handcuffs. As soon as Jugga saw them he lost his temper and abused them. They protested and refused to leave the reporting room veranda. Iqbal wondered who the new prisoners were. From the snatches of conversation that he had overheard, it seemed that everyone was on a spree, killing and looting. Even in Chundunnugger, a few yards from the police station, there had been killing. Iqbal had seen the pink glow of fire and heard people yelling, but the police had made no arrests. The prisoners must be quite out of the ordinary. While he was trying to figure out who the newcomers were, his cell was unlocked and Jugga came in with a constable. Jugga was in a good humour.

'Sat Sri Akal, Babuji,' he said. 'I am going to be the servant of your feet. I will learn something.'

'Iqbal Sahib,' the constable added, relocking the cell, 'teach this badmash how to go on the straight and narrow path.'

'Get away with you,' Jugga said. 'Babuji thinks it is you and the government who have made me a badmash. Isn't that so, Babuji?'

Iqbal did not answer. He put his feet in the extra chair and gazed at the pile of papers. Jugga took Iqbal's feet off the chair and began pressing them with his enormous hands.

'Babuji, my kismet has woken up at last. I will serve you if you teach me some English. Just a few sentences so that I can do a little *git mit*.'

'Who is going to occupy the next cell?'

Jugga continued pressing Iqbal's feet and legs.

'I don't know,' he answered hesitantly. 'They tell me they have arrested Ram Lal's murderers.'

'I thought they had arrested you for the murder,' said Iqbal.

'Me, too,' smiled Jugga, baring his row of even white teeth studded with gold points. 'They always arrest me when anything goes wrong in Mano Majra. You see, I am a badmash.'

'Didn't you kill Ram Lal?'

Jugga stopped pressing. He caught his ears with his hands and stuck out his tongue. 'Toba, toba! Kill my own village bania? Babuji, who kills a hen which lays eggs? Besides, Ram Lal gave me money to pay lawyers when my father was in jail. I would not act like a bastard.'

'I suppose they will let you off now.'

'The police are the kings of the country. They will let me off when they feel like it. If they want to keep me in, they will trump up a case of keeping a spear without a license or going out of the village without permission—or just anything.'

'But you were out of the village that night. Weren't you?'

Jugga sat down on his haunches, took Iqbal's feet in his lap, and started massaging his soles.

'I was out of the village,' he answered with a mischievous twinkle in his eye, 'but I was not murdering anyone. I was being murdered.'

Iqbal knew the expression. He did not want to encourage Jugga to make further disclosure. But once the subject had been suggested, there was no keeping Jugga back. He began to press Iqbal's feet with greater fervour.

'You have been in Europe many years?' asked Jugga lowering his voice.

'Yes, many,' answered Iqbal, vainly trying to evade the inevitable.

'Then, Babuji,' asked Jugga lowering his voice further, 'you must have slept with many memsahibs. Yes?'

Iqbal felt irritated. It was not possible to keep Indians off the subject of sex for long. It obsessed their minds. It came out in their art, literature and religion. One saw it on the hoardings in the cities advertising aphrodisiacs and curatives for ill effects of masturbation. One saw it in the law courts and marketplaces, where hawkers did a thriving trade selling oil made of the skin of sand lizards to put life into tired groins and increase the size of the phallus. One read it in the advertisements of quacks who claimed to possess remedies for barrenness and medicines to induce wombs to yield male children. One heard about it all the time. No people used incestuous abuse quite as casually as did the Indians. Terms like *sala*, wife's brother ('I would like to sleep with your sister'), and *susra*, father-in-law ('I would like to sleep with your daughter') were as often terms of affection for one's friends and relatives as expressions of anger to insult one's enemies. Conversation on any topic—politics, philosophy, sport—soon came down to sex, which everyone enjoyed with a lot of giggling and hand-slapping.

'Yes, I have,' Iqbal said, casually. 'With many.'

'*Wah, wah*,' exclaimed Jugga with enthusiasm and vigorous pressing of Iqbal's feet. '*Wah*, Babuji—great. You must have had lots of fun. The memsahibs are like *houris* from paradise— white and soft, like silk. All we have here are black buffaloes.'

'There is no difference between women. As a matter of fact, white women are not very exciting. Are you married?'

'No, Babuji. Who will give his daughter to a badmash? I have to get my pleasure where I can get it.'

'Do you get much of it?'

'Sometimes . . . When I go to Ferozepur for a hearing and if I save money from lawyers and their clerks, I have a good time. I make a bargain for the whole night. Women think, as with other men, that means two, or at the most three times.' He twirled his moustache. 'But when Juggut Singh leaves them, they cry "hai, hai", touch their ears, say "toba, toba" and beg me in the name of God to leave them and take the money back.'

Iqbal knew it was a lie. Most young men talked like that.

'When you get married, you will find your wife a match for you,' Iqbal said. 'You will be holding your ears and saying "toba, toba".'

'There is no fun in marriage, Babuji. Where is the time or place for fun? In summer, everyone sleeps out in the open and all you can do is to slip away for a little while and get over with things before your relations miss you. In winter, men and women sleep separately. You have to pretend to answer the call of nature at the same time at night.'

'You seem to know a lot about it, without being married.'

Jugga laughed. 'I don't keep my eyes shut. Besides, even if I am not married, I do a married man's work.'

'You also answer calls of nature by arrangement?'

Jugga laughed louder. 'Yes, Babuji, I do. That is what has brought me to this lockup. But I say to myself: if I had not been out that night, I would not have had the good fortune of meeting you, Babuji. I would not have the chance to learn English from you. Teach me some git mit like "good morning". Will you, Babuji-sahib?'

'What will you do with English?' Iqbal asked. 'The sahibs have left. You should learn your own language.'

Jugga did not seem pleased with the suggestion. For him, education meant knowing English. Clerks and letter writers who wrote Urdu or Gurmukhi were literate, but not educated.

'I can learn that from anyone. Bhai Meet Singh has promised to teach me Gurumukhi, but I never seem to get started. Babuji, how many classes have you read up to? You must have passed the tenth?'

Tenth was the school-leaving examination.

'Yes, I have passed the tenth. Actually I have passed sixteen.'

'Sixteen! *Wah, wah*! I have never met anyone who has done that. In our village only Ram Lal has done four. Now he is dead, the only one who can read anything is Meet Singh. In the neighbouring villages they haven't even got a bhai. Our Inspector Sahib has only read up to seven and the Deputy Sahib to ten. Sixteen! You must have lots of brain.'

Iqbal felt embarrassed at the effusive compliments.

'Can you read or write anything?' he asked.

'I? No. My uncle's son taught me a little verse he learned at school. It is half English and half Hindustani:

Pigeon—kabootur, oodan—*fly*
Look—dekho, usman—*sky*

Do you know this?'

'No. Didn't he teach you the alphabet?'

'The A.B.C.? He did not know it himself. He knew as much as
I do:

A. B. C. *where have you been?*
Edward's dead, I went to mourn.

You must know this one?'

'No, I don't know this either.'

'Well, you tell me something in English.'

Iqbal obliged. He taught Jugga how to say 'good morning'
and 'goodnight'. When Jugga wanted to know the English for
some of the vital functions of life, Iqbal became impatient. Then
the five new prisoners were brought into the neighbouring cell.
Jugga's jovial mood vanished as fast as it had come.

By eleven o'clock the rain had dwindled to a drizzle. The day
became brighter. The subinspector looked up from his cycling.
Some distance ahead of him, the clouds opened up, unfolding a
rich blue sky. A shaft of sunlight slanted across the rain. Its saffron
beams played about on the sodden fields. The rainbows spanned
the sky, framing the town of Chundunnugger in a multicoloured
arc.

The subinspector drove faster. He wanted to get to the police
station before his head constable made an entry about Malli's
arrest. It would be awkward to have to tear off pages from the
station diary and then face a whole lot of questions from some
impertinent lawyer. The head constable was a man of experience,
but after the arrests of Jugga and Iqbal the subinspector's
confidence in him had been somewhat shaken. He could not be
relied on to handle a situation which was not routine. Would he
know where to lock up the prisoners? He was a peasant, full of
awe of the educated middle class. He would not have the nerve
to disturb Iqbal (in whose cell he had put a charpai and a chair
and table). And if he had put Jugga and Malli together in the
other cell, they would by now have discussed the murder and
dacoity and decided to help each other.

As the subinspector cycled into the police station, a couple of policemen sitting on a bench on the veranda got up to receive him. One took his cycle; the other helped him with his raincoat, murmuring something about having to go out in the rain.

'Duty,' said the subinspector pompously, 'duty. Rain is nothing. Even if there was an earthquake, duty first! Is the head constable back?'

'Yes, sir. He brought in Malli's gang a few minutes ago and has gone to his quarters to have tea.'

'Has he made any entry in the daily diary?'

'No, sir, he said he would wait for you to do that.'

The subinspector was relieved. He went into the reporting room, hung his turban on a peg and sat down in a chair. The table was stacked with registers of all kinds. One large one with its yellow pages all divided into columns lay open before him. He glanced at the last entry. It was in his own hand, about his leaving Mano Majra rest house earlier that morning.

'Good,' he said aloud, rubbing his hands. He slapped his thighs and ran both his hands across his forehead and through his hair. 'Right,' he said loudly to himself. 'Right.'

A constable brought him a cup of tea, stirring it all the time.

'Your clothes must be wet!' he said, putting the tea on the table and giving it a last violent stir.

The subinspector picked it up without looking at the constable. 'Have you locked Malli's gang in the same cell as Jugga?'

'Toba! Toba!' exclaimed the constable, holding his hands up to his shoulder. 'Sir, there would have been a murder in the police station. You should have been here when we brought Malli in. As soon as Jugga saw him he went mad. I have never heard such abuse. Mother, sister, daughter—he did not leave one out. He shook the bars till they rattled. We thought the door would come off its hinges. There was no question of putting Malli in there. And Malli would not have gone in, any more than a lamb would into a lion's cage.'

The subinspector smiled. 'Didn't Malli swear back?'

'No. He really looked frightened and kept saying that he had nothing to do with the Mano Majra dacoity. Jugga yelled back saying that he had seen him with his own eyes and he would settle scores with all of them and their mothers, sisters and daughters, once he was out. Malli said he was not afraid of him any more since all Jugga could do now was to sleep with his weaver girl. You should really have seen Jugga then! He behaved like an animal. His eyes turned red; he put his hand on his mouth and yelled; he beat his chest and shook the iron bars; he swore that he would tear Malli limb from limb. I have never seen anyone in a rage like that. We could not take any chances, so we kept Malli in the reporting room till Jugga's temper was down. Then we moved Jugga into the Babu's cell and put Malli's men in Jugga's.'

'It must have been a good tamasha,' said the subinspector with a grin. 'We will have some more. I am going to release Malli's men.'

The constable looked puzzled. Before he could ask any questions, the subinspector dismissed him with a lordly wave of the hand.

'Policy, you know! You will learn when you have been in the service as long as I have. Go and see if the head constable has had his tea. Say it is important.'

A little later the head constable arrived, belching contentment. He had the smug expression of one ready to protest against any commendation of his efficiency. The subinspector ignored the modest smile the other wore and asked him to shut the door and sit down. The head constable's expression changed from contentment to concern. He shut the door and stood on the other side of the table. 'Yes, sir. What are the orders?'

'Sit down. Sit down,' the subinspector said. His voice was cool. 'There is no hurry.'

The head constable sat down.

The subinspector rotated the sharp end of a pencil in his ear and examined the brown wax which stuck to it. He got a cigarette out of his pocket and tapped its tip on the matchbox several times before lighting it. He sucked it noisily. The smoke poured out of his nostrils, rebounded off the table and spread into the room.

'Head Constable Sahib,' he said at last, removing a tiny bit of tobacco from his tongue. 'Head Constable Sahib, there are lots of things to be done today, and I want you to do them personally.'

'Yes. sir,' answered the head constable gravely.

'First, take Malli and his men to Mano Majra. Release them where the villagers can see them being released. Near the temple, perhaps. Then inquire casually from the villagers if anyone has seen Sultana or any of his gang about. You need not say why. Just make the inquires.'

'But, sir, Sultana and his lot went away to Pakistan. Everyone knows that.'

The Inspector put the end of his pencil in his ear again and rubbed the wax on the table. He took a couple of pulls at the cigarette and this time pouted his lips and sent jets of smoke bounding off the register into the head constable's face.

'I do not know that Sultana has gone to Pakistan. Anyway, he left after the dacoity in Mano Majra. There is no harm in asking the villagers if they know when he left, is there?'

The head constable's face lit up.

'I understand, sir. Are there any other orders?'

'Yes. Also inquire from the villagers if they know anything about the mischief the Muslim Leaguer Iqbal had been up to when he was in Mano Majra.'

The head constable looked puzzled again.

'Sir, the Babu's name is Iqbal Singh. He is a Sikh. He has been living in England and had his long hair cut.'

The subinspector fixed the head constable with a stare and smiled. 'There are many Iqbals. I am talking of a Mohammed Iqbal, you are thinking of Iqbal Singh. Mohammed Iqbal can be a member of the Muslim League.'

'I understand, sir,' repeated the head constable, but he had not really understood. He hoped he would catch up with the scheme in due course. 'Your orders will be carried out.'

'Just one thing more,' added the subinspector, getting up from the table. 'Get a constable to take a letter from me to the commander of the Muslim refugee camp. Also, remind me to send some constables to Mano Majra tomorrow when the Pakistan army chaps come to evacuate Muslim villagers.'

The head constable realized that this was meant to help him understand the plan. He made a mental note of it, saluted a second time and clicked his heels. 'Yes, sir,' he said, and went out.

The subinspector put on his turban. He stood by the door looking into the courtyard of the station. The railway creeper on the wall facing him had been washed by the rain. Its leaves glistened in the sun. Policemen's dormitories on the left side had rows of charpais with bedding neatly rolled on them. Opposite the dormitories were the station's two cells—in reality just ordinary rooms with iron bars instead of bricks for the front wall. One could see everything inside them from anywhere in the courtyard. In the nearer cell, Iqbal sat in a chair with his feet on the charpai, reading a magazine. Several newspapers lay scattered on the floor. Juggut Singh was sitting, holding the bars with his hands, idly staring at the policemen's quarters. In the other cell, Malli and his companions lay sprawled on the floor talking to each other. They got up as the head constable and three policemen with rifles entered carrying handcuffs. Juggut Singh took no notice of the policemen going into the adjoining cell. He thought that Malli was probably being taken to court for a hearing.

Malli had been shaken by Juggut Singh's outburst. He was frightened of Juggut Singh and would sooner have made peace on the other's terms than go about in fear of violence—for Jugga was the most violent man in the district. Juggut Singh's abuse had made that impossible. Malli was the leader of his own band and felt that after Jugga's insults he had to say something to regain his prestige in the eyes of his companions. He thought of several nasty things he could have said, if he had known that Juggut Singh was going to return his offer of friendship with abuse. He felt hurt and angry. If he got another chance he would give it back to Jugga, abuse for abuse. Iron bars separated them and in any case there were armed policemen about.

The policemen handcuffed Malli and his companions and linked all the handcuffs to one long chain attached to a constable's belt. The head constable led them away. Two men armed with rifles kept the rear. As they emerged from their cell, Jugga looked up at Malli and then looked away.

'You forget old friends,' said Malli with mock friendliness. 'You don't even look at us and we pine away for you.'

His companions laughed. 'Let him be. Let him be.'

Jugga sat still with his eyes fixed on the ground.

'Why are you so angry, my dear? Why so sad? Is it somebody's love that torments your soul?'

'Come along, keep moving,' said the policemen reluctantly. They were enjoying the scene.

'Why can't we say Sat Sri Akal to our old friend? Sat Sri Akal, Sardar Juggut Singhji. Is there any message we can convey for you? A love message maybe? To the weaver's daughter?'

Jugga kept staring through the bars as if he had not heard. He turned pale with anger. All the blood drained from his face. His hands tightened around the iron bars.

Malli turned round to his smiling companions. 'Sardar Juggut Singh seems a little upset today. He will not answer our Sat Sri Akal. We do not mind. We will say Sat Sri Akal to him again.'

Malli joined his manacled hands and bent low near Juggut Singh's iron bar door and started loudly, 'Sat Sri . . .'

Jugga's hands shot through the bars and gripped Malli by the hair protruding from the back of his turban. Malli's turban fell off. Jugga yelled murderously and with a jerk brought Malli's head crashing against the bars. He shook Malli as a terrier shakes a piece of rag from side to side, forward and backward, smashing his head repeatedly against the bars. Each jerk was accompanied by abuse: 'This to rape your mother. This your sister. This your daughter. This for your mother again. And this . . . and this.'

Iqbal, who had been watching the earlier proceedings from his chair, stood up in a corner and started shouting to the policemen: 'Why don't you do something? Don't you see he will kill the man?'

The policemen began to shout. One of them tried to push the butt end of his rifle in Jugga's face, but Jugga dodged. Malli's head was spattered with blood. His skull and forehead were bruised all over. He began to wail. The subinspector ran up to the cell and hit Jugga violently on the hand with his swagger stick several times. Jugga would not let go. The subinspector drew his revolver and pointed it at Jugga. 'Let go, you swine, or I will shoot.'

Jugga held up Malli's head with both his hands and spat in his face. He pushed him away with more abuse. Malli fell in a heap with his hair all over his face and shoulders. His companions helped him up and wiped the blood and spit off his face with his turban. He cried like a child, swearing all the time, 'May your mother die . . . you son of a pig . . . I will settle this with you.' Malli and his men were led away. Malli could be heard crying till he was a long way from the police station.

Jugga sank back into the stupor he had been in before he lost his temper. He examined the marks the subinspector's swagger stick had left on the back of his hands. Iqbal continued shouting agitatedly. Jugga turned round angrily. 'Shut up, you babu! What have I done to you that you talk so much?'

Jugga had not spoken rudely to him before. That scared Iqbal all the more.

'Inspector Sahib, now that the other cell is vacant, can't you shift me there?' he pleaded.

The subinspector smiled contemptuously. 'Certainly, Mr Iqbal, we will do all we can to make you comfortable. Tables, chairs—an electric fan maybe?'

Mano Majra

When it was discovered that the train had brought a full loud of corpses, a heavy brooding silence descended on the village. People barricaded their doors and many stayed up all night talking in whispers. Everyone felt his neighbour's hand against him, and thought of finding friends and allies. They did not notice the clouds blot out the stars nor smell the cool damp breeze. When they woke up in the morning and saw it was raining, their first thoughts were about the train and the burning corpses. The whole village was on the roofs looking towards the station.

The train had disappeared as mysteriously as it had come. The station was deserted. The soldier's tents were soaked with water and looked depressing. There was no smouldering fire nor smoke. In fact there was no sign of life—or death. Still people watched: perhaps there would be another train with more corpses!

By afternoon the clouds had rolled away to the west. Rain had cleared the atmosphere and one could see for miles around. Villagers ventured forth from their homes to find out if anyone knew more than they. Then they went back to their roofs. Although it had stopped raining, no one could be seen on the station platform or in the passenger shed or the military camp. A row of vultures sat on the parapet of the station building and kites were flying in circles high above it.

The head constable, with his posse of policemen and prisoners, was spotted a long way away from the village. People shouted the information to each other. The lambardar was summoned.

When the head constable arrived with his party, there was quite a crowd assembled under the peepul tree near the temple.

The head constable unlocked the handcuffs of the prisoners in front of the villagers. They were made to put their thumb impressions on pieces of paper and told to report to the police station twice a week. The villagers looked on sullenly. They knew that Jugga badmash and the stranger had nothing to do with the dacoity. They were equally certain that in arresting Malli's gang the police were on the right track. Perhaps they were not all involved; some of the five might have been arrested mistakenly. It was scarcely possible that none of them had had anything to do with it. Yet there were the police letting them loose—not in their own village, but in Mano Majra where they had committed the murder. The police must be certain of their innocence to take such a risk.

The head constable took the lambardar aside and the two spoke to each other for some time. The lambardar came back and addressed the villagers saying: 'The Sentry Sahib wants to know if anyone here has seen or heard anything about Sultana badmash or any of his gang.'

Several villagers came out with news. He was known to have gone away to Pakistan along with his gang. They were all Muslims, and Muslims of their village had been evacuated.

'Was it before or after the murder of the Lala that he left?' inquired the head constable, coming up beside the lambardar.

'After,' they answered in a chorus. There was a long pause. The villagers looked at each other somewhat puzzled. Was it them? Before they could ask the policemen any questions, the head constable was speaking again.

'Did any of you see or talk to a young Mussulman babu called Mohammed Iqbal who was a member of the Muslim League?'

The lambardar was taken aback. He did not know Iqbal was a Muslim. He vaguely recalled Meet Singh and Imam Baksh calling him Iqbal Singh. He looked in the crowd for Imam Baksh but could not find him. Several villagers started telling the head constable excitedly of having seen Iqbal go to the fields and loiter about the railway track near the bridge.

'Did you notice anything suspicious about him?'

'Suspicious? Well . . .'

'Did you notice anything suspicious about the fellow?'

'Did you?'

No one was sure. One could never be sure about educated people; they were all suspiciously cunning. Surely Meet Singh was the one to answer questions about the babu; some of the babu's things were still with him in the gurdwara.

Meet Singh was pushed up to the front.

The head constable ignored Meet Singh and again addressed the group that had been answering him. 'I will speak to the bhai later,' he said. 'Can any one of you say whether this man came to Mano Majra before or after the dacoity?'

This was another shock. What would an urban babu have to do with dacoity or murder? Maybe it was not for money after all! No one was quite sure. Now they were not sure of anything. The head constable dismissed the meeting with: 'If anyone has any authentic information about the moneylender's murder or about Sultana or about Mohammed Iqbal, report at the police station at once.'

The crowd broke into small groups, talking and gesticulating animatedly. Meet Singh went up to the head constable who was getting his constables ready to march back.

'Sentry Sahib, the young man you arrested the other day is not a Mussulman. He is a Sikh—Iqbal Singh.'

The head constable took no notice of him. He was busy writing something on a piece of yellow paper. Meet Singh waited patiently.

'Sentry Sahib,' he started again as the other was folding the paper. The head constable did not even look at him. He beckoned one of the constables and handed him the paper saying:

'Get a bicycle or a tonga and take this letter to the commandant of the Pakistan military unit. Also tell him yourself that you have come from Mano Majra and the situation is serious. He must send his trucks and soldiers to evacuate the Muslims as early as possible. At once.'

'Yes, sir,' answered the constable clicking his heels.

'Sentry Sahib,' implored Meet Singh.

'Sentry Sahib, Sentry Sahib, Sentry Sahib,' repeated the head constable angrily. 'You have been eating my ears with your "Sentry Sahibs". What do you want?'

'Iqbal Singh is a Sikh.'

'Did you open the fly-buttons of his pants to see whether he was a Sikh or a Mussulman? You are a simple bhai of a temple. Go and pray.'

The head constable took his place in front of the policemen standing in double file.

'Attention! By the left, quick march.'

Meet Singh turned back to the temple without answering the eager queries of the villagers.

The head constable's visit had divided Mano Majra into two halves as neatly as a knife cuts through a pat of butter.

Muslims sat and moped in their houses. Rumours of atrocities committed by Sikhs on Muslims in Patiala, Ambala and Kapurthala, which they had heard and dismissed, came back to their minds. They had heard of gentlewomen having their veils taken off, being stripped and marched down crowded streets to be raped in the marketplace. Many had eluded their would-be ravishers by killing themselves. They had heard of mosques being desecrated by the slaughter of pigs on the premises, and of copies of the holy Quran being torn up by infidels. Quite suddenly, every Sikh in Mano Majra became a stranger with an evil intent. His long hair and beard appeared barbarous, his kirpan menacingly anti-Muslim. For the first time, the name Pakistan came to mean something to them—a refuge where there were no Sikhs.

The Sikhs were sullen and angry. 'Never trust a Mussulman,' they said. The last Guru had warned them that Muslims had no loyalties. He was right. All through the Muslim period of Indian history, sons had imprisoned or killed their own fathers and brothers had blinded brothers to get the throne. And what had they done to the Sikhs? Executed two of their Gurus, assassinated another and butchered his infant children; hundreds of thousands had been put to the sword for no other offence than refusing to accept Islam; their temples had been desecrated by the slaughter of kine; the holy Granth had been torn to bits. And Muslims were never ones to respect women. Sikh refugees had told of women jumping into wells and burning themselves rather than fall into the hands of Muslims. Those who did not commit suicide were paraded naked in the streets, raped in public, and then murdered. Now a trainload of Sikhs massacred by Muslims had been cremated in Mano Majra. Hindus and Sikhs were fleeing from their homes in Pakistan and having to find shelter in Mano Majra. Then there was the murder of Ram Lal. No one knew who had killed him, but everyone knew Ram Lal was a Hindu; Sultana and his gang were Muslims and had fled to Pakistan. An unknown character—without turban or beard—had been loitering about the village. These were reasons enough to be angry with someone. So they decided to be angry with the Muslims; Muslims were basely ungrateful. Logic was never a strong point with Sikhs; when they were roused, logic did not matter at all.

It was a gloomy night. The breeze that had swept away the clouds blew them back again. At first they came in fleecy strands of white. The moon wiped them off its face. Then they came in large billows, blotted out the moonlight and turned the sky a dull grey. The moon fought its way through, and occasionally, patches of the plain sparkled like silver. Later, clouds came in monstrous black formations and spread across the sky. Then, without any lightning or thunder, it began to rain.

A group of Sikh peasants gathered together in the house of the lambardar. They sat in a circle around a hurricane lantern— some on a charpai, others on the floor. Meet Singh was amongst them.

For a long time nobody said anything apart from repeating, 'God is punishing us for our sins.'

'Yes, God is punishing us for our sins.'

'There is a lot of zulum in Pakistan.'

'That is because He wants to punish us for our sins. Bad acts yield a bitter harvest.'

Then one of the younger men spoke. 'What have we done to deserve this? We have looked upon the Muslims as our brothers and sisters. Why should they send somebody to spy on us?'

'You mean Iqbal?' Meet Singh said. 'I had quite a long conversation with him. He had an iron bangle on his wrist like all of us Sikhs and told me that his mother had wanted him to wear it, so he wore it. He is a shaven Sikh. He does not smoke. And he came the day after the moneylender's murder.'

'Bhai, you get taken in easily,' replied the same youth. 'Does it hurt a Mussulman to wear an iron bangle or not smoke for a day—particularly if he has some important work to do?'

'I may be a simple bhai,' protested Meet Singh warmly, 'but I know as well as you that the babu had nothing to do with the murder; he would not have been in the village afterwards if he had. That any fathead would understand.'

The youth felt a little abashed.

'Besides that,' continued Meet Singh more confidently, 'they had already arrested Malli for the dacoity . . .'

'How do you know what they had arrested Malli for?' interrupted the youth triumphantly.

'Yes, how do you know what the police know? They have released Malli. Have you ever known them to release murderers without a trial and acquittal?' asked some others.

'Bhai, you always talk without reason.'

'Achha, if you are the ones with all the reason, tell me who threw the packet of bangles into Jugga's house.'

'How should we know?' answered a chorus.

'I will tell you. It was Jugga's enemy Malli. You all know they had fallen out. Who else would dare insult Jugga except he?'

No one answered the question. Meet Singh went on aggressively to drive his point home. 'And all this about Sultana, Sultana! What has that to do with the dacoity?'

'Yes, Bhaiji, you may be right,' said another youth. 'But Lal is

dead: why bother about him? The police will do that. Let Jugga,
Malli and Sultana settle their quarrels. As for the babu, for all
we care he can sleep with his mother. Our problem is: what are
we to do with all these pigs we have with us? They have been
eating our salt for generations and see what they have done! We
have treated them like our own brothers. They have behaved
like snakes.'

The temperature of the meeting went up suddenly. Meet Singh
spoke angrily.

'What have they done to you? Have they ousted you from
your lands or occupied your houses? Have they seduced your
womenfolk? Tell me, what have they done?'

'Ask the refugees what they have done to them,' answered the
truculent youth who had started the argument. 'You mean to
tell us that they are lying when they say that gurdwaras have
been burned and people massacred?'

'I was only talking of Mano Majra. What have our tenants
done?'

'They are Muslims.'

Meet Singh shrugged his shoulders.

The lambardar felt it was up to him to settle the argument.

'What had to happen has happened,' he said wisely. 'We have
to decide what we are to do now. These refugees who have turned
up at the temple may do something which will bring a bad name
on the village.'

The reference to 'something' changed the mood of the meeting.
How could outsiders dare do 'something' to their fellow villagers?
Here was another stumbling block to logic. Group loyalty was
above reason. The youth who had referred to Muslims as pigs
spoke haughtily: 'We would like to see somebody raise his little
finger against our tenants while we live!'

The lambardar snubbed him. 'You are a hotheaded one.
Sometimes you want to kill Muslims. Sometimes you want to
kill refugees. We say something and you drag the talk to
something else.'

'All right, all right, Lambardara,' retorted the young man, 'if you are all that clever, you say something.'

'Listen, brothers,' said the lambardar lowering his voice. 'This is no time to lose tempers. Nobody here wants to kill anyone. But who knows the intentions of other people? Today we have forty or fifty refugees, who by the grace of the Guru are a peaceful lot and they only talk. Tomorrow we may get others who may have lost their mothers or sisters. Are we going to tell them: "Do not come to this village"? And if they do come, will we let them wreak vengeance on our tenants?'

'You have said something worth a hundred thousand rupees,' said an old man. 'We should think about it.'

The peasants thought about their problem. They could not refuse shelter to refugees: hospitality was not a pastime but a sacred duty when those who sought it were homeless. Could they ask their Muslims to go? Quite emphatically not! Loyalty to a fellow villager was above all other considerations. Despite the words they had used, no one had the nerve to suggest throwing them out, even in a purely Sikh gathering. The mood of the assembly changed from anger to bewilderment.

After some time the lambardar spoke.

'All Muslims of the neighbouring villages have been evacuated and taken to the refugee camp near Chundunnugger. Some have already gone away to Pakistan. Others have been sent to the bigger camp at Jullundur.'

'Yes,' added another. 'Kapoora and Gujjoo Matta were evacuated last week. Mano Majra is the only place left where there are Muslims. What I would like to know is how these people asked their fellow villagers to leave. We could never say anything like that to our tenants, any more than we could tell our sons to get out of our homes. Is there anyone here who could say to the Muslims, "Brothers, you should go away from Mano Majra"?

Before anyone could answer, another villager came in and stood on the threshold. Everyone turned round to see, but they could not recognize him in the dim lamplight.

'Who is it?' asked the lambardar, shading his eyes from the lamp. 'Come in.'

Imam Baksh came in. Two others followed him. They also were Muslims.

'Salaam, Chacha Imam Baksh. Salaam, Khair Dina. Salaam, salaam.'

'Sat Sri Akal, Lambardara. Sat Sri Akal,' answered the Muslims.

People made room for them and waited for Imam Baksh to begin.

Imam Baksh combed his beard with his fingers.

'Well, brothers, what is your decision about us?' he asked quietly.

There was an awkward silence. Everyone looked at the lambardar.

'Why ask us?' answered the lambardar. 'This is your village as much as ours.'

'You have heard what is being said! All the neighbouring villages have been evacuated. Only we are left. If you want us to go too, we will go.'

Meet Singh began to sniff. He felt it was not for him to speak. He had said his bit. Besides, he was only a priest who lived on what the villagers gave him. One of the younger men spoke.

'It is like this, Uncle Imam Baksh. As long as we are here nobody will dare to touch you. We die first and then you can look after yourselves.'

'Yes,' added another warmly, 'we first, then you. If anyone raises his eyebrows at you we will rape his mother.'

'Mother, sister and daughter,' added the others.

Imam Baksh wiped a tear from his eyes and blew his nose in the hem of his shirt.

'What have we to do with Pakistan? We were born here. So were our ancestors. We have lived amongst you as brothers.' Imam Baksh broke down. Meet Singh clasped him in his arms and began to sob. Several of the people started crying quietly and blowing their noses.

The lambardar spoke: 'Yes, you are our brothers. As far as we are concerned, you and your children and your grandchildren can live here as long as you like. If anyone speaks rudely to you, your wives or your children, it will be us first and our wives and children before a single hair of your heads is touched. But Chacha, we are so few and the strangers coming from Pakistan are coming in thousands. Who will be responsible for what they do?'

'Yes,' agreed the others, 'as far as we are concerned you are all right, but what about these refugees?'

'I have heard that some villages were surrounded by mobs many thousands strong, all armed with guns and spears. There was no question of resistance.'

'We are not afraid of mobs,' replied another quickly. 'Let them come! We will give them such a beating they will not dare to look at Mano Majra again.'

Nobody took notice of the challenger; the boast sounded too hollow to be taken seriously. Imam Baksh blew his nose again, 'What do you advice us to do then, brothers?' he asked, choking with emotion.

'Uncle,' said the lambardar in a heavy voice, 'it is very hard for me to say, but seeing the sort of time we live in, I would advise you to go to the refugee camp while this trouble is on. You lock your houses with your belongings. We will look after your cattle till you come back.'

The lambardar's voice created a tense stillness. Villagers held their breath for fear of being heard. The lambardar himself felt that he ought to say something quickly to dispel the effect of his words.

'Until yesterday,' he began again loudly, 'in case of trouble we could have helped you to cross the river by the ford. Now it has been raining for two days; the river has risen. The only crossings are by trains and road bridges—you know what is happening there! It is for your own safety that I advise you to take shelter in the camp for a few days, and then you can come back. As far as we are concerned,' he repeated warmly, 'if you decide to stay on, you are most welcome to do so. We will defend you with our lives.'

No one had any doubts about the import of the lambardar's

words. They sat with their heads bowed till Imam Baksh stood up.

'All right,' he said solemnly, 'if we have to go, we better pack up our bedding and belongings. It will take us more than one night to clear out of homes it has taken our fathers and grandfathers hundreds of years to make.'

The lambardar felt a strong sense of guilt and was overcome with emotion. He got up and embraced Imam Baksh and started to cry loudly. Sikh and Muslim villagers fell into each other's arms and wept like children. Imam Baksh gently got out of the lambardar's embrace. 'There is no need to cry,' he said between sobs. 'This is the way of the world—

Not forever does the bulbul sing
In balmy shades of bowers,
Not forever lasts the spring
Nor ever blossom flowers.
Not forever reigneth joy,
Sets the sun on days of bliss,
Friendships not forever last,
They know not life, who know not this.

'They know not life, who know not this,' repeated many others with sighs. 'Yes, Uncle Imam Baksh. This is life.'

Imam Baksh and his companions left the meeting in tears.

Before going round to other Muslim homes, Imam Baksh went to his own hut attached to the mosque. Nooran was already in bed. An oil lamp burned in a niche in the wall.

'Nooro, Nooro,' he shouted, shaking her by the shoulder. 'Get up, Nooro.'

The girl opened her eyes. 'What is the matter?'

'Get up and pack. We have to go away tomorrow morning.' he announced dramatically.

'Go away? Where?'

'I don't know . . . Pakistan!'

The girl sat up with a jerk. 'I will not go to Pakistan,' she said defiantly.

Imam Baksh pretended he had not heard. 'Put all the clothes in the trunks and the cooking utensils in a gunny bag. Also take something for the buffalo. We will have to take her too.'

'I will not go to Pakistan,' the girl repeated fiercely.

'You may not want to go, but they will throw you out. All Muslims are leaving for the camp tomorrow.'

'Who will throw us out? This is our village. Are the police and the government dead?'

'Don't be silly, girl. Do as you are told. Hundreds of thousands of people are going to Pakistan and as many coming out. Those who stay behind are killed. Hurry up and pack. I have to go and tell the others that they must get ready.'

Imam Baksh left the girl sitting up in bed. Nooran rubbed her face with her hands and stared at the wall. She did not know what to do. She could spend the night out and come back when all the others had gone. But she could not do it alone; and it was raining. Her only chance was Jugga. Malli had been released, maybe Jugga had also come home. She knew that was not true, but the hope persisted and it gave her something to do.

Nooran went out in the rain. She passed many people in the lanes, going about with gunny bags covering their heads and shoulders. The whole village was awake. In most houses she could see the dim flickers of oil lamps. Some were packing; others were helping them to pack. Most just talked with their friends. The women sat on the floors hugging each other and crying. It was as if in every home there had been a death.

Nooran shook the door of Jugga's house. The chain on the other side rattled but there was no response. In the grey light she noticed the door was bolted from the outside. She undid the iron ring and went in. Jugga's mother was out, probably visiting some Muslim friends. There was no light at all. Nooran sat down on a charpai. She did not want to face Jugga's mother alone nor did she want to go back home. She hoped something would happen— something which would make Jugga walk in. She sat and waited and hoped.

For an hour Nooran watched the grey shadows of clouds chasing each other. It drizzled and poured and poured and drizzled alternately. She heard the sound of footsteps cautiously picking their way through the muddy lane. They stopped outside the door. Someone shook the door.

'Who is it?' asked an old woman's voice.

Nooran lost her nerve; she did not move.

'Who is it?' demanded the voice angrily. 'Why don't you speak?'

Nooran stood up and mumbled indistinctly, '*Beybey.*'

The old woman stepped in and quickly shut the door behind her.

'Jugga! Jugga, is it you?' she whispered. 'Have they let you off?'

'No, Beybey, it is I—Nooran. Chacha Imam Baksh's daughter,' answered the girl timidly.

'Nooro? What brings you here at this hour?' the old woman asked angrily.

'Has Jugga come back?'

'What have you to do with Jugga?' his mother snapped. 'You have sent him to jail. You have made him a badmash. Does your father know you go about to strangers' houses at midnight like a tart?'

Nooran began to cry. 'We are going away tomorrow.'

That did not soften the old woman's heart.

'What relation are you to us that you want to come and see us? You can go where you like.'

Nooran played her last card. 'I cannot leave. Jugga has promised to marry me.'

'Get out, you bitch!' the old woman hissed. 'You, a Muslim weaver's daughter, marry a Sikh peasant! Get out, or I will go and tell your father and the whole village. Go to Pakistan! Leave my Jugga alone.'

Nooran felt heavy and lifeless. 'All right, Beybey, I will go. Don't be angry with me. When Jugga comes back just tell him I came to say Sat Sri Akal.' The girl went down on her knees, clasped the old woman's legs and began to sob. 'Beybey, I am going away and will never come back again. Don't be harsh to me just when I am leaving.'

Jugga's mother stood stiff, without a trace of emotion on her face. Inside her, she felt a little weak and soft. 'I will tell Jugga.'

Nooran stopped crying. Her sobs came at long intervals. She still held onto Jugga's mother. Her head sank lower and lower till it touched the old woman's feet.

'Beybey.'

'What have you to say now?' She had a premonition of what was coming.

'Beybey.'

'Beybey! Beybey! Why don't you say something?' asked the woman, pushing Nooran away. 'What is it?'

The girl swallowed the spittle in her mouth.

'Beybey, I have Jugga's child inside me. If I go to Pakistan they will kill it when they know it has a Sikh father.'

The old woman let Nooran's head drop back on her feet. Nooran clutched them hard and began to cry again.

'How long have you had it?'

'I have just found out. It is the second month.'

Jugga's mother helped Nooran up and the two sat down on the charpai. Nooran stopped sobbing.

'I cannot keep you here,' said the old woman at last. 'I have enough trouble with the police already. When all this is over and Jugga comes back, he will go and get you from wherever you are. Does your father know?'

'No! If he finds out he will marry me off to someone or murder me.' She started crying again.

'Oh, stop this whining,' commanded the old woman sternly. 'Why didn't you think of it when you were at the mischief? I have already told you Jugga will get you as soon as he is out.'

Nooran stifled her sobs.

'Beybey, don't let him be too long.'

'He will hurry for his own sake. If he does not get you he will have to buy a wife and there is not a pice or trinket left with us. He will get you if he wants a wife. Have no fear.'

A vague hope filled Nooran's being. She felt as if she belonged to the house and the house to her; the charpai she sat on, the buffalo, Jugga's mother, all were hers. She would come back even if Jugga failed to turn up. She could tell them she was married. The thought of her father came like a dark cloud over her lunar hopes. She would slip away without telling him. The moon shone again.

'Beybey, if I get the chance I will come to say Sat Sri Akal in the morning. Sat Sri Akal. I must go and pack.' Nooran hugged the old woman passionately. 'Sat Sri Akal,' she said a little breathlessly again and went out.

Jugga's mother sat on her charpai staring into the dark for several hours.

Not many people slept in Mano Majra that night. They went from house to house—talking, crying, swearing love and friendship, assuring each other that this would soon be over. Life, they said, would be as it always had been.

Imam Baksh came back from his round of Muslim homes before Nooran had returned. Nothing had been packed. He was too depressed to be angry with her. It was as hard on the young as the old. She must have gone to see some of her friends. He started pottering around looking for gunny bags, tin canisters and trunks. A few minutes later Nooran came in.

'Have you seen all your girl friends? Let us get this done before we sleep,' said Imam Baksh.

'You go to bed. I will put the things in. there is not much to do—and you must be tired,' she answered.

'Yes, I am a little tired,' he said sitting down on his charpai. 'You pack the clothes now. We can put in the cooking utensils in the morning after you have cooked something for the journey.' Imam Baksh stretched himself on the bed and fell asleep.

There was not much for Nooran to do. A Punjabi peasant's baggage consists of little besides a change of clothes, a quilt and a pillow, a couple of pitchers, cooking utensils, and perhaps a brass plate and a copper tumbler or two. All that can be put on the only piece of furniture they possess—a charpai. Nooran put her own and her father's clothes in a grey battered steel trunk which had been with them ever since she could remember. She lit a fire in the hearth to bake a few chapattis for the next day. Within half an hour she had done the cooking. She rinsed the utensils and put them in a gunny bag. Flour, salt and the spices that remained went in biscuit and cigarette tins, which in their turn went inside an empty kerosene oil can with a wood top. The packing was over. All that remained was to roll her quilt round the pillow, put the odds and ends on the charpai and the charpai on the buffalo. She could carry the piece of broken mirror in her hand.

It rained intermittently all night. Early in the morning it became a regular downpour. Villagers who had stayed up most of the night fell asleep in the monotonous patter of rain and the opiate of the fresh morning breeze.

The tooting of motor horns and the high note of truck engines in low gear plowing their way through the slush and mud woke the entire village. The convoy went around Mano Majra looking for a lane wide enough to let their trucks in. In front was a jeep fitted with a loud-speaker. There were two officers in it—a Sikh (the one who had come after the ghost train) and a Muslim. Behind the jeep were a dozen trucks. One of the trucks was full of Pathan soldiers and another one full of Sikhs. They were all armed with sten guns.

The convoy came to a halt outside the village. Only the jeep could make its way through. It drove up to the centre and stopped beside the platform under the peepul tree. The two officers stepped out. The Sikh asked one of the villagers to fetch the lambardar. The Muslim was joined by the Pathan soldiers. He sent them out in batches of three to knock at every door and ask the Muslims to come out. For a few minutes Mano Majra echoed to cries of 'All Muslims going to Pakistan come out at once.

Come! All Muslims. Out at once.'

Slowly the Muslims began to come out of their homes, driving their cattle and their bullock carts loaded with charpais, rolls of bedding, tin trunks, kerosene oil tins, earthen pitchers and brass utensils. The rest of Mano Majra came out to see them off.

The two officers and the lambardar were the last to come out of the village. The jeep followed them. They were talking and gesticulating animatedly. Most of the talking was between the Muslim officer and the lambardar.

'I have no arrangement to take all this luggage with bullock carts, beds, pots and pans. This convoy is not going to Pakistan by road. We are taking them to the Chundunnugger refugee camp and from there by train to Lahore. They can only take their clothes, bedding, cash and jewellery. Tell them to leave everything else here. You can look after it.'

The news that the Mano Majra Muslims were going to Pakistan came as a surprise. The lambardar had believed they would only go to the refugee came for a few days and then return.

'No, Sahib, we cannot say anything,' replied the lambardar. 'If it was for a day or two we could look after their belongings. As you are going to Pakistan, it may be many months before they return. Property is a bad thing; it poisons people's minds. No, we will not touch anything. We will only look after their houses.'

The Muslim officer was irritated. 'I have no time to argue. You see yourself that all I have is a dozen trucks. I cannot put buffaloes and bullock carts in them.'

'No, Sahib,' retorted the lambardar stubbornly. 'You can say what you like and you can be angry with us, but we will not touch our brothers' properties. You want us to become enemies?'

'Wah, wah, Lambardar Sahib,' answered the Muslim laughing loudly. 'Shabash! Yesterday you wanted to kill them, today you call them brothers. You may change your mind again tomorrow.'

'Do not taunt us like this, Captain Sahib. We are brothers and will always remain brothers.'

'All right, all right, Lambardara. You are brothers,' the officer said. 'I grant you that, but I still cannot take all this stuff. You consult the Sardar Officer and your fellow villagers about it. I will deal with the Muslims.'

The Muslim officer got on the jeep and addressed the crowd. He chose his words carefully.

'We have a dozen trucks and all you people who are going to Pakistan must get on them in ten minutes. We have other villages to evacuate later on. The only luggage you can take with you is what you can carry—nothing more. You can leave your cattle, bullock carts, charpais, pitchers, and so on with your friends in the village. If we get a chance, we will bring these things out for you later. I give you ten minutes to settle your affairs. Then the convoy will move.'

The Muslims left their bullock carts and thronged round the jeep, protesting and talking loudly. The Muslims officer who had stepped off the jeep went back to the microphone.

'Silence! I warn you, the convoy will move in ten minutes; whether you are on it or not will be no concern of mine.'

Sikh peasants who had stood apart heard the order and went up to the Sikh officer for advice. The officer took no notice of them; he continued staring contemptuously over the upturned collar of his raincoat at the men, cattle, carts and trucks steaming in the slush and rain.

'Why, Sardar Sahib,' asked Meet Singh nervously, 'is not the lambardar right? One should not touch another's property. There is always danger of misunderstanding.'

The officer looked Meet Singh up and down.

'You are quite right, Bhaiji, there is some danger of being misunderstood. One should never touch another's property; one should never look at another's woman. One should just let others take one's goods and sleep with one's sisters. The only way people like you will understand anything is by being sent over to Pakistan: have your sisters and mothers raped in front of you, have your clothes taken off, and be sent back with a kick and spit on your behinds.'

The officer's speech was a slap in the face to all the peasants.

But someone sniggered. Everyone turned around to look. It was Malli with his five companions. With them were a few young refugees who were staying at the Sikh temple. None of them belonged to Mano Majra.

'Sir, the people of this village are famous for their charity,' said Malli smiling. 'They cannot look after themselves, how can they look after other people? But do not bother, Sardar Sahib, we will take care of Muslim property. You can tell the other officer to leave it with us. It will be quite safe if you can detail some of your soldiers to prevent looting by these people.'

There was complete confusion. People ran hither and thither shouting at the tops of their voices. Despite the Muslim officer's tone of finality, villagers clamoured around him protesting and full of suggestions. He came up to his Sikh colleague surrounded by his bewildered co-religionists.

'Can you make arrangements for taking over what is left behind?'

Before the Sikh could answer, a babel of protests burst from all sides. The Sikh remained tight-lipped and aloof.

The Muslim officer turned around sharply. 'Shut up!' he yelled.

The murmuring died down. He spoke again, punctuating each word with a stab of his forefinger.

'I give you five minutes to get into the trucks with just as much luggage as you can carry in your hands. Those who are not in will be left behind. And this is the last time I will say it.'

'It is all settled,' said the Sikh officer, speaking softly in Punjabi. 'I have arranged that these people from the next village will look after the cattle, carts, and houses till it is over. I will have a list made and sent over to you.'

His colleague did not reply. He had a sardonic smile on his face. Mano Majra Sikhs and Muslims looked on helplessly.

There was no time to make arrangements. There was no time even to say goodbye. Truck engines were started. Pathan soldiers rounded up the Muslims, drove them back to the carts for a brief minute or two, and then onto the trucks. In the confusion of rain, mud and soldiers herding the peasants about with the muzzles of their sten guns sticking in their backs, the villagers saw little of each other. All they could do was to shout their last farewells from the trucks. The Muslim officer drove his jeep round the convoy to see that all was in order and then came to say goodbye to his Sikh colleague. The two shook hands mechanically, without a smile or a trace of emotion. The jeep took its place in front of the line of trucks. The microphone blared forth once more to announce that they were ready to move. The officer shouted 'Pakistan!' His soldiers answered in a chorus 'Forever!' The convoy slushed its way towards Chundunnugger. The Sikhs watched them till they were out of sight. They wiped the tears off their faces and turned back to their homes with heavy hearts.

Mano Majra's cup of sorrow was not yet full. The Sikh officer summoned the lambardar. All the villagers came with him—no one wanted to be left alone. Sikh soldiers threw a cordon round them. The officer told the villagers that he had decided to appoint Malli custodian of the evacuated Muslims' property. Anyone interfering with him or his men would be shot.

Malli's gang and the refugees then unyoked the bullocks, looted the carts, and drove the cows and buffaloes away.

KARMA

All that morning, people sat in their homes and stared despondently through their open doors. They saw Malli's men and the refugees ransack Muslim houses. They saw Sikh soldiers come and go as if on their beats. They heard the piteous lowing of cattle as they were beaten and dragged along. They heard the loud cackle of hens and roosters silenced by the slash of the knife. But they did nothing but sit and sigh.

A shepherd boy, who had been out gathering mushrooms, came back with the news that the river had risen. No one took any notice of him. They only wished that it would rise more and drown the whole of Mano Majra along with them, their women, children, and cattle—provided it also drowned Malli, his gang, the refugees, and the soldiers.

While the men sighed and groaned, the rain fell in a steady downpour and the Sutlej continued to rise. It spread on either side of the central piers which normally contained the winter channels, and joined the pools round the other piers into one broad stream. It stretched right across the bridge, licking the dam which separated it from the fields of Mano Majra. It ran over the many little islands in the river bed till only the tops of the bushes that grew on them could be seen. Colonies of cormorants and terns which were used to roosting there flew over to the banks and then to the bridge—over which no trains had run for several days.

In the afternoon, another villager went around to the houses shouting, 'Oi Banta Singh, the river is rising! Oi Daleep Singha, the river has risen! Oi listen, it is already up to the dam!' The people just looked up with their melancholy eyes signifying, 'We have heard that before.' Then another man came with the same message, 'The river has risen'; then another, and another, till everyone was saying, 'Do you know, the river has risen!'

At last the lambardar went out to see for himself. Yes, the river had risen. Two days of rain could not have caused it; it must have poured in the mountains after the melting of the snows. Sluice gates of canals had probably been closed to prevent the flood from bursting their banks; so there was no outlet except the river. The friendly sluggish stream of grey had become a menacing and tumultuous spread of muddy brown. The piers of the bridge were all that remained solid and contemptuously defiant of the river. Their pointed edges clove through the sheet of water and let it vent its impotent rage in a swirl of eddies and whirlpools. Rain beat upon the surface, pockmarking it all over. The Sutlej was a terrifying sight.

By evening, Mano Majra had forgotten about its Muslims and Malli's misdeeds. The river had become the main topic of conversation. Once more women stood on the rooftops looking to the west. Men started going in turns to the embankment to report on the situation.

Before sunset the lambardar went up again to see the river. It had risen more since his visit in the afternoon. Some of the clusters of pampas which had been above the water level were now partly submerged. Their stalks had gone limp and their sodden snow-white plumes floated on the water. He had never known the Sutlej to rise so high in so short a time. Mano Majra was still a long way off and the mud dam looked solid and safe. Nevertheless he arranged for a watch to be kept all through the night. Four parties of three men each were to take turns and be on the embankment from sunset to sunrise and report every hour. The rest were to stay in their houses.

The lambardar's decision was a quilt under which the village slept snug and safe. The lambardar himself had little sleep. Soon after midnight the three men on watch came back talking loudly, in a high state of excitement. They could not tell in the grey muffled moonlight whether the river had risen more, but they had heard human voices calling for help. The cries came from over the water. They may have been from the other side or from the river itself. The lambardar went out with them. He took his chromium-plated flashlight.

The four men stood on the embankment and surveyed the Sutlej, which looked like a sheet of black. The white beam of the lambardar's torch scanned the surface of the river. They could see nothing but the swirling water. They held their breath and listened, but they could hear nothing except the noise of the rain falling on the water. Each time the lambardar asked if they were sure that what they had heard were human voices and not jackals, they felt more and more uncertain and had to ask each other: 'It was clear, wasn't it, Karnaila?'

'Oh yes. It was clear enough. "Hai, hai"—like someone in pain.'

The four men sat under a tree, huddled around a hurricane lamp. The gunny sacks they used as raincoats were soaking wet; so were all their clothes. An hour later there was a break in the clouds. The rain slowed down to a drizzle and then stopped. The moon broke through the clouds just above the western horizon. Its reflection on the river made a broad path of shimmering tinfoil running from the opposite bank to the men under the tree. On this shining patch of moonlight even little ripples of water could be seen distinctly.

A black oval object hit the bridge pier and was swept by the stream towardss the Mano Majra embankment. It looked like a big drum with sticks on its sides. It moved forward, backward and sideways until the current caught it again and brought it into the silvery path not far from where the men were sitting. It was a dead cow with its belly bloated like a massive barrel and its legs stiffly stretched upward. Then followed some blocks of thatch straw and bundles of clothing.

'It looks as if some village has been swept away by the flood,' said the lambardar.

'Quiet! Listen,' said one of the villagers in a whisper. The faint sound of a moan was wafted across the waters.

'Did you hear?'

'Quiet!'

They held their breath and listened.

No, it could not have been human. There was a rumbling sound. They listened again. Of course, it was a rumble; it was a train. Its puffing became clearer and clearer. Then they saw the outlines of the engine and the train itself. It had no lights. There was not even a headlight on the engine. Sparks flew out of the engine funnel like fireworks. As the train came over the bridge, cormorants flew silently down the river and terns flew up with shrill cries. The train came to a halt at Mano Majra station. It was from Pakistan.

'There are no lights on the train.'

'The engine did not whistle.'

'It is like a ghost.'

'In the name of the Lord do not talk like this,' said the lambardar. 'It may be a goods train. It must have been the siren you heard. These new American engines wail like someone being murdered.'

'No, Lambardara, we heard the sound more than an hour ago; and again the same one before the train came on,' replied one of the villagers.

'You cannot hear it any more. The train is not making any noise now.'

From across the railway line, where some days earlier over a thousand dead bodies had been burned, a jackal sent up a long plaintive howl. A pack joined him. The men shuddered.

'Must have been the jackals. They sound like women crying when somebody dies,' said the lambardar.

'No, no,' protested the other. 'No, it was a human voice as clear as you are talking to me now.'

They sat and listened and watched strange indistinguishable forms floating on the floodwaters. The moon went down. After a brief period of darkness the eastern horizon turned grey. Long lines of bats flew across noiselessly. Crows began to caw in their sleep. The shrill cry of a koel came bursting through a clump of trees and all the world was awake.

The clouds had rolled away to the north. Slowly the sun came up and flooded the rain-soaked plain with a dazzling orange brilliance; everything glistened in the sunlight. The river had risen further. Its turbid water carried carts with the bloated carcasses of bulls still yoked to them. Horses rolled from side to side as if they were scratching their backs. There were also men and women with their clothes clinging to their bodies; little children sleeping on their bellies with their arms clutching the water and their tiny buttocks dipping in and out. The sky was soon full of kites and vultures. They flew down and landed on the floating carcasses. They pecked till the corpses themselves rolled over and shooed them off with hands which rose stiffly into the air and splashed back into the water.

'Some villages must have been flooded at night,' said the lambardar gravely.

'Who yokes bulls to carts at night?' asked one of his companions.

'Yes, that is true. Why should the bullocks be yoked?'

More human forms could be seen coming through the arches of the bridge. They rebounded off the piers, paused, pirouetted at the whirlpools, and then came bouncing down the river. The men moved up towards the bridge to see some corpses which had drifted near the bank.

They stood and stared.

'Lambardara, they were not drowned. They were murdered.'

An old peasant with a grey beard lay flat on the water. His arms were stretched out as if he had been crucified. His mouth was wide open and showed his toothless gums, his eyes were covered with film, his hair floated about his head like a halo. He had a deep wound on his neck which slanted down from the side to the chest. A child's head butted into the old man's armpit. There was a hole in its back. There were many others coming down the river like logs hewn on the mountains and cast into streams to be carried down to the plains. A few passed through the middle of the arches and sped onward faster. Others bumped into the piers and turned over to show their wounds till the current turned them over again. Some were without limbs, some had their bellies torn open, many women's breasts were slashed. They floated down the sunlit river, bobbing up and down. Overhead hung the kites and vultures.

The lambardar and the villagers drew the ends of their turbans across their faces. 'The Guru have mercy on us,' someone whispered. 'There has been a massacre somewhere. We must inform the police.'

'Police?' a small man said bitterly. 'What will they do? Write a first information report?'

Sick and with heavy hearts, the party turned back to Mano Majra. They did not know what to say to people when they got back. The river had risen further? Some villages had been flooded? There had been a massacre somewhere upstream? There were hundreds of corpses floating on the Sutlej? Or, just keep quiet?

When they came back to the village nobody was about to hear what they had to say. They were all on the rooftops looking at the station. After several days a train had drawn up at Mano Majra in the daytime. Since the engine faced eastward, it must have come from Pakistan. This time too the place was full of soldiers and policemen and the station had been cordoned off. The news of the corpses on the river was shouted from the housetops. People told each other about the mutilation of women and children. Nobody wanted to know who the dead people were nor wanted to go to the river to find out. There was a new interest at the station, with promise of worse horrors than the last one.

There was no doubt in anyone's mind what the train contained. They were sure that the soldiers would come for oil and wood. They had no more oil to spare and the wood they had left was too damp to burn. But the soldiers did not come. Instead, a bulldozer arrived from somewhere. It began dragging its lower jaw into the ground just outside the station on the Mano Majra side. It went along, eating up the earth, chewing it, casting it aside. It did this for several hours, until there was a rectangular trench almost fifty yards long with mounds of earth on either side. Then it paused for a break. The soldiers and policemen who had been idly watching the bulldozer at work were called to order and marched back to the platform. They came back in twos carrying canvas stretchers. They tipped the stretchers into the pit and went back to the train for more. This went on all day till sunset. Then the bulldozer woke up again. It opened its jaws and ate up the earth it had thrown out before and vomited it into the trench till it was level with the ground. The place looked like the scar of a healed-up wound. Two soldiers were left to guard the grave from the depredations of jackals and badgers.

That evening, the entire village turned up for the evening prayers at the gurdwara. This had never happened before, except on Gurus' birthdays or on the New Year's Day in April. The only regular visitors to the temple were old men and women. Others came to have their children named, for baptisms, weddings and funerals. Attendance at prayers had been steadily going up since the murder of the moneylender; people did not want to be alone. Since the Muslims had gone, their deserted houses with doors swinging wide open had acquired an eerie, haunted look. Villagers walked past them quickly without turning their heads. The one place of refuge to which people could go without much explanation was the gurdwara. Men came pretending that they would be needed; women just to be with them, and they brought the children. The main hall where the scripture was kept and the two rooms on the side were jammed with refugees and villagers. Their shoes were neatly arranged in rows on the other side of the threshold.

Meet Singh read the evening prayer by the light of the hurricane lamp. One of the men stood behind him waving a fly whisk. When the prayer was over, the congregation sang a hymn while Meet Singh folded the Granth in gaudy silk scarfs and laid it to rest for the night. The worshippers stood up and folded their hands. Meet Singh took his place in front. He repeated the names of the ten Gurus, the Sikh martyrs and the Sikh shrines and invoked their blessing; the crowd shouted their amens with loud 'Wah Gurus' at the end of each supplication. They went down on their knees, rubbed their foreheads on the ground, and the ceremony was over. Meet Singh came and joined the men.

It was a solemn assembly. Only the children played. They chased each other around the room, laughing and arguing. The adults scolded the children. One by one, the children returned to their mothers' laps and fell asleep. Then the men and women also stretched themselves on the floor in the different parts of the room.

The day's events were not likely to be forgotten in sleep. Many could not sleep at all. Others slept fitfully and woke up with startled cries if a neighbour's leg or arm so much as touched them. Even the ones who snored with apparent abandon, dreamed and relived the scenes of the day. They heard the sound of motor vehicles, the lowing of cattle and people crying. They sobbed in their sleep and their beards were moist with their tears.

When the sound of a motor horn was heard once more, those who were awake but drowsy thought they were dreaming. Those that were dreaming thought they were hearing it in their dreams. In their dreams they even said 'Yes, yes' to the voice which kept asking 'Are you all dead?'

The late night visitor was a jeep like the one in which the army officers had come in the morning. It seemed to know its way about the village. It went from door to door with a voice inquiring, 'Is there anyone there?' Only the dogs barked in reply. Then it came to the temple and the engine was switched off. Two men walked into the courtyard and shouted again: 'Is there anyone here or are you all dead?'

Everyone got up. Some children began to cry. Meet Singh turned up the wick of his hurricane lantern. He and the lambardar went out to meet the visitors.

The men saw the commotion they had created. They ignored the lambardar and Meet Singh and walked up to the threshold of the large room. One looked in at the bewildered crowd and asked:

'Are you all dead?'

'Any one of you alive?' added the other.

The lambardar answered angrily, 'No one is dead in this village. What do you want?'

Before the men could answer two of their companions joined them. All were Sikhs. They wore khaki uniforms and had rifles slung on their shoulders.

'This village looks quite dead,' repeated one of the strangers, loudly addressing his own companions.

'The Guru has been merciful to this village. No one has died here,' answered Meet Singh with quiet dignity.

'Well, if the village is not dead, then it should be. It should be drowned in a palmful of water. It consists of eunuchs,' said the visitor fiercely with a flourish of his hand.

The strangers took off their shoes and came inside the large hall. The lambardar and Meet Singh followed them. Men sat up and tied their turbans. Women put their children in their laps and tried to rock them to sleep again.

One of the group, who appeared to be the leader, motioned the others to sit down. Everyone sat down. The leader had an aggressive bossy manner. He was a boy in his teens with a little beard which was glued to his chin with brilliantine. He was small in size, slight of build and altogether somewhat effeminate; a glossy red ribbon showed under the acute angle of his bright blue turban. His khaki army shirt hung loosely from his round drooping shoulders. He wore a black leather Sam Browne: the strap across his narrow chest charged with bullets and the broad belt clamped about his still narrower waist. On one side it had a holster with the butt of a revolver protruding; on the other side there was a dagger. He looked as if his mother had dressed him up as an American cowboy.

The boy caressed the holster of his revolver and ran his fingers over the silver noses of the bullets. He looked around him with complete confidence.

'Is this a Sikh village?' he asked insolently. It was obvious to the villagers that he was an educated city-dweller. Such men always assumed a superior air when talking to peasants. They had no regard for age or status.

'Yes, sir,' answered the lambardar. 'It has always been a Sikh village. We had Muslim tenants but they have gone.'

'What sort of Sikhs are you?' asked the boy, glowering menacingly. He elaborated his question: 'Potent or impotent?'

No one knew what to say. No one protested that this was not the sort of language one used in a gurdwara with women and children sitting by.

'Do you know how many trainloads of dead Sikhs and Hindus have come over? Do you know of the massacres in Rawalpindi and Multan, Gujranwala and Sheikhupura? What are you doing about it? You just eat and sleep and you call yourselves Sikhs— the brave Sikhs! The martial class!' he added, raising both his arms to emphasize his sarcasm. He surveyed his audience with the bright eyes daring anyone to contradict him. People looked down somewhat ashamed of themselves.

'What can we do, Sardarji?' questioned the lambardar. 'If our government goes to war against Pakistan, we will fight. What can we do sitting in Mano Majra?'

'Government!' sneered the boy contemptuously. 'You expect the government to do anything? A government consisting of cowardly bania moneylenders! Do the Mussalmans in Pakistan apply for permission from their government when they rape your sisters? Do they apply for permission when they stop trains and kill everyone, old, young, women and children? You want the government to do something! That is great! Shabash! Brave!' He gave the holster on his side a jaunty smack.

'But, Sardar Sahib,' said the lambardar falteringly, 'Do tell us what we can do.'

'That is better,' answered the lad. 'Now we can talk. Listen and listen very carefully.' He paused, looked around and started again. He spoke slowly, emphasizing each sentence by stabbing the air with his forefinger. 'For each Hindu or Sikh they kill, kill two Mussulmans. For each woman they abduct or rape, abduct two. For each home they loot, loot two. For each trainload of dead they send over, send two across. For each road convoy that is attacked, attack two. That will stop the killing on the other side. It will teach them that we also play this game of killing and looting.'

He stopped to gauge the effect he had created. People listened to him with rapt open-mouthed attention. Only Meet Singh did not took up; he cleared his throat but stopped.

'Well, brother, why do you keep quiet?' asked the lad, throwing a challenge.

'I was going to say,' said Meet Singh haltingly, 'I was going to say,' he repeated, 'what have the Muslims here done to us for us to kill them in revenge for what Muslims in Pakistan are doing. Only people who have committed crimes should be punished.'

The lad glared angrily at Meet Singh. 'What had the Sikhs and Hindus in Pakistan done that they were butchered? Weren't they innocent? Had the women committed crimes for which they were ravished? Had the children committed murder for which they were spiked in front of their parents?'

Meet Singh was subdued. The boy wanted to squash him further. 'Why, brother? Now speak and say what you want to.'

'I am an old Bhai; I could not lift my hands against anyone—fight in battle or kill the killer. What bravery is there in killing unarmed innocent people? As for women, you know that the last Guru, Gobind Singh, made it a part of a baptismal oath that no Sikh was to touch the person of a Muslim woman. And God alone knows how he suffered at the hands of the Mussulmans! They killed all his four sons.'

'Teach this sort of Sikhism to someone else,' snapped the boy contemptuously. 'It is your sort of people who have been the curse of this country. You quote the Guru about women; why don't you tell us what he said about the Mussulmans? "Only befriend the Turk when all other communities are dead." Is that correct?'

'Yes,' answered Meet Singh meekly, 'but nobody is asking

you to befriend them. Besides, the Guru himself had Muslims in his army . . .'

'And one of them stabbed him while he slept.'

Meet Singh felt uneasy.

'One of them stabbed him while he slept,' repeated the boy.

'Yes . . . but there are bad ones and . . .'

'Show me a good one.'

Meet Singh could not keep up with the repartee. He just looked down at his feet. His silence was taken as an admission of defeat.

'Let him be. He is an old bhai. Let him stick to his prayers,' said many in a chorus.

The speaker was appeased. He addressed the assembly again in pompous tones. 'Remember,' he said like an oracle, 'remember and never forget—a Muslim knows no argument but the sword.'

The crowd murmured approval.

'Is there anyone beloved of the Guru here? Anyone who wants to sacrifice his life for the Sikh community? Anyone with courage?' He hurled each sentence like a challenge.

The villagers felt very uncomfortable. The harangue had made them angry and they wanted to prove their manliness. At the same time Meet Singh's presence made them uneasy and they felt they were being disloyal to him.

'What are we supposed to do?' asked the lambardar plaintively.

'I will tell you what we are to do,' answered the boy, pointing to himself. 'If you have the courage to do it.' He continued after a pause. 'Tomorrow a trainload of Muslims is to cross the bridge to Pakistan. If you are men, this train should carry as many people dead to the other side as you have received.'

A cold clammy feeling spread among the audience. People coughed nervously.

'The train will have Mano Majra Muslims on it,' said Meet Singh without looking up.

'Bhai, you seem to know everything, don't you?' yelled the youth furiously. 'Did you give them the tickets or is your son a Railway Babu? I don't know who the Muslims on the train are; I do not care. It is enough for me to know that they are Muslims.

They will not cross this river alive. If you people agree with me, we can talk; if you are frightened, then say so and we will say Sat Sri Akal to you and look for real men elsewhere.'

Another long period of silence ensued. The lad beat a tattoo on his holster and patiently scanned the faces around him.

'There is a military guard at the bridge.' It was Malli. He had been standing outside in the dark. He would not have dared to come back to Mano Majra alone. Yet there he was, boldly stepping into the gurdwara. Several members of his gang appeared at the door.

'You need not bother about the military or the police. No one will interfere. We will see to that,' answered the lad looking back at him. 'Are there any volunteers?'

'My life is at your disposal,' said Malli heroically. The story of Jugga beating him had gone round the village. His reputation had to be redeemed.

'Bravo,' said the speaker. 'At least one man. The Guru asked for five lives when he made the Sikhs. Those Sikhs were supermen. We need many more than five. Who else is willing to lay down his life?'

Four of Malli's companions stepped over the threshold. They were followed by many others, mostly refugees. Some villagers who had only recently wept at the departure of their Muslim friends also stood up to volunteer. Each time anyone raised his hand the youth said 'Bravo,' and asked him to come and sit apart. More than fifty agreed to join in the escapade.

'That is enough,' said the lad, raising his hand. 'If I need any more volunteers, I will ask for them. Let us pray for the success of our venture.'

Everyone stood up. Women put their children on the floor and joined the menfolk. The assembly faced the little cot on which the Granth lay wrapped, and folded their hands in prayer. The boy turned round to Meet Singh.

'Will you lead the prayer, Bhaiji?' he asked tauntingly.

'It is your mission, Sardar Sahib,' replied Meet Singh humbly. 'You lead the prayer.'

The boy cleared his throat, shut his eyes and began to recite the names of the Gurus. He ended by asking for the Gurus' blessings for the venture. The assembly went down on their knees and rubbed their foreheads on the ground, loudly proclaiming:

In the name of Nanak,
By the hope that faith doth instill,
By the Grace of God,
We bear the world nothing but good will.

The crowd stood up again and began to chant:

The Sikhs will rule
Their enemies will be scattered
Only they that seek refuge will be saved!

The little ceremonial ended with triumphant cries of Sat Sri Akal. Everyone sat down except the boy leader. The prayer had given him a veneer of humility. He joined his hands and apologized to the assembly.

'Sisters and brothers, forgive me for disturbing you at this late hour; you too, Bhaiji, and you, Lambardar Sahib, please forgive us for this inconvenience and for any angry words that I may have uttered; but this is in the service of the Guru. Volunteers will now adjourn to the other room; the others may rest. Sat Sri Akal.'

'Sat Sri Akal,' replied some of the audience.

Meet Singh's room on the side of the courtyard was cleared of women and children. The visitors moved in with the volunteers. More lamps were brought in. The leader spread out a map on one of the beds. He held up a hurricane lantern. The volunteers crowded round him to study the map.

'Can you all see the position of the bridge and the river from where you are?' he asked.

'Yes, yes,' they answered impatiently.

'Have any of you got guns?'

They all looked at each other. No, no one had a gun.

'It does not matter,' continued the leader. 'We still have six or seven rifles, and probably a couple of sten guns as well. Bring your swords and spears. They will be more useful than guns.' He paused.

'The plan is this. Tomorrow after sunset, when it is dark, we will stretch a rope across the first span of the bridge. It will be a foot above the height of the funnel of the engine. When the train passes under it, it will sweep off all the people sitting on the roof of the train. That will account for at least four to five hundred.'

The eyes of the listeners sparkled with admiration. They nodded to each other and looked around. The lambardar and Meet Singh stood at the door listening. The boy turned round angrily:

'Bhaiji, what have you to do with this? Why don't you go and say your prayers?'

Both the lambardar and Meet Singh turned away sheepishly. The lambardar knew he too would be told off if he hung around.

'And you, Lambardar Sahib,' said the boy. 'You should be going to the police station to report.'

Everyone laughed.

The boy silenced his audience by raising his hand. He continued: 'The train is due to leave Chundunnugger after midnight. It will have no lights, not even on the engine. We will post people with flashlights along the track every hundred yards. Each one will give the signal to the next person as the train passes him. In any case, you will be able to hear it. People with swords and spears will be right at the bridge to deal with those that fall off the roof of the train. They will have to be killed and thrown into the river. Men with guns will be a few yards up the track and will shoot at the windows. There will be no danger of fire being returned. There are only a dozen Pakistani soldiers on the train. In the dark, they will not know where to shoot. They will not have time to load their guns. If they stop the train, we will take care of them and kill many more into the bargain.'

It seemed a perfect plan, without the slightest danger of

retaliation. Everyone was pleased.

'It is already past midnight,' said the boy, folding up the map. 'You'd all better get some sleep. Tomorrow morning we will go to the bridge and decide where each one is to be posted. The Sikhs are the chosen of God. Victory be to our God.'

'Victory to our God,' answered the others.

The meeting dispersed. Visitors found room in the gurdwara. So did Malli and his gang. Many of the villagers had gone away to their homes lest they get implicated in the crime by being present at the temple when the conspiracy was being hatched. The lambardar took two of the villagers with him and left for the police station at Chundunnugger.

'Well, Inspector Sahib, let them kill,' said Hukum Chand wearily. 'Let everyone kill. Just ask for help from other stations and keep a record of the messages you send. We must be able to prove that we did our best to stop them.'

Hukum Chand looked a tired man. One week had aged him beyond recognition. The white at the roots of his hair had become longer. He had been shaving in a hurry and had cut himself in several places. His cheeks sagged and folds of flesh fell like dewlaps about his chin. He kept rubbing the corners of his eyes for the yellow which was not there.

'What am I to do?' he wailed. 'The whole world has gone mad. Let it go mad! What does it matter if another thousand get killed? We will get a bulldozer and bury them as we did the others. We may not even need the bulldozer if this time it is going to be on the river. Just throw the corpses in the water. What is a few hundred out of four hundred million anyway? An epidemic takes ten times the number and no one even bothers.'

The subinspector knew that this was not the real Hukum Chand. He was only trying to get the melancholia out of his system. The subinspector waited patiently, and then dropped a feeler.

'Yes, sir. I am keeping a record of all that is happening and what we are doing. Last evening, we had to evacuate Chundunnugger. I could not rely on the army nor my own constables. The best I could do was to ward off the attackers by telling them that Pakistan troops were in the town. That frightened them and I got the Muslims out in the nick of time. When the attackers discovered the trick, they looted and burned every Muslim house they could. I believe some of them planned to come to the police station for me, but better counsel prevailed. So you see, sir, all I got was abuse from the Muslims for evicting them from their homes; abuse from the Sikhs for having robbed them of the loot they were expecting. Now I suppose the government will also abuse me for something or the other. All I really have is my big thumb.' The subinspector stuck out his thumb and smiled.

Hukum Chand's mind was not itself that morning. He did not seem to realize the full import of the subinspector's report.

'Yes, Inspector Sahib, you and I are going to get nothing out of this except a bad name. What can we do? Everyone has gone trigger-happy. People empty their rifle magazines into densely packed trains, motor convoys, columns of marching refugees, as if they were squirting red water at the Holi festival; it is a bloody Holi. What sense is there in going to a place where bullets fly? The bullet does not pause and consider, "This is Hukum Chand, I must not touch him." Nor does a bullet have a name written on it saying "Sent by So-and-so". Even if it did bear a name— once inside, what consolation would it be to us to know who fired it? No, Inspector Sahib, the only thing a sane person can do in a lunatic asylum is to pretend that he is as mad as the others and at the first opportunity scale the walls and get out.'

The subinspector was used to these sermons and knew how little they represented the magistrate's real self. But Hukum Chand's apparent inability to take a hint was surprising. He was known for never saying a thing straight; he considered it stupid. To him the art of diplomacy was to state a simple thing in an involved manner. It never got one into trouble. It could never be quoted as having implied this or that. At the same time, it gave one the reputation of being shrewd and clever. Hukum Chand was as adept at discovering innuendoes as he was at making them. This morning he seemed to be giving his mind a rest.

'You should have been in Chundunnugger yesterday,' said the subinspector, bringing the conversation back to the actual problem which faced him. 'If I had been five minutes later, there would not have been one Muslim left alive. As it is, not one was killed. I was able to take them all out.'

The subinspector emphasized 'not one' and 'all'. He watched Hukum Chand's reaction.

It worked. Hukum Chand stopped rubbing the corners of his eyes and asked casually, as if he were only seeking information, 'You mean to tell me there is not one Muslim family left in Chundunnugger?'

'No, sir, not one.'

'I suppose,' said Hukum Chand, clearing his throat, 'they will came back when all this blows over?'

'Maybe,' the subinspector answered. 'There is not much for them to come back to. Their homes have been burned or occupied. And if anyone did come back, his or her life would not be worth the tiniest shell in the sea.'

'It will not last forever. You see how things change. Within a week they will be back in Chundunnugger and the Sikhs and Muslims will be drinking water out of the same pitcher.' Hukum Chand detected the note of false hope in his own voice. So did the subinspector.

'You may be right, sir. But it will certainly take more than a week for that to happen. Chundunnugger refugees are being taken to Pakistan by train tonight. God alone knows how many will go across the bridge alive; those that do are not likely to want to come back in a hurry.'

The subinspector had hit the mark. Hukum Chand's face went pale. He could no longer keep up the pretense.

'How do you know that Chundunnugger refugees are going by the night train?' he asked.

'I got it from the camp commander. There was danger of attack on the camp itself, so he decided to get the first train available to take the refugees out. If they do not go, probably no one will be left alive. If they do, some at least may get through, if the train is running at some speed. They are not planning to derail the train; they want it to go on to Pakistan with a cargo of corpses.'

Hukum Chand clutched the arms of his chair convulsively.

'Why don't you warn the camp commander about it? He may decide not to go.'

'Cherisher of the poor,' explained the subinspector patiently, 'I have not told him anything about the proposed attack on the train because if he does not go the whole camp may be destroyed. There are mobs of twenty to thirty thousand armed villagers thirsting for blood. I have fifty policemen with me and not one of them would fire a shot at a Sikh. But if your honour can use influence with these mobs, I can tell the camp commander about the plans to ambush the train and persuade him not to go.'

The subinspector was hitting below the belt.

'No, no,' stuttered the magistrate. 'What can influence do with armed mobs? No. We must think.'

Hukum Chand sank back in his chair. He covered his face with his hands. He beat his forehead gently with his clenched fist. He tugged at his hair as if he could pull ideas out of his brain.

'What has happened to those two men you arrested for the moneylender's murder?' he asked after some time.

The subinspector did not see the relevance of the inquiry.

'They are still in the lockup. You ordered me to keep them till the trouble was over. At this rate it seems I will have to keep them for some months.'

'Are there any Muslim females, or any stray Muslims who have refused to leave Mano Majra?'

'No, sir, not one remains. Men, women, children, all have left,' answered the subinspector. He was still unable to catch up with Hukum Chand's train of thought.

'What about Jugga's weaver girl you told me about? What was her name?'

'Nooran.'

'Ah yes, Nooran. Where is she?'

'She has left. Her father was a sort of leader of the Muslims of Mano Majra. The lambardar told me a great deal about him. He had just one child, this girl Nooran; she is the one alleged to be carrying on with the dacoit Jugga.'

'And this other fellow, didn't you say he was a political worker of some sort?'

'Yes, sir. People's Party or something like that. I think he is a Muslim Leaguer masquerading under a false label. I examined . . .'

'Have you got any blank official papers for orders?' cut in Hukum Chand impatiently.

'Yes, sir,' answered the subinspector. He fished out several pieces of yellow printed paper and handed them to the magistrate.

Hukum Chand stretched out his hand and plucked the subinspector's fountain pen from his pocket.

'What are the names of the prisoners?' he asked, spreading out the sheets on the table.

'Jugga badmash and . . .'

'Jugga badmash,' interrupted Hukum Chand, filling in a blank and signing it. 'Jugga badmash, and . . . ?' he asked taking the other paper.

'Iqbal Mohammed or Mohammed Iqbal. I am not sure which.'

'Not Iqbal Mohammed, Inspector Sahib. Nor Mohammed Iqbal. Iqbal Singh,' he said, writing with a flourish. The subinspector looked a little stupefied. How did Hukum Chand know? Had Meet Singh been around calling on the magistrate?

'Sir, you should not believe everyone. I examined . . .'

'Do you really believe an educated Muslim would dare to come to these parts in times like these? Do you think any party would be so foolish as to send a Muslim to preach peace to Sikh peasants thirsting for Muslim blood, Inspector Sahib? Where is your imagination?'

The subinspector was subdued. It did seem unlikely that an educated man would risk his neck for any cause. Besides, he had noticed on Iqbal's right wrist the steel bangle all Sikhs wear.

'Your honour must be right, but what has this to do with the preventing of an attack on the train?'

'My honour *is* right,' said Hukum Chand triumphantly. 'And you will soon know why. Think about it on your way to Chundunnugger. As soon as you get there, release both the men and see that they leave for Mano Majra immediately. If necessary, get them a tonga. They must be in the village by the evening.'

The subinspector took the papers, and saluted. He sped back to the police station on his cycle. Gradually, the clouds of confusion lifted from his mind. Hukum Chand's plan became as crystal clear as a day after heavy rain.

'You will find Mano Majra somewhat changed,' the subinspector remarked, casually addressing the table in front of him. Iqbal and Jugga stood facing him on the other side.

'Why don't you sit down, Babu Sahib?' said the subinspector. This time he spoke directly to Iqbal. 'Please take a chair. Oi, what is your name? Why don't you bring a chair for the Babu Sahib?' he shouted at a constable. 'I know you are angry with me, but it is not my fault,' he continued. 'I have my duty to do. You as an educated man know what would happen if I were to treat people differently.'

The constable brought a chair for Iqbal.

'Do sit down. Shall I get you a cup of tea or something before you go?' The subinspector smiled unctuously.

'It is very kind of you. I would rather keep standing; I have been sitting in the cell all these days. If you do not mind, I would like to leave as soon as you have finished with the formalities,' answered Iqbal without responding to the other's smile.

'You are free to go whenever and wherever you want to go. I have sent for a tonga to take you to Mano Majra. I will send an armed constable to accompany you. It is not safe to be about in Chundunnugger or to travel unescorted.'

The subinspector picked up a yellow paper and read: 'Juggut Singh, son of Alam Singh, age twenty-four, caste Sikh of village

Mano Majra, badmash number ten.'

'Yes, sir,' interrupted Jugga, smiling. The treatment he had received from the police had not made any difference to him. His equation with authority was simple: he was on the other side. Personalities did not come into it. Subinspectors and policemen were people in khaki who frequently arrested him, always abused him, and sometimes beat him. Since they abused and beat him without anger or hate, they were not human beings with names. They were only denominations one tried to get the better of. If one failed, it was just bad luck.

'You are being released, but you must appear before Mr Hukum Chand, Deputy Commissioner, on the first of October 1947, at ten a.m. Put your thumb impression on this.'

The subinspector opened a flat tin box with a black gauze padding inside it. He caught Juggut Singh's thumb in his hand, rubbed it on the damp pad and pressed it on the paper.

'Have I permission to go?' asked Jugga.

'You can go with Babu Sahib in the tonga; otherwise you will not get home before dark.' He looked up at Jugga and repeated slowly, 'You will not find Mano Majra the same.'

Neither of the men showed any interest in the subinspector's remark about Mano Majra. The subinspector spread out another piece of paper and read: 'Mr Iqbal Singh, social worker.'

Iqbal looked at the paper cynically.

'Not Mohammed Iqbal, member of the Muslim League? You seem to fabricate facts and documents as it pleases you.'

The subinspector grinned. 'Everyone makes mistakes. To err is human, to forgive divine,' he added in English. 'I admit my mistake.'

'That is very generous of you,' answered Iqbal. 'I had always believed that the Indian Police were infallible.'

'You can make fun of me if you like; you do not realize that if you had been going about lecturing as you intended and had fallen into the hands of a Sikh mob, they would not have listened to your arguments. They would have stripped you to find out whether or not you were circumcised. That is the only test they have these days for a person who has not got long hair and a beard. Then they kill. You should be grateful to me.'

Iqbal was in no mood to talk. Besides, the subject was not one he wanted to discuss with anyone. He resented the way the subinspector took the liberty of mentioning it.

'You will find big changes in Mano Majra!' warned the subinspector for the third time; neither Jugga nor Iqbal showed any response. Iqbal laid down on the table the book he had been holding and turned away without a word of thanks or farewell. Jugga felt the floor with his feet for his shoes.

'All Mussulmans have gone from Mano Majra,' said the subinspector dramatically.

Jugga stopped shuffling his feet. 'Where have they gone?'

'Yesterday they were taken to the refugee camp. Tonight they will go by train to Pakistan.'

'Was there any trouble in the village, Inspector Sahib? Why did they have to go?'

'There would have been if they had not gone. There are lots of outsiders going about with guns killing Muslims; Malli and his men have joined them. If the Muslims had not left Mano Majra, Malli would have finished them off by now. He has taken all their things—cows, buffaloes, oxen, mares, chicken, utensils. Malli has done well.'

Jugga's temper shot up at once. 'That penis of a pig who sleeps with his mother, pimps for his sister and daughter, if he puts his foot in Mano Majra I will stick my bamboo pole up his behind!'

The subinspector pursed his lips in a taunting smile. 'You talk big, Sardara. Just because you caught him unawares by his hair and beat him, you think you are a lion. Malli is not a woman with henna on his palms or bangles on his wrists. He has been in Mano Majra and taken all the things he wanted; he is still there. You will see him when you get back.'

'He will run like a jackal when he hears my name.'

'Men of his gang are with him. So are many others, all armed with guns and pistols. You had better behave sensibly if you hold your life dear.'

Jugga nodded his head. 'Right, Inspector Sahib. We will meet again. Then ask me about Malli.' His temper got the better of him. 'If I do not spit in his bottom, my name is not Juggut Singh.' He rubbed his mouth with the back of his hand. 'If I do not spit in Malli's mouth, my name is not Juggut Singh.' This time Juggut Singh spat on his own hand and rubbed it on his thigh. His temper rose to fever heat. 'If it had not been for your policemen in their uniforms, I would like to meet the father of a son who could dare to bat an eyelid before Juggut Singh,' he added, throwing out his chest.

'All right, all right, Sardar Juggut Singh, we agree you are a big brave man. At least you think so,' smiled the subinspector. 'You had better get home before dark. Take the Babu Sahib with you. Babu Sahib, you need have no fear. You have the district's bravest man to look after you.'

Before Juggut Singh could reply to the subinspector's sarcasm, a constable came in to announce that he had got a tonga.

'Sat Sri Akal, Inspector Sahib. When Malli comes crying to lodge a report against me, then you will believe that Juggut Singh is not a man of hollow words.'

The subinspector laughed. 'Sat Sri Akal, Juggut Singha. Sat Sri Akal, Iqbal Singhji.'

Iqbal walked away without turning back.

The tonga left Chundunnugger in the afternoon. It was a long, uneventful journey. This time Jugga sat on the front seat with the policeman and the driver, leaving the rear seat all to Iqbal. No one was in a mood to talk. Bhola, the driver, had been pressed into service by the police at a time when it was not safe to step out of the house. He took it out on his skinny brown horse, whipping and swearing continuously. The others were absorbed in their own thoughts.

The countryside also was still. There were large expanses of water which made it look flatter than usual. There were no men or women in the fields. Not even cattle grazing. The two villages they passed seemed deserted except for the dogs. Once or twice they caught a fleeting glimpse of someone stepping behind a wall or peering round a corner—and that someone carried a gun or a spear.

Iqbal realized that it was the company of Jugga and the constable, who were known Sikhs, that really saved him from being stopped and questioned. He wished he could get out of this place where he had to prove his Sikhism to save his life. He would pick up his things from Mano Majra and catch the first train. Perhaps there were no trains. And if there were, could he risk getting onto one? He cursed his luck for having a name like Iqbal, and then for being a . . . Where on earth except in India would a man's life depend on whether or not his foreskin had been removed? It would be laughable if it were not tragic. He would have to stay in Mano Majra for several days and stay close to Meet Singh for protection—Meet Singh with his unkempt appearance and two trips a day to the fields to defecate. The thought was revolting. If only he could get out to Delhi and to civilization! He would report on his arrest; the party paper would frontpage the news with his photograph: ANGLO-AMERICAN CAPITALIST CONSPIRACY TO CREATE CHAOS (lovely alliteration). COMRADE IQBAL IMPRISONED ON BORDER. It would all go to make him a hero.

Jugga's immediate concern was the fate of Nooran. He did not look at his companions in the tonga or at the village. He had forgotten about Malli. At the back of his mind persisted a feeling that Nooran would be in Mano Majra. No one could have wanted Imam Baksh to go. Even if he had left with the other Muslims Nooran would be hiding somewhere in the fields, or would have come to his mother. He hoped his mother had not turned her out. If she had, he would let her have it. He would walk out and never come back. She would spend the rest of her days regretting having done it.

Jugga was lost in his thoughts, concerned and angry alternately, when the tonga slowed down to pass through the lane to the Sikh temple. He jumped off the moving vehicle and disappeared into the darkness without a word of farewell.

Iqbal stepped off the tonga and stretched his limbs. The driver and the constable had a whispered consultation.

'Can I be of any more service to you, Babu Sahib?' asked the policeman.

'No. No, thank you. I am all right. It is very kind of you.' Iqbal did not like the prospect of going into the gurdwara alone, but he could not bring himself to ask the others to come with him.

'Babuji, we have a long way to go. My horse has been out all day without any food or water; and you know the times.'

'Yes, you can go back. Thank you. Sat Sri Akal.'

'Sat Sri Akal.'

The courtyard of the gurdwara was spotted with rings of light cast by hurricane lamps and fires on improvised hearths over which women were cooking the evening meal. Inside the main hall was a circle of people around Meet Singh, who was reciting the evening prayer. The room in which Iqbal had left his things was locked.

Iqbal took off his shoes, covered his head with a handkerchief and joined the gathering. Some people shifted to make room for him. Iqbal noticed people looking at him and whispering to each other. Most of them were old men dressed like town folk. It was quite obvious that they were refugees.

When the prayer was over, Meet Singh wrapped the massive volume in velvet and laid it to rest on the cot on which it had been lying open. He spoke to Iqbal before anyone else could start asking questions.

'Sat Sri Akal, Iqbal Singhji. I am glad you are back. You must be hungry.'

Iqbal realized that Meet Singh had deliberately mentioned his surname. He could feel the tension relax. Some of the men turned around and said 'Sat Sri Akal.'

'Sat Sri Akal,' answered Iqbal and got up to join Meet Singh.

'Sardar Iqbal Singh,' said Meet Singh, introducing him to the others, 'is a social worker. He has been in England for many years.'

A host of admiring eyes were turned on Iqbal, 'the England returned'. The 'Sat Sri Akals' were repeated. Iqbal felt embarrassed.

'You are Sikh, Iqbal Singhji?' inquired one of the men.

'Yes.' A fortnight earlier he would have replied emphatically 'No', or 'I have no religion' or 'Religion is irrelevant.' The situation was different now, and in any case it was true that he was born a Sikh.

'Was it in England you cut your hair?' asked the same person.

'No, sir,' answered Iqbal, completely confused. 'I never grew my hair long. I am just a Sikh without long hair and beard.'

'Your parents must have been unorthodox,' said Meet Singh coming to his aid. The statement allayed suspicion but left Iqbal with an uneasy conscience.

Meet Singh fumbled with the cord of his shorts and pulled up a bunch of keys dangling at the end. He picked up the hurricane lantern from the stool beside the scriptures and led the way through the courtyard to the room.

'I kept your things locked in the room. You can take them. I will get you some food.'

'No, Bhaiji, do not bother, I have enough with me. Tell me, what has happened in the village since I left? Who are all these people?'

The bhai unlocked the door and lit an oil lamp in the niche. Iqbal opened his kit bag and emptied its contents on a charpai. There were several copper-gold tins of fish paste, butter and cheese; aluminum forks, knives and spoons, and celluloid cups and saucers.

'Bhaiji, what has been happening?' Iqbal asked again.

'What has been happening? Ask me what has not been happening. Trainloads of dead people came to Mano Majra. We burned one lot and buried another. The river was flooded with corpses. Muslims were evacuated, and in their place, refugees have come from Pakistan. What more do you want to know?'

Iqbal wiped a celluloid plate and tumbler with his

handkerchief. He fished out his silver hip flask and shook it. It was full.

'What have you in that silver bottle?'

'Oh this? Medicine,' faltered Iqbal. 'It gives me an appetite for food,' he added with a smile.

'And then you take pills to digest it?'

Iqbal laughed. 'Yes, and more to make the bowels work. Tell me, was there any killing in the village?'

'No,' said the bhai casually. He was more interested in watching Iqbal inflating the air mattress. 'But there will be. Is it nice sleeping on this? Does everyone in England sleep on these?'

'What do you mean—there will be killing?' asked Iqbal, plugging the end of the mattress. 'All Muslims have left, haven't they?'

'Yes, but they are going to attack the train near the bridge tonight. It is taking Muslims of Chundunnugger and Mano Majra to Pakistan. Your pillow is also full of air.'

'Yes. Who are they? Not the villagers?'

'I do not know all of them. Some people in uniforms came in military cars. They had pistols and guns. The refugees have joined them. So have Malli badmash and his gang—and some villagers. Wouldn't this burst if a heavy person slept on it?' asked Meet Singh, tapping the mattress.

'I see,' said Iqbal, ignoring Meet Singh's question. 'I see the trick now. That is why the police released Malli. Now I suppose Jugga will join them, too. It is all arranged.' He stretched himself on the mattress and tucked the pillow under his armpit. 'Bhaiji, can't you stop it? They all listen to you.'

Meet Singh patted and smoothed the air mattress and sat down on the floor.

'Who listens to an old bhai? These are bad times, Iqbal Singhji, very bad times. There is no faith or religion. All one can do is to crouch in a safe corner till the storm blows over. This would not do for a newly married couple,' he added, slapping the mattress affectionately.

Iqbal was agitated. 'You cannot let this sort of thing happen!

Can't you tell them that the people on the train are the very same people they were addressing as uncles, aunts, brothers and sisters?'

Meet Singh sighed. He wiped a tear with the scarf on his shoulder.

'What difference will my telling them make? They know what they are doing. They will kill. If it is a success, they will come to the gurdwara for thanksgiving. They will also make offerings to wash away their sins. Iqbal Singhji, tell me about yourself. Have you been well? Did they treat you properly at the police station?'

'Yes, yes, I was all right,' snapped Iqbal impatiently. 'Why don't you do something? You must!'

'I have done all I could. My duty is to tell people what is right and what is not. If they insist on doing evil, I ask God to forgive them. I can only pray; the rest is for the police and the magistrate. And for you.'

'Me? Why me?' asked Iqbal with a startled innocence. 'What have I to do with it? I do not know these people. Why should they listen to a stranger?'

'When you came you were going to speak to them about something. Why don't you tell them now?'

Iqbal felt concerned. 'Bhaiji, when people go about with guns and spears you can only talk back with guns and spears. If you cannot do that, then it is best to keep out of their way.'

'That is exactly what I say. I thought you with your European ideas had some other remedy. Let me get you some hot spinach. I have just cooked it,' added Meet Singh getting up.

'No, no, Bhaiji, I have all I want in my tins. If I want something I will ask you for it. I have a little work to do before I eat.'

Meet Singh put the hurricane lantern on a stool by the bed and went back to the hall.

Iqbal put his plates, knife, fork, and tins back into the haversack. He felt a little feverish, the sort of feverishness one feels when one is about to make a declaration of love. It was time for a declaration of something. Only he was not sure what it should be.

Should he go out, face the mob and tell them in clear ringing tones that this was wrong—immoral? Walk right up to them with his eyes fixing the armed crowd in a frame—without flinching, without turning, like the heroes on the screen who become bigger and bigger as they walk right into the camera. Then with dignity fall under a volley of blows, or preferably a volley of rifleshots. A cold thrill went down Iqbal's spine.

There would be no one to see this supreme act of sacrifice. They would kill him just as they would kill the others. He was not neutral in their eyes. They would just strip him and see. Circumcised, therefore Muslim. It would be an utter waste of life! And what would it gain? A few subhuman species were going to slaughter some of their own kind—a mild setback to the annual increase of four million. It was not as if you were going to save good people from bad. If the others had the chance, they would do as much. In fact they were doing so, just a little beyond the river. It was pointless. In a state of chaos self-preservation is the supreme duty.

Iqbal unscrewed the top of his hip flask and poured out a large whisky in a celluloid tumbler. He gulped it down neat.

When bullets fly about, what is the point of sticking out your head and getting shot? The bullet is neutral. It hits the good and the bad, the important and the insignificant, without distinction. If there were people to see the act of self-immolation, as on a cinema screen, the sacrifice might be worth while: a moral lesson might be conveyed. If all that was likely to happen was that next morning your corpse would be found among thousands of others, looking just like them—cropped hair, shaven chin . . . even circumcised—who would know that you were not a Muslim victim of a massacre? Who would know that you were a Sikh who, with full knowledge of the consequences, had walked into the face of a firing squad to prove that it was important that good should triumph over evil? And God—no, not God; He was irrelevant.

Iqbal poured another whisky. It seemed to sharpen his mind. The point of sacrifice, he thought, is the purpose. For the purpose, it is not enough that a thing is intrinsically good: it must be known to be good. It is not enough only to know within one's self that one is in the right: the satisfaction would be posthumous. This was not the same thing as taking punishment at school to save some friend. In that case you could feel good and live to enjoy the sacrifice; in this one you were going to be killed. It would do no good to society: society would never know. Nor to yourself: you would be dead. That figure on the screen, facing thousands of people who looked tense and concerned! They were ready to receive the lesson. That was the crux of the whole thing. The doer must do only when the receiver is ready to receive. Otherwise, the act is wasted.

He filled the glass again. Everything was becoming clearer.

If you really believe that things are so rotten that your first duty is to destroy—to wipe the slate clean—then you should not turn green at small acts of destruction. Your duty is to connive with those who make the conflagration, not to turn a moral hose-pipe on them—to create such a mighty chaos that all that is rotten like selfishness, intolerance, greed, falsehood, sycophancy, is drowned. In blood, if necessary.

India is constipated with a lot of humbug. Take religion. For the Hindu, it means little besides caste and cow-protection. For the Muslim, circumcision and kosher meat. For the Sikh, long hair and hatred of the Muslim. For the Christian, Hinduism with a sola topee. For the Parsi, fire-worship and feeding vultures. Ethics, which should be the kernel of a religious code, has been carefully removed. Take philosophy, about which there is so much hoo-ha. It is just muddle-headedness masquerading as mysticism. And Yoga, particularly Yoga, that excellent earner of dollars! Stand on your head. Sit cross-legged and tickle your navel with your nose. Have perfect control over the senses. Make women come till they cry 'Enough!' and you can say 'Next, please' without opening your eyes. And all the mumbo-jumbo of reincarnation. Man into ox into ape into beetle into eight million four hundred thousand kinds of animate things. Proof? We do not go in for such pedestrian pastimes as proof! That is Western.

We are of the mysterious East. No proof, just faith. No reason; just faith. Thought, which should be the sine qua non of a philosophical code, is dispensed with. We climb to sublime heights on the wings of fancy. We do the rope trick in all spheres of creative life. As long as the world credulously believes in our capacity to make a rope rise skyward and a little boy climb it till he is out of view, so long will our brand of humbug thrive.

Take art and music. Why has contemporary Indian painting, music, architecture and sculpture been such a flop? Because it keeps harking back to BC. Harking back would be all right if it did not become a pattern—a deadweight. If it does, then we are in a cul-de-sac of art forms. We explain the unattractive by pretending it is esoteric. Or we break out altogether—like modern Indian music of the films. It is all tango and rhumba or samba played on Hawaiian guitars, violins, accordions and clarinets. It is ugly. It must be scrapped like the rest.

He wasn't quite sure what he meant. He poured another whisky.

Consciousness of the bad is an essential prerequisite to the promotion of the good. It is no use trying to build a second storey on a house whose walls are rotten. It is best to demolish it. It is both cowardly and foolhardy to kowtow to social standards when one believes neither in the society nor in its standards. Their courage is your cowardice, their cowardice your courage. It is all a matter of nomenclature. One could say it needs courage to be a coward. A conundrum, but a quotable one. Make a note of it.

And have another whisky. The whisky was like water. It had no taste. Iqbal shook the flask. He heard a faint splashing. It wasn't empty. Thank God, it wasn't empty.

If you look at things as they are, he told himself, there does not seem to be a code either of man or of God on which one can pattern one's conduct. Wrong triumphs over right as much as right over wrong. Sometimes its triumphs are greater. What happens ultimately, you do not know. In such circumstances what can you do but cultivate an utter indifference to all values?

Nothing matters. Nothing whatever . . .

Iqbal fell asleep, with the celluloid glass in his hand and the lamp burning on the stool beside him.

In the courtyard of the gurdwara, the fires on the hearths had burned to ashes. A gust of wind occasionally fanned a glowing ember. Lamps had been dimmed. Men, women and children lay sprawled about on the floor of the main room. Meet Singh was awake. He was sweeping the floor and tidying up the mess.

Somebody started banging at the door with his fists. Meet Singh stopped sweeping and went across the courtyard muttering, 'Who is it?'

He undid the latch. Jugga stepped inside. In the dark he looked larger than ever. His figure filled the doorway.

'Why, Juggut Singhji, what business have you here at this hour?' asked Meet Singh.

'Bhai,' he whispered, 'I want the Guru's word. Will you read me a verse?'

'I have laid the Granth Sahib to rest for the night,' Meet Singh said. 'What is it that you want to do?'

'It does not matter about that,' said Jugga impatiently. He put a heavy hand on Meet Singh's shoulder. 'Will you just read me a few lines quickly?'

Meet Singh led the way, grumbling. 'You never came to the gurdwara any other time. Now when the scripture is resting and people are asleep, you want me to read the Guru's word. It is not proper. I will read you a piece from the Morning Prayer.'

'It does not matter what you read. Just read it.'

Meet Singh turned up the wick of one of the lanterns. Its sooty chimney became bright. He sat down beside the cot on which the scripture lay. Jugga picked up the fly whisk from beneath the cot and began waving it over Meet Singh's head. Meet Singh got out a small prayer book, put it to his forehead and began to read the verse on the page which he happened to have opened to:

He who made the night and day,
The days of the week and seasons.

He who made the breezes blow, the waters run,
The fires and the lower regions.
Made the earth—the temple of law.
He who made creatures of diverse kinds
With a multitude of names,
Made this the law—
By thought and deed be judged forsooth,
For God is True and dispenseth Truth.
There the elect his court adorn,
And God Himself their actions honours.
There are sorted deeds that were done and bore fruit,
From those that to action could never ripen.
This, O Nanak, shall hereafter happen.

Meet Singh shut the prayer book and again put it to his forehead. He began to mumble the epilogue to the morning prayer:

Air, water and earth,
Of these are we made,
Air like the Guru's word gives the breath of life
To the babe born of the great mother Earth
Sired by the waters.

His voice tapered off to an inaudible whisper. Juggut Singh put back the fly whisk and rubbed his forehead on the ground in front of the scripture.

'Is that good?' he asked naïvely.

'All the Guru's word is good,' answered Meet Singh solemnly.

'What does it mean?'

'What have you to do with meaning? It is just the Guru's word. If you are going to do something good, the Guru will help you; if you are going to do something bad, the Guru will stand in your way. If you persist in doing it, he will punish you till you repent, and then forgive you.'

'Yes, what will I do with the meaning? All right, Bhaiji. Sat

Sri Akal.'

'Sat Sri Akal.'

Jugga rubbed his forehead on the ground again and got up. He threaded his way through the sleeping assembly and picked up his shoes. There was a light in one of the rooms. Jugga looked in. He recognized the head with tousled hair on the pillow. Iqbal was sleeping with the silver hip flask lying on his chest.

'Sat Sri Akal, Babuji.' he said softly. There was no reply. 'Are you asleep?'

'Do not disturb him,' interrupted Meet Singh in a whisper. 'He is not feeling well. He has been taking medicine to sleep.'

'Achha, Bhaiji, you say Sat Sri Akal to him for me.' Juggut Singh went out of the gurdwara.

'No fool like an old fool.' The sentence kept recurring in Hukum Chand's mind. He tried to dismiss it, but it came back again and again: 'No fool like an old fool.' It was bad enough for a married man in his fifties to go picking up women. To get emotionally involved with a girl young enough to be his daughter and a Muslim prostitute at that! That was *too* ludicrous. He must be losing his grip on things. He was getting senile and stupid.

The feeling of elation which his plan had given him in the morning was gone. Instead there was one of anxiety, uncertainty and old age. He had released the badmash and the social worker without knowing much about them. They probably had no more nerve than he. Some of the leftist social workers were known to be a daring lot. This one, however, was an intellectual, the sort people contemptuously describe as the armchair variety. He would probably do nothing except criticize others for failing to do their duty. The badmash was a notorious daredevil. He had been in train robberies, car hold-ups, dacoities and murders. It was money he was after, or revenge. The only chance of his doing anything was to settle scores with Malli. If Malli had fled when he heard of Jugga's arrival, Jugga would lose interest and might even join the gang in killing and looting the victims of the ambush. His type never risked their necks for women. If Nooran was killed, he would pick up another girl.

Hukum Chand was also uneasy about his own role. Was it enough to get others to do the work for him? Magistrates were responsible for maintenance of law and order. But they maintained order with power behind them; not opposing them. Where was the power? What were the people in Delhi doing? Making fine speeches in the assembly! Loudspeakers magnifying their egos; lovely-looking foreign women in the visitors' galleries in breathless admiration. 'He is a great man, this Mr Nehru of yours. I do think he is the greatest man in the world today. And how handsome! Wasn't that a wonderful thing to say? "Long ago we made a tryst with destiny and now the time comes when we shall redeem our pledge, not wholly or in full measure but very substantially."' Yes, Mr Prime Minister, you made your tryst. So did many others.

There was Hukum Chand's colleague Prem Singh who went back to fetch his wife's jewellery from Lahore. He made his tryst at Feletti's Hotel where European sahibs used to flirt with each other's wives. It is next door to the Punjab Assembly building where Pakistani parliamentarians talked democracy and made laws. Prem Singh whiled away time drinking beer and offering it to the Englishmen staying in the hotel. Over the privet hedge a dozen heads with fez caps and Pathan turbans waited for him. He drank more beer and forced it on his English friends and on the orchestra. His dates across the hedge waited patiently. The Englishmen drank a lot of beer and whisky and said Prem Singh was a grand chap. But it was late for dinner so they said, 'Good night Mr . . . Did not catch your name. Yes, of course, Mr Singh. Thank you very much, Mr Singh. See you again.' . . . 'Nice old Wog. Can hold his drink too,' they said in the dining room. Even the orchestra had more beer than ever before. 'What would you like us to play, sir?' asked Mendoza the Goan bandleader. 'It is rather late and we must close down now.' Prem Singh did not know the name of any European piece of music. He thought hard. He remembered one of the Englishmen had asked for something which sounded like 'bananas'. 'Bananas,' said Prem

Singh. '"We'll Have No Bananas Today." Yes, sir.' Mendoza, McMello, DeSilva, DeSaram and Gomes strummed 'Bananas'. Prem Singh walked across the lawn to the gate. His dates also moved along to the hedge gate. The band saw Prem Singh leave so they switched onto 'God Save the King'.

There was Sundari, the daughter of Hukum Chand's orderly. She had made her tryst with destiny on the road to Gujranwala. She had been married four days and both her arms were covered with red lacquer bangles and the henna on her palms was still a deep vermilion. She had not yet slept with Mansa Ram. Their relatives had not left them alone for a minute. She had hardly seen his face through her veil. Now he was taking her to Gujranwala where he worked as a peon and had a little room of his own in the Sessions Court compound. There would be no relatives and he would certainly try it. He did not seem particularly keen, sitting in the bus talking loudly to all the other passengers. Men often pretended indifference. No one would really believe that she wanted him either—what with the veil across her face and not a word! 'Do not take any of the lacquer bangles off. It brings bad luck,' her girl friends had said to her. 'Let him break them when he makes love to you and mauls you.' There were a dozen on each of her arms, covering them from the wrists to the elbows. She felt them with her fingers. They were hard and brittle. He would have to do a lot of hugging and savaging to break them. She stopped daydreaming as the bus pulled up. There were large stones on the road. Then hundreds of people surrounded them. Everyone was ordered off the bus. Sikhs were just hacked to death. The clean-shaven were stripped. Those that were circumcised were forgiven. Those that were not, were circumcised. Not just the foreskin: the whole thing was cut off. She who had not really had a good look at Mansa Ram was shown her husband completely naked. They held him by the arms and legs and one man cut off his penis and gave it to her. The mob made love to her. She did not have to take off any of her bangles. They were all smashed as she lay in the road, being taken by one man and another and another. That should have brought her a lot of good luck!

Sunder Singh's case was different. Hukum Chand had had him recruited for the army. He had done well. He was a big, brave Sikh with a row of medals won in battles in Burma, Eritrea and Italy. The government had given him land in Sindh. He came to his tryst by train, along with his wife and three children. There were over five hundred men and women in a compartment meant to carry '40 sitting, 12 sleeping'. There was just one little lavatory in the corner without any water in the cistern. It was 115° in the shade; but there was no shade—not a shrub within miles. Only the sun and the sand . . . and no water. At all stations there were people with spears along the railings. Then the train was held up at a station for four days. No one was allowed to get off. Sunder Singh's children cried for water and food. So did everyone else. Sunder Singh gave them his urine to drink. Then that dried up too. So he pulled out his revolver and shot them all. Shangara Singh aged six with his long brown-blonde hair tied up in a topknot, Deepo aged four with curling eyelashes, and Amro, four months old, who tugged at her mother's dry breasts with her gums and puckered up her face till it was full of wrinkles, crying frantically. Sunder Singh also shot his wife. Then he lost his nerve. He put the revolver to his temple but did not fire. There was no point in killing himself. The train had begun to move. He heaved out the corpses of his wife and children and came along to India. He did not redeem the pledge. Only his family did.

Hukum Chand felt wretched. The night had fallen. Frogs called from the river. Fireflies twinkled about the jasmines near the veranda. The bearer had brought whisky and Hukum Chand had sent it away. The bearer had laid out the dinner but he had not touched the food. He had the lamp removed and sat alone in the dark, staring into space.

Why had he let the girl go back to Chundunnugger? Why? he asked himself, hitting his forehead with his fist. If only she were here in the rest house with him, he would not bother if the rest of the world went to hell. But she was not here; she was in the train. He could hear its rumble.

Hukum Chand slid off his chair, covered his face with his arms and started to cry. Then he raised his face to the sky and began to pray.

A little after eleven, the moon came up. It looked tired and dissipated. It flooded the plain with a weary pale light in which everything was a little blurred. Near the bridge there was very little moonlight. The high railway embankment cast a wall of dark shadow.

Sandbags, which had guarded the machine-gun nest near the signal, were littered about on either side of the railway tracks. The signal scaffolding stood like an enormous sentry watching over the scene. Two large oval eyes, one on top of the other, glowed red. The two hands of the signal stood stiffly parallel to each other. The bushes along the bank looked like a jungle. The river did not glisten; it was like a sheet of slate with just a suspicion of a ripple here and there.

A good distance from the embankment, behind a thick cluster of pampas, was a jeep with its engine purring gently. There was no one in it. The men had spread themselves on either side of the railway line a few feet from each other. They sat on their haunches with their rifles and spears between their legs. On the first steel span of the bridge a thick rope was tied horizontally above the railway line. It was about twenty feet above the track.

It was too dark for the men to recognize each other. So they talked loudly. Then somebody called.

'Silence! Listen!'

They listened. It was nothing. Only the wind in the reeds.

'Silence anyhow,' came the command of the leader. 'If you talk like this, you will not hear the train in time.'

They began to talk in whispers.

There was a shimmy-shammy noise of trembling steel wires as one of the signals came down. Its oval eye changed from red to a bright green. The whispering stopped. The men got up and took their positions ten yards away from the track.

There was a steady rumbling sound punctuated by soft puff-puffs. A man ran up to the line and put his ear on the steel rail.

'Come back, you fool,' yelled the leader in a hoarse whisper.

'It is the train,' he announced triumphantly.

'Get back!' repeated the leader fiercely.

All eyes strained towards the grey space where the rumbling of the train came from. Then they shifted to the rope, stiff as a shaft of steel. If the train was fast it might cut many people in two like a knife slicing cucumbers. They shuddered.

A long way beyond the station, there was a dot of light. It went out and another came up nearer. Then another and another, getting nearer and nearer as the train came on. The men looked at the lights and listened to the sound of the train. No one looked at the bridge any more.

A man started climbing on the steel span. He was noticed only when he had got to the top where the rope was tied. They thought he was testing the knot. He was tugging it. It was well tied; even if the engine funnel hit it, the rope might snap but the knot would not give. The man stretched himself on the rope. His feet were near the knot; his hands almost reached the centre of the rope. He was a big man.

The train got closer and closer. The demon form of the engine with sparks flying from its funnel came up along the track. Its puffing was drowned in the roar of the train itself. The whole train could be seen clearly against the wan moonlight. From the coal-tender to the tail end, there was a solid crust of human beings on the roof.

The man was still stretched on the rope.

The leader stood up and shouted hysterically: 'Come off, you ass! You will be killed. Come off at once!'

The man turned round towards the voice. He whipped out a small kirpan from his waist and began to slash at the rope.

'Who is this? What is he . . . ?'

There was no time. They looked from the bridge to the train, from the train to the bridge. The man hacked the rope vigorously.

The leader raised his rifle to his shoulder and fired. He hit his mark and one of the man's legs came off the rope and dangled in the air. The other was still twined round the rope. He slashed away in frantic haste. The engine was only a few yards off, throwing embers high up in the sky with each blast of the whistle. Somebody fired another shot. The man's body slid off the rope, but he clung to it with his hands and chin. He pulled himself up, caught the rope under his left armpit, and again started hacking with his right hand. The rope had been cut in shreds. Only a thin tough strand remained. He went at it with the knife, and then with his teeth. The engine was almost on him. There was a volley of shots. The man shivered and collapsed. The rope snapped in the centre as he fell. The train went over him, and went on to Pakistan.

TAMAS

BHISHAM SAHNI

Translated from the Hindi
by Bhisham Sahni

The clay lamp in the alcove flickered. Close to it, where the wall joined the ceiling, two bricks had been removed from the wall, leaving behind a gaping hole. With every gust of wind, the flame in the clay lamp quivered violently and long shadows flitted across the walls. But as soon as the flame steadied again, a thin line of smoke would rise from it in a straight line, licking, as it went, the side of the alcove.

Nathu was already breathless. He thought, perhaps it was his heavy breathing which caused the flame to quiver so violently. He slumped on the floor, his back resting against the wall. His eyes again fell on the pig. The pig grunted and put its snout to some sticky peel or rind in the garbage which littered the entire floor. With its pinkish snout, it had already licked Nathu thrice on his shins, causing him searing pain. At times the pig would begin walking along a wall, its eyes on the floor as though looking for something. It would then suddenly squeal and start running, its little tail curling and uncurling. Rheum, oozing from its left eye had trickled down its snout. Its bulging belly swayed from side to side as it walked or ran. By constantly trampling over the garbage, the pig had scattered it all over the floor and now a foul stench from the garbage, the pig's heavy breathing and from the pungent smoke of the linseed oil burning in the clay lamp pervaded the room making it unbearably stuffy.

Though drops of blood lay spattered on the floor, the pig did not seem to have received a scratch on its body. It was as if for the last two hours Nathu had been plunging his knife into water or a heap of sand. He had struck the pig several times on its belly and shoulders, but on pulling out the knife, only a few drops of blood would ooze out and trickle down to the floor. There was no trace of any wound or stab. A thin, red line of a scratch or a tiny blot were the only visible signs of his efforts. Every now and then, with an angry grunt, the pig would either rush towards Nathu's legs or begin running along a wall. Nathu's blade had not gone beyond the thick layers of fat to reach the pig's intestines.

Why of all the creatures, Nathu thought, had this despicable brute with its fat, bulging body, a snout covered with thick white hair like that of a rabbit's, thorny bristles on its back, fallen to his lot to tackle?

Nathu had once heard someone say that in order to kill a pig, one should, first of all, pour boiling water on it. But where was he to get boiling water from? On another occasion, one of his fellow-chamars, while cleaning a hide, had casually remarked, 'The best way to kill a pig is to catch it by its hind legs, twist them hard and turn the pig over on its back. While it is struggling to rise, one should cut open its jugular vein. That will finish off the pig.' Nathu had tried all the devices but not one had worked. Instead, his shins and ankles were badly bruised. It is one thing to clean a hide, it is quite another to slaughter a pig. He cursed the evil moment he had agreed to do the job. Even now, had he not accepted the money in advance, he would have pushed the damned creature out of the hut and gone home.

'The veterinary surgeon needs a pig for his experiments,' Murad Ali had said, as Nathu stood washing his hands and feet at the municipal water tap after cleaning a hide.

'A pig?' Nathu had exclaimed, surprised. 'What am I to do with it?'

'Get one and slaughter it,' Murad Ali had said, 'There are many pigs roaming around the nearby piggery, push one into your hut and kill it.'

Nathu had looked askance at Murad Ali's face.

'But I have never killed a pig, Master. If it were flaying an animal, or cleaning a hide, I would have been glad to do it for you. But killing a pig, I am sorry, I have never done it. It is only the people in the piggery who know how to do it.'

'Why should I come to you then knowing that the piggery people can do it? You and you alone shall do this job.' And Murad Ali had shoved a rustling five-rupee note into his pocket.

'It is not much of a job for you. I couldn't say no to the vet sahib, could I?' said Murad Ali, then added rather casually, 'There are any number of pigs roaming about on the other side of the cremation ground. Just catch one of them. The vet sahib will himself do the explaining to the piggery people.'

And before Nathu could so much as open his mouth, Murad Ali had turned round to leave. Then, stroking his legs softly with his thin cane stick, he had added:

'The job must be done this very night. At dawn the jamadar will come with his pushcart and take the carcass away. Don't forget. I shall tell the fellow myself to take it to the vet sahib's residence. Understand?'

Nathu had stood with folded hands. The rustling five-rupee note that had gone into his pocket had made it impossible for him to open his mouth.

'People living in this area are mostly Muslims. If anyone sees it, there can be trouble. So be careful. I too don't like getting such jobs done. But what to do? I couldn't say no to the vet sahib.' And flapping the cane against his legs, Murad Ali had left.

Nathu could not refuse either. How could he? He dealt with Murad Ali almost every day. Whenever a horse or a cow or a buffalo died anywhere in the town, Murad Ali would get it for him to skin. It meant giving an eight-anna piece or a rupee to Murad Ali but Nathu would get the hide. Besides, Murad Ali was a man of contacts. There was hardly a person, connected with the Municipal Committee, with whom he did not have dealings.

Waving his thin cane stick and walking jauntily along the road, Murad Ali was a common sight in the town. He would suddenly appear in one or another of the lanes or by-lanes. Everything about him, his swarthy face, his bristling, black moustaches, his small, ferrety eyes, the knee-length khaki coat he wore over a white salwar, even the turban on his head, all combined to make him look distinctive. Without any of these, even without his thin cane stick, or the well-bound turban, he would not be what he was.

Murad Ali had left after issuing his instructions, leaving Nathu in a tight spot. How was he to catch hold of a pig? At one time he had even thought of going straight to the piggery which stood on the outskirts of the town and telling the folks there to get a pig slaughtered and have it sent to the veterinary surgeon. But he could not so much as lift his foot in the direction of the piggery.

It had not been easy to draw the pig into the hut. The pigs were there, roaming about and sniffing at the rubbish that lay around. But it was a different matter altogether to lure one into the hut. All that Nathu could think of was to carry armfuls of wet hay and put it in piles outside his dilapidated hut.

Three straying pigs, wandering along dung-heaps and pools of stagnant water, chanced to come towards his hut. One of them sauntered into the courtyard and began sniffing at the pile. Nathu promptly shut the gate behind him. He then ran across the courtyard, opened the door of the hut, and picking up his lathi, drove the pig inside. Fearing that someone from the piggery might come that way and become suspicious on hearing the grunts of the pig, Nathu carried an armful of wilted hay into the hut and made small piles of it on the floor. The pig was soon absorbed in picking at the piles and Nathu, greatly relieved, came out and sat in the courtyard to have a quiet smoke. He smoked one bidi after another and waited for night to fall. When, at last, he went inside it was already dark. But what he saw in the unsteady light of the clay lamp, made his heart sink. The entire floor was littered with rubbish and a foul smell filled the room. As his eyes fell on the ugly, bloated pig, Nathu cursed himself for having taken on so repulsive and hazardous a task. He was half-inclined to throw open the door and drive the despicable creature out.

And now it was past midnight. The pig was still strutting about leisurely in the midst of the rubbish littered on the floor. All that Nathu had achieved was a few drops of blood on the floor, a couple of scratches on the pig's belly, and a few nasty bruises on his own shins where he had been butted by the pig's snout. Panting for breath and sweating profusely, Nathu could see no way out of the mess into which he had landed.

Far away, the tower-clock in the Sheikh's garden struck two. Nathu stood up, nervous and perplexed. His eyes fell on the pig standing in the middle of the room. It urinated, and as though irritated by what it had done, began running along the right-hand wall of the hut. The wick in the clay lamp spluttered and long shadows swayed eerily across the walls. Nathu's situation had not changed a whit. The pig, its head bent, would now and then stop to sniff at some bit of rubbish, then resume walking along a wall, or grunt and start running, its thin little tail curling and uncurling itself like an insect.

'This won't do,' muttered Nathu, grinding his teeth. 'It is beyond me to kill a pig. This damned pig will be my undoing.'

It occurred to him to try turning the pig over on its back by twisting its hind leg. He slowly moved towards the middle of the room, his left hand aloft, holding a dagger. The pig, which was walking along the left-hand wall, on seeing Nathu, stopped in its tracks and instead of breaking into a trot, turned and started walking towards Nathu. It grunted menacingly. Nathu slowly stepped back, his eyes on the pig's snout. Both confronted each other. The pig advanced towards Nathu, making it impossible for the latter to catch hold of its hind legs. The pig's eyes looked red with rage. Who could tell what the pig was up to? Nathu was losing his nerve. It was already past two in the morning. There was little chance that the job over which he had been straining so hard since last evening would be done before daybreak. The sweeper would be there with his push-cart, and Murad Ali would turn from a friend into a bitter enemy. Anything could be expected of him if the job was not done. It could mean the end of getting hides to clean; the fellow could have him evicted from the premises he was occupying, get him thrashed by a goonda and harass him no end. Nathu felt extremely nervous. He feared that even if he succeeded in catching the hind legs of the pig, the pig might kick him and free itself.

Suddenly a wave of anger rose within him and he felt furious. 'It is now or never for me,' he muttered and turning around picked up a slab of stone lying on the floor below the alcove. Holding it high over his head, he came and stood in the middle of the room. The pig was sniffing at the rind of a watermelon close to its forelegs, its bloodshot eyes blinking and its little tail swishing. 'If it does not move,' thought Nathu, 'and the slab falls pat on it, it may break a bone or two or maybe one of its legs. That too will be something. At least the damned creature will not be able to walk.'

Balancing the slab in his hands Nathu threw it down with all his might. The flame in the clay lamp trembled and shadows flitted across the walls. The slab fell on the pig with a loud thud. Nathu stepped back and looked hard at the pig. It was still blinking its small eyes and its snout still rested on its forelegs. Nathu could not say whether the slab had caused any injury.

The pig grunted and began to move, its bulky frame swaying. Nathu stepped aside and crept close to the door opening into the courtyard. In the quivering light of the clay lamp, the pig appeared to be moving like a dark shadow. The slab had hit it on the forehead, due to which, it seemed to Nathu, its vision had been affected. The pig was heading towards Nathu, and fearing that he might be attacked, Nathu opened the door and rushed out of the hut.

'What a nasty trap I am caught in,' moaned Nathu as he came and stood by the low wall of the courtyard.

The cool fresh air brought him some relief. It caressed his sweating body and rejuvenated him. 'To hell with all this! I care a damn whether the vet gets the pig or not. I am through with the whole business. Tomorrow I shall hand back the five-rupee note to Murad Ali and with folded hands tell him that I couldn't do the job, that it was too much for me. The fellow will be cross for a few days but I shall manage to bring him round.'

He stood by the low wall and waited. The moon had risen and the entire area around bore a mysterious and unfamiliar look. The mud-track in front of the hut which, during the day, resounded with the creaking of bullock-carts and the jingle of bells round the bullocks' necks was now silent and deserted. Deep fissures had been cut into the road by the rolling wheels which had ground the soil into powdery dust so deep that if an unwary person walked into it he would find himself knee-deep in fine dust. On the other side of the road was a sharp slope that descended to the flat ground. It was strewn with dust-laden thorny bushes which, under the light of the moon, looked washed and clean. At some distance was the cremation ground with two mud huts, one of which was occupied by the caretaker. There was no light burning in them. The caretaker had got drunk the previous evening and had babbled away till late in the night, but now all was silent. Nathu suddenly thought of his wife, who would be sleeping peacefully at this moment in the colony of the chamars. Had he not got into this mess, he too would have been in bed beside her, her buxom body in his arms. Suddenly he felt an intense longing to hold her in his arms. She must have waited for him, God knows for how long. He had come away without telling her anything. And now he missed her terribly, even though he had been away from her for hardly a few hours.

The dusty track, after some distance, turned towards the right and sloped downward. A little removed from the track stood a country well, which too, with its wheel and string of pots looked quite picturesque in the light of the moon. At some distance, the track joined the metalled road going towards the city, turning its back, as it were, on the lonely, flat, deserted area.

Far away, towards the left, stood the piggery, while all around was a vast, barren tract of land, with thorny bushes and stunted trees growing here and there. Far into the distance, hours of walking distance away, stood rows of military barracks, one long row behind the other.

Nathu felt weak and limp. How he would have loved to rest his head against the low wall and gone to sleep! Coming out of the hut had been like stepping into a different world, bathed in moonlight, with a cool breeze blowing. He felt like crying over his nightmarish situation. The dagger in his hand looked odd and irrelevant. He felt like running away from it all. The next day the *purbia* would come looking for the pig and, on seeing the scattered hay, would locate the pig inside the hut and drive it back to the piggery.

Nathu thought of his wife again. His troubled mind would find comfort only when he lay by her side and conversed with her in soft, confiding tones. He longed for the torture to end and to go back to the haven of his tenement in the chamars' colony.

The tower-clock struck three causing Nathu to tremble from head to foot. His eyes turned to the dagger in his hand. The thought of his predicament and the fate that awaited him was like a stab of pain. What was he doing here when the pig was still alive? The sweeper would be here any minute. What would he tell him? A faint, yellowish tint had already streaked the inky darkness of the sky. Dawn was breaking and his task was far from over.

In desperation he turned towards the hut. He opened the door softly and peeped in. In the dim light of the clay lamp, the pig lay motionless in the middle of the room. It looked tired and exhausted. 'It should not be difficult now to kill the beast,' thought Nathu. He shut the door behind him and came and stood under the alcove, his eyes on the pig.

The pig lifted its snout which had turned red. Its eyes appeared to have shrunk. Behind it, at some distance, lay the stone slab which had been thrown upon it. The flame in the clay lamp flickered again and in its unsteady light Nathu thought the pig had stirred. He stared hard at it. The pig had actually moved. It walked ponderously towards Nathu. It had hardly taken a couple of steps when it staggered and emitted a strange sound. Nathu, with his dagger raised high, sat down on the floor. The pig took another couple of steps when its snout drooped to its feet, and before it could move further, it suddenly fell down on its side. There was a violent tremor in its legs and they soon stiffened in midair. The pig was dead.

Nathu put the dagger down. Just then, far away, in some house, a cock fluttered its wings and crowed. Soon after, a jolting pushcart came creaking on the dusty track. Nathu heaved a sigh of relief.

2

At the start of the *prabhat pheri*, before daybreak, only a handful of Congress activists would be present. But as it advanced and passed through lanes and by-lanes, whosoever lived en route would step out of his house yawning and scratching his belly, and join in.

It was the fag-end of winter: the air was dry and people still slept inside, swathed in blankets. Quite a few elderly people in the prabhat pheri were wearing woollen caps.

The clock-tower in the Sheikh's garden struck four. In front of the Congress office, three or four people stood waiting for their compatriots. Two constables from the Intelligence Department were already there standing on one side at some distance.

Just then a glimpse of light was seen far away. A man with a hurricane lamp had turned the corner of the Bara Bazaar and was coming towards the Congress office. The light of the lamp fell only on the man's legs so it seemed as though only a pair of pyjamas was walking along.

'Here comes Bakshiji,' exclaimed Aziz recognizing the pyjamas.

Bakshiji was a stickler for punctuality. 'Four o'clock means four o'clock,' he used to say. 'Not a minute past nor a minute to.' But on that day he was late.

Yes, it was Bakshiji, the thickset secretary of the District Congress Committee. His presence was essential to the programme.

As he drew near, Aziz greeted him by reciting a satirical couplet:

The mullah, the preacher and the
torch-bearer—all have one thing in
common—they show light to others while
themselves walk in darkness.

'I got up late because I slept late last night,' Bakshiji explained
apologetically. Then, after the usual exchange of courtesies,
suddenly remarked, 'But where is Master Ram Das? Hasn't he
arrived?'

To this too Aziz answered, 'He will come after he has milked
his cow. He can't come earlier.'

'He used to come running even at midnight when he wanted a
raise in his salary. Now that he has got it, why should he bother
about coming on time?'

In the surrounding darkness, a tall man, dressed in white, was
seen coming up the slope from the side of the Naya Mohalla.

'Here comes piety personified,' remarked Aziz. 'Doesn't
Mehtaji look every inch a leader?'

As he arrived, Mehtaji looked around and on noticing the
absence of Ajit Singh, Shankar and Master Ram Das, turned to
Bakshiji and said, 'Didn't I tell you not to fix so early an hour
for the prabhat pheri? Four o'clock is too early.'

'It is only when you call the members at four o'clock can you
expect the prabhat pheri to start at five o'clock,' Bakshiji
answered. 'Had I fixed five o'clock as the time, they wouldn't
have been here even after sunrise. And how does it matter to
you, Mehtaji, when you yourself are so late?' Bakshiji said and
put his hand under his shawl to take out a packet of cigarettes
from his waistcoat pocket.

'From a distance you look every inch a leader, Mehtaji.'

A condescending smile flickered on Mehtaji's lips. Putting his
hand on Aziz's shoulder, he said, 'The other day I was standing
at the taxi stand when I overheard someone ask another person,
"Is that Jawaharalal Nehru standing there?"' Giving a little tilt
to the Gandhi cap on his head, he added, 'Many people make
this mistake.'

'You are in no way less great Mehtaji. You have a personality all your own.'

'I am slightly taller than Jawaharlal,' Mehtaji said.

'Did you take a bath before coming here, Mehtaji?' put in Kashmiri Lal.

'What a question to ask! As a rule I always take a bath before coming out, summer or winter. And it is a must so far as the prabhat pheri is concerned. Tell us about yourself, Kashmiri Lal, did you even wash your face?'

Just then someone's voice was heard from the direction of the slope: 'Left...left...right, left...left...'

Everyone laughed.

'Here comes the Jarnail,' said Bakshiji.

As the Jarnail (colloquial for General) arrived, the light from the hurricane lamp fell on his tattered shoes. It was difficult to make out whether what he was wearing was a pair of slippers or shoes. Nearly six inches above his shoes, appeared the lower end of his khaki trousers. A crumpled khaki coat hung over his emaciated body. It was covered with innumerable medallions and badges of Gandhi and Nehru along with ribbons and strings of diverse colours. He had a sparse greying beard and wore a dark-green turban on his head.

The Jarnail was the only one among the Congress activists who courted imprisonment irrespective of whether a movement was on or not. He went about making speeches all over town and took a roughing-up every other day. But that did not deter him. A thin cane stick under his arm, he would be seen 'marching' in one street or another. Whenever an announcement regarding a public meeting was to be made, and a tonga went round the town for the purpose, he would be the one sitting in the back seat, beating the drum. And when a meeting took place, he would be the first to jump on to the dais to address the gathering in his hoarse, husky voice, hardly audible even to the first row of listeners.

As the Jarnail drew near, Kashmiri Lal made a dig at him, 'Jarnail, why did you run away from the public meeting yesterday?'

The Jarnail peered hard into the darkness and on recognizing Kashmiri Lal by his voice, tucked his cane stick under his arm and shouted, 'I don't want to have any truck with fellows like you early in the morning. You'd better keep out of my way.'

Bakshiji turned to Kashmiri Lal, 'This is no time for your tomfoolery, you had better keep quiet.'

But the Jarnail was already furious, 'I shall expose you and your doings. You keep the company of communists. I saw you with my own eyes, eating sweets at the hunchbacked sweetmeat-seller's shop, in the company of that communist—Dev Datt.'

'Enough, enough, Jarnail. Don't expose him further,' said Bakshiji, trying to pacify him.

Just then Shankarlal arrived, his loose wide pyjamas flapping.

Dawn was breaking. Tints of yellow and orange coloured the sky. From the high wall of the bank building another layer of darkness had been peeled off. Across the road, smoke was already rising from the open furnace of the sweetmeat-seller's shop located in the Arya School building. Now and then, men emerged for their morning walk, coughing and pattering the ground with their walking sticks. Here and there a woman, her head and shoulders heavily covered, made her way to a temple or a gurdwara.

Bakshiji, lifting the hurricane lamp close to his face blew into it and put out the light.

'Why has the lamp been extinguished? And that too on my arrival, Bakshiji?'said, Shankar, the man who made announcements regarding public meetings.

'Why, do you want to look at my face or Mehtaji's?' Bakshi said, 'I cannot afford to waste oil. The lamp does not belong to the Congress Committee, it is my personal property. Get the oil sanctioned by the Congress Committee and I shall keep the lamp burning day and night.'

At this Shankar, who was standing behind Kashmiri Lal, commented in a low voice, 'When no sanction is needed for your cigarettes, why should one be required for kerosene oil?'

Bakshiji had heard Shankar but swallowed the bitter pill. It was demeaning to talk to such 'loafers'.

'You are the boss, Bakshiji. Even a sparrow cannot flap its wings without your permission. What do you need a sanction for?' said Shankar, then turning towards Mehtaji said, 'Jai Hind, Mehtaji. Forgive me. I did not see you.'

'Why should you take notice of us poor folks, Shankar? You are fortune's favourite these days.'

'Where is your bag, Mehtaji, by the way? You are not carrying it today.'

'Who needs a handbag on a prabhat pheri, Shankar?'

'Why, it is a handy thing. A client can be trapped at any time.'

Mehta kept quiet. Besides Congress work Mehtaji did insurance business.

'Why can't you keep your mouth shut sometimes, Shankar? Mehtaji is thrice your age. You must have regard for age.'

'I didn't say anything offensive. I didn't ask him whether he had succeeded in bagging the fifty-thousand-rupee insurance policy from Sethi.'

Shankar had shot the arrow. Generally the fellow was not given to talking in oblique, insinuating terms. He was a blunt, outspoken person. The reference to the fifty-thousand-rupee policy, however, was hitting below the belt.

Mehta squirmed. He had spent sixteen years of his life in jail and was the president of the District Congress Committee. He was always dressed in spotless white khadi. To level such an accusation was unmannerly, to say the least. But a rumour had been gaining ground that he was about to secure a fifty-thousand-rupee insurance policy from Sethi, a contractor, in lieu of which, Mehta would help him secure the Congress ticket for the next General Elections.

'He is a wag, Mehtaji, don't listen to what he says.'

'I never said that Mehtaji has promised to get him the ticket. Only the Provincial Committee has the authority to do that. The District Congress Committee can only make recommendations. Of course, if the president and the secretary of the District

Committee come to a secret understanding, it is a different matter.
And both are present here, listening to what I am saying. If big
contractors succeed in getting tickets in this manner, it will spell
doom for the Congress.'

Mehtaji moved away and struck up a conversation with
Kashmiri Lal. Bakshiji lit another cigarette. The fact of the matter
was that Shankar and Mehta did not get along with each other.
They had fallen apart ever since Mehtaji had struck off Shankar's
name from the list of district representatives for a conference to
be addressed by Pandit Nehru in Lahore. Ever since then Shankar
had looked upon Mehtaji as his sworn enemy. Shankar had,
nonetheless, gone to Lahore on his own and attended the
conference. He had also attended the lunch meant exclusively
for the delegates. The District Committee, on behalf of its
members, was required to pay a nominal subscription for lunch,
but Mehtaji had declined to pay for Shankar. At the lunch party,
Shankar had made it a point to sit right opposite Mehtaji. He
had gobbled the food like a hungry wolf, shouted at the volunteers
serving the guests and, in general, caused much embarrassment
to Mehtaji. When asked by Mehtaji to mind his manners and
not bring disgrace on the District Committee, Shankar had
retorted, 'Keep your advice to yourself, Mehtaji, I am eating
from my own pocket. I shall settle scores with you when we go
back home.'

'What will you do to me when we are back home? You are
nothing but a babbler.' Mehtaji had said.

On their return from Lahore, Shankar had succeeded in playing
his master-stroke. The elections to the Provincial Congress
Committee were at hand and every District Committee was
required to send four representatives. Mehtaji had proposed
Kohli's name as the fourth representative. He would certainly
have been elected had Shankar not spoken out. The meeting of
the Scrutiny Committee was on, when Shankar suddenly stood
up.

'Excuse me, I have a question to ask.' Mehta felt alarmed. He
realized that Shankar was spoiling for trouble and said, 'This is

the meeting of the Scrutiny Committee. You can put your question to me later.'

'It is to the Scrutiny Committee that I want to address my question,' Shankar said, standing in a theatrical pose waiting for the chairman's ruling.

'What is your question?' asked the chairman.

'I wish to know the rules for the nomination of candidates.'

'Come to the point. This is not the time to discuss irrelevant things.' Mehtaji had retorted, only to be snubbed by Shankar's, 'Please keep quiet, Mehatji, I am not talking to you.'

'Let him speak,' said the chairman. 'Son, you want to know the rules of the Congress membership? Well, a member is required to pay an annual subscription of four annas, ply the spinning wheel daily and wear clothes made from handspun, handwoven cloth...'

'That is so,' said Shankar, adding, 'Now may I ask Mr Kohli to stand up for a minute?'

There was silence on all sides.

'Excuse me, but everyone has the right to seek clarification from the Scrutiny Committee.'

At which Mehtaji grunted.

'Mehtaji, you do not have to play the high and mighty here. My queries are addressed to the chairman of the Scrutiny Committee.' Then turning to Kohli, 'Yes, Mr Kohli, will you stand up for a minute?'

Kohli stood up.

'You wear khadi, don't you?'

'What's all this? Get to the point. What is it you want to know?'

'Can I see the cord with which you have tied your pyjamas?'

'The fellow is being rude to an honourable member. What nonsense is this?'

'Please keep out of this, Mehtaji. You have no right to speak without the chairman's permission. Now, Mr Kohli, I would ask you again to show me your pyjama cord.'

'What if I don't?'

'You have to. The cord must be shown so that I can prove my

point.'

'Show it, Kohli yaar. This good-for-nothing will not let us get any work done, otherwise. All kinds of riff-raff have come into the Congress.'

'What did you say, Mehtaji? That I am riff-raff and you are a gentleman? Don't force me to speak. I know black from white well enough. Yes, Mr Kohli... I don't want you to untie your pyjamas. Only show us the cord with which you have tied them.'

'Show it, Kohli. Get it over, otherwise this man will...'

Kohli lifted his khadi kurta. Below it, a yellow cord was hanging.

Shankar leapt forward and caught the cord. 'See gentlemen. The cord is made of artificial silk. It is not handspun cotton.'

'So what? What if it isn't? It is only a cord.'

'It is incumbent on a Congress member to wear khadi. That he should be wearing an artificial silk cord compromises the principles the Congress stands for. And you propose to send his name as candidate for the Provincial Committee?'

Members of the Scrutiny Committee looked at one another. They were forced to strike out Kohli's name. Since that day, Mehtaji could not bear the sight of Shankar.

Bakshiji was becoming restless. Neither Ram Das nor Desraj had turned up. Who would lead the singing? There had to be at least one person who sang well. If neither came, then Bakshiji would manage it himself somehow, but then, those who were paid for the job were expected to be more responsible.

'I can tell you what will happen, Mehtaji,' Bakshiji said. 'When we have already covered three lanes, Master Ram Das will come running. "The calf had sucked all the cow's milk." That's the excuse he will make. That is how these people work.' Then, turning to the other members, he added, 'We can't go on waiting indefinitely. Let's start. Kashmiri Lal, you lead the song.'

Kashmiri Lal, who enjoyed pulling people's legs turned to Jarnail and said, 'We must have a speech, Jarnail. Come on, give us a speech.'

Nothing suited the Jarnail better. Waving his cane and

marching military-style, he went and climbed up a stone by the roadside.

'What nonsense is this, Kashmiri? What are you up to?' shouted Bakshiji. 'There is a time for everything. If you don't want the prabhat pheri, tell us so.' Then he turned towards the Jarnail, but the latter had already begun his speech, 'Sahiban...'

'No Sahiban business. Come down!' shouted Bakshiji. 'Get him down, someone. Why are you out to make a tamasha of the whole thing? Making a public exhibition of ourselves early in the morning.'

'No one in the world can silence me,' the Jarnail said, commencing his speech. 'Sahiban...' he again said, in his grating, hoarse voice.

The Jarnail was a middle-aged man of fifty years or so, with a worn-out, emaciated body—the result of long spells of imprisonment as a political prisoner. Whereas other Congress activists would invariably be given 'B' class cells, he would be huddled into 'C' class cells, which meant, among other things, eating food mixed with sand. But the Jarnail neither relented, nor took off his self-designed 'military' uniform. During his younger days, he had attended the Congress session in Lahore as a volunteer. There the famous resolution calling for full Independence had been proclaimed. The national flag had been unfurled on the banks of the Ravi and Pandit Nehru had danced with joy along with other activists. The Jarnail too had been one of them. Ever since then, he had always worn his volunteer's uniform. As and when he had money, additions would be made to the uniform, a whistle, or a few more badges or a new string the colours of the national flag. But, in general, the uniform was crumpled and unwashed. The Jarnail never did any work, nor could he have secured one. He received a sum of fifteen rupees every month from the Congress office as propagandist's fee. If Bakshiji was not prompt in making the payment, the Jarnail would then and there, come out with a long speech. A passion had gripped his soul, and on the strength of that passion he was able to bear the troubles and tribulations of life. He had neither a home, nor a wife or child, neither a regular job, nor a regular roof over his head. Two or three times a week he would be roughed-up somewhere or the other in the town. Every time there was a lathi-charge by the police, while other activists would manage to get away to safer places, he would bare his narrow, shrivelled chest and get his ribs broken.

'Get him down, Kashmiri Lal; why are you out to create a scene?'

It was Mehtaji who had shouted this time. But the Jarnail became all the more adamant.

'Sahiban, I am sorry to say that the president of the District Congress Committee has betrayed the country. We shall live up to the pledge we took on the banks of the Ravi in 1929 to our last breath. Without taking much of your time, all I would say is, no man is born yet who can flout the rules of the Congress. Mehtaji is a nobody. We shall deal with him and his sycophants, namely Kishori Lal, Shankar Lal, Jit Singh and such other traitors.'

There was a guffaw of laughter.

'He won't come down like this,' whispered Kashmiri Lal, who had started this mischief, to Bakshiji. 'The more we try to stop him, the more adamant he'll get.' And Kashmiri Lal stepped forward and clapped his hands. Others followed suit.

'Fine, well said, Jarnail! Wonderful!'

'Sahiban, I am thankful to you for giving a patient ear to my stray thoughts. Not taking much of your valuable time, I would like to assure you that the day is not far when Hindustan will be free. The Congress shall achieve its goal and the pledge I had taken on the banks of the Ravi...'

There was a loud applause.

'Fine. Well said.'

'Sahiban, I thank you from the bottom of my heart. I shall address you again one of these days. Now, I would request you to repeat with me...' and raising his voice, shouted, 'Inquilab!' 'Inquilab... Zindabad!'

In response to which a few faint voices were heard saying

'Zindabad!'

'Can't you shout loudly?' said the Jarnail. 'Don't you eat two meals a day?'

A loud answer came from somewhere:

'Zindabad!'

And the Jarnail, putting his cane stick under his arm stepped down from the stone slab.

'Zindabad!' The voice had come from the side of the slope; it was Master Ram Das who came, panting for breath.

'Is this the time to come?' Bakshiji asked him sharply.

To which the answer came from Kashmiri Lal: 'He got late because the calf sucked up all the cow's milk.'

Everyone burst out laughing. But Master Ram Das said soberly, 'There will be no prabhat pheri today.'

'Why not?'

'Today's been set aside for community work. That's what was decided.'

'Who took the decision?'

'It was Gosainji who told me that the drains in the locality behind Imam Din street would be cleaned this morning.'

'You are making excuses for coming late.'

'Why do you say that? I have even left brooms and shovels in that locality. I left some last night and some more were deposited there this morning. In all there are five shovels, twelve brooms and five iron pans. They are all kept in Sher Khan's house.'

'Why were we not told about it?'

'That's why I have come running. When I came earlier, there was no one here.'

'But there are no drains in that locality. What are you going to clean? Are you in your senses?' said Kashmiri Lal.

'There may be no regular drains there, but there are certainly kuchcha ones.'

'There must be years of filth in those drains. Who's going to clean them?'

'We shall!' shouted the Jarnail. 'You are a coward and a traitor!' He was suddenly peeved.

'Programmes are changed without any prior intimation. If Gosainji had already decided, why were we not informed?'

It was getting brighter. Those who had come prepared for prabhat pheri felt odd and uncomfortable at the sudden change in the programme.

'Let's at least get out of here,' said Bakshiji, picking up his lantern. 'We shall go singing from here. Start off, Ram Das,' he added and stepped forward.

Kashmiri Lal picked up the tricolour. 'Left, right, left,' shouted the Jarnail, marching right ahead. Ram Das cleared his throat and began singing the old, time-honoured song with which prabhat pheris invariably began and which was also invariably sung out of tune:

Those wedded to the cause of freedom
Are like the legendary lover, Majnu
Deserts and forests are their home...

Master Ram Das sang the first line and the group of activists, keeping time with their feet as they walked, repeated the lines, one after the other and headed towards Dhok Qutab-ud-Din.

3

Nathu heaved a sigh of relief as he stepped into the lane. It was still dark there, although on the roads, it was already daylight. He was eager to reach home as quickly as possible, and he hurried through the maze of lanes. Coming out of that stuffy, stinking hut into open air had refreshed him somewhat. After the hectic business of the night his mind was finally at rest in the half-awake dark lanes.

In the distance, he saw two or three women with their earthen pitchers beside them, sitting by the municipal water tap, chatting in low tones, their glass bangles making a soft, jingling sound. They were waiting for the water to be turned on by the municipality. The familiar morning scene gladdened his heart.

He had hardly covered some distance when suddenly his foot struck against something, and he felt as though the thing had got scattered. It did not take long for Nathu to understand what it was, and the thought sent a shiver down his spine. Some unfortunate woman had placed a 'spell' right opposite someone's house—a few pebbles tied in a rag, along with an image made from kneaded dough and pierced through with wooden needles— intended to transfer her misfortunes on to someone else. Nathu regarded it as a bad omen. After having spent such an awful night, the incident shook him in the extreme, but soon enough he regained his composure. Such a practice was generally carried out to protect a child from an evil eye. The thought gave Nathu some consolation, since he was himself childless.

He was quite familiar with the area through which he was

passing. The entire row of houses in this lane was inhabited by Muslim families. Some were washermen while some others butchers who had their meatshops at the corner of the lane. Mahamdu, the *hamam*-keeper too lived in that lane. Further down, there were houses in which Hindus and Sikhs lived. Beyond which again there were some Muslim houses. The houses at the far end of the lane were inhabited by Sikh families.

As he passed by one of the houses, he heard someone praying: 'Ya Allah, Kul Ki Khair, Kul Ka Bhala'. It was some old man arising uttering his little prayer, followed by yawning and coughing. People were waking up to greet the new day.

At one place his foot fell into something sticky and slimy with a strong, pungent smell like that of cow dung. He steadied himself, extricated his foot from the half-broken pitcher. A swear-word was about to escape his lips when he suddenly understood what it was and a broad smile came to his lips. The ill effect of the 'spell' had been neutralized by this collision. Whenever the weather became hot and sultry, it was customary among young fellows in the town to fill a pitcher with cow dung and horse urine, and fling it into the entrance of some tight-fisted miser of the locality. It was commonly believed that the act would induce a shower.

Opposite another house in the lane, a man was mixing fodder for his cow. From another house close by came the sound of cups and saucers and the jingle of glass bangles. Tea was being prepared. Just then, a woman, her head and shoulders covered, stepped out of a house with a katori in her hand, mumbling words of prayer. She was obviously going to a temple or a gurdwara to offer her morning prayers. How calm and peaceful were the beginnings of the day's business. To cap it all came the sound of an *ektaara* from somewhere. It was some fakir on his morning round. Nathu was familiar with the voice but had never set eyes on the fakir. He had heard him singing softly, particularly during the Ramadan. As he drew near, Nathu saw that the fakir was a tall, elderly person, with a benign countenance like that of a dervish. Frail in body, with a sparse white beard, he was wearing a long cloak. A cloth bag was slung on one shoulder and he had on a skull cap. Nathu stopped to listen to the words of the fakir's song.

The birds are chirping merrily,
while you, ignorant one,
are still fast asleep...

Nathu had often heard this song to the accompaniment of the fakir's ektaara. Nathu took out a paisa from his shirt-pocket and gave it to the fakir.

'May God be with you! May you be blessed with plenty!' said the fakir.

Nathu moved on.

As he stepped out of the lane he found that it was much brighter outside. He was now in the street of the tongawallahs. Two or three tongas, with their shafts raised towards the sky, as though in prayer, stood by the roadside. One of the tongawallahs was brushing his horse; close by two women sat on the ground making flat dung-cakes and sticking them on the wall behind them; a horse with a harness still on its back walked leisurely up and down the road, all by itself. Here too the day's business was starting in a calm, peaceful atmosphere.

Nathu felt as though he had come out to have a stroll. He did not want to be seen by anyone. His mind at peace, he strolled from one street to another.

Where would the pushcart be at this time, the thought suddenly crossed Nathu's mind. In which direction would it be going? It was a pointless question, but the thought impelled Nathu to walk faster. It might have already entered the cantonment, it might be at that very moment standing right at the gate of the veterinary hospital. To hell with it—Nathu uttered a swear-word. What did the veterinary surgeon need a pig for? It must have been to sell its meat somewhere. The thought of what he had gone through made him shiver, what with the stench in that stuffy room, the sweat, the grunts of the wretched creature which had licked his shins so hard that the skin had come off. To hell with Murad Ali. Nathu would wander wherever he liked. He put his hand on his pocket and felt the rustle of the five-rupee note. 'What do I care? It is my well-earned money.'

At the corner of the street stood the horses' trough, Nathu turned to the right. Far away, he heard the chiming of the Sheikh's tower-clock. Perhaps it was striking the hour of four. How clear the chimes were at that hour! During the day it was muffled by street noises. It appeared as though the sound was coming from the sky. Soon after came the sound of temple-bells, from the temple on top of a mound in the centre of the city. City sounds were increasing every minute—of doors opening, of men going out on their morning walk, coughing, pattering of sticks on the ground. A goatherd with his three goats was already on his round to sell goats' milk. Nathu slowed his pace. He was enjoying his stroll in the cool morning air.

The tongawallahs' street had been left behind. Nathu walked along the railing of the spacious municipal grounds opposite the Imam Din Street. On the other side of the railing was the slope that joined the municipal grounds—the hub of activities in the town. In winter there were dog fights every Sunday morning with people betting heavily. If a badly-mauled dog tried to escape the field, those who had betted on it would block its way. The grounds were also the venue for pegging contests, drawing huge crowds, circus shows from touring circus companies such as Miss Tarabai's Circus or Parshuram's Circus. Baisakhi was celebrated here with drumbeats and wrestling bouts. Of late, it had become the centre for political meetings primarily of the Muslim League and of the Belcha Party—meetings of the Congress took place in the grain market at a considerable distance from there.

Nathu took out a bidi from his pocket and sat down on the railing to have a leisurely puff.

Just then the sound of the Azan rang out from the mosque behind the Imam Din Street. It had became brighter by now and things looked clearer in the morning light. Nathu got down from the railing and putting out the bidi, headed towards the Imam

Din Street. He had suddenly remembered that Murad Ali lived somewhere nearby, on the other side of the municipal grounds. He had seen Murad Ali coming from that direction once or twice. But then, Murad Ali was seen everywhere in the town—walking in the middle of the road, swinging his cane, his thick, bushy moustache almost covering his lips, so that even when he smiled or laughed his teeth could not be seen. Only his chubby cheeks bulged prominently and his small, penetrating eyes would blink. Maybe Murad Ali was strolling somewhere nearby even at that time. He had better leave the place, thought Nathu and quickened his pace. The fellow would be cross if he saw him loitering there. Murad Ali had given clear instructions that after delivering the carcass of the pig, Nathu should wait for him in the hut. But Nathu had run away from there. 'Why the hell should I have stuck in that filthy hole? Besides, I have got my remuneration.' Nathu again mumbled to himself.

Nathu turned into a narrow lane and after walking a short distance, turned into another lane to the right which zigzaged towards the north. The sound of a song, sung by a group fell on his ears. As he walked further, the sound became louder and clearer. Nathu understood that the group was out on a prabhat pheri. In those days public meetings, processions, demonstrations, and prabhat pheris were a frequent sight. Nathu did not have a clear grasp of developments that were taking place around him. The air was thick with slogans of all sorts. Soon enough he saw a group of persons coming from the other side. It appeared to be a group of Congressmen because the man walking in front was carrying the tricolour flag of the Congress. As the group drew near, Nathu stepped to one side, and it passed him by, singing. There were eight or ten persons in all, a couple of them had Gandhi caps on their heads, while some wore fez caps. A couple of Sikhs too were among them. Both young and old comprised the group.

As they passed by him, one of them raised a slogan: '*Quomi Nara*!'

And the others answered, 'Bande Mataram!'

Hardly had they finished, when from a distance, the sound of another slogan was heard:

'Pakistan Zindabad!'

'*Qaid-e-Azam* Zindabad!' (referring to Mr Jinnah).

Nathu turned round. Three persons had suddenly appeared at the turn of the lane shouting slogans. It appeared to Nathu that they were standing in the middle of the lane trying to block the other group from proceeding further. One of them with gold-rimmed spectacles and a Turkish cap on his head, said challengingly: 'Congress is the body of the Hindus. The Musalmans have nothing to do with it.'

To which an elderly person from the other group replied: 'Congress is everyone's organization, of Hindus, Sikhs, Muslims. You know this well enough, Mahmud Sahib. There was a time when you too were with us.' Saying so the elderly man stepped forward and put his arms around the man with the Turkish cap. Some persons laughed. Disengaging himself from the elderly man's embrace, the man with the Turkish cap said, 'It is the chicanery of the Hindus. We know this well enough, Bakshiji. You may say whatever you like but the incontrovertible truth is that the Congress is the body of the Hindus, and the Muslim League of the Muslims. The Congress cannot speak for the Muslims.'

Both groups stood facing each other. They talked like friends, and they also exchanged diatribes.

'See for yourself,' Bakshiji said. 'In our group there are Sikhs, Hindus and Muslims. There stands Aziz. Here is Hakimji.'

'Aziz and Hakim are the dogs of the Hindus. We do not hate the Hindus, but we detest their dogs.'

He said it with such vehemence that both the Muslim members of the Congress looked crestfallen.

'Is Maulana Azad a Hindu or a Muslim?'

'Maulana Azad is the biggest dog of the Hindus who goes wagging his tail before you.'

The elderly man continued to listen patiently.

'Freedom of Hindustan will be for the Hindus. It is in sovereign

Pakistan alone that Muslims will be really free.'

Just then, a thin emaciated Sardar, in soiled, crumpled clothes stepped forward, shouting: 'Pakistan over my dead body!'

Some members of the Congress laughed.

'Silence, Jarnail!' someone shouted.

To Nathu too the Sardar's loud exclamation had sounded odd. Seeing his friends laugh, Nathu concluded that the man must be crazy.

But the man kept on shouting: 'Gandhiji has said that Pakistan can only be formed over his dead body. I too say the same.'

'Spit out your anger, Jarnail.'

'Enough, Jarnail. Learn to keep quiet sometimes.'

The Jarnail became furious.

'No one can silence me. I am a soldier of Netaji Subhash Bose's army. I know each one of you well enough...'

There was much laughter.

But when the group of Congressmen moved forward, resuming their prabhat pheri, the man with the Turkish cap blocked their way: 'Muslims reside in this street. You can't go there.'

'Why can't we go there? You go raising slogans for Pakistan all over the town without let or hindrance, while here we are only singing patriotic songs.'

The man with the Turkish cap softened somewhat.

'You can go if you wish, but we shall not allow these dogs of yours to enter our street.'

And he stretched his arms sideways so as to block the way.

Just then Nathu's eyes fell on Murad Ali. He was standing at the street-corner, at some distance from the man with the Turkish cap. Nathu trembled from head to foot.

What is the man doing here? Nathu slowly crept to one side so as to hide behind the singing group. 'Has the fellow seen me?' When he felt that he was completely covered, and from where he stood he himself could not see Murad Ali, he tilted his head a little to see if Murad Ali was still there. The fellow was very much there, listening intently to what those people were saying.

Nathu stepped back and slowly began to withdraw from the

place. So long as those people kept arguing, he thought, Murad Ali would continue to stand there. 'I had better get away from here.' He said to himself. 'If Murad Ali sees me, he will surely come to my tenement and demand an explanation.' He continued to step backward for some distance, then turned round, and taking long strides turned a corner in the lane and then took to his heels.

4

They reined in their horses on reaching the top of the hill. Before them lay a vast plain stretching far into the distance, interspersed with mounds and small hillocks. A blue haze hung over the horizon. High above in the cerulean sky, kites glided with outstretched wings. Beyond the valley, the hill on their left tapered sharply down while the eastern flank, covered in a shimmering haze, barely revealed a range of low, reddish hills stretching far into the distance.

Richard had succeeded in persuading Liza, his wife, to accompany him on his morning ride that day. He had long been eager to show her the spectacle of a sunrise over the valley, to present it to her as a kind of gift.

The cool morning breeze gently ruffled Liza's golden hair. Her blue eyes looked clear and bright though tiny lines had begun to appear under her eyes, a result of boredom, long hours of sleep and excessive consumption of beer.

It was to provide Liza with some diversion that Richard had brought her here. She had returned from England after a long absence of six months, and Richard could not risk a repetition of what had transpired earlier. If Liza did not take kindly to the new place and resolved to return to England, life for both of them would inevitably turn into a veritable hell. When he returned home from his office after the day's work, the exchange of courtesies between them would often turn into a heated argument which soon degenerated to shouting, yelling and cursing. Richard now made a firm resolve to spend the mornings with her. Ever since she had arrived, hardly a week ago, he had been taking her out every morning to a different place—the Mall, the Topi Park or horse riding. Liza too, on her part had been trying hard to take interest in her new surroundings and in Richard's work in order to keep herself occupied. Sometimes she would venture out alone to the cantonment where, being the wife of the Deputy Commissioner of the district, the natives would fawn on her, bow low to offer their salutations and would eagerly want to be of service to her. But for how long can a person go about alone, and the Deputy Commissioner is not the master of his own time. Therefore, neither was sure whether the new arrangement, despite earnest efforts on both sides, would work and, if it did, for how long.

'Very nice!' Liza exclaimed. 'What mountain is that, Richard? Is it part of the Himalayan range?'

'Yes, one might say so,' replied Richard, greatly encouraged by her interest. 'The valley down below extends far into the mountains for hundreds of miles.'

'What a desolate valley!' Liza muttered under her breath.

'But Liza, the valley has great historical significance. All the invaders that attacked India came through this valley, whether they came from Central Asia or Mongolia.' Richard was warming up to the subject. 'Alexander too came through here. Farther away, the valley gets divided into two routes, one leading to Tibet, the other to Afghanistan. Traders, monks, dervishes for centuries used these routes, covering long distances. It is truly a historic area. I have been exploring these parts for the last one month. For a historian no area could be more fascinating. At numerous places you find ruins of ancient buildings, Buddhist monasteries, fortresses, caravanserais...'

'Richard, you talk as though this was your own country.'

'It is not my country, Liza, but its history is certainly of great interest to me.' Richard replied smiling. Then, pointing his whip towards the high hill, said, 'On the other side of that hill, nearly seventeen miles from here are the ruins of Taxila. You know about Taxila, don't you?'

'Yes, I have heard the name.'

There was a time when it used to be renowned for its university.

Liza smiled. She knew that now Richard would narrate the entire history of that region. She liked Richard's enthusiasm. He could talk with so much zest even about rugged rocks. There was something childlike about him, despite his being the Deputy Commissioner. How she wished she too could take interest in such things.

'There is a museum there too. I am sure you will like it. Recently, I brought a sculpted head of the Buddha from there.'

'Why, you already have a huge collection of the Buddha heads. Why did you need another?'

'Excavations are going on nearby. They found quite a large number of such heads. The curator presented one to me.'

Liza saw before her mind's eye their large living room which housed Richard's collection of statuettes and specimens of Indian folk art. The almirahs were crammed with books on the subject. Richard had had a similar obsession in Kenya too, while serving there. He had amassed a collection of African folk art—bows and arrows, all kinds of beads, feathers of birds, totems and the like. And here, in India, it was the Buddha heads.

Liza again turned her eyes towards the surrounding view. Down below, towards the left was a cluster of low, stunted trees through which they had come. The vista before them opened on crossing that patch of trees.

'The colour of the soil is red,' observed Liza, looking at the hills in front of her. 'There is no road to be seen down below. Shall we go back the way we came, through the shrubbery?' Then, turning to Richard, added half in jest, 'Where is the road by which Alexander came to India, Richard?'

'There were no pucca roads in those days, Liza, but there is surely a route, thousands of years old which lies on the other side of that hill.'

Liza looked at Richard. Below his thick-rimmed glasses, the lower part of his face looked very sensitive. Liza wished he would stop talking about ancient routes and ruins and talk to her about love. But Richard's attention was focused on his subject.

'The inhabitants of this area too have been living here since times immemorial. Have you noticed their features? A broad forehead, brownish tint in the colour of their eyes. They all belong to the same racial stock.'

'How can they be of the same racial stock, Richard, when invaders from all over, as you say, have been here?'

'This is precisely the mistake some people make,' Richard said vehemently, as though trying to prove some pet theory of his. 'The first wave of migrants who came from Central Asia three or four thousand year ago and the bands of invaders who came two thousand years or so later, both belonged to the same racial stock. The former were known as Aryans and the latter Muslims. But both had the same roots.'

'The people here too must know all this.'

'These people know only what we tell them.' After a little pause he added, 'Most people have no knowledge of their history. They only live it.'

Liza was getting bored. Once he got started on the subject there was no getting off it, she thought. At such moments, Liza felt relegated to the background. Though he was very fond of her, he had little time for her. Standing in front of a bookshelf, while leafing through a book he would get so absorbed in it that he would become oblivious of everything else. Inevitably, once again Liza would begin to have fits of boredom, everything around her would become insufferable, the natives would look abhorrent, and ultimately she would either have a nervous breakdown or leave for England for another six months or a year.

'Is there a picnic spot nearby?' Liza asked, interrupting Richard.

Richard was taken aback, but the query was not so irrelevant.

'Oh, there are many.' Pointing his whip towards the hill to the left, added, 'There are lovely water springs at the foot of that hill under the shade of the tall banyan trees. Water has spurted out from the inner recesses of the hill. The Hindus have turned them into bathing pools and named them after their mythological characters, like Rama and Sita.' Richard smiled as he said this, thinking that these names must sound very odd to Liza's ears, odd and unfamiliar. 'There are many such spots around,' he went on, then, pointing his whip towards another cluster of trees, said, 'Not far from it, there is another lovely place. A fair is held there, once a year, for a full fortnight, during the month of March. Singing girls come from all over India to participate in it. The fair has some religious sanctity to it because there is the tomb of a Muslim pir there. Devotees light clay lamps on it.' Then smiling, added, 'There is singing and dancing during the night, and gambling during the day. I shall take you there one evening.'

'Is the fair on, these days?'

'Yes, it is. But it is not advisable to go there now.'

'Why not?'

'There is some tension between the Hindus and Muslims. We fear a riot might break out.'

Liza had vaguely heard about the tension but she knew very little about it.

'I still cannot make out a Hindu from a Muslim. Can you, Richard? Can you immediately know whether a person is Hindu or Muslim?'

'Yes, I can.'

'What about our cook? Is he Hindu or Muslim?'

'He is Muslim.'

'How do you know?'

'From his name, the cut of his beard; he offers namaz. Even his eating habits are different.'

'You are so clever, Richard. Do you really know all this?'

'Yes, I do. Quite a bit.'

'You know so much. You must teach me, Richard, I too want to understand things. And that fellow, your stenographer, the man who came to the railway station, the fellow with glistening white teeth. Is he a Hindu or Muslim?'

'He is Hindu.'

'How do you know?'

'From his name.'

'From his name alone?'

'It is quite simple, Liza. The names of Muslims end with such suffixes as Ali, Din, Ahmed, whereas the names of Hindus end with Lal, Chand or Ram. If the name is Roshanlal the man is Hindu, but if it is Roshan Din, he is Muslim. If it is Iqbal Chand, he is Hindu, if Iqbal Ahmed, he is Muslim.'

'I will never be able to understand all this,' Liza said, discouraged. 'And what about the fellow who wears a turban, your chauffeur who has a long beard?'

'He is a Sardar, a Sikh,' Richard said, laughing.

'It is not difficult to make out such a person,' Liza said, laughing.

'Every Sikh's name ends with the word "Singh",' Richard said.

They began to go down the slope. The day was warming up. The sun had risen and the thin curtain of haze which had lent an aura of mystery to the atmosphere was dispersing.

'It is great fun roaming in these parts. You will like it. We'll come out every weekend.'

As they were crossing the bed of a dry stream strewn with round pebbles and stones, Richard leading the way, Liza said, 'Where will you take me this weekend, Richard? To Taxila?'

Richard did not miss the touch of sarcasm in Liza's voice. Taxila drew Richard like magnet, he could wander there for hours. But what about Liza? Would she like to wander about in the midst of ruins?

'No, not to Taxila for a few days, Liza dear. There is some tension in the town as I told you. We shall go there when the situation improves somewhat. As for this weekend...'

Richard did not know what to say. He couldn't tell what sort of a weekend it was going to be.

'We'll go somewhere,' he said, as they reached the bottom of the slope and spurred the horses homewards.

Before sitting down to breakfast, Liza and Richard, passing through the numerous rooms of their bungalow, came and stood in the spacious living room. With the approach of April, curtains would be drawn over doors and windows immediately after sunrise to keep out the heat and harsh daylight. One needed to use electric light even during daytime. Along all the walls stood shelves sagging with books. In between them, on wooden stands, rested heads of the Buddha or the busts of Bodhisattvas. Each statuette had been provided with a separate electric light which illuminated the face or a profile from a well-studied, favourable angle. The walls were covered with Indian paintings. On the mantelpiece stood a colourful doll beside which lay an ancient manuscript on copper plates. On a wooden pedestal by the side of the fireplace stood a rock-edict, while in front of the fireplace were placed three cane stools with a long, low, mahogany teapoy. Richard often sat there, his pipe in hand and browsed through his books and ancient manuscripts. The cook had been instructed to put the kettle on a stove close by with the necessary tea-service as Richard was fond of making his own tea. On the long teapoy lay half-open books and periodicals. At one end of it stood a pipe stand with half a dozen pipes of different shapes and sizes hanging in it. The round lampshade over the teapoy had been so arranged that, switched on, the light fell only on the three cane stools and the teapoy, leaving the rest of the room in semi-darkness.

His arm round Liza's waist, Richard was showing her the busts and statuettes that he had collected in her absence.

'When I step out of my bungalow, I find myself in some part of India; but when I am back in my bungalow, I return to the whole of India.'

Wearing an old tweed coat with leather-patches on its elbows, loose corduroy trousers, a pair of thick, black-framed spectacles, Richard looked very much like the curator of a museum.

They stopped in front of a Buddha.

'The most beautiful thing about a Buddha is the serene smile. The light should so fall on the face that it highlights that smile. Let me show you,' Richard said turning the Buddha head slightly to the right and switching on the light above the statuette.

'See? See the difference?' Richard exclaimed. To Liza too it appeared that the smile on Buddha's face had become more pronounced—calm, soft, yet slightly ironical.

'The smile always rests in the corners of the lips. If you shift the angle even slightly, the smile will become faint.'

Liza turned round and looked at Richard's face. Men are such odd creatures, she thought. A woman would notice all these things and yet not be so childishly excited about them. She pressed Richard's arm, resting her cheek on his shoulder.

'This is the most significant thing about a Buddha head—the soft mysterious smile,' Richard said bending down to kiss Liza on the head.

Every room in the bungalow had been fitted with all sorts of electrical devices. Wherever they chose to sit, a call-bell was available close by, linking them to the kitchen as also to the veranda outside.

Looking at Richard, going from one room to another, nobody could tell that the man was the highest executive officer of the district. He looked more like a connoisseur of Indian art and a scholar of history. But when he sat in his administrator's chair, he was the representative of the British Empire carrying out the behests and policies laid down in England. He was a pastmaster at keeping the two identities distinctly separate from each other as also the emotions involved with either. That was the hallmark of his mental make-up. He would, with the greatest ease, shift from one kind of activity into another, even though each might be diametrically different from the other. He could draw the line between private interests and official concerns. His life moved, impelled by a peculiar kind of discipline. Three days in a week he held court in his capacity as the District Magistrate. Sitting in the judge's chair he would forget that he was the rulers' representative and dispense justice in strict conformity with the rules of the Indian Penal Code. It was difficult to say what his own beliefs were, if at all he had any. Perhaps Richard had never put this question to himself. As a matter of fact, there was no room for personal beliefs in his life. The thought that one's actions should conform to one's beliefs was considered juvenile idealism to be dispensed with the day a person joined the Civil Service. As a Civil Servant, Richard was required to implement policies, grasp the essentials of a situation, take quick decisions and enforce them without the least fuss or noise. Personal beliefs or convictions had no place in such a role. Besides, who has ever bothered to consider the moral or ethical aspects of the profession he or she was in?

Arm in arm, they proceeded towards the dining room. It was Liza's favourite room. In its centre stood a big, circular dining table, of black mahogany. A lampshade hanging low from the ceiling right above the table shed its light on a copper vase filled with red roses. The room spoke of Richard's taste and Liza was well aware that if she was to live with Richard she would have to adapt herself to his idiosyncrasies.

Richard paused a little before stepping into the room.

'What's on your mind?' asked Liza, her head resting on his shoulder.

'Well, what exactly was I thinking? Where should I begin...?'

'Begin what, Richard?'

'You wish to know about the situation in the town, isn't it?'

'I don't want to know anything. All I want to know is when you'll be back from your office,' said Liza caressing Richard's chest. Richard bent down and kissed her on her lips.

'Getting bored already?'

Richard felt as though a small cloud had appeared on the horizon which could only grow bigger and darker till it covered the entire sky.

He drew Liza closer but his heart was not in it. Behind his affection lurked the fear that things might not turn out well again this time between them. Though his lips passed over her hair, her forehead, her eyes and her lips, he felt strangely removed from her. The ardour and passion of the night had now been replaced with indifference. He was only playing at love, observing a formality.

The *khansama*, who had been standing in a corner of the room, stepped forward, the red waistband over his white uniform shining brightly in the light. Walking softly, he began laying the table for breakfast.

Liza and Richard continued to hold each other in their arms. Earlier, if a servant suddenly appeared, Liza would try to extricate herself from Richard's arms. Richard would continue to hold her close, and the servant would go on doing his work. Embarrassed, Liza would close her eyes to forget the servant's presence. But gradually, she came to realize that the servant was a mere native and that his presence was beneath notice.

'You had better start taking interest in some activity. A Deputy Commissioner's wife is looked upon as the first lady of the district. The officers' wives will be only too willing to help you in whatever you take up.'

'I know. I know. Collect donations for the Red Cross, hold flower shows; children's fêtes; collect shoes and clothes for disabled soldiers' wives...'

'There is another association which we propose to set up for the care and protection of animals. The stray dogs roaming freely on the cantonment roads may be rabid and bite people. Then some people make lame horses pull carriages...'

'What do you propose to do with such animals?'

'Have them put to sleep. It is cruel to harness a lame horse to a vehicle, and stray dogs spread disease. You can choose any activity that may be of interest to you.'

'No, thank you. That I should go about killing stray dogs while you go ruling over the district... You are always pulling my leg, you never take me seriously.'

'I am not joking, Liza. I really want you to take interest in something.'

'I do take interest in your work. Tell me more of what you were telling me this morning. About the Indians.'

Richard smiled.

'Well, all Indians are quick-tempered. They flare up over trivial things. They fly at one another's throat in the name of religion. They are all terribly self-centred. And they all adore white women.'

His last words again made her feel as though he was pulling her leg. She regarded Richard as a very capable, erudite person and suspected that he considered her an ignoramus and would not miss any opportunity of making a dig at her. His conversations with her were often laced with sarcasm directed at her.

'You never take me seriously, Richard.'

'Why should anything be taken seriously, Liza?' Richard said in a tone of disenchantment. 'Listen, darling, we may have some trouble here.'

Liza looked up.

'What sort of trouble, Richard? Will there be a war again?'

'No. A riot may break out in the city. Tension is mounting between the Hindus and the Muslims.'

'Will they fight one another? In London you used to tell me that they were fighting against you.'

'They are fighting both against us and against one another.'

'You are again joking, Richard. Aren't you?'

'In the name of religion they fight one another; in the name of freedom they fight against us.'

'Don't try to be too clever, Richard. I also know a thing or two. In the name of freedom they fight against you, but in the name of religion you make them fight one another. Isn't that right?'

'It is not we who make them fight. They fight of their own accord.'

'You can stop them from fighting, Richard. After all they are from the same racial stock. Didn't you say so?'

Richard was charmed by his wife's simplicity. He bent down and kissed her on the cheek.

'Darling, rulers have their eyes only on differences that divide their subjects, not on what unites them.'

Just then the khansama came in with a tray. On seeing him, Liza said, 'Is he a Hindu or a Musalman?'

'What do you think?' asked Richard.

Liza stared at the khansama for a while who, after putting

down the tray, had stepped aside and was standing motionless like a statue.

'He is a Hindu.'

Richard laughed. 'Wrong.'

'How is it wrong?'

'Have a good look at him again.'

Liza looked hard at the man.

'He is a Sikh. He has a beard. He is wearing a turban on his head.'

Richard laughed even more loudly. The khansama continued to stand motionless, without a muscle of his face moving.

'The Sikhs do not trim beards. It is against their religion.'

'You did not tell me that.'

'There is a lot else that I did not tell you.'

'For example?'

'That the Sikhs, besides keeping their hair long, adhere to four other commandments; that many Hindus keep a tuft of hair on their heads; that the Muslims too have their dos and don'ts, they do not eat pork while the Hindus do not eat beef; that the Sikhs eat jhatka meat while the Muslims eat halal...'

'Which means, you do not want me to learn anything. Who can remember all this?' She looked at the khansama. 'When I have mastered all these details, shall I be able to tell, just by looking at a person, whether he is Hindu or Muslim? How can one tell without looking at those particular signs?' Liza said, and, laughing, added, 'I bet these people themselves cannot tell one from the other, who among them is Hindu or Muslim. I bet you too cannot tell.'

And turning towards the khansama she said, 'Khansama, are you Muslim?'

'Yes, Memsahib.'

'Will you kill a Hindu?'

The khansama was taken aback at the question. He looked at Liza. Then smiling, turned his eyes towards the Sahib. He came forward and placing a plate in front of Richard, stepped back into the semi-darkness. Richard picked up the paper on the plate, glanced through it and put it back on the plate.

'What is it, Richard?'

'Just a report, Liza.' Richard replied softly and was soon lost in his thoughts.

'What sort of report, Richard?'

'About the situation in the town, Liza. Every morning I receive reports from the heads of three or four departments—from the superintendent of police, from the health officer, the civil supplies officer... Excuse me, Liza...' Richard said abruptly and went out of the dining room.

Liza felt confused at Richard's abrupt departure. He had not even finished his coffee. She didn't know whether she should wait for him or drink her coffee. But Richard came back soon enough.

'Where was that report from, Richard?'

'From the superintendent of police,' he said, then added in a reassuring voice, 'Only a routine report.'

But Liza felt as though Richard was hiding something from her.

'There is something you are keeping from me, Richard.'

'Why should I keep anything from you? We have nothing to do with what happens in the town.'

'Still, there seems to be something urgent in the report. What has the superintendent of police written?'

'That there is some tension in the town between the Hindus and the Muslims. Nothing new. This kind of tension prevails in many parts of India these days.'

'What do you propose to do?'

'You tell me what I should do. I think I shall carry on the administration. What else?'

Liza looked up.

'You are again joking.'

'I am not joking, Liza. What can I do if there is tension between the Hindus and the Muslims?'

'You can resolve their differences.'

Richard smiled and taking a sip of his coffee said in a calm voice, 'All I can say to them is that their religious disputes are their affairs and should be resolved by them. The administration can only render any help that they may want.'

'Also tell them that they belong to the same racial stock and therefore should not fight one another. That is what you told me, Richard. Didn't you?'

'I shall certainly tell them, Liza,' Richard replied, with an ironic smile playing on his lips.

They sipped their coffee. Suddenly Liza grew anxious and her face looked bleak.

'I hope there is no danger to you, Richard.'

'No, Liza. If the subjects fight among themselves, the ruler is safe.'

She felt greatly relieved and an expression of profound respect for Richard shone in her eyes, as the implication of what he had said sank into her.

'Right you are, Richard. You know so much, I suddenly felt so frightened. Jackson's wife had once told me that on one occasion, Jackson, holding a revolver in his hand ran after a crowd of natives, trying to disperse them. And his wife, who stood watching from the balcony, got terribly scared. Just think, Richard, Jackson, all alone, revolver in hand, running after a huge crowd. Anything could have happened.'

'Don't be alarmed, Liza,' said Richard, getting up from his chair, he patted Liza on the cheek, got up, and left the room.

5

By the time the group of prabhat pheri activists, making their way through the maze of lanes, reached the Imam Din Mohalla, dawn was giving way to bright morning. Along the way they had picked up brooms, shovels and *taslas* from Sher Khan's house. In the early morning light, the exhaustion on their pale, wrinkled faces was clearly visible. Barring Mehtaji, they were all in crumpled, home-washed clothes. The Gandhi cap on Bakshiji's head was askew looking as though a heavy load had been lifted off it. Shankar, Master Ram Das and Aziz carried brooms on their shoulders while Des Raj and Sher Khan had taslas in their hands. The Jarnail carried a big bamboo pole. As the day broke, Master Ram Das, a Brahmin by caste, was acutely embarrassed at the thought of being seen with a broom in his hand.

'Oh Gandhi Baba, you have put a scavenger's broom in a Brahmin's hand. You are capable of anything. Isn't that so, friends?' and he tittered, putting the broom behind his back. Unable to catch anyone's attention, he turned to Bakshiji.

'I am telling you now, Bakshiji, I will not clean drains.'

'Why not? Are you from a royal family or what?'

'I can't be expected to clean drains at my age, surely?'

'If Gandhiji can clean his lavatory, why can't you clean a drain?'

'The fact is, I cannot bend. Honest to God, each time I bend I get a shooting pain in my back. Apparently, there is a stone in my kidney.'

'How is it that the stone in your bladder does not act up when you're milking your cow or mixing fodder for it? It only pops up when you have to do community work.'

At this Shankar turned round and said, 'We have come here to spread a message, not to actually clean the drains. But if you feel so awkward, Masterji, I shall do the cleaning and you carry the refuse in the tasla.'

They had hardly gone a few yards and turned into a lane when Gosainji, who was at the back of the group, shouted, 'Why are we going by this route today?'

Des Raj, walking in front, had taken a turn to the right and the others had merely followed suit.

'Tell him to stop,' shouted Bakshiji. He too had realized that they were not on the right route. 'This is their time for offering namaz. We should avoid going by the masjid. O Kashmiri! Have you gone out of your mind? Why have you taken this route? Are you listening?'

Kashmiri Lal stoppped and turned round.

'Sher Khan and Des Raj turned in here by mistake,' he said, 'But don't worry. We'll stop the singing when we pass by the mosque.'

'Why go in that direction at all? You know the times we are living in. Turn back and take the lane that leads straight to the crossing. We shall enter the Imam Din Mohalla from that side.'

They turned back and took the new route which was unfamiliar to the prabhat pheris. Generally, the Congress activists did not go to far-flung colonies located outside the town. Even otherwise the route was long, for it involved crossing the sprawling municipal grounds.

They stopped as they reached a cattle water-trough and Kashmiri Lal, who held the tricolour in his hand, raised a full-throated slogan: 'Inquilab!'

To which the others replied in a spirited voice:

'Zindabad!'

'Bharat Mata ki'

'Jai!'

At the sound of the slogans, little children came running out

of their houses, and women peeped through curtains. A cock
with a red crest climbed up a mud wall and flapping its wings
crowed loudly, as though in answer to the slogans.

'The cock did a lot better than you, Kashmiri. See how proudly
it crowed!' commented Sher Khan.

'Kashmiri is no less than any cock! Kashmiri is the cock of the
Congress.'

Shankar added, 'Put a red cap on his head and Kashmiri will
have a red crest too. Get him a red cap, Bakshiji.'

'Why, Kashmiri doesn't need any crest. He is the female of
the species, a hen. Kashmiri hen!'

Such leg-pulling and broad humour were an integral part of
the activities of fellow activists.

'Enough, enough! Let's get to work,' said Bakshiji as he put
the lantern on the low wall of the trough.

Most of the houses in the locality were small, single-storeyed
houses, built in two paralled lanes on either side of a spacious
courtyard. Gunny-cloth curtains hung over the front doors of
most of them. The lanes were not paved. Only one of the lanes
had a kachcha drain, the other one had no drain at all. In some
lanes, cattle were tied. From the houses, now and then, women
emerged with earthen pitchers balanced on their heads to fetch
water. A small boy was collecting dung from under a buffalo.
Near the trough, two little boys sat on the ground, opposite each
other, relieving themselves and chatting away merrily.

'Why is your shit so thin?' one asked the other.

'I drink goats' milk. That's why. What do you drink?'

In one corner of the open ground, stood a tandoor.

Entering the locality one felt as though one was in a village.

'Pick up your shovels and start working!' shouted Bakshiji.

Mehtaji and Master Ram Das picked a tasla each and went to
work in the yard. Shankar and Kashmiri Lal, armed with shovels
headed for the drain, while Sher Khan, Des Raj and Bakshiji
began sweeping the courtyard with brooms.

The residents of the locality watched them, puzzled. A tonga-
driver came out of his house, and squatting on the ground,

watched the goings-on. As his eyes fell on Bakshiji, sweeping the ground, he went over to him and tried to stop him.

'Why do you put us to shame, Babuji? It is highly improper that you should sweep the ground of our locality. Pray, hand over the broom to me.'

'No, no don't worry. That's what we have come here for,' Bakshiji answered.

'No, good sir, I won't let you. You are well-educated men from good families. How can we let you sweep our floors? Heaven forbid! Please hand over your broom to me. Why must you push us into the fires of hell?'

Bakshiji was deeply touched by the man's warm sympathy. 'The community work is having its effect. This is precisely what constructive work stands for,' Bakshiji muttered to himself.

Kashmiri Lal and Shankar were shovelling out the mud from the kachcha drain which ran alongside the row of houses. Ever since the drain had been dug, dirty water had been accumulating in it and now it had turned into slimy mud of dark colour. So long as the mud had been inside the drain, foul smell did not emanate from it, but when Kashmiri Lal and Shankar took out shovelfuls of it and piled it by the side of the drain at different places, an unbearable smell filled the air attracting a horde of mosquitoes. The drain was about a foot deep and it was filled with mud right up to the top.

'O good fellow! What are you up to?'

It was the voice of an elderly man with a henna-dyed beard standing behind the low parapet wall on the roof of one of the houses. 'Have you come to spread disease here? Why can't you leave the filth where it is, inside the drain? By taking it out and leaving it to scatter all over the place you are making it a potential source of disease. Who will clean it when you are gone? You'll leave the place a lot dirtier than before.'

Bakshiji who was sweeping the lane close by, straightened his back and stood up. He felt angry with Shankar and Kashmiri Lal. 'These young fellows will never understand anything,' he muttered under his breath. 'Constructive work does not mean that you should actually clean the drains. It is only a symbolic gesture to make the residents aware of the need for civic sanitation and gradually earn their trust and participation in the struggle for Independence.'

The old man, having made his comments withdrew from the parapet wall and Bakshiji resumed sweeping the lane with his broom.

Just then another elderly man, with a flowing white beard and a rosary in his hand, emerged from the lane opposite. Obviously, he was on his way to the mosque for his morning prayer. In his white salwar and kurta, an open waistcoat embroidered with a fancy design, a mushaddi lungi on his head, he looked a very pious man. He stood watching the 'constructive' programme for some time, then turning to Master Ram Das, who was covered with dust from sweeping the yard, said in a voice trembling with emotion: 'We shall remain indebted to you for all this.' His eyes turned towards the other activists. 'God bless you! What goodness of heart! What nobility of purpose!' He muttered again and again.

Bakshiji walked over to the old patriarch. 'It is nothing,' he said in a self-effacing tone. 'We are contributing in our small way to social welfare.'

'It is not the work, it is the lofty sentiment behind it that is so inspiring! Congratulations! Wah, Wah! Wonderful!' and smiling, walked out of the locality at a leisurely pace. Hearing words of such high praise, Bakshiji felt gratified. 'Today's work has yielded rich dividends,' he muttered to himself.

'Look at Mehtaji and Aziz,' Sher Khan said, laughing. Neither of them has even touched his broom. Mehtaji can't risk soiling his clothes.'

Careful, lest his fingers should become dirty, Mehta was picking up a stone at a time from the ground, very daintily with his forefinger and thumb and dropping it into the pan. Master Ram Das already had a thick coating of dust on his hair and thick moustaches.

By then, besides children, quite a few residents of the locality had gathered. Women and young girls stood behind curtains while men stood on roof-tops, interestedly observing the goings-on.

The Jarnail, who had been standing with his long bamboo pole near the trough, moved slowly to where the drain was being cleaned.

'Is the drain blocked? Do you want me to open it with the bamboo pole?' People standing around burst out laughing at his military abruptness.

'This constructive programme is really worthless, if you ask me,' said Shankar to Kashmiri Lal as he straightened his back. 'Shovelling mud out of drains will not bring freedom.'

Sweating profusely, both Shankar and Kashmiri Lal had by then made three piles of slimy mud along the drain.

'Don't go blurting whatever comes into your head, Shankar.' Bakshi had overheard Shankar's remark. He stood in the middle of the lane, broom in hand.

'I credited you with more intelligence than that. Is Bapu a fool to want us to ply the *charkha* and do constructive work?'

'What else am I doing if not that? Still, it makes no sense to me.'

Bakshi was in no mood to get into an argument with a fellow like Shankar who was unerringly blunt and outspoken. Even so, he couldn't help adding, 'Try to understand, Shankar, what we are doing is only the symbolic expression of our patriotism; it brings us close to our people, to the poor. When we come, clad in khadi, brooms and shovels in our hands to their locality, they regard us as their own; it inspires confidence in them, which it won't if we came to them in the Western attire of coat and pant.'

'Ever since you got involved in this constructive work the freedom struggle has come to a standstill,' retorted Shankar. 'Go on plying the charkha and sweeping lanes with brooms,' he said angrily as he threw a shovelful of mud on the pile.

'You are a traitor,' the Jarnail shouted. 'I know you well enough. You hobnob with the communists.'

'Enough, Jarnail,' Bakshiji intervened. To let the Jarnail continue would only aggravate matters. Turning to Shankar, he said, 'Can't you hold your tongue, Shankar? Must you go on babbling all the time? Is this the place for an argument?'

Just then, a man came running from the direction of the municipal grounds, past the lane where Sher Khan lived and went straight to where the knot of local residents stood. He had on a black waistcoat and looked very agitated. He spoke to the residents in low whispers, all the while gesticulating furiously. The manner of his arrival seemed very odd. Suddenly the local residents began to disperse. Only a few children continued to stand in the lane. Soon enough, the women standing behind gunny-cloth curtains also withdrew and doors began to shut. One of the women hurriedly came out of her house, caught hold of one of the two children who had been easing themselves near the trough, and pulling him by the arm, took him inside the house.

An uncanny silence fell on all sides. The Congress workers were bewildered by the turn of events.

They saw the white-haired man, who a little while earlier had praised the Congress workers so effusively, coming towards them. Mehta and Bakshi were standing together trying to understand the situation and what had caused the sudden commotion. They wondered whether they should ask the old man about it, when the latter, swinging his rosary stopped in front of them.

'Clear out of here at once if you don't want to be skinned alive!' he shouted in his high-pitched voice. His chin trembled and his cheeks turned pale. 'Enough of your nonsense! Just get out of here. Aren't you listening? Rascals, clear out of here.' And turning round, he strode away.

The singing party was stunned. They looked at one another. It was Bakshi's surmise that perhaps, Shankar and Kashmiri Lal, who were given to loose talk, had said something offensive to the local residents. But did it warrant the scathing outburst of the old man?

Just then a stone came flying from somewhere and fell near Bakshiji. Shankar and Kashmiri Lal, confused and bewildered, looked at Bakshiji.

'There is something amiss. What do you think could have happened?' asked Master Ram Das, coming closer.

'There is something wrong somewhere. Let's get away from here,' said Bakshiji, 'it was a mistake to have come here in the first place. Where is Des Raj who had been so insistent that we should come to this locality?'

But Des Raj was nowhere to be seen. Nobody knew when he had slunk away.

'Some mischief is afoot.'

Two or three stones came flying, one after the other and one of them hit Master Ram Das on the shoulder.

'Let's get away at once. Let's not linger here, even for a minute.'

The group rushed towards the end of the lane.

Holding the bamboo pole in his hand, the Jarnail shouted, 'You are all cowards! I know each one of you well enough! I shall leave only after I have completed my job.'

At this Bakshiji shouted to the Jarnail like a military commander, 'Jarnail, pick up the flag! At once!'

The Jarnail at once stood to attention and marched in step towards the trough, against which stood the national flag.

Two more stones came flying, hurled from somewhere. At the same time three men came out of a lane and stood at its entrance.

Kashmiri Lal took the flag from the Jarnail's hand and the party of Congress workers started on their way out of the locality. Mehta overturned the tasla in which he had been collecting pebbles, and carrying it in his hand joined the others who were leaving the locality. The hurricane lamp once again swung from Bakshiji's hand, but Bakshiji's head was bowed as he walked out.

'Shall we put back the shovels and taslas in Sher Khan's house?' Master Ram Das asked Bakshiji.

'Keep walking. Don't stop anywhere.'

Kashmiri Lal turned round to look back. Instead of three, five men were now standing at the entrance to the lane. Across the yard too, some men had gathered and were staring at them. As the party entered the Qutab Din street the scene that confronted

them was similar to the one they had left behind. Here too,
opposite the Nanbai's shop, stood three men, silently watching
them.

'Something is amiss,' Bakshi said to Mehta.

'For all we know, Shankar or Kashmiri might have misbehaved
with someone in the locality. You have let in all kinds of riff-raff
into the Congress.'

'What are you saying, Mehtaji? Kashmiri was busy cleaning
the drain the whole time. Something else seems to be the matter.'

On entering the Mohyals' lane, they again saw a knot of men
standing ominously at the far end of the lane.

They were suddenly stopped by a tall resident of the Mohyal
street.

'Don't go to that side, Bakshiji,' he said, stepping forward.

'Why, what's the matter?'

'Don't go that way.'

'Why not?'

By then, Kashmiri, Jarnail and Master Ram Das had come to
where Bakshi and Mehta were standing.

'Can you see anything lying at the end of the lane?' Bakshiji
strained his eyes to look. Outside the farther end of the lane,
across the road stood a mosque, known in the locality as the
Khailon ki Masjid.

'What is it?'

'Look towards the steps, at the entrance of the mosque.'

'Something blackish, like a bundle seems to be lying there.'

'It is the carcass of a pig, Bakshiji. Someone has left a dead pig
there.'

Bakshiji looked at Mehta's face, as though to say, 'See? Didn't
I tell you something unusual has happened?'

Everyone was looking hard in that direction. On the steps of
the mosque, lay a black bag from which two legs were sticking
out. The green door of the mosque was closed.

'Let's turn back from here,' whispered Master Ram Das.

Kashmiri Lal spat on the ground when he saw the pig and
turned his face away.

'Bakshiji, let's turn back. Beyond the lane is a Muslim locality,' Ram Das said again.

'A foul mischief has been played by someone,' Mehta muttered under his breath. 'But are you sure it is the carcass of a pig lying there? It may be some other animal.'

'Had it been some other animal, the Muslims would not have reacted so sharply,' Bakshiji said, somewhat peeved.

The Jarnail with his small eyes under his bushy eyebrows stared hard at the pig and exclaimed in a loud voice, 'It is the Englishman's doing.'

His nostrils were quivering as he said again at the top of his voice, 'It is the Englishman's mischief. I know it for sure.'

'Yes, yes, Jarnail, it is the Englishman's mischief. But right now you had better keep quiet,' Bakshiji said to him persuasively.

'Let's return by the back lane,' suggested Master Ram Das once again. But the Jarnail pulled him up sharply, 'You are a coward. It is the Englishman's doing. I shall not spare him. I shall expose him.'

Mehtaji whispered into Bakshiji's ear: 'Why do you bring this lunatic with you wherever you go? He will be our undoing one day. Why don't you expel him from the Congress?'

Whenever the eye of a Muslim pedestrian walking along the road fell on the steps of the mosque, he would at first stare hard in that direction, then abruptly turn his face away and quicken his pace, muttering something under his breath.

Suddenly a tonga dashed along the road. Soon after, sounds of running footsteps were heard from the side of the mosque. A few paces away, a butcher hurriedly covered the carcasses of four goats hanging in his shop with cloth and pulled down the shutters. Doors began to shut in the Mohyals' lane too.

Bakshiji turned round. Master Ram Das, walking fast, had reached almost the end of the lane. Behind him, at some distance were Shankar and Aziz. Here and there in the lane, stood small groups of local residents.

Bakshiji's Mohyal friend advised, 'You too should leave the place, Bakshiji, your presence here will add to the tension.'

Bakshiji looked at the man and turning to Kashmiri Lal said, 'Fold up the flag, Kashmiri. Take it off the staff.' Turning to his Mohyal friend, said, 'We must remove the carcass of the pig from the steps of the mosque. Tension will keep mounting so long as the carcass is there.'

'What? Are you suggesting that you will remove the carcass from the steps of the mosque? I think you should not even go near the place.'

'He is right,' said Mehtaji. 'We should keep away from it all. The situation can get worse.'

'Won't it be worse if we walk away from it? Do you think the Muslims will remove the pig's carcass from the steps of the mosque?'

'They can get it done by a scavenger or a sweeper. Anyway, under no circumstance should we get involved in it.'

Bakshiji put down the lamp on the steps of a nearby house, and turning to Mehtaji said, 'What did you say, Mehtaji? That we should slink away and allow the tension to aggravate? It would have been a different matter if we had not seen the carcass.' Then, turning to the Jarnail and Kashmiri Lal, added, 'Come with me,' and went out of the lane towards the mosque.

Kashmiri was nonplussed. He couldn't decide whether to follow Bakshiji or not. Stones had been hurled at them in the Imam Din Mohalla. God alone knew what lay in store for them here. Drops of perspiration appeared on his forehead. He put the flagpole alongside a wall and for a while stood wavering. But then, with a sudden resolve followed Bakshiji out of the lane.

On reaching the road, he turned round. The Mohyal too had left. Only Mehtaji was still standing in the deserted lane. The three or four shops standing in a row were all closed. Shops down the road near the well too were closed. Only four or five persons, stood in a knot there. They were all looking towards the mosque. People stood on their balconies or on rooftops with the doors of their houses shut tight.

'We must first remove the carcass from the steps of the mosque,'

Bakshiji was saying.

The carcass was that of a pig with jet-black bristles. It was covered with a gunny bag from under which the pig's legs, its snout and a part of its belly peeped out.

Mehtaji, still undecided, stood inside the lane, close to a wall. Removing the carcass was not only risky it was a dirty business too, for it meant soiling his clothes of pure white khadi. The Jarnail and Bakshiji had, in the meantime, caught the pig by its legs and pulled it off the steps of the mosque. Dragging it across the road they had pushed it behind a pile of bricks, thereby concealing it from view.

'Let it be here for the present. The doors of the mosque can now be opened. Let us now wash the steps of the mosque.' Bakshiji said and turning to Kashmiri, added, 'The municipal corporation scavengers live in the lane at the back. Tell one of them to bring his pushcart and we'll get the carcass removed from here.'

Just then, sounds of commotion were heard from the direction of the well. A cow came running towards them, followed at some distance by a young man whose face was half-covered and who carried a big stick in his hand. His chest was bare and on it dangled a talisman. The cow was young, with an almond-coloured hide and big startled eyes. Its tail was raised from sheer terror. It looked as though it had lost its way. All three of them stood perplexed, their minds filled with apprehensions. The youth with the half-covered face drove the cow and took it into a side-lane towards the right.

Bakshiji stood transfixed as it were, anxiety writ large on his face. He slowly nodded his head and muttered: 'It seems kites and vultures will hover over the town for a long time.'

His face had turned pale and gloomy.

6

Before the dispersal of the weekly congregation, the *vanaprasthi* led the chanting of sacred hymns. He believed that such chanting of hymns and sacred verses was like the last oblation offered at a sacred rite and that the weekly congregation was in the nature of such a rite. He considered the hymns, carefully chosen by him, the very essence of Indian thought and culture. After years of persuasion, the vanaprasthi had succeeded in making the members of the congregation memorize them. Sitting cross-legged on the platform, his eyes closed and head bowed, with folded hands resting in his lap, he began chanting the holy verses:

'*Sarve Bhavantu Sukhina...*' (May every living being in the world be happy and live a contented life...)

The vanaprasthi was the only one in the congregation well-versed in Vedic lore and recited the mantras in chaste Sanskrit. Every word uttered by him seemed to emerge from the depths of his soul. The members of the congregation hummed or recited the verse after him. Some of them could not keep pace with the vanaprasthi, and invariably, their humming would continue long after the verse had been fully chanted.

Shanti Path was recited last. It was a prayer for universal peace. The entire congregation stood up and chanted it in a full-throated voice, since this was a mantra they were all familiar with. The invocation filled the hall with an atmosphere of serenity. It seemed as though this prayer for peace expressed so resonantly was reaching out to every home. It filled every heart with deep satisfaction. After the chanting of hymns, a prayer seeking the well-being of every living being was sung. The vanaprasthi kept the rhythm by softly clapping his hands.

Grant mercy O Lord, to everyone
Grant every living creature your blessing...

On his insistence the practice of chanting the traditional aarati had almost been given up, because it contained such mortifying expressions as 'I am a fool, a lout, O Lord,' which, the vanaprasthi thought, had a demoralizing effect on the singer. Similarly a song composed by some Khanna rhymester which comprised the line, 'We, your sons, O Lord, are utterly worthless,' had been discarded.

The prayers over, the congregation would normally have dispersed, but the members continued sitting because the secretary was expected to make an important announcement. The secretary stood up and requested the members comprising the core group to stay back to deliberate over an important matter. The members already had a hunch of what it was about, for in his discourse, the vanaprasthi had hined at it. Not only that, while making references to it he had got excited and agitated, and even recited, in a deeply anguished voice, the lines of a couplet:

Much blighted has this land been by
the sins of the Muslims, even the
Divine has refused us this grace,
and the earth its bounty.

After the announcement, the congregation dispersed. Members exited from the seven big doors of the hall into a long veranda and began putting on their shoes. Some members, at the time of entering the hall, had deliberately left one shoe outside one door and the other outside another to ensure that no one pinched the pair. This caused some confusion and crowding in the veranda. Even otherwise, after congregational meetings, members would hang around in the veranda, chatting and exchanging views. It was even more so on that particular day when the situation in the town was on everyone's mind. The vanaprasthi, after his impassioned discourse, continued to sit on the raised platform. His face was flushed and he still appeared to be agitated.

Just then some people were seen coming towards the hall from outside. They were important functionaries of another Hindu organization in town. They were soon followed by a group of six or seven Sikhs, representatives of the local gurdwara committee. They too had been invited to participate in the deliberations of the core group.

The secretary, a gaunt, wiry and very fiery person, gave a telling account of the deteriorating situation in the town, of the rumours that were rampant; he even spoke about the carcass of a pig found on the steps of a mosque and made a special mention of the fact that for the last several days, lathis, lances and other weapons were being stored in large quantities in the Jama Masjid. He then made a fervent appeal to give serious thought to the gravity of the situation and devise ways and means to combat it effectively.

'This place is not suitable for such deliberations' said the vanaprasthi, raising his hand. 'Let us move to some other place. It is only proper that the subject is discussed in a more suitable place.'

So saying, he got down from the *chowki* and proceeded towards the back of the hall. The members of the core group followed suit. Climbing up a winding satircase, the vanaprasthi led them into a small room on the first floor in which lay a few benches and some chairs.

After they had all sat down, the vanaprasthi continued in his sombre voice, 'Our primary concern is self-defence and safety. Everything must be done to ensure this. Every householder must immediately store in his house, a canister of linseed oil and a bag of coke and charcoal. Boiling oil can be poured over the enemy from the roof-top, red-hot coals can be flung...'

It was straight talk, members listened with close attention, but to some ears the suggestions, coming as they did from the mouth of a vanaprasthi, sounded rather odd. Most of the members present were elderly businessmen, a couple of them were lawyers or men in service. They were all anxious and concerned, no doubt, but not so agitated as the vanaprasthi. They were still not convinced that the situation had deteriorated to such an extent that people should store canisters of oil in their houses. They were largely of the view that even if a few untoward incidents did take place, the situation would eventually be brought under control by the administration.

One of the members, turning towards the secretary, said, 'How is it that our youth wing has gone into hibernation? You have put Shri Dev Vrat to all sorts of other jobs. It is absolutely necessary that our young men are activized. They must be given training in lathi-wielding. I would suggest that two hundred lathis be purchased today and distributed among them.'

At this, the chairman of the core group, a well-known merchant of the town and philanthropist, nodded his head and said, 'I shall pay for these two hundred lathis.'

'Oh how generous!' some voices were heard saying. The gesture of the chairman was received with high acclaim.

A voice was heard saying, 'This is the biggest shortcoming of the Hindu character. We think of digging a well only when we are thirsty. The situation is fast deteriorating; the Muslims have already stocked weapons in the Jama Masjid, whereas we are thinking now of buying lathis.'

To which the secretary was quick to retort, 'Our Youth Wing is fully active and alert. The matter has received our full attention. Vanaprasthiji himself is taking keen, personal interest in the activities. Besides the study of scriptures and performance of rites and rituals, vanaprasthiji is devoting heart and soul to the sacred task of Hindu unity. I, however, welcome the generous offer of our esteemed chairman. His generosity always helps us tide over many a difficult situation. But I assure you, no stone will be left unturned in our preparations.'

Just then an elderly gentleman, who had been listening with his chin resting on his walking stick, and both legs drawn up under him on the seat of the chair, said in his thin, squeaking voice, 'Brothers, all this is very fine. But I would say, first go and meet the deputy commissioner. Don't wait even to drink a glass of water. Just go and meet him. This nuisance is not going to end soon. Meet him and tell him that the life and property of the Hindus is in grave danger.'

'It is necessary to go to the deputy commissioner, no doubt, but Lalaji,' said the vanaprasthi, intervening, 'we have to depend on our own resources for our defence.'

'O Maharaj, give training to your young men in lathi-wielding. Teach them to handle lances and swords also. But first go and meet the deputy commissioner. He is the man in authority. Not a sparrow can flutter its wings without his consent.'

'But we cannot meet him today, it is Sunday.'

'I say, go to his bungalow and meet him there. This is just the right time to do so.'

At this a Sikh gentleman raised his hand and said, 'I am told that a deputation has already gone to meet the deputy commissioner.'

'What sort of deputation? Who are the members of the deputation?'

'It consists of some Congressmen and some members of the Muslim League.'

Silence fell on all sides.

'Of what use is such a delegation? A separate delegation of Hindus and Sikhs must wait upon the deputy commissioner and tell him of the doings of the Muslims. If you go arm in arm with the Muslims what can you tell the deputy commissioner? The whole thing has been spoiled by the Congressmen. They keep pampering the Muslims.'

'The mischief is spreading fast. I have heard that a cow too has been slaughtered and its limbs thrown outside the dharmashala of Mai Satto. I do not know if it is true, but it is strongly rumoured.' The face of the vanaprasthi grew red with anger and his eyes became bloodshot. But he restrained himself and did not utter a word.

'Streams of blood shall flow if a cow has been slaughtered,' said the secretary, greatly agitated.

Everyone was silent. They all felt that some big mischief was afoot and that the Muslims would not stop at committing any outrage.

Thereupon they began considering seriously how best to unite the Hindus and the Sikhs on a large scale and draw up plans for joint defence. 'What is the position of the Mohalla Committees?' someone asked. 'It is not easy to set up Mohalla Committees here. Muslims have infiltrated every mohalla. After the riots in 1926, two or three such mohallas did come up which had exclusive Hindu and Sikh population such as the Naya Mohalla, Rajpura, but in other mohallas the Muslims and Hindus are present in a mixed population. How can you form Mohalla Committees there?'

The question of mohalla committees received serious attention and was discussed for a long time. A subcommittee was formed to forge links with the Mohalla Committees wherever they existed forthwith and devise ways by which they could be activized at short notice, and quick contact established among them. A plan was drawn up to this effect.

'What about the alarm-bell that was installed in the Shivala temple?' An elderly gentleman said, 'I think it should be checked too.'

'Why, is there anything amiss?'

'We should assure ourselves that it is in working order. It shouldn't happen that when we need to ring the bell, we pull the rope and the rope snaps. We shouldn't leave things to chance.'

Shivala temple stood on a high mound right in the heart of the city. It was surrounded by a cluster of shops.

'Many years have passed since the bell was installed. It is time we got it overhauled.' The old gentleman was saying. 'It was way back in 1927 if I am not mistaken.'

'God forbid that it should have to ring again.' One of the persons suddenly exclaimed.

The remark infuriated the vanaprasthi.

'It is such thinking that has made cowards of Hindus,' he said. 'To be afraid of danger at every step. That is why we are given the derogatory nickname of *karars* and banias by the *mlecchas*.'

They all fell silent again. Everyone present held the same views, though they were agitated to a lesser degree than the vanaprasthi. They too believed that the Muslims were at the root of all mischief, but at the same time they did not want a riot to break out, for that would pose a serious danger to the life and property of both Hindus and Sikhs.

The deliberations went on for a long time. Matters concerning self-defence and measures for the prevention of a riot were discussed. Several suggestions were put forward concerning mohalla committees, formation of a volunteer corps to maintain contact with the Hindu and Sikh organizations of the town, provision for canisters of linseed oil, bags of sand, storage of water. During all these deliberations, like the refrain of a song, the elderly gentleman kept repeating his suggestion:

'O Brothers, first of all, wait upon the deputy commissioner; don't wait even to drink a glass of water, go and meet the deputy commissioner; as soon as this meeting ends, go straight to meet him. I too am willing to accompany you...'

It was finally decided that after the meeting, the secretary would stay back and through a peon circulate to all the members of the congregation the decisions concerning the storage of oil and coal. The secretary would establish contact with like-minded organizations, engage Gurkhas to serve as watchmen, speak to the secretary of the Sanatan Dharm Sabha to get the alarm-bell repaired and alert the Youth Wing. The other members of the core group except the vanasprasthi, would forthwith get into tongas and proceed to the bungalow of the deputy commissioner. The vanaprasthi, however, being a spiritual man, could not be expected to concern himself with mundane matters of the worldly householders.

On reaching home, the philanthropic chairman learnt that his son was not at home. It was a disturbing piece of information. He had a lurking fear that his young son might have been caught in the whirl of developments that were taking place in the town.

At the time when the chairman was returning home, Ranvir,

his son, was somewhere in the narrow dingy lanes of the town, walking with bowed head behind his preceptor, Master Dev Vrat, the organizer of the Youth Wing's *akhara*. The clatter of Master Dev Vrat's heavy boots resounded in the lanes, while in the heart of the fifteen-year-old Ranvir, eager aspirations rose like ripples as he walked behind him. Every pore in his body throbbed with expectations. He was to be examined today and if he came out successful, he would receive his initiation.

It seemed that the town consisted of only crooked lanes; there was hardly a straight lane anywhere. For some distance a lane would appear to be moving straight, but then, from somewhere, a slanting lane, bent, as it were, under the weight of single-storeyed houses on either side, would join it and the lane would lose its sense of direction. Sometimes it would appear to them as though they were walking in a blind alley and that they would soon face a wall, but just as they would reach the end they would find a narrow slit and the lane would open out in a different direction. Dev Vrat's heavy boots were familiar with all the lanes.

Ranvir was as yet only a boy, his eyes shone with simple trust and eager curiosity. He lacked that sobriety which was so necessary for the initiation test. But the lack of sobriety was amply made up for by his enthusiasm, his sense of dedication to the cause, and by a strong determination to lay down his life at Masterji's command.

When he was small, Master Dev Vrat used to tell Ranvir stories of valour. There was one of how Rana Pratap, for the first time, became conscious of his helpless situation when the only piece of bread left with him was eaten up by a cat. Ranvir would imagine Chetak, Rana Pratap's horse, galloping away on the hills on the town's outskirts. He would see Shivaji on horseback, poised on a high rock looking toward the Turkish hordes in the distance, or holding in his iron embrace the mleccha chief. It was Masterji who had taught him to tie different kinds of knots, to scale a wall with the help of a rope, about arrows that produced fire or rain on striking against their target.

'The fire-arrow, when shot, goes piercing through the air,

sparks flying from its head. Such fire-arrows were shot during the great Mahabharata war. The arrow would go flying at top-speed and eventually strike against the shield of a Kaurava warrior causing it to erupt in flames. It would continue coursing through the air—the arrow never fell to the ground; instead it flew round and round the entire battlefield and flames of fire leapt up from all sides. Its point had only to strike against the head-gear of a warrior, or merely grate against the canopy of a chariot and flames of fire would erupt. The fire-arrow turned back only after setting fire to the enemy's entire camp like a victorious warrior, with dazzling light shooting out of it as though it had set the whole firmament on fire.'

It was Masteriji who had told him that the technique to make a bomb or an aeroplane was inscribed in the Vedas. It was from his mouth too that Ranvir had heard about the powers of Yoga-Shakti. 'A man who has Yoga-Shakti can accomplish anything. Once, on the slopes of the Himalayas, a Yogiraj, already at the peak of his yogic powers, was in deep meditation when a mleccha tried to distract him. Mlecchas are unclean people—they don't bathe, don't even wash their hands after their toilet, eat from one another's plate, they have no regular hour of going to the toilet. The mleccha came and stood right in front of the yogi and stared hard at him. His abominable shadow had hardly fallen on the yogi when the yogi opened his eyes. The next moment, a ray of light shot out of the yogi's eyes, and the mleccha was reduced to a heap of ashes.'

The mleccha would appear before Ranvir's eyes again and again—in his neighbourhood, the cobbler who sat by the roadside was a mleccha, the tonga-driver who lived right opposite his house was a mleccha; Hamid, his classmate, was a mleccha too; the fakir who came to beg for alms was a mleccha; the family that lived in his immediate neighbourhood was also a mleccha family. It must have been one such mleccha who had gone to interfere with the *samadhi* of the Yogiraj, on the Himalayas.

Ranvir was the only one, from among the eight aspirants who had been chosen for the initiation test. Everyone was scared stiff of Master Dev Vrat who, in his heavy black boots, his khaki shorts, his loud thunderous voice and his menacing demeanour would strike terror in every heart. He could thrash anyone at any time. But this test was an undercover affair; only those young men knew anything about it who had passed the test and they would never divulge its contents to anyone.

The lanes looked deserted. It would sometimes appear to Ranvir as though the lane, at some distance was plunged in darkness, but on drawing near he would find that it was only a gaping dark hole in a wall, caused by the partial collapse of another wall.

Master Dev Vrat came to a halt opposite a discoloured, drab-looking door in a long wall. He pushed the door open. Ranvir's heart pounded with expectations, although when they had entered the dark lane, he had felt somewhat nervous. They stepped into a spacious courtyard on the other side of which stood a *kothari* with a tarpaulin curtain hanging over the door. A pile of bricks and stones lay on one side towards the left of the courtyard. The place sent shivers down Ranvir's spine. Masterji crossed the courtyard to the other side and knocked at the door. Someone inside coughed and the shuffling of feet was heard. 'It is I, Dev Vrat', Masterji called out. The door opened. In front of them stood an elderly Gurkha chowkidar, who folded his hands immediately on seeing Dev Vrat. It was dark inside the room. A charpai lay on one side. Against the right-hand wall stood a lathi. On the floor lay an upturned hookah. From a peg in the wall hung the chowkidar's khaki woollen overcoat and a bayonet.

Just then they heard the clucking of hens. Ranvir turned round and saw five or six white hens in a big basket.

Masterji put his arms round Ranvir's shoulders and led him into the backyard, a narrow slit of a place, across which stood the high wall of the adjoining house. The Gurkha followed, carrying a cackling hen in one hand and a big knife in the other.

'Ranvir, you slaughter this hen. This is your initiation test. You have to prove how mentally tough you are.' So saying, Dev Vrat guided Ranvir to the middle of the yard.

'An Arya youth must possess strength of mind, speech and action. Here, take this knife and get down to work.'

Ranvir felt as though an eerie silence had fallen on all sides. A pile of broken bricks and blood-stained feathers lay scattered about. Close by was a stone slab blackened with the blood of slaughtered hens.

'Sit down and put one foot of the hen tightly under your right foot.' Dev Vrat twisted the hen's wings together and after a while the hen lay still. All it could do was croak fiercely.

'Hold it tight,' he shouted and sat down by Ranvir's side, 'Now get going.'

Ranvir's forehead was covered with cold sweat and his face turned deathly pale. Masterji saw that the boy was feeling sick.

'Ranvir!' he shouted and gave the boy a stinging slap. Ranvir bent double and fell on the floor. His head was reeling. The Gurkha stood where he was. Ranvir looked as though he was about to burst into tears but his nausea abated.

'Get up, Ranvir,' said Masterji in a stern voice. Ranvir slowly rose and looked at Masterji with scared eyes.

'There is nothing difficult about it. Let me show you.'

He put the hen's foot under the heel of his heavy boot. The hen's eyes became glazed and then closed. Masterji held the neck of the hen in his left hand and moved the blade of the knife on it just once. Blood spurted out, some spilling on Masterji's hand. The hen's head fell on the floor, near his heavy boot, but Dev Vrat continued to press the hen's artery, a white little thing which struggled as if to free itself. The bird's body heaved and trembled, and became motionless. Feathers soaked in blood, lay on the floor close to Ranvir. Masterji flung the dead hen to one side and stood up. 'Go, fetch another one from inside,' he ordered the Gurkha.

Master Dev Vrat saw that Ranvir had vomited and was sitting with his head in both his hands, breathing hard. He felt like giving him another slap but restrained himself. A little later, he said, somewhat persuasively, 'You are being given another chance. How will a young man who cannot slaughter a hen, kill an enemy? You are being given another five minutes to prove your mettle. If you fail again you will not be inducted.' So saying Masterji turned round and went into the room.

Five minutes later when he came out, the hen lay convulsing on the floor near the wall, its blood, splashed all over the place. Ranvir was sitting on the ground with his right hand pressed tightly between his thighs. Masterji immediately guessed that the hen had pecked at his hand which meant that Ranvir had succeeded only in wounding the bird, not in beheading it. Unable to control the bird, he had used the knife on its wriggling head, and at the sight of blood spurting out of its neck, had forthwith, released the bird.

The wounded hen leapt up again and again in agony, splattering blood as it flew about. Blood spurted from its neck.

But Ranvir had passed the test.

'Stand up, Ranvir!' Masterji said, patting him on the back. 'You have the necessary strength of will, you have determination too, even though your hand is still not very steady. You have passed the initiation test.' He bent down, dipped his finger in the blood on the stone slab and put a teeka with it on Ranvir's forehead, thus inducting him into the category of the initiates.

Ranvir still stood in a daze, his head reeling. But on hearing Masterji's words, though vaguely, he felt gratified.

They had managed to procure all the necessary things except cauldrons that were needed for boiling oil. Everything had been arranged neatly on the window-sill —three knives, a dagger, and a kirpan. Ten lathis had been stacked in one corner of the room, each had a brass-head with spikes at the other end. On the wall hung three bows and arrows. Bodhraj could shoot an arrow lying down. He could take aim at a target by listening to a sound, or by looking at its reflection in a mirror. He could even cut a hanging thread into two with his arrow. He had pointed metal-heads fixed to his arrows, and expatiated on their special features to his fellow 'warriors'.

'If you rub arsenic on the arrow tip, it will become a poison-arrow; if you rub camphor on it, it will become a fire-arrow, that is, it will produce fire wherever it strikes; if you put blue vitriol on it, it will produce poison gas on striking its target.'

Dharam Vir had managed to filch his uncle's leather-belt which had empty cartridges fitted into it. That too was hanging on the wall. The room looked like an arsenal store, and in acknowledgement to that, Ranvir had put up a sign-board saying 'Arsenal' in bold letters right above the door.

But the most important of vanaprasthiji's instructions concerning the boiling of linseed oil had not yet been implemented. None of the young men had been able to secure a cauldron big enough to boil a canful of oil. A can of oil however had been obtained and it was lying against a wall on one side. Each representative of the youth committee had contributed four annas from his pocket money to meet part of its cost, the balance was to be paid to the provision store later. Now, the cauldron was the only hitch. Even the temple, where every other day congregational lunches took place, did not have one.

Suddenly Bodhraj thought of a way out. Why not get a cauldron from the halwai's shop?

'His shop is closed.'

'Where does he live?'

'He lives in Naya Mohalla.'

'Has anyone seen his house?'

Bodhraj had, but at that time, being the group leader, could not take upon himself so petty a job.

Ranvir suggested breaking into his shop.

Though the others did not feel comfortable with the idea, it was the only option in the present situation.

For a while the group leader stood looking at the roof, pondering over the situation. To be a group leader was no joke, it was a highly responsible job. The youngsters must not be seen breaking open a lock. The group leader was the son of a clerk who worked in the commissariat and was a first-year student in a local college. He was the only one in the group wearing an army shirt with two pockets, much to the envy of others.

'Yes, you may break open the lock, but the work must be done on the sly. No one must see you doing it. Who will volunteer himself for this work?'

'I shall do it,' said Ranvir stepping forward.

The group leader glanced at Ranvir from head to toe and shook his head.

'No. You are too short for the job. Your hand will not reach the lock if it is high up on the door.'

'The lock is in the middle of the door. I have seen it several times,' Ranvir replied somewhat boastfully, as was his habit, which often irritated the group leader. Nevertheless, he was a smart boy, ran very fast too, but he lacked discipline.

The group leader believed that Ranvir would procure the cauldron, come what may, but the boy could be lackadaisical in his approach, make some mistake, and thereby land the group into trouble.

'You have my permission. But you will not go alone. Dharamdev will go with you,' said the group leader in a decisive voice. 'No one must see you breaking the lock. Go at a time when there is no one around. And don't go together. Go separately, one by one.'

The halwai's shop stood at the road-crossing, on the other side of the ditch. As they approached the shop, Ranvir saw something moving behind the shop, something white, like a turban. Perhaps the halwai had come to open his shop. But what was he doing, standing at the back of his shop? Maybe it was not the halwai but someone else. Who could it be? Maybe a mleccha had come to loot the shop. Ranvir looked closely. It was none other than the halwai opening the backdoor of his shop.

There was no one around. Even otherwise, at that time of the day, except for an occasional hawker or a plying tonga, the road was empty. It was only in the evening that the road was frequented.

Both the boys went over to the shop. The plan was that while one would engage him in conversation the other would go in and pick up the cauldron.

'It won't be necessary to steal the cauldron. He will give it to us on his own. He is our Hindu brother,' said Ranvir's companion.

'What nonsense. Who do you think you are, you midget?'

Both boys moved towards the back of the shop. The door was open. The halwai seemed to have gone in.

It was dark inside the shop. A swarm of flies buzzed over the greasy shelves. The place smelt of stale samosas. Ranvir peeped in.

'Who is it?' A voice came from inside the shop. 'The shop is closed today.'

The two boys went in. The halwai was standing in a corner of the shop pouring a tin of fine wheat-flour into a bag. He was taken aback on seeing someone standing at the door.

'Come in. Please come in,' he said smiling. 'No sweetmeats have been made today. I thought I would take some of the provisions home. The situation in the town is not good. Sons, you too should not stir out on a day like this. It is better to stay indoors.'

'Pick up the cauldron,' Ranvir ordered Dharamdev.

Dharamdev moved towards the row of utensils lying against the wall.

'The cauldron is being taken away for the defence of the nation. You will get it back at the right time.'

The halwai did not understand what the boy was talking about.

'What is the matter? Who are you? What do you need the cauldron for? Is it for some wedding?'

Neither of the boys answered.

'Pick up the one in the middle. It is lying right in front of you,' Ranvir said in a commanding voice.

'Wait! What is all this?' shouted the bewildered halwai. 'Why are you taking my cauldron?'

'You will know at the right time.'

'That's no way of doing things,' exclaimed the halwai. 'You can't just pick up a thing and take it away. You have to take my permission for it. Who are you, anyway?'

Just then Ranvir put his hand in his shirt pocket and shouted fiercely. 'Are you refusing us?' He advanced threateningly towards him and struck him.

Before the halwai could open his mouth to say something, blood was streaming down his right cheek. Ranvir put his hand back into his shirt pocket. The halwai sat down on the floor, both hands covering his face, moaning in pain, drops of blood falling on the floor.

'No one should know about it or you will be finished off.'

Dharamdev had meanwhile carried the cauldron across the ditch towards the other side of the road. After a short pause, Ranvir too left the shop and walked a few paces behind Dharamdev. 'Killing is not difficult,' Ranvir thought, 'I could have killed this man easily. One has only to raise one's hand and it is done. It is fighting that is difficult, particularly when the other person stands up against you. To stab a man to death is far easier. It poses no problem, killing poses no problem.'

On entering the house, Dharamdev paused in the doorway 'Why did you hit him?'

'Why did he not carry out my order immediately? Why was he dilli-dallying?'

But Dharamdev's throat had gone dry and he stammered as he spoke. 'What if anyone had seen? What if the halwai had cried out for help?'

'We are not afraid of anyone. Let the fellow do his worst. You too may do your worst,' Ranvir said in a menacing voice and went towards the staircase.

7

'There must be something important, gentlemen, that has brought you to my residence, and that too on a Sunday,' Richard said smiling.

The peon lifted the bamboo curtain and members of the deputation entered the room one by one. Richard stood at the door, his eyes taking in each member as he went in. Then he too entered and sat at his table. Four of the men wore turbans while one had a Turkish cap on, and two were wearing Gandhi caps. The very composition of the deputation convinced him that it would not be difficult to handle them.

'What can I do for you, gentlemen?'

Members were pleased with the courtesy shown to them by the deputy commissioner. His predecessor was an insolent man who didn't believe in meeting anyone or discussing anything.

Richard had previously, with the help of police diaries, conducted an investigation on each member of the delegation. The unkempt, carelessly dressed man with the Gandhian cap must be Bakshi who had spent sixteen years in jail. The fellow sitting in a corner with a Turkish cap must be Hayat Baksh, a prominent member of the Muslim League. Mr Herbert, the American principal of a local college had also come along as a member of the deputation. And there was Professor Raghu Nath too, a lecturer in literature. He must have been included because he was on friendly terms with the deputy commissioner. The rest belonged to different organizations.

Looking towards Bakshi, Richard said, 'I am told there is some tension in the town.'

'It is precisely because of that that we have come to meet you,' Bakshi said. Bakshi looked anxious and agitated. Every occurrence since morning had been upsetting him. He had, on his own, called on the president of the Muslim League, but finding him indifferent, had decided to form a deputation and take it to the deputy commissioner. That too had not been easy. He had gone from house to house to get some local leaders together.

'Immediate action must be taken by the government to control the situation. Otherwise, my fear is that kites and vultures will hover for a long time over the town,' he said, repeating the expression which had been going round in his head.

The others were worried but not so agitated as Bakshi was.

Just then Richard and Raghu Nath's eyes met. The professor was the only Indian among them with whom Richard socialized, since he regarded him as a knowledgeable, well-cultivated person and since both were keenly interested in literature and ancient Indian history. Their eyes lit up, as if to say, 'We have been willy-nilly drawn by these people into mundane matters, otherwise we belong to a different world.'

Richard nodded his head and tapped the table with his pencil. 'The administration does not enjoy a good reputation with you gentlemen. I am a British officer, and you have little faith in the British government. You won't very much care to listen to what I have to say,' he said in an ironical vein and tapped the table with his pencil.

'But the reins of power are in the hands of the British government. And you represent British authority. To preserve law and order in the town is your direct responsibility,' Bakshi said, his chin trembling and his face turning pale in agitation.

'At this time, power rests in the hands of Pandit Nehru,' Richard said, in a low voice, a flicker of a smile playing on his lips. Then, turning to Bakshiji, he said, 'The British government is always to blame, whether you have differences with it or among yourselves.'

The smile still played on his lips. Then, restraining himself, as it were, he continued, 'But I believe, with our joint efforts we can tackle and resolve the situation.' He turned his eyes towards Hayat Baksh.

'If the police is alerted, the situation can be brought under control in no time,' said Hayat Baksh, 'despite the mischief played by the Hindus. You know what was found on the steps of the mosque?'

'How can you say that the Hindus had a hand in it?' shouted Lakshmi Narain, the philanthropist, jumping up in his seat.

For Richard the problem was resolving itself.

'Blaming one another will not serve any purpose,' he said persuasively. 'You gentlemen have obviously come to me with the intention of resolving the issue.'

'Of course we do not want rioting and bloodshed in the city,' said Hayat Baksh.

Lakshmi Narain felt isolated and angry. Had his colleagues been present, he wouldn't have had to face the Muslims all by himself. They would have supported him and told the deputy commissioner how weapons were being stored in the Jama Masjid, about the killing of the cow and a hundred other things. A deputation comprising exclusively of Hindus should have called on the deputy commissioner and apprised him of the real situation.

'If the police were to patrol the city and army pickets were set up at different places, there would be no rioting,' said Bakshiji.

Richard nodded his head, smiled and said, 'The army is not under my command, even though some army contingents are stationed in the cantonment.'

'The cantonment is as much under British rule as the city is,' said Bakshiji. 'If you set up army pickets, the situation will come under control in no time.'

Richard shook his head, 'The deputy commissioner has no such authority.'

'If you cannot set up army pickets you can at least clamp curfew on the town. That might help bring the situation under control. Police pickets can be set up, too.'

'Don't you think clamping curfew will make the people more nervous?' Richard said. He picked up a piece of paper from the rack and jotted down something on it, and then looked at his watch.

'The administration will certainly do whatever it can, gentlemen,' he said in a reassuring tone. 'But you are the prominent leaders of the town, your word carries more weight with the people. I believe a joint appeal from you addressed to the people to keep peace will have a salutary effect.'

Two or three heads nodded.

'Leaders of both the Congress and the Muslim League are present here. A joint Peace Committee can be formed forthwith, with the inclusion of Sardarji and start its work. The administration will do all it can to help you,' said Richard.

'We shall of course do that,' said Bakshiji, still agitated. 'But the situation is critical and calls for immediate action. Once rioting starts, it will be difficult to control. If an aeroplane were to fly over the town, it will serve as a kind of warning to the people. They will know that the administration is alert. This small measure itself will prevent a riot from breaking out.'

Richard again nodded his head, and jotted down something on the piece of paper. 'I have no authority over aeroplanes either,' said Richard, smiling.

'Everything is under your authority, Sahib, only if you want to exercise it.'

The man was becoming over-assertive, thought Richard, he must be shown his place.

'It was wrong of you gentlemen, to have come to me with your complaint. You should have addressed it directly to Mr Nehru or the Minister of Defence, Mr Baldev Singh. It is they who are running the government now,' said Richard laughing.

On seeing the attitude of the deputy commissioner some people fell silent, but Bakshi's agitation increased.

'We have been told that hardly an hour ago, your police officer, Mr Robert forcibly ejected a family of Muslim tenants from a house, due to which tension has mounted in the entire area. The house belonged to a Hindu landlord. I believe, in the prevailing situation, such an action need not have been taken.'

Richard knew about the incident. As a matter of fact, the officer had consulted him before taking action. And Richard had asked him to go ahead, since implementation of a law-court judgement was a matter of daily routine and there was no point in postponing it. But before the deputation, he pretended not to know anything about it. He jotted down something on the piece of paper and said, 'I shall make the necessary enquiries,' and again looked at his watch.

At this Herbert, the elderly American pincipal of the local Mission College, said in a persuasive voice, 'Keeping peace in the city is not a political matter. It is above all political considerations; it concerns all the people. We are required to rise above our party affiliations. The administration too has a vital role to play. We should all join hands and bring the situation under control. Without losing another minute we should go round the entire city and make a fervent appeal to the people to desist from fighting one another.'

Richard at once supported the proposal, adding, further 'I would suggest that we engage a bus, duly fitted with a loudspeaker. All you gentlemen should sit in it and go round the town, making a fervent appeal to the people to keep peace.'

Hardly had these words been uttered by Richard when strange, disturbing sounds were heard from the road outside.

'A Hindu has been done to death on the other side of the bridge,' someone was saying to the peon sitting outside. 'All the shops are closed.'

The members of the deputation sat up greatly perturbed. The deputy commissioner's bungalow was located far from the city. If the riot had actually broken out, it would be a problem reaching home. Then came the sound of a tonga rattling away at top speed on the road, followed by someone's running footsteps.

'It seems the trouble has started,' exclaimed Lakshmi Narain nervously and got up.

'Everything possible shall be done, gentlemen,' said Richard.

'Too bad if the trouble has started.'

One by one the members of the deputation stepped out of the room, lifting the bamboo curtain. The deputy commissioner accompanied them to the door.

'I can arrange for a police escort for you, gentlemen,' Richard said and turned towards the telephone lying on the table.

'You need not worry about us. It is more important that the trouble does not spread,' said Bakshiji, stepping out. 'There is still time. I would say, clamp curfew on the town.'

The sahib smiled, nodding his head.

On coming out of the bungalow all the members of the deputation felt confused. They exited from the gate and found themselves on the road without speaking to one another. They walked along, side by side, for some distance, then suddenly Lakshmi Narain and the Sardarji hurriedly crossed over to the other side of the road. Lakshmi Narain had taken off his turban and tucked it under his arm. The road here sloped down and went straight up to the bridge which separated the city from the cantonment.

Herbert, the principal, had come on his bicycle. He went slowly down the slope. For a moment he paused, with the intention of asking them as to when or where the meeting of the proposed Peace Committee would take place, but, seeing them so nervous, desisted from saying anything. How can a meeting take place now, if a riot has actually broken out?

Hayat Baksh strode briskly looking over his shoulder from time to time. All of them, in fact turned to look back now and again.

'I need not walk fast. It is a Muslim locality,' Hayat Baksh mumbled reassuring himself.

On the other side of the road, the Sardarji was walking fast. The bulky Lakshmi Narain was trailing nearly two yards behind. He was breathless and had to slow down to wipe the perspiration from his neck again and again. Bakshiji and Mehta stood undecided for some time at the gate, but then they too walked down the slope.

'Let us take a tonga, that will be much quicker,' suggested Mehta. Bakshiji stopped. A tonga was approaching from the other side. Hearing the patter of the horse's hoofs, Mehta waved his hand to stop it.

'Where do you want to go?' asked the young, swarthy tonga driver, reining in his horse.

'Take us to the tonga stand.'

'It will be two rupees.'

'What? Two rupees? That is scandalous,' Bakshi said out of sheer habit. The tonga began to move on.

'Let us take it, Bakshiji. This is no time to bargain.' And Mehta jumped in and occupied the back seat. 'Take us to the city. Make it quick.'

Seeing them get into the tonga, Lakshmi Narain turned and went towards them. But the tonga was already moving away. Lakshmi Narain stood in the middle of the road staring at them.

'That is how a Hindu treats another Hindu. This has been so since times immemorial. Such is their character.'

Hurt and angry, he went stomping back to the pavement.

By now the others were walking down the slope, each on his own. A little ahead of Lakṣhmi Narain walked Hakim Abdul Ghani, an old Congress activist. At some distance ahead of him was Sardarji, while Hayat Baksh was walking ahead of all of them. He had taken off his coat and hung it over his right shoulder.

Sitting down in the tonga, Bakshi had said, 'Let us ask them if anyone wants a lift,' to which Mehta's reply had been categorical. 'No one need be asked. How many can you accommodate? Let us get away from here as soon as possible. You can't ask one and not ask the other. We can even take a turn to the left and get out of sight.'

Bakshiji felt uneasy sitting in the tonga. It had been a bad decision getting into it. He felt irritated, as much with Mehta as with himself. 'Why do I allow myself to be persuaded by fellows like Mehta. The members of the deputation had all come together. That is how we should have gone back too.' Nevertheless there was nothing much he could do about it now.

As the tonga drove past Hayat Baksh he remarked jokingly, 'Running away, Bakshi? The karars that you are! You first stoke the fires and then run away!'

They were on informal terms with each other, having grown up together in the same town. They could share a joke.

Seing the Sardarji coming at some distance, Hayat Baksh remarked, 'Bakshiji has decamped! Such is the character of these people!'

But the Sardar continued walking with his head bent, without uttering a word.

Walking at the tail-end of the line, Lakshmi Narain felt that he should increase his pace and join Hayat Baksh. They were passing through a Muslim locality and it would be safer to walk alongside Hayat Baksh.

'What's the big hurry? Let's walk slowly,' he shouted.

Hearing his voice all three stopped. But Lakshmi Narain, taking long strides, went straight ahead, pattering his stick and joined Hayat Baksh.

'It will be awful if a riot breaks out in the city,' he said, as he joined Hayat Baksh.

Hayat Baksh had sensed Lakshmi Narain's motive. In a way it served Hayat Baksh's interest too, because the locality on the other side of the bridge was predominantly Hindu and Hayat Baksh had to go through it in order to reach his house. The fear was largely baseless because all these gentlemen were well-known figures of the town, and it would not have been easy for anyone to raise his hand against any of them.

Sitting in the tonga, Bakshi felt uneasy and irritated. Whenever he was overwhelmed by events or circumstances he would lose his equilibrium and clarity of mind.

'Kites and vultures shall hover over the town, Mehtaji,' he repeated peeping out of the tonga. 'Take it from me, kites and vultures...'

'We shall see what happens. The first thing is to reach the town.'

'What difference will that make?' said Bakshi irritably. 'We are already in deep trouble.'

Mehta was anxious but not as worked up as Bakshi.

'The deputy commissioner at least gave us a patient hearing. The previous DC was such a haughty fellow, he would not even talk decently with us.'

'What does he care? He doesn't give a damn,' Bakshi said irritably. 'What patient hearing has he given us?'

Bakshi's thoughts then turned towards something else.

'No one can be trusted,' said Mehta.

That further irritated Bakshi. 'If Muslims cannot be trusted, can Hindus be trusted?'

'Look Bakshiji, I shall tell you something. It may be a trivial thing, but for an intelligent person it is like a straw in the wind. This fellow, Mubarak Ali, who is a member of the District Congress Committee wears a khadi kurta and salwar, but his cap is not a Gandhi cap, it is a Peshawari fur cap. Muzaffar is the only Muslim Congressman who wears a Gandhi cap.'

Bakshi took his handkerchief and wiped the perspiration off his face.

'The Hindu Sabha people have formed Mohalla Committees but we have not done anything of the kind. We should at least have formed Peace Committees in every mohalla,' said Mehta, wiping his neck.

'You should be ashamed of yourself, Mehta,' Bakshi said, quivering with rage.

'Why? Why should I be ashamed of myself? What sin have I committed?'

'It is never good to try to ride in two boats at the same time. And that is exactly what you have been doing all along—one foot in the Congress and the other foot in the Hindu Sabha. You think nobody knows about it; well, everyone does.'

'Will you come to save my life when a riot breaks out?' said Mehta. 'The entire area on the other side of the ditch is inhabited by Muslims, and my house is on the edge of it. In the event of a riot, will you come to protect me? Will Bapu come to save my life? In a situation like this, I can only rely on the Hindus of the locality. The fellow who comes with a big knife to attack me will not ask me whether I was a member of the Congress or of the Hindu Sabha... Why have you gone dumb now? Why don't you speak?'

'You should be ashamed of yourself, Mehta. It is in such times that a man's integrity is put to test. You have gathered a lot of wealth and your brain is covered with thick layers of fat. If your house is located near the mohalla of the Muslims, is mine located in that of the Hindus?'

'It makes no difference to you. You are a sadhu, without a wife or family. What will a fellow gain by killing you?' Mehta said, getting excited. 'I told you to throw out Latif from the Congress organization. I can give you in writing that he has links with the CID. He gives information to the police about each one of us. You know this as well as I do. But you would not do a thing. You would go on feeding the snake in the grass. Then there is Mubarak Ali. He is always hobnobbing with the League fellows. Gets money out of us and out of the Muslim League. He has had a house built of pucca bricks. And yet you choose to turn a blind eye to it.'

'There are only a handful of Muslims in the organization. Shall we throw them out? Are you in your senses? If Latif is undesirable, does that mean everyone else is undesirable too? Is Hakimji who joined the Congress long before you did, undesirable? Is Aziz Ahmed undesirable?'

The tonga had by then reached the end of the slope and turned towards the bridge.

Across the bridge, on the right, the Islamia school, was closed. Very few persons or vehicles were to be seen on the road. A few persons stood in a knot in the school compound.

The other four members of the deputation were still walking down the slope. As Hayat Baksh passed by the offices of the Electric Supply Company, he met Maula Dad, standing by the roadside. Maula Dad worked as a clerk in the Electric Supply Company and was also a Muslim League activist.

'What have you achieved by going to the deputy commissioner? You had gone to meet him, hadn't you?'

'Hardly had we sat down when there was some noise outside and the meeting dispersed. Everyone got up and left. What news of the town?'

'Tension is mounting, they say. There has been some disturbance near Ratta. How is the situation there, at the back, from where you are coming?'

By that time Hakim Abdul Ghani and the Sardar also had arrived. After having walked separately for some distance, they had begun to walk together. Since Hakimji was a Congress Muslim, the Sardar had little hesitation in walking alongside him.

'A riot must not break out. It is an awful thing,' said Lakshmi Narain.

Maula Dad looked searchingly at Lakshmi Narain. 'If it were left to the Hindus, a riot would certainly break out. It is we Muslims who are putting up with all kinds of provocations.' His eyes fell on Hakimji and his temper rose. 'This dog of the Hindus too had accompanied you? Whom does he represent?'

Both fell silent. Pretending not to hear what Maula Dad had said, Hakimji, with his head turned, kept looking towards the bridge. But Maula Dad was exasperated. 'It is not the Hindu who is the enemy of the Muslims, it is the tail-wagging Musalman who goes after the Hindus and lives on the crumbs thrown to him.'

'Listen, Maula Dad Sahib,' Hakimji said patiently. 'You can call me by any names you like, but the most important question is that of the freedom of India, of freeing the country from the British yoke. Hindu-Muslim differences are not the primary question.'

'Shut up, you despicable dog,' shouted Maula Dad, his eyes turning red and his lips trembling.

'No, no, no, this is no time for an argument.'

Lakshmi Narain suddenly felt weak in the legs, but the elderly Hayat Baksh was there to control the situation.

'Move on, Hakimji, but your patrons have already gone in a tonga, leaving you in the lurch.'

Hakimji slowly moved away. The Sardar went along with him. But Lakshmi Narain kept standing wbere he was.

'Are you going home?' Maula Dad asked Hayat Baksh. 'Won't you come to the League Office?'

'I shall be there later. You go along.'

Maula Dad understood why Hayat Baksh had tagged Lakshmi Narain to himself. Putting his hand on his heart he said respectfully to Lakshmi Narain: 'Rest assured, Lalaji, as long as we are there, nobody dare touch even a hair on your head.'

Hayat Baksh and Lakshmi Narain too moved on.

By twelve noon, Liza leisurely walked towards the door opening in the veranda outside. Pushing aside the curtain, she looked out. Dazzling hot sun, like a shimmering sheet of glass covered the garden. Trembling vapour seemed to rise from the ground. It was already scorching hot. Liza pulled back the curtain.

As she passed by the fireplace, her eyes fell on a statuette in the middle of the mantelpiece. Some Hindu god, with a big paunch, red and white lines drawn across his forehead, sat there laughing. Liza felt sick. It looked so awfully ugly. Wherefrom had Richard picked it up?

She came into the large drawing room. With idols and statuettes all over the place, she felt as though everything around her had become lifeless, as though they were not statuettes but heads of the dead Buddha. It gave her the creeps. She felt suffocated in a house so stacked with books and statuettes. Wherever she went, she felt as though the Buddha heads were peeping at her through the corner of their eyes. Richard had only to go out of the house when these objects became dead-wood for her. And yet she had to spend the endlessly long day, in the company of these statuettes and piles of books. She couldn't take her eyes off them, even if she wanted to, as she went from one room to another. Inadvertently, she came and stood in front of a Buddha statue. Out of idle curiosity she pressed an electric button. Truly enough, Buddha's face lit up with a soft smile. She switched off the light. The smile vanished. She pressed the button again. The smile returned. But it also appeared as though the Buddha was eyeing her through the corner of his eyes. She immediately switched off the light.

Liza returned to her room. As she entered, she was greeted by a soft, tinkling sound. Right in front of the window, above the bedstead, hung a tiny brass bell. With every whiff of air, the tiny bell tinkled softly, as though wafting from far away. This sweet, musical sound could be heard throughout the day. It was a new addition to the house, brought by Richard from somewhere before Liza's arrival, to welcome her with.

Just then, a sharp sound suddenly fell on Liza's ears. She looked around but for some time could not see anything. Then her eyes fell on a lizard lying on her dressing table. It had apparently fallen from the wall, close to the electric lamp. It was in convulsions, gasping for breath. Then, suddenly, it stopped moving and lay still. It was dead. The hot summer caused lizards to die everyday. Despite its numerous spacious rooms, the bungalow in which they lived was an old one, built at a time when the British rule had just struck roots in the Punjab.

Two years earlier when they were living in a different bungalow, a snake, nearly a yard-and-a-half long, had once crawled out of the servants' quarter. It would sometimes get under the cots, or would be seen slithering along the wall in the veranda. Liza had got so scared that for several days after that, she would not open the window leading into the veranda. Nor would she open her wardrobe, fearing that a cobra might be lying curled in it. Within days after that incident, she had left for England.

Liza pressed the button of the call bell and came out into the veranda.

Before coming to India, Liza had made many plans. She would collect specimens of village handicrafts, travel extensively, practise photography, get herself photographed sitting on the back of a tiger, go about wearing a sari. But now it seemed to her that she was destined to endure the scorching heat, imprisonment in a big bungalow, never-ending days, Buddha statuettes, lizards and snakes. Life outside the bungalow was no less monotonous. There was the British officers' club no doubt, but in the hierarchical relationship that existed there—the overassertive commissioner's wife, about whom it was said that she exercised the commissioner's authority more than the commissioner himself, the Brigadier's wife who socialized with other officers' wives strictly on the basis of seniority, while Richard was comparatively a junior officer—Liza felt ignored. Though there were parties every other day and dance parties every Saturday night, the days seemed interminably long. It was then that she got into the habit of drinking beer. Getting bored with going from one room to another the whole day long, she found in beer the only way to keep off boredom.

'You must have German blood in your veins that makes you so fond of beer,' Richard would say in jest. But Liza's addiction increased with time. Sometimes, when Richard would come home for lunch, he would find Liza sprawled on a sofa, her eyes swollen. Amidst hugs and kisses and hiccups, she would swear again and again that she would give up the habit. But the next day again she would find it impossible to pass time.

This time however, she had returned with a more positive frame of mind. She had come fully resolved to take interest in Richard's activities, both administrative and otherwise, as also in those relating to public welfare.

She tried to figure out for herself the kind of work the Association for Prevention of Cruelty to Animals was doing and how she could associate herself with it. 'What assignment should I take in it?' Liza was thus ruminating when the khansama came into the room and Liza was strongly tempted to tell him to get her some beer, but she desisted. The khansama was a new recruit and did not know anything about her weakness. 'What sort of assignment will it be? Shall I be required to go from street to street, getting stray dogs and old horses shot one by one? Or, being the first lady of the district, be only a presiding officer and the actual work will be done by the underlings?'

Liza was in a queer state of mind. There was the horror of boredom, but there was also the consciousness of being the wife of the virtual ruler of the district with a huge bungalow to live in and a retinue of servants and waiters; there was insufferable boredom, but there was also the strong sense of personal importance as the mistress of the house.

'Memsahib!'

The khansama stood before her, waiting for her orders.

'There is a dead lizard on the dressing table in my room. Go and remove it.'

'Huzoor!' said the khansama, then bowed and left.

Liza walked over to the window opening into the veranda. On lifting the curtain she was again faced with the glaring light of the midday sun. But she also noticed Richard's office-clerk sitting behind a small table on one side of the veranda. He was sorting out letters—a dark-complexioned young clerk with glistening white teeth who would say 'Yes sir' twice to every sentence uttered by Richard, always shaking his head sideways. On seeing him Liza smiled. The babu knew English. It was always interesting to talk to him. Liza came over into the veranda by way of the dining room.

'Babu!' Liza shouted, in the same way as Richard did, and sat down in a chair near the door.

The babu shut his file and came running.

'Yes sir, yes madam!'

Besides his dark complexion and glistening white teeth it seemed as though every limb of his body had been screwed into his torso, because one or the other of his limbs would always hang down to one side with a jerk. Sometimes it would be his right shoulder that would bend down or the left knee while his mouth would always remain open.

'You Hindu, babu?' 'Yes, Madam,' the babu replied somewhat embarrassed. Liza was pleased with her discovery. 'I guessed right!' 'Yes, madam!'

Liza stared at him. But the longer she looked, the more

confused she became. On what basis had she surmised that he was a Hindu? Surely not on the basis of the clothes—coat, a pair of trousers and necktie that he was wearing. She became contemplative. What are those signs by which a Hindu can be recognized? She got up, and putting out her hand searched through his hair for that distinctive something that distinguished a Hindu from a Muslim.

The babu became nervous. A man of nearly thirty years of age, he had been working as a stenographer in the deputy commissioner's office for the last ten years. Liza was the first woman, and that too the wife of a deputy commissioner, who spoke to him with such familiarity. The wives of other deputy commissioners had always been curt and indifferent towards him.

At the far end of the veranda, near the passage that led to the kitchen, stood the khansama, the gardener and the cook, all looking towards them.

'No, it isn't here!' Liza said.

The babu again became nervous. The faint smile that had appeared on his lips vanished.

'You are no Hindu. You told a lie.'

'No, madam, I am a Hindu, a Brahmin Hindu.'

'Oh, no. Where is your tuft, in that case?'

There was danger of a riot breaking out in the city and he had, with great difficulty, managed to reach the office. He had felt somewhat reassured by the way the lady was treating him, and a broad smile appeared on his swarthy face, showing his glistening white teeth.

'I have no tuft, madam.'

'Then you are no Hindu,' Liza said, laughing, shaking her forefinger at him. 'You told a lie!'

'No, madam, I am a Hindu.'

'Take off your coat, babu.' Liza commanded.

'Oh, madam!' said the babu acutely embarrassed.

'Take it off, take it off. Hurry!'

Smiling, the babu took off his coat.

'Good. Now unbutton your shirt.'

'What, madam?'

'Don't say "What madam!" Say, "I beg your pardon, madam". All right. Unbutton your shirt.'

The babu stood perplexed. Then putting his hand under his necktie, he undid all the three buttons.

'Show me your thread.'

'What, madam?'

'Your thread.'

'What madam?'

'Show me your Hindu thread.'

The babu understood what the lady meant. The Memsahib was asking about the sacred thread, the *yagyopaveet*. The babu was not wearing any. After passing his matriculation examination he had cut off the tuft on his head, and on joining the intermediate class, had cast off the sacred thread.

'I am not wearing any thread, madam.'

'No thread? Then you are no Hindu.'

'I am a Hindu, madam. I swear by God I am a Hindu.'

He was getting nervous again.

'No, you are no Hindu. You told a lie. I shall tell your boss about it.'

The babu's face suddenly turned pale.

'I tell you sincerely, madam, I am a Hindu. My name is Roshan Lal,' he said, as he buttoned his shirt and put on his coat.

'Roshan Lal? But the cook's name is Roshan Din and he is a Musalman.'

'Yes, madam,' the babu replied. It was difficult for him to explain the difference.

'He is Roshan Din, madam. I am Roshan Lal. I am a Hindu. He is a Muslim.'

'No. My husband told me you people have different names.'

Then, raising her forefinger, she said in a mock-angry voice, 'No, babu, you told a lie. I shall tell your boss.'

The babu's throat became parched and his heart started pounding. 'There is trouble brewing in the city. It may be that the lady's questions have something to do with it. What does the memsahib want?'

Suddenly Liza felt bored and sick at heart.

'Go babu. I shall tell your boss everything.'

The babu picked up his file from the floor and went towards his table.

'Babu!' Liza shouted again.

The babu turned round.

'Where is your boss?'

'He is in his office, madam. He is very busy.'

'Go. Get out of here... You and your boss!' she almost shrieked.

'Yes, madam!' and the babu turned away, trembling in every limb.

As the babu left, her playful mood had turned into intense disgust. An acute sense of loneliness and desolation came over her. The babu, walking away with his shoulders bent, looked to her a slimy creature. How can Richard work with such people day in and day out? She heaved a long, painful sigh and turned to go in.

8

Each community in the town pursued a trade that was exclusive to them. Textile business was mostly in the hands of Hindus, business in leather goods was owned by Muslims; transport was run by Muslims, and grain merchants were Hindus. Petty jobs and professions, however, were pursued by both Hindus and Muslims.

The Shivala market was doing brisk business. Looking at it, no one could say that there was tension in the town. The goldsmiths' shops were crowded with village women in burkas buying or placing orders for silver jewellery. In front of Hakim Labh Ram's dispensary two Kashmiri Muslims, pestles in hand, were pounding away at medicinal herbs, their noses covered with pieces of cloth; the hunchbacked halwai had, as usual, a crowd of customers at his shop; Santram, the vendor had arrived with his pushcart, punctually at one o'clock, as was his wont, and was slowly moving through the goldsmiths' market towards the Shivala Bazaar, serving half a *chhatank* or more of halwa on a pipal leaf to every customer on the way. At the Shivala Bazaar, the tailor Khuda Baksh and his two brothers were Santram's daily customers, besides many others.

The general atmosphere was calm and stable. There was the usual traffic on the roads. The tension caused by the incident that morning had partly been diffused and partly submerged. Opposite Khuda Baksh's shop at the corner of the lane, a municipal worker was standing on a ladder cleaning the chimney of the oil lamp fixed in the wall and replenishing it with oil.

Every activity in the business of life appeared to be moving as rhythmically as part of a symphony. When Ibrahim the pedlar selling scents and oils with the bag on his back full of bottles big and small and another bag hanging from his shoulder, went from lane to lane shouting about his wares, it appeared as though his movements too were in keeping with that rhythm. So were the movements of the women with their earthen pitchers going to the water-taps, tongas plying on the roads, children going to school. Every activity gave the impression of having combined to create an inner harmony to which the heart of the town throbbed. It was to the same rhythm that people were born, grew up and became old, that generations came and went. This rhythm or symphony was the creation of centuries of communal living, of the inhabitants having come together in harmony. One would think that every activity was like a chord in a musical instrument, and if even one string snapped the instrument would produce only jarring notes.

It cannot be said that the even tenor of the town's life was never disturbed. In recent years there had been the ebb and flow of many a current and cross-current. During the days of the freedom struggle, every now and then, the town would shake under the impact of surging emotions and movements. Then there were disturbing developments. Once every year, on the occasion of Guru Nanak's birthday, a Sikh procession would be taken out and tension would grip the city. Will the procession pass in front of the Jama Masjid, with its band playing or will it take some other route? There was the fear that even a stray stone flung on the procession might lead to a communal riot. Similarly, on the occasion of Muharram, tension would mount when Muslims would take out tazias, beat their bare chests and shout 'Ya Hussein! Ya Hussein!', perspiration dripping from their bodies, and pass through the streets of the town. But soon after, the atmosphere would cool down and life would regain its even tenor, linking itself once again with the inner rhythm. Once again its innate cheerfulness would return.

At the shop of Khuda Baksh the tailor, Sardar Hukam Singh's

wife was complaining loudly: 'O Bakshe, when will you ever learn to keep your word? Why aren't my clothes ready? Why must I have to come to your shop again and again?'

Khuda Baksh smiled. He was familiarly addressed as Bakshe by the women of Hindu and Sikh families of the town. His shelves were heavily stacked with bundles of unstitched cloth, meant primarily for wedding dresses.

'Bibi, you never bothered to send me the required cloth in time. Didn't I keep reminding you of it throughout winter? You never bothered. After all it takes time to stitch clothes. God has given me only two hands, Bibi, not sixteen.'

'What is the man saying? Throughout winter?'

'Why, wasn't your daughter betrothed fifteen days after the wedding of Shiv Ram's son? Isn't that so? Which month was it?'

Hukam Singh's wife laughed. 'He even remembers the dates. Now tell me clearly—when will my daughter's suit be ready?'

'Which is the auspicious day, Bibi, of the wedding?'

'Look at the fellow. He knows the day of the girl's betrothal but not her wedding day.'

'Don't I know? It is on the twenty-fifth of this month. Isn't that so? Today is fifth. Have no fear, the suit will be ready on time.'

'Nothing doing. Tell me the exact date. Don't I know you? On the wedding day itself you will make us run to your shop again and again. Didn't this happen on my Vidya's marriage? The wedding party was already on its way and I was sending my man again and again for her gold-embroidered suit. Tell me the exact date when the suit will be ready.'

She had not yet finished talking when someone standing behind her threw a packet of light-green silken cloth and a spool of gold-thread border into Bakshe's lap.

'Get the cloth measured, Bakshe, and if more cloth is required get it in my account from Budh Singh's shop.'

It was another lady customer. Bakshe wet a corner of the cloth with his tongue and, taking his pencil from behind his right ear, put a mark on it and threw the packet and the spool on to the shelf by his side. The whole almirah was full of bundles and packets meant for wedding dresses.

'Yes, yes, the suit will be ready. I shall deliver it at your house myself.'

'You only know how to talk. If this time you fail me I shall never set foot in your shop again.' And Hukam Singh's wife turned and left the shop.

As she turned away, Khuda Baksh's eyes fell on the wall of the Shivala opposite. He noticed some movement there. He looked intently. A man was standing on top of the wall doing something. It was the Gurkha watchman. What was he doing there? On the other side of the wall was the old temple whose shining dome could be seen from far and near. A bell had been installed on top of the wall and the Gurkha watchman appeared to be cleaning it.

'What is he doing that for?' Khuda Baksh said to one of his assistants, who sat working on a sewing machine close by.

'The bell is being repaired, it seems,' the shop assistant answered.

'God forbid that it should ring again,' Khuda Baksh exclaimed. Both fell silent.

The bell had been put up after the communal riots of 1926. Its weather-beaten metal was no longer as bright as it used to be. Much of the plaster on the wall too had cracked and fallen off. Khuda Baksh was then a young man of twenty or so, madly interested in body-building exercises, and had just joined his father in the tailoring business. It was in those very days that the bell had been installed. Khuda Baksh was now an elderly man; there was hardly a wedding in the town for which his services as a tailor were not sought after. The man perched on the wall too was the same Gurkha chowkidar—Ram Bali by name—who had originally installed the bell. After the riots, his services had been retained because of his alertness, integrity and spirit of service. Wrinkles had since appeared on his face and his hair had greyed. But as a watchman he was still as alert as he used to be.

A low ringing sound emanated from the bell. Khuda Baksh's

eyes again turned towards the wall. The Gurkha chowkidar was tying a new rope to the bell. The pulley had been oiled and the bell was once again shining and ringing as before.

'I tremble when I hear that sound,' Khuda Baksh said. 'The first time the alarm bell was rung when the grain market had been set on fire and half the sky was covered with the glow of its flames.'

Perched on the wall, the Gurkha was still rubbing the bell with a duster so as to bring out its shine, as though for some festival or an auspicious day. A new, white rope was now hanging by its side.

From the wall, Khuda Baksh's eyes turned towards the neighbouring goldsmith's shop where an elderly villager and his wife were persuading their young daughter to buy a pair of earrings.

'Why don't you take it if it has caught your fancy? Only hurry up. We have a lot else to do before going back to the village.'

The girl's eyes were shining. She would put the earrings to her ears again and again and show them to her mother.

'How do they look on me, Ma?'

She was unable to make up her mind.

Khuda Baksh's eyes again went back towards the wall of the temple. The old watchman was now getting down from the wall.

'Ya Allah!' muttered Khuda Baksh and turned his face away.

It was a common practice at Fazal-din, the *nanbai*'s shop, in the afternoons, when the hot sun was on the decline and there was little work to do, for friends from here and there to gather for a leisurely chat. With the hookah going around, all subjects under the sun would be discussed.

To begin with, the discussion had centred round the morning incident that the whole town was talking about. But then it branched out to other topics. Old Karim Khan was rambling on how impossible it was for an ordinary man to fathom what was in the mind of the ruler. 'The man in authority takes a long view of things; each one of his actions reflects his far-sightedness. It is beyond the ken of an ordinary man to see what the man in authority can see.'

'Musa said to Khizr one day,' continued Karim Khan, "Please take me on as your pupil..." Listen Jilani, listen attentively. This is a very instructive story. . . Now Musa was much younger in age, but he was aspiring to become a seer, a prophet. Till then he had not become one. Khizr was already a prophet. You are following me, aren't you? And was older in age too. Everyone held him in very high esteem.' Karim Khan went on. There was a glint of a smile in his eyes. Whenever he laughed, he would slap his thigh and all those sitting around would smile too.

'So, one day, Musa said to Khizr, "Make me your pupil" and Khizr replied "All right, I shall make you my pupil, but on one condition."

"What is that?" asked Musa.

"That you will keep your mouth shut at whatever I do. You will not utter a word."

"I agree," replied Musa.

'And so Khizr took him on as his pupil. Now Khizr wanted to impart to him an important lesson. What was that lesson? The lesson was: It is God Almighty alone who sees everything. It is not given to us humans to see everything. We may rack our brains and go into cause and effect but to no purpose. It is God who is all-seeing; it is God the Merciful who alone is omnipotent. And Khizr said, "You will not utter a word. I may do anything, say anything, and you will keep your mouth shut."'

Karim Khan had passed on the hookah and Jilani was now puffing away at it. The afternoon was on the decline, the water-carrier had already sprinkled water on the ground in front of the shop, the odour of wet earth filled the air, the traffic on the road had eased, and only occasionally a man would be seen going towards the Jama Masjid for his afternoon prayer.

'So, God bless you,' continued Karim Khan. 'The next day, Khizr set out on a journey to the next village, and Musa went along with him. Later on Musa became a great seer, a great prophet, but at that time he was only a pupil of Khizr. Now listen, Jilani. Are you listening? It is a very instructive story. So, both set out. On the way they came to a river. They found a boat tied to the river-bank, it was used by people to cross the river. Both sat down in the boat and the boatman began to row them across. After a little while Musa saw that Khizr was making a hole in the bottom of the boat. It was a brand new boat, probably bought only the day before, and here was Khizr boring a hole in its bottom. He finished boring one hole and started drilling another. Musa cried out, "What in God's name are you doing? The boat will sink and we shall both be drowned."

'Khizr put his forefinger to his lips making a sign to him to keep quiet. Musa was extremely nervous, because the boat was getting flooded with water, but he kept his peace, since he had given his word to Khizr. After some time Khizr put stoppers in each one of the holes he had made, but by then the bottom of the boat had been badly damaged. Reaching the other side, both of them stepped out of the boat and, God be praised, resumed their journey.

'They had walked a little distance when they saw a little boy playing on the ground. As they passed by, Khizr picked up the boy and without a word, wrung his neck and strangled him to death. "What?" shrieked Musa. "You have put an innocent child to death!" But Khizr put his finger to his lips, ordering him to keep quiet.

'"How can I keep quiet?" shouted Musa. "You have twisted the neck of a little child, and you want me to keep quiet! You did not even know him. Never before have you set foot in this village. How had this innocent child offended you?" Musa was deeply troubled. In reality he too was a prophet, only a prophet in the making.' Karim Khan said, shaking his head, 'Now, God be praised, both of them again resumed their journey. After covering some distance, they passed through a village. On reaching the other end of the village they came across a dilapidated boundary wall. Musa jumped over to the other side at one go, but as he turned round he saw Khizr standing by it, picking up the bricks lying on the ground, one by one, and putting them on the wall, as though repairing it.

'Musa turned back. "Sir, you put to death the little boy who had merely opened his eyes on the world, and here you are, repairing an old, dilapidated wall. What is the matter? I can't make head or tail of what you are doing." Khizr again put his forefinger to his lips to indicate to Musa to keep quiet. Musa again fell silent.

'They went further, on and on, till they came to a garden in which, under the shade of a big tree, bubbled a lovely spring. Both washed their hands and feet and sat down to rest. Khizr said:

'"Listen, my dear. You had strongly protested when I bore holes into the bottom of that boat. Well, the fact of the matter is that the ruler of that village is a tyrant. For his own merry-making he takes away the boats of poor people. I thought if I made holes in the bottom of the boat, his men will not carry it away and the boatman will not be deprived of his livelihood."

'Musa was listening with rapt attention. "But why did you kill that innocent child?" he asked.

'"Well," Khizr said "That boy was a bastard, born of sin, the progeny of a cruel and wicked man. I could foresee that when he grew up, he too would be a heartless, vicious man, a torment for innocent people. Now tell me, was my conduct right or wrong?"

'Musa fell to thinking, his head bowed.

'"Why did you repair that broken-down wall? For whose benefit did you do that?"

'And Khizr's reply was:

'"There is an explanation to that also. Under that wall lies buried a treasure, a fabulous treasure. But the villagers know nothing about it. They are poor, needy people. I wanted to help them. While ploughing their fields when they come upon the wall, they will find it an impediment, an obstacle in their way and will, one day, pull it down and throw the bricks out of their fields. They will then discover this treasure which will make them wealthy and prosperous. They will then have bread to eat and clothes to wear. Now tell me, how was I wrong in what I did?"'

Having narrated the parable, Karim Khan turned his eyes

towards his listeners, one after the other and said, 'The moral of the story is: a ruler can see what you and I, ordinary folk, cannot see. The British ruler has all-seeing eyes, otherwise how can it be possible that a handful of firanghis coming from across the seven seas should rule over so big a country? The firanghis are very wise, very subtle, very far-sighted...'

'Of course, of course!' said many of the listeners, nodding their heads.

Nathu too was sitting at the nanbai's shop, a glass of tea before him and in his hand a piece of dry rusk, which he would dip into his tea and nibble at, bit by bit. He too had been listening to Karim Khan's story and it gave him a sense of reassurance. Ever since he had come out of that despicable hole, he had been wandering from one street to the other. He would prick up his ears every time he heard people talking about the pig. Sometimes he would think that people were talking about some other pig, and not the one he had killed. Nevertheless his heart would miss a beat. In the nanbai's shop too, they had earlier been talking about the pig. But the narration of the elderly gentleman had given him considerable relief. If a riot did not break out, the incident would begin to look trivial. Since the ruler was far-sighted and alert, nothing untoward would happen.

Nathu again put his hand on his pocket to feel the currency note lying in it. The crisp note rustled. That pleased him. It was nice of Murad Ali to have paid the entire amount in advance. Even if he had put an eight-anna piece on the palm of his hand, saying that the rest would be paid later, he couldn't have refused, the poor skinner that he was. Since Murad Ali had been a man of his word, he too was expected to stand by him. But he had run away from that filthy hole; unmindful of Murad Ali's clear instructions that he should wait for him there. But it was so suffocating in that room. On reaching the town, however, when he found everyone talking about the pig his heart sank.

Nathu had been feeling extremely restless. The more nervous he became, the more confused he felt. He could not talk to anyone. He had been tricked. Using the veterinary surgeon as an alibi,

Murad Ali had got the pig slaughtered by him, and got it thrown outside the mosque. But who could tell if it was the same pig? He had not seen the carcass on the steps of the mosque. What if people came to know that he was the man who had killed the pig? At times he wanted to go home and shut himself in. At others he felt like just knocking about the streets, from one lane to the other. There were other thoughts too that oppressed him. No, he wouldn't go home. When night fell, he would go to Motia, the prostitute. If she asked for one rupee, he would pay her five. He would pass the whole night with her.

The whole day passed thus, wandering about the streets, but when evening fell he suddenly began to miss his wife. Had he been in his colony he would have been sitting and chatting with his fellow-skinners, smoking his hookah. 'No I shall go home' he suddenly said to himself. 'I'll bathe, change my shirt, make my wife sit by my side and talk to her. As soon as I reach home I shall take her in my arms, I won't even mention the name of Murad Ali; it is not necessary to tell her anything; no need to talk about that hateful business. It is only when I rest my head on her bosom that I shall have peace of mind. If I go to a prostitute, she will talk nastily, even abuse me. My wife is a quiet kind, she will give me comfort and courage. Instead of wasting money on the prostitute I will buy something for my wife. She will be pleased. She will say, "Why did you have to bring anything for me? I have everything." She never makes any demands.' He felt the warmth of her body in his close embrace, despite the distance that lay between them. He felt as though his mental anguish was ebbing out. It is only to one's wife that one turns in moments of pain; she alone can relieve him of his mental suffering. She is blessed with infinite patience, her bosom is brimming with love.

It was smoky inside the nanbai's shop. On the two benches lying outside, sat two load-carriers cross-legged on each bench eating their meal out of tin plates. Dipping their morsels of naan into the plate of lentils they ate hungrily. The water-carrier was again sprinkling the road.

Suddenly the sound of a drumbeat was heard from far away. The porters turned their heads towards the sound. The drum was heard closer now. People sitting inside the nanbai's shop fell silent; some of them came out.

'What is it?'

'Some announcement, it seems,' someone answered. Soon enough, a tonga appeared with the tricolour fluttering on its top. Someone sitting inside was beating away at the drum. The tonga came and stopped right in front of the nanbai's shop. A man, sitting by the side of the tonga-driver, stood up. He began to make the announcement by first reciting a couplet, the purport of which was:

'Pray, think for once of your country. Calamity is knocking at your door, and confabulations are going on high above, plotting to bring about your ruin.

'Fellow countrymen, this is to inform you that a public meeting, under the auspices of the District Congress Committee will take place this evening at six o'clock sharp, in Ganj Mandi, in which the efforts of the British rulers to disrupt India's struggle for freedom through their perfidious policy of divide and rule will be fully exposed, and a fervent appeal will be made to all the citizens to preserve peace and tranquillity in the city at all costs. Citizens are requested to attend the meeting in large numbers.'

On the back seat of the tonga sat the Jarnail with a big drum between his knees. It was Shankar who had stood up to make the announcement. He sat down in his seat. The drumbeat was resumed and the tonga moved away.

As the tonga left, one coolie said to the other, 'I was carrying a babu's load from the Ganj Mandi when the babu said, "Azadi is coming. India will soon be free." I laughed and said, "Babuji, what is that to me? I am carrying loads now and shall continue carrying them then."' And he burst out laughing, revealing the bright-red gums over his teeth. 'Our lot is to carry loads,' he repeated laughing.

An elderly man with a beard, sitting inside the shop said, 'Has that rascal been arrested or not who defiled the mosque? The swine! May his body be eaten up by worms, limb by limb.'

'What happened was awful!'

At this Karim Khan, the jolly old man with a twinkle in his eyes, said solemnly, 'It is said in the Holy Book, "Man's crops are standing by my orders; all man's schemes work by my orders; without my command, standing crops shall wilt and perish, floods shall inundate the lands, causing havoc to city after city." Everything is in God's hands. Every task is accomplished by His divine will. His and His alone will be done.'

People sitting around nodded their heads. The hookah continued to do its rounds. Outside the shop, one of the two coolies burst into song:

O why are you bending so low.
To stare at the folds of my salwar!

It was the same coolie who, a little while earlier, had been laughing and reproducing the dialogue he had had with the babu.

Nathu envied the man for his carefree, happy-go-lucky temperament.

There were again some stirrings on the road. Pedestrians on their way stopped and stepped aside, their eyes turned towards the Jama Masjid nearby.

'The Pir of Golra Sharif is here!' Someone standing by the roadside said to the nanbai, and putting his hand on his heart waited for the Pir Sahib.

The nanbai too stood up. All those sitting inside the shop came out and devoutly stood waiting for the Pir sahib's arrival.

A tall, bearded man appeared. He was dressed in a long, black robe and had numerous necklaces of large beads round his neck. His long, flowing hair fell on the nape of his neck from under his turban. He had a bright, pious face and in his hand was a rosary. He was surrounded by a band of devoted followers.

The nanbai went and stood in the middle of the road, his head bent and his hands on his thighs. As the pir put out his left hand, the nanbai touched both his eyes to it one by one, and then putting his right hand on his heart continued to stand with his head bowed. The pir raised his hand a little, and without uttering a word moved on. Almost everyone standing by the roadside went up to him, put the pir's hand to his eyes and received his blessing.

'He is not a pir, he is a sage!' said the nanbai coming back into his shop. 'What radiance! What a glowing forehead!'

Among the customers, some came back into the shop, while some others left for their homes. The Pir sahib was now the topic of discussion inside the shop.

'He is a pir with very high spiritual attainments. He can read a person's mind merely by looking at him,' the nanbai said. Then, turning towards those who were sitting inside the shop, said, 'I once went on a pilgrimage to Golra Sharif. As I stood in his holy presence, he said to me, "Pick up some grains from that heap. What are you looking at me for?" From the heap of grains that lay on the ground in front of him, I bent down and picked up a handful, at which the Pir sahib remarked, "Is that all? Only a hundred and seventy grains? You could have picked up more." Amazed, I sat down and counted them. Not a grain more, not a grain less than a hundred and seventy.'

'He can cure any disease,' remarked Karim Khan. 'My grandson, now a grown-up lad by God's grace, when only a small child, developed mumps. Both his cheeks were swollen. Someone advised me to take the child to Golra Sharif, and so I did. As I stood in his presence, the Pir sahib asked me to put down the child before him. He picked up a big knife lying by his side and touched the child's cheeks twice with it. Then, putting his right hand to his mouth, he spat on it, and smeared the sputum on the child's cheeks. Just that, and asked me to take away the child. I made my obeisance and left. By the time we reached home the swelling had subsided and the child's fever was gone.'

'Holy men are blessed with healing powers. Near here, in Masiadi, there is a Baba Roda—the bald sadhu—he too has the healing touch.'

'But the Pir sahib does not touch kafirs with his hands. He hates infidels. Earlier, it was different. Anyone could go to him.

Only, if an infidel came for treatment, he would feel his pulse with a stick—putting one end of the stick on his pulse and the other to his ear, and thus diagnose the disease. But now he does not permit any kafir to come near him.'

'It is surprising how he has come to the town at this time of the year. Usually he comes in late summer.'

'What difference does it make to holy men whether it is summer or winter.'

'It may be that the news about the defiling of the mosque has reached him.'

'He needs no telling. He must have come to know of it, on his own, intuitively.'

'It is the holy man's goodwill that is of paramount importance. Otherwise a pir-fakir has only to pronounce a curse and a whole city will be in ruins, reduced to dust!'

'True! Very true!'

'Will he deliver a sermon while he is here?'

'He will certainly do so, if he stays on till Friday.'

'Now that he has come, he will not go back without purging the city clean.'

Shades of the afternoon were lengthening when Nathu left the nanbai's shop. He felt light at heart. The apprehensions that had been gnawing at his heart had almost subsided. There was a lot of bustle and gaiety on the roads. Why should he allow that petty incident to torment him so much? People would curse the fellow who had put the carcass on the steps of the mosque and then dismiss it from their minds, calling the fellow a mad man. Besides, no one seemed to know how the pig was killed and by whom. Murad Ali was the only one who knew about it, and he, being a Muslim, would not tell anyone that he had got the heinous deed done.

Nathu was intrigued by the surrounding scene. Outside a small shoe-shop, a man from a village was persuading his wife to buy a new pair of shoes for herself. 'Why don't you buy it? You don't have an extra pair and the one you are wearing is worn-out.'

'No, no, it is you who needs a good pair of shoes. You have to do so much of running about. Mine is serving me well still.'

Nathu moved on. He felt good. He crossed the road and turned towards the right, and began walking at a leisurely pace. He passed by another row of nanbais' shops. Spicy aromas arose from huge metal pots of cooked meat and the piles of naans heaped one on top of another. Nanbais' shops were bursting with customers, most of them coolies or families from surrounding villages who would come to these eating shops, tired and hungry after the day's work. That particular bazaar was located at one end of the town, from where the villagers, after satisfying their hunger, would get on to their bullock-carts and set off on the long road towards their respective villages.

Behind the row of nanbais' shops, stood the imposing Jama Masjid. In the declining afternoon sun, it looked milky white as though newly washed. The mosque presented the familiar, everyday scene, with beggars sitting on the steps, labourers reclining or lying about and devotees going in or coming out. Suddenly Nathu saw a crowd of people coming out of its vaulted entrance. Everyone was picking up or puting on his pair of shoes and hurriedly coming down the steps. Nathu just stood and watched. It was only on rare occasions, such as Id, that people in such large numbers would be seen emerging from the mosque. Was there some sermon? Suddenly the Pir of Golra Sharif came to his mind. It may be that he had delivered the sermon and people were returning from it. His heart missed a beat. Perhaps all these hundreds of people had gathered to discuss the awful deed committed by him. The pir too must have come to deliver a sermon concerning that deed.

Nathu walked past the Jama Masjid. At the farther end of the building was a ditch. All the dirty water of the town flowed into it and was carried out of the city. Nathu came and stood against the railing of the ditch. As he looked down, his eyes fell on a man of dark complexion lying utterly naked on a narrow ledge below the railing, with a talisman round his neck. A tin-box was hanging by a nail driven into the wall above him. The ledge was so narrow that if the man turned on to his side while asleep, he would surely fall into the ditch. Nathu thought that for all he knew, this man too might be a fakir of high spiritual attainments. He gazed at him intently.

Suddenly the fakir sat up, stared at him and began shaking his head violently, as a man who is crazy or in a trance does.

Nathu turned away and began looking towards the bazaar. After a while when he looked back, the man was no longer shaking his head; instead, he was beckoning him with his forefinger. Nathu felt confused. He was afraid lest the fakir should cast a magic spell on him or pronounce a curse. He took out a one-anna coin from his pocket and threw it in front of the fakir. The latter picked it up and threw it into the ditch, and staring hard at Nathu, again beckoned him. Nathu trembled with fear and left the place.

The Bara Bazaar, the main market of the town, bore a festive look. At the two shops of aerated water, which stood side by side and were decked with long rows of coloured bottles, sat the neatly dressed shopkeepers, filling glass after glass with lemon squash and passing them on to customers. Those who sold flower-garlands on the pavement, had already arrived. Close to the aerated water shops were stalls selling meat cutlets and kababs. Round the corner was the prostitutes' lane with a wine-shop in front. Nathu stood undecided by the roadside.

By the roadside, stood a few tongas with shining well-polished harnesses and feather-plumes fluttering on the heads of horses, lending a festive air to the atmosphere. Now and then a tonga would stop in the middle of the road, with some wealthy landlord sitting inside chatting with a couple of friends, all of them in their well-starched clothes and turbans.

Nathu again felt reassured and relaxed and continued strolling about. People had come out to have a good time. As evening fell, the fun and gaiety increased. And Nathu, elated, went straight to the stall of meat kababs and bought eight-annas worth of kababs. Then walking over to the wine-shop, he settled down on a bench outside. He ate the kababs with zest and then put the glass of country wine to his lips.

The street lights went up. The odour of wet earth from the sprinkling of water blended with the smell of flowers and Nathu felt inebriated. He did not remember when he had bought a garland of flowers and put it round his neck. He even did not remember that after getting up from the wine-shop he had crossed the wide Raja Bazaar Road and gone into the prostitutes' lane.

It was then that he saw Murad Ali coming towards him. It was Murad Ali, wasn't it?—in his long coat coming down to his knees, his thin cane-stick, his bristling black moustaches—the short, stoutish figure of Murad Ali. Or was he dreaming? Like an apparition Murad Ali moved from street to street, swinging his cane-stick. Did a man, with the name of Murad Ali really exist or was he a figment of his imagination? No, no, it was really Murad Ali, coming from the side of the grain market, by way of the lane. Had Nathu not been a little high, he would have hidden behind the projection of some house. But Nathu was in high spirits. He came and stood right in the middle of the street. He had not had much to drink. For a low-caste skinner, two tumblers of wine are like water. It was only that after having knocked about the whole day, he had seen someone he knew, to whom he could talk. Of a sudden, Nathu felt elated and confident. 'Whatever job we take up, we do it to perfection!' he mumbled to himself.

'Salaam huzoor!'

Nathu stepped forward and greeted him jovially.

'Salaam huzoor!' he said again, standing erect, with his chest out.

Murad Ali, taken aback, stopped in his tracks, but only for a moment. Looking at Nathu with his sharp, piercing eyes, he grasped the situation and without acknowledging Nathu's greetings or uttering a word, moved on.

'Salaam huzoor! I am Nathu. Don't you recognize me?' Nathu said and laughed.

By then, Murad Ali had moved ahead.

Confused, Nathu stood in the middle of the street and again

shouted: 'Huzoor! Murad Ali Sahib!'

But Murad Ali did not stop or turn round.

Suddenly a thought occurred to Nathu: 'Murad Ali must know that I have done the job. He must not be under any misapprehension. He must not think that I am loitering about without doing the job.'

Nathu moved forward on his unsteady legs. The lane became more dark as he went farther; but he had his eyes on the receding figure of Murad Ali. He followed him. 'The huzoor has to be told that the job was done.'

He felt as though he had overtaken Murad Ali. That part of the lane was lonely, and it had seemed to him that Murad Ali had slowed his pace.

'I forgot to tell you, huzoor, that the job was duly done! The thing was despatched on time! The fellow with the pushcart had duly arrived!'

Nathu saw that Murad Ali had stopped, and with his cane lifted, was looking at him.

Soon enough Murad Ali would move towards him, but why was he holding up his cane? And why didn't he speak? At one end of the dark lane, they stood staring at each other.

'The work was done, huzoor!' Nathu said again. 'The stuff was sent off to the right place!'

Hardly had he uttered these words when it seemed to him that Murad Ali had again turned round and moved away, taking long strides. At the dark end of the lane, there was a slope and Murad Ali was going up the slope.

Nathu looked up. Murad Ali had moved farther away. He was now going up the slope which led towards the Shivala. He again looked like an apparition to Nathu, going farther and farther away, and yet not vanishing from sight!

When she opened the door and saw Nathu standing on the threshold, Nathu's wife felt so relieved that tears welled up in her eyes. 'I have been on tenterhooks waiting for you'.

She went in and sat down on the cot, crying. 'I was so anxious, my heart was sinking. I kept wondering where you could have gone. I was so miserable.'

Wiping her tears with a corner of her sari she looked at him and suddenly smiled.

'You are looking like a clown, a garland hanging from one ear. Whom have you been visiting?'

Nathu went in and without uttering a word sat down on the cot.

'Oh, you have been drinking. But then, why aren't you laughing and singing as you always do when you come home drunk?'

Nathu's wife was a woman blessed with infinite patience. Even when Nathu, in a fit of rage, abused her, she would not answer back. She would only say: 'Go on, say whatever is on your mind, you will feel lighter that way.' Or, she would stand quietly on one side and putting her finger to her lips say, 'Enough, enough, don't say anything more otherwise you will regret your outburst later on.' Now, you can drive a pin into a person's flesh, but what is the point in driving it into a lump of clay? Seeing her cool temperament, Nathu too would keep his temper under control. In the neighbouring row of huts, no fewer than twenty chamar families lived, and she was on good terms with all of them, sharing their joys and sorrows. A God-fearing woman, she was content with whatever little she had. There is a quality of character which some people possess, an inner balance which strikes an equation with any situation, and does not make any demands on life that are beyond their reach. Such people are always cheerful and are like flowers that have blossomed fully.

Nathu had still not uttered a word.

'Why don't you say something? You have been away for so long. I felt a like a fish out of water.'

Nathu lifted his eyes and looked at her. Something welled up within him. He shook his head. 'To hell with Murad Ali and his pig,' he muttered to himself. 'I am safely back home.'

'Did the people in the colony enquire after me?' he asked.

'Yes, they did. Once or twice.'

'What did you tell them?'

'I said that you had gone out on some work and would be back shortly.'

'Did they ask about me many times?'

'No. Don't people go to work? In the evening, the woman next door asked about you. I said you had gone to skin a horse.'

A faint smile appeared on Nathu's lips.

'But where were you? Where did you go?'

'I shall tell you some other time.' Nathu's wife looked at him. There had never been an occasion in the past when he had hidden anything from her. But it was better to remain silent.

'I won't insist. Don't tell me if you don't want to... Would you like to eat something? I shall make chapattis for you. You can have them with a glass of tea. Good, hot chapattis.' And she got down from the cot. Impelled by some inner urge, Nathu pulled her back and made her sit by his side.

'No, no, just sit here.'

And she sat down.

'Have you eaten?'

'Yes, I have.'

Nathu's wife noticed that he was behaving oddly.

'Don't lie,' he said. 'Tell me the truth. Have you had your meal?'

She again looked up at him and said, laughing: 'I cooked the meal all right, but I couldn't eat anything.'

'Did you eat in the morning?'

'Yes, I did.'

'You are lying again. Tell the truth. Did you eat?'

She looked at her husband and laughed.

'No, I didn't. I was waiting for you. How could I eat?'

'What if I had not come home even tonight?'

'You had to come. I knew you would come.'

A vague uneasiness still troubled him. It was this uneasiness which had impelled him to wander about the streets the whole day long and later to get drunk at the wine-shop. Even as he sat by his wife, it was gnawing at his heart. Suddenly he thought he heard something. It seemed to him that Murad Ali was standing outside, the point of his cane-stick resting on the door. Nathu's heart missed a beat. He tried to reassure himself, 'But Murad Ali might not have recognized me. He would have spoken to me otherwise. He just went away. He must have taken me for some drunken lout who was bothering him. After all it was Murad Ali who had put the five-rupee note in my hand.'

'I knew there was something bothering you. That's why I was so worried.'

Nathu turned to look at her. Her anxious eyes were staring at his face.

'People said there was some trouble brewing in the town. Someone had killed a pig and thrown it outside a mosque. That also made me nervous. I said to myself "If some trouble broke out, where shall I look for you? How shall I find you?"'

Nathu was taken aback.

'Which pig? What sort of pig?'

'Don't you know what a pig is?' His wife laughed. She was relieved that Nathu had come back. She only wished that they would just keep sitting and chatting with each other.

'What colour was the pig? Black or white?' Nathu asked. He was all ears to hear his wife's answer.

'What difference does that make?'

'Did you see it?'

'Shall I go to see a pig? What have I to do with it?'

'Has anyone in our colony seen it?'

'What are you saying? Will people from the colony go to see a dead pig? They were only repeating what they had heard.'

The night was deepening. Voices from the neighbouring tenements had virtually ceased.

'Where would you like to sleep? Out in the open or inside?' she asked, looking sideways at her husband.

'Why do you ask?'

'How can I be sure about you? When we are sleeping outside, you sometimes lift me and carry me inside. I thought I might as well ask you beforehand. If you have any shady intentions we may as well stay indoors, even though it is rather stuffy inside.' Saying so she sat down and began untying her hair. 'You have not told me whether you would like to eat something. Shall I make you some tea? Why are you so glum? I felt so lonely when you were not here.'

Listening to his wife talk a wave of emotion, at once painful and ecstatic, welled up within him and he put his arms round her and his eager lips sought her cheeks, her lips, her hair, her eyes hungrily, over and over again. His frenzy increased with every passing moment and he felt as though every pore of his body was melting into her warm flesh and her excited breathing.

'I cried three times during the day. Standing in the veranda I waited for you for hours and hours and then came into the room to cry. I thought you would never come back.'

His craving for mental peace would take him to her lips, then to her breasts, from one part of her body to another, seeking solace and comfort.

Just then dogs began to bark fiercely in the yard outside, and muffled noises were heard from far away. Nathu was oblivious of everything. A little while later however, his wife noticed something on the wall of their room, near the ceiling. It was a trembling glow of light on the wall opposite the ventilator. From far away, muffled sounds continued to come.

'What is that?' said his wife pointing towards the wall. 'What light is that on the wall? Looks like a fire has broken out somewhere. Just listen.'

Nathu looked up and a low moan escaped his lips. The dogs were barking even more fiercely than before; the distant noises had become louder too, their echoes filling the atmosphere like the sound of approaching armies. The unsteady glow of light too had become brighter and looked more like the reflection of flames.

'Fire has broken out somewhere,' Nathu cried out and sat up.

Just then, as though floating over the muffled, indistinct sounds, came the ringing of an alarm bell. For both of them it was an unfamiliar sound. Normally, they used to hear the chimes of a tower-clock in the Sheikh's garden during the night. After winding up her kitchen work for the day, as both of them prepared to retire for the night, the tower-clock would strike the hour and Nathu's wife would invariably count the number of chimes. They would be ten, sometimes even eleven. But this was not the sound of the Sheikh's tower-clock. The bell was ringing insistently and continuously. Its sound would get lost in the midst of increasing noises, but after some time, it would again be heard in all its clarity above other sounds.

The noises from far away were getting louder and louder. Now voices began to be heard inside the colony too. Neighbours were getting up and coming out of their tenements.

'The grain market is on fire!' someone shouted. Soon enough, from far away, was heard a voice, loud and clear: 'Allah-o-Akbar!'

Nathu trembled in every limb of his body. With wide open eyes he stared at the ceiling, as though struck with paralysis.

'Let's go out and find out,' whispered his wife, 'I feel so frightened. Let's ask our people.'

But Nathu, stone-stiff, continued sitting on the cot, holding on to her.

A little while later, a unison of voice rose over all other sounds: 'Har... Har... Har... Mahadev!' The last word of the slogan was shouted loud and long.

In the midst of the increasing noises and the incessant ringing of the alarm-bell, the slogans began to be heard more and more loudly and frequently. It seemed as though celebrations of some big festival had begun!

Nathu's wife could not restrain herself any longer. Extricating herself from Nathu's arms she got up, opened the door and went out. Nathu was still looking at the ceiling with wide-open eyes.

This confused mixture of sounds, like notes from a cracked musical instrument, had begun to strike against the walls of Richard's distant bungalow too. Now and then, another sound, that of an alarm bell too would come floating in the air. Richard was fast asleep, but the sound had woken up Liza. At first, on hearing it she mistook it for the soft tinkle of the little bell that hung in their living room and chimed softly with every gust of air. But on waking up fully she realized that the sound was different. Sometimes it would be lost among other sounds, and then suddenly it would again come floating through the distant caverns of darkness. Liza's eyes were heavy with sleep. The sound seemed to her as though it was the alarm bell of some ship, lost in a storm, desperately trying to find its way.

She raised herself on her elbows and looked at Richard. Richard was snoring softly. Richard had only to put his head on the pillow and he would be fast asleep. Such was his remarkable nature, unattached, untroubled by what was going on around him.

It was oppressively dark in the room for Liza. At the gate outside, the loud pattering of the watchman's heavy boots could be heard.

'What sound is that, Richard?' said Liza, nestling close to Richard.

'What? What is it?'

'What sound is that?'

'There's nothing. Go to sleep,' and Richard turned on to his side.

'Some sort of bell is ringing somewhere, Richard. It sounds like a church bell.'

Richard woke up. He raised himself on his elbows and listened attentively.

'A church bell has a deeper sound. This is more like the sound of a Hindu temple.'

'Why is it ringing at this time of the night, Richard? Is there some Hindu festival today? The sound makes one feel as though there was a storm on the sea and some ship was sounding the alarm bell.'

Richard remained silent.

The confused din from the side of the city grew louder. Now and then a voice would be heard above the din, as though someone was calling someone, but it would again sink into that din. Just then, another voice was heard, loud and clear, as though wafting on the waves of darkness.

'Allah-o-Akbar!'

Every muscle in Richard's body became taut. But soon enough, he relaxed.

'What sound is that? What does it mean?'

'It means God is great!' said Richard.

'Why is this being raised at this time? Is it some religious occasion?'

Richard laughed. 'It is not a religious occasion, dear Liza, a riot has broken out in the city between the Hindus and the Muslims.'

'What? A riot while you are present in the town?'

Richard felt that Liza, who was fairly well-informed, was purposely putting such an embarrassing question to him.

'We do not interfere in their religious matters. You know that well enough, don't you?'

For a fleeting moment Liza felt as though she was in the midst of a thick jungle and that the sounds she heard were coming from its depths.

'Why don't you stop it, Richard? I am frightened.' Richard was again silent. His mind was at work again, as to what should be his role in the new situation and how best he should implement the policy of the government.

Liza put her arm round Richard's neck.

'They may be fighting among themselves but it puts your life in danger too, Richard,' she said and a surge of sympathy rose in her heart for Richard. Richard was so frail and sensitive, and was surrounded by such ferocious people. It is not easy to rule over such subjects.

Now and then, the sound of the alarm bell would be heard.

'But Richard, it is such a horrid thing that these people should fight among themselves.'

Richard laughed.

'Will it be less horrid if they stopped fighting among themselves and joined hands to attack me, to shed my blood?' Richard said and turning on to his side, began stroking Liza's hair. 'How would you feel if at this moment, slogans were raised in front of our house and people stood with axes and lances ready to attack me?'

Liza shuddered and snuggled close to Richard, trying to look at his face in the dark. It seemed to her that human values were of little consequence, that it was only values that related to governance that mattered. Meanwhile Richard had again sat up. 'There is trouble in the city, Liza. You go to sleep. I have to make some enquiries.' Just then, the telephone bell rang.

9

'It is such a disorderly family, one can never find anything even if one rummages the whole house for it,' grumbled Lala Lakshmi Narain standing in front of his cupboard. He was looking for a small woodchopper that he had put in the lower drawer of his cupboard under a pile of clothes. In the city, a riot had already broken out. He had come out of his room twice to ask his wife if she had seen it lying anywhere, and each time his wife had given two answers to his single question

'How should I know where the woodchopper is? I don't have to cut twigs with it to clean my teeth. Nor do I need your tiny woodchopper to cut firewood for the kitchen. Why do you ask me about it again and again, good sir?'

'Is it a crime to ask about it? If I can't find the woodchopper whom should I ask, if not you?'

'My good man, don't get panicky. Have faith in God and sit quietly. How many people will you be able to protect with that tiny woodchopper?'

The woodchopper was truly a small one. Its yellow wooden handle was painted with green and red creepers and flowers. Lalaji had once taken his children to a fair and there the woodchopper had caught his fancy. Thereafter, whenever he went for his morning walks, he took along, instead of his walking stick, the woodchopper since it came in handy for cutting twigs from keekar trees. With the result, within a short time, quite a pile of twigs had gathered in the house. His own need did not go beyond one small piece from a twig every day. Now if a whole branch is cut and while walking home, the person keeps filing it, he automatically gets a few twigs out of a single branch. Whenever his wife wanted to throw them into the garbage can, he would get annoyed.

'Who throws away fresh twigs from the tree?'

'Fresh or stale, they are of no use to anyone. What's the use of storing them?'

'You can use them for cleaning your teeth.'

'My teeth are no longer strong. It is thanks to your twigs that they have become shaky. Earlier they used to be as strong as steel.' Saying that she would carry them towards the staircase where the garbage tin stood.

'At least you could wait till they dried and withered.'

The woodchopper could not be traced. With the woodchopper near at hand, Lalaji felt a sense of security; with it missing, he felt exposed to all kinds of dangers. Apart from the woodchopper, there was nothing in the house which could serve as a weapon apart from a few sticks used to hold up the mosquito nets and some kitchen knives. As for oil and charcoal, there was one small bottle of linseed oil and a tiny quantity of charcoal barely sufficient for the needs of the kitchen. Despite the vanaprasthi's behest, he had not been able to procure more. Besides, he was inwardly convinced that the government would not allow a riot to break out, and even if it did, his family would not be immediately affected by it.

The small woodchopper at that time was adding lustre to the arsenal of the Youth League. It was lying on the window-sill along with the arrowheads tidily arranged by Ranvir.

'It is such a disorderly house. Where shall I look for it now?' Lalaji grumbled again. He called over the servant and asked him: 'Have you seen the woodchopper?'

'It was somewhere in the house, Lalaji, but I have not seen it recently.'

'If it was in the house, then, has it suddenly sprouted wings and flown away? Are you trying to fool me? Where has it disappeared?'

'Honest to God, I do not know, Lalaji,' Nanku said, standing in the doorway.

That very morning, out of anxiety for the safety of the Hindus, Lalaji had made a strong exhortation at the meeting held to discuss the deteriorating situation in the town. 'It is imperative that we train our young men to wield a lathi. This cannot brook delay. And for this work I hereby donate five hundred rupees.' Encouraged by his sense of concern, other members too had come forth and within a few minutes no less than two-thousand-five-hundred rupees had been collected. At that time he was hell-bent on confronting the enemy and had no thought of his own safety.

In reality, he was quite safe too. He was a man of means and lived in a spacious house, and was, besides, a prominent citizen. Who would lift his hand against a man of means? Muslim families lived in his immediate neighbourhood, but most of them belonged to the lower strata of society. Besides, being a businessman he had dealings with many Muslim traders and was on cordial terms with them. What was there to be afraid of?

But now, with the fire raging in the grain market, the situation had radically changed and his heart sank within him as he thought of it.

'Are you listening? It seems our darling son has taken away the woodchopper and given it to the Youth League.'

'How does it concern me? It is between you and your son. You have always regarded me as a know-nothing. Why should I meddle in your affairs?'

'Did he tell you where he was going before he left?'

'Who?'

'What do you mean who? Ranvir, of course, who else?'

'He didn't say anything to me. It is to your speeches and sermons that he keeps listening, day in and day out. How should I know where he has gone? On a dreadful night like this, the boy is not at home.'

With an angry wave of his hand, Lalaji went back into the room. But what was the point—the woodchopper was not there.

He picked up the four long sticks of the mosquito net standing in a corner of the room and came out. He gave one of the sticks to Nanku, the servant.

'Now go downstairs and sit by the front door, holding this stick in your hand.'

He put the second stick against the wall near the bedstead on which sat his wife and their grown-up daughter. He held the third one in his own hand. But soon enough he felt rather odd holding the stick and put it back against the wall. Thereafter he went towards the staircase which led up to the family lavatory on the roof.

In the earlier riot too, the grain market had been set on fire. But there had been no killing then. This time the atmosphere was more tense and full of hatred.

The fire was spreading. Nearly half the sky had already turned copper-red with its glow. Down below, near the horizon, it rose in whirls, flames leapt up, curling like tongues of monstrous snakes towards the sky. The fire was spreading north. The scene reminded one of the Dussehra festival when Lanka was in flames and the fire enveloped the effigy of Ravana. Now and then a cloud of red dust would rise upward, turn into red smoke and disperse in the sky. The stars had lost their lustre. A little above the horizon the sky was burnished red, but above it a certain pallor blending with it gave it a pale-red colour.

Coming out of the lavatory, Lalaji stood at the parapet of his double-storeyed house. Against the background of the glowing sky, the sprawling clusters of flat-roofed single-storeyed houses spread far into the distance, looked like a picture in relief. On the roofs of neighbouring houses and even beyond, stood men and women and children, looking towards the grain market. Lalaji's godown was located in a lane close to the Burra Bazaar, at some distance north-west of the grain market. He was somewhat relieved to find that the fire had not as yet spread in that direction.

From behind the parapet wall, as Lalaji viewed the scene his eyes fell on three men standing on the roof of the neighbouring house looking towards the raging fire. They were none other than Fateh Din, his younger brother and their elderly father. Fateh Din turned his head and saw Lalaji standing behind the parapet wall. 'Hell-fire has broken loose, Lalaji! How terrible!' Lalaji did not answer, and Fateh Din added in a reassuring tone: 'Have no fear, Lalaji. No one will dare look with an evil eye towards your house. He will have to settle with us before he raises his hand against you.'

'Of course, of course!' Lalaji said. 'A neighbour is like one's right hand. I am fortunate to have neighbours like you.'

'Have no fear! It is hooligans who create trouble and harass decent people. All of us have to live in the same town after all, so why should there be any conflict? What do you say, Lalaji?'

'Of course, of course!' said Lalaji.

Lalaji trusted Fateh Din's words and yet did not trust them. For the last twenty years that he had been living in that house, not once had he had any complaint. Yet the fact remained that they were Muslims. As things stood he had little reason to feel unsafe. If anyone set fire to his house, the fire would spread and engulf the entire mohalla of Muslim houses. Besides, that very morning a person no less than the president of the Muslim League, Hayat Baksh, had assured him that so long as he was around, none dare do any harm to him. As for his godown, there was little to worry either. The entire lot of goods was insured. Even so the situation could worsen any time and the Muslims could not be trusted.

It was primarily about Ranvir that Lalaji was worried. Ranvir had chosen to be away from home on such a dreadful night. Being of an impetuous nature the boy might land himself in trouble. Most likely, Master Dev Vrat would keep him back at his place. One of Ranvir's friends too had told him that evening that all the boys were with Masterji. Yet who could tell, the boy might turn his steps towards the grain market.

It was then that the sound of the alarm bell fell on his ears. It came as a reassuring sound for him. He had strongly proposed at the meeting that the old bell should be repaired and a new rope attached to it, and he was happy that his proposal had been implemented. But at the same time the sound of the alarm bell appeared to be too feeble to be of much use against the raging fire.

'On one side the alarm bell is ringing and on the other, the grain market is being gutted down. It will be the undoing of the Hindus,' Lalaji muttered as he strolled up and down, with his hands joined behind his back. Each time he thought of his daughter in the house, his heart would skip a beat. 'If the trouble worsens, how will I cope with the situation? And Ranvir is loitering about God knows where. An unruly boy who doesn't listen to anyone, always harping on social service, service to the nation. What social service can a fellow do who has no thought of his parents?' At times he would imagine Ranvir heading towards the grain market where the fires were raging and the thought would send a shiver down his spine. 'Other people too have sons who go to learn to wield a lathi. But they don't loiter about the streets at a time like this. Thinks he is a great hero, or something.' Lalaji was angry with himself too. 'At the meetings while others keep their counsels to themselves and do not utter a word, I go on babbling. They made me part with no less than five hundred rupees, whereas no one else donated more than a hundred rupees. If any untoward thing happens to me, none of those good-for-nothings will come to my help. And here I am, like a forsaken man doomed in a Muslim locality.'

Standing behind the parapet wall Lalaji looked below. It was very dark there. Near the railing, both mother and daughter were sitting on a cot, close to each other. His wife was asking their daughter to pray. 'Recite the GAYATRI MANTRA, child. Pray.' And their daughter putting her clasped hands in her lap had begun to recite the holy GAYATRI MANTRA.

From the roof Lalaji asked in a low voice: 'Are you listening, Ranvir's mother? Has Ranvir come?'

'No, he has not.'

'Speak in low tones. Can't you speak in low tones?'

Lalaji again began pacing the roof. He would try to reassure himself again and again, 'If they set fire to my house, the entire lane will be gutted.' But at last he could not hold out any longer and came down.

On coming down, however, he felt differently: 'Why are you sitting so glumly, Ranvir's mother? What is there to be nervous about? Have courage. Buck up!'

Lalaji's wife remained silent. She was of course anxious about Ranvir. 'He is telling me to buck up, whereas he himself has been to the lavatory three times.'

Lalaji moved away from the railing—and went towards his room.

A little later Lalaji's wife became somewhat suspicious. 'Vidya, go and see why your father has gone into his room.'

Vidya went and found Lalaji changing his clothes; he had taken off his small dhoti and was putting on his pyjamas.

'He is getting ready to go out.' Vidya came back and told her mother.

'O Lord, no one can tell what your father may be up to,' and getting down from the cot went straight to her husband's room: 'You will see me dead if you step out of the house.'

'What? Shall I keep sitting at home feeling helpless? I must find out where the boy is.'

'And you will leave your grown-up daughter in my care on a night like this?' she said nervously.

'My son has gone out of the house. Should I, like a woman, put on bangles and sit at home?'

'He is not your son alone, he is my son too. Where will you go looking for him? The school is long since closed. He is a sensible boy, he must have stayed back somewhere. One of his friends too had told us that all the boys were at Masterji's house. How many times did I tell you that you should not try to make a Hindu warrior out of your son; that he should devote his time to study, play games, eat well and become a strong boy. But you wouldn't listen. You insisted on his taking part in drills and exercises and lathi-wielding, knowing fully well that we were destined to live our whole life in a Muslim city. To live in the ocean and make an enemy of crocodiles, who will call it wise? You are seeing the result now...'

'Don't keep lecturing me all the time. What is wrong with him being in the Youth League? One must do some work for the country and society.'

'Then work for the country and society and face the consequences. But on a night like this, I won't let you go out, whatever you may say.'

Lalaji gave up the idea of going out of the house. He had not expected that the riot would take such a fierce turn. He hated the Muslims, and he was sure that the British authority would keep them under control.

His wife was saying: 'Other people make it a point to be on the right side of government officers, they socialize with their neighbours, whether Hindus or Muslims. Look at your own in-laws, their Muslim friends keep walking in and out of their house all the time, whereas you have not cultivated anyone, neither officers nor neighbours.'

The fact of the matter was that he too had been thinking on these very lines. His wife had, as it were, taken the words out of his mouth. Their in-laws were certainly on very cordial terms with some Muslims, with Shah Nawaz, for instance, who was a very influential person, ran a transport company and a petrol pump. They even ate together. Why not get in touch with Shah Nawaz and with his help get away with our daughter to a safer place, even for a few days, say to the cantonment area? But how to go about it?

Somewhere far away slogans were being raised. The sound of 'Allah-O-Akbar!' came again and again. Soon the same slogan began to be raised in the near vicinity, and to Lalaji's consternation, began to be repeated from the roofs of neighbouring houses too! The whole atmosphere resounded with slogans. From the side of the Shivala temple the Hindu slogan: 'Har Har Mahadev!' was also heard occasionally, but it was not repeated anywhere in Lalaji's neighbourhood. It made Lalaji shiver with apprehension.

'Tell Nanku to come upstairs,' Lalaji said to his wife.

'Why, what's the matter?'

'Don't question everything I say. Just call him. I want him to carry a letter from me.'

Dumbfounded, she stared at her husband's face.

'At this time of the night? Where do you want to send him?' She thought that he wanted to send Nanku in search of Ranvir.

'Where will he go looking for Ranvir? We have had word that the boy is with Masterji. Why should you be so nervous? Have faith in God and wait patiently till morning.'

'I am not sending him to look for Ranvir; it is some other work.'

'Listen, my good sir, why do you want to send this poor man anywhere at this time of the night when hell has broken loose? He does not know anybody, nor does anyone know him.'

'Why must you oppose whatever I say? We have young Vidya on our hands. It is not advisable that we should continue to stay here. I want him to take a letter to the in-laws. I want them to ask their friend Shah Nawaz to take us out of here.'

The wife pondered for a while and then said, 'This work too can wait till morning. This is not the time for it. Do you think, on getting your letter, our in-laws will go running to Shah Nawaz's house to seek his help? What are you saying?'

But Lalaji would not budge.

'Once an idea gets stuck in his head, it's impossible to make him change his mind,' she muttered to herself.

'How do you know he will take your letter to the right place? He is such an idiot.'

'Why not, he has to. What are we keeping him for, otherwise? He has only to cross a few lanes and he will be at their house in no time.'

'Why must you be so adamant? Even if we have to move out of this place, it cannot be done before morning. Of what use is it to write to anyone at this time? You will only embarrass the in-laws.' Lalaji paused a little as though undecided. 'No,' he said in a low voice. 'We must leave this house this very night.'

'Why should you be so worried? Are you afraid of the neighbours? I am not. Pray to God and relax,' said his wife and thereafter did not utter a word.

At the thought of their grown-up daughter, the mother too lost her equanimity of mind. 'Maybe he is right, maybe we should get away from here without any loss of time. There must be some good reason why he has become so restless. If anything untoward happens, where shall we conceal our daughter?'

'Tell Nanku to take one of the sticks of the mosquito net with him,' said Lalaji, expressing his sense of concern for Nanku's safety.

Handing the letter to Nanku, Lalaji gave him detailed instructions: 'If you find that there is trouble anywhere along the way, avoid that route and get into some by-lane. Try to take the Gurkha chowkidar from the temple with you. But the letter must be delivered. Understand? Now, go.'

But before Nanku left, Lalaji's wife again protested, greatly perturbed: 'I would again beseech you, wait patiently till morning. Leave yourself in God's hands. We shall see what can be done tomorrow. Nanku too is the son of some mother. Don't push him into the jaws of death.'

'No, no, nothing will happen to him. He is not a weakling.'

Just then the sound of running footsteps was heard from the sidelane. The sound became louder as the footsteps drew near. On that night every sound seemed abnormally loud. It struck the ears as well as the heart. Someone was running for his life.

Lalaji stopped in his tracks. He suddenly felt weak in the legs. His heart began to throb violently. Are these Ranvir's footsteps? Is it Ranvir running back home?

But how can anyone make out by merely listening to the sound of running footsteps?

Suddenly, the sound of another pair of running feet was heard. It seemed someone, having turned the corner and coming into the lane, was chasing the person who was trying to run away.

Then suddenly, a cry was heard, piercing the darkness of the night, 'Bachao! Bachao!'

The sound of running feet, not of one but of two persons, coming from the back part of the lane was heard by both the mother and the daughter sitting on the cot. It was also heard by those standing on the roofs of nearby houses.

'Help! Help! Help!'

The terror-stricken voice was heard again. It was a shrill voice of some desperate, terribly frightened person. It was impossible to make out if it was Ranvir's voice. The voice of frightened people, running for their lives and crying for help has the same tenor.

Then came the sound of some object being thrown—either a stick or a stone, which hit the nearby wall and making a loud, pattering sound fell on the ground.

'Get him! Catch hold of him! Kill him!'

Then the person who had been shouting for help seemed to have gone out of the lane for the patter of his running feet suddenly grew faint and distant while that of his pursuers grew louder.

Was the object thrown on Ranvir? Has he escaped unhurt? Has Ranvir reached home safe? Then, any moment, there should be a knock on the door.

The pursuing feet too had gone out of the lane. Lalaji's heart was pounding while his ears were glued to the door down below, opening into the street.

But there was no knock on the door.

Lalaji felt somewhat relieved and his limp feet came back to life. He walked over to the balcony to see if he could make out who the pursuers were and who the pursued. But the road was empty. Across the road, on the roof of the mud-house, stood men, women and children, motionless as statues. They too must have heard the sound of running feet.

Then three persons emerged from the lane opposite and crossed the road. Their faces were half-covered and they had lathis in their hands, and they were all breathless.

'The Sikh has escaped. If he had not started running, we wouldn't have chased him,' one of them was saying.

They re-entered the sidelane and the sound of their footsteps gradually receded into the distance.

Lalaji heaved a sigh of relief and once again, with his hands joined behind his back began strolling up and down the room. Nanku too picked up the mosquito-net stick, went downstairs and sat down behind the door opening into the street.

10

As the day dawned, the town, as though stung by a cobra, bore a half-dead, half-alive appearance. The grain market was still burning; the fire-brigades of the municipality had long since given up fighting the fire. The smoke billowing from it continued to darken the sky, although during the night the sky had looked glowing red. Seventeen shops had been reduced to ashes.

Shops all over the town were closed, except a shop here and there selling milk. Outside such shops stood small groups of people talking about the happenings of the previous night. Information about the killings was largely based on rumours. Residents of Gawalmandi said that many people had been killed in Ratta, while those in Ratta said that a lot of killing had taken place in the Committee Mohalla.

At a road-crossing in Naya Mohalla lay the dead body of a horse. On the outskirts of the city, by the side of a road that led to the villages, the dead body of a middle-aged man had been found. Another dead body had been found in a graveyard on the western edge of the town. It was the dead body of an elderly Hindu in whose pocket some loose coins and a list of clothes required for some wedding had been found. A shoe shop on College Road and a tailoring shop adjoining it had been looted.

Overnight, dividing lines had been drawn among the residential localities. No Muslim now dared go into a Hindu locality, nor a Hindu into a Muslim locality. Everyone was filled with fear and suspicion. At the entrance to the lanes and at road-crossings, small groups of people sat hidden from view, their faces half-covered, holding lances, knives and lathis in their hands. Wherever Hindu and Muslim neighbours stood together, their conversation contained one and only sentence repeated over and over again. 'Very bad! What is happening is very bad!' The conversation would come to a standstill there. The atmosphere had become heavy. Inwardly everyone knew that the crisis was not over, but no one knew what course the events would take.

Doors of houses were shut tight. All business had come to a halt. All schools, colleges, offices were closed. A man walking in a street had the eerie feeling that he was being watched all the time from behind half-shut windows, from the dark entrances of houses, from crevices and peep-holes. People had shut themselves in. The only contact was through rumours. Those belonging to well-off families were preoccupied only with the question of their safety. In one day all public activity—the prabhat pheris, the constructive programmes and the like—had come to an end. Only the Jarnail, as was his wont, acting under his own compulsions, went along diverse roads and lanes and managed to reach the Congress office at the break of day, but seeing a big lock on the door waited for his comrades for a while, then climbed up the stone slab over the drain and began his speech:

'Sahiban! I am sorry to say that since all the cowards are sitting in their houses like rats in their holes, we shall not be able to hold the prabhat pheri this morning. I would beg forgiveness of all of you and would appeal to you to maintain peace in the town at all costs. It is all the mischief of the British who make brother fight brother and shed his blood. Jai Hind!' and alighting from the stone slab, marching in military style went out of sight in the darkness of a nearby lane.

Ranvir did not return home that night, but Master Dev Vrat had managed to send word about his safety. That morning, Lalaji was still worried and did not know which way to turn when a blue-coloured Buick car stopped outside his house and the man who alighted from it was none other than Shah Nawaz himself. The tall, impressive-looking Shah Nawaz had come on his own. Though both of them knew each other well enough they were not on intimate terms. Within minutes of his arrival, the family—Lalaji, his wife and Vidya, their daughter—were seated in the car. Nanku alone had been left behind to guard the house.

'Don't go to sleep, Nanku. Be alert and guard the house. We are leaving the entire house in your charge,' Lalaji had said.

And the car sped away through the deserted streets in the direction of the cantonment. Here and there, stray individuals and groups standing by the roadside would turn round to look at them—Shah Nawaz, with his fair, shining face, a trusted friend among friends, a swanky tuft of his turban fluttering in the air, sat in the driver's seat and Lala Lakshmi Narain sat by his side while the ladies were in the back seat. It was an act of courage to come out like this. Wherever Lalaji noticed a knot of persons standing by the roadside he would turn his face and look in another direction. His wife, on the other hand, sitting on the back seat was all praise for Shah Nawaz, showering blessings on him incessantly. 'God lives in the hearts of people who help others in distress,' she would say again and again.

After dropping Lalaji and his family in the cantonment at a relative's house, the Buick car again sped along the roads of the city. Shah Nawaz was now on his way to the house of his bosom friend, Raghu Nath. Shah Nawaz was not in the least worried about his own safety.

The car went past the Jama Masjid in the direction of Mai Satto's water tank. Drab, single-storeyed houses lined either side of the road; small dingy shops, their canvas awnings supported by bamboo dotted the road. The area bore a dilapidated look. It was a Muslim locality. After crossing a ramshackle bridge the car proceeded towards Syed Mohalla. Here the scene changed radically. Pucca double-storeyed houses with balconies and terraces, and here and there window-panes of tinted glass, stood on both sides of the road. Mostly Hindu lawyers, contractors and businessmen lived here. Shah Nawaz was on friendly terms with many of them. As he drove, Shah Nawaz was quite conscious of the fact that many a curious pair of eyes was looking at him from behind windows and half-shut doors. But he was also confident that all those who saw him knew well enough the kind of man he was. Despite this, he accelerated the speed of the car.

On reaching Mai Satto's tank, he turned towards the right. He was now passing through a mixed locality. All sorts of people lived or worked here—there was a long row of shoe-makers' shops who were all Sikhs hailing originally from Hoshiarpur and who specialized in making jooties. The shops were closed. A little beyond, stood a row of mud-houses, their walls covered with hundreds of dung-cakes. The locality wore a deserted look. A little farther, was the scavengers' colony. Shah Nawaz had by then considerably slowed the speed of the car. It did not look like a riot-affected area. Two little children were chasing each other round an electric pole. Nearby was a group of urchins standing in a circle. Shah Nawaz could not help looking at them. Inside the circle lay a little girl on the ground, her shirt uplifted, and on her bare thighs sat a little boy who too had lifted up his shirt. The children around them were roaring with laughter. 'Bastards!' muttered Shah Nawaz, and laughed. 'They couldn't think of another game.' This part of the town appeared to be free from tension.

Looking at Shah Nawaz, a man with an imposing personality, a firm physique, elegantly dressed with polished shoes and a fluttering *turra*, one could not imagine that he could harbour any mean or petty thoughts. It was said about him that if on seeing a girl he smiled at her, the girl would smile back. But that was years ago. Now he was a staid, worldly-wise person, owner of two petrol pumps and a transport company whose cars and trucks plied in all directions, a dependable friend and a sociable, cheerful fellow.

Loyalty to friends was an article of faith with him. When the trouble started he had gone to Raghu Nath's house to find out how the family was faring. In close proximity to Raghu Nath's house was the shop of a nanbai, Fakira by name.

'Look Fakira,' Shah Nawaz had said to him 'Listen, with your ears open. If anyone dares look at my friend's house with an evil eye, I shall catch hold of you and skin you alive. Nobody must go near this house.'

The car was now speeding along one of the main roads. It was now a more open area, the road was broad and the houses on either side at a distance from the road. It was a Muslim locality and the speed of the car was slow. Maula Dad was standing at the turn of the road, which led to Bhabarkhana. Behind him, on the projection of a shop sat five or six persons with lathis and lances in their hands, their faces half-covered. Maula Dad was, as usual, dressed in a queer costume—khaki breeches and a green silken kerchief round his neck. He stepped forward when he saw Shah Nawaz's car approaching.

'What news?' Shah Nawaz asked applying brakes to his car.

'What news should I give you, Khanji? The kafirs have done to death a poor Musalman in the mohalla at the back,' Maula Dad said angrily, almost foaming at the mouth.

Maula Dad's eyes blazed with anger. 'You go about hugging kafirs,' he seemed to say, 'and socialize with them while the Muslims are being butchered,' but he did not say anything. Maula Dad knew well enough that he could not dream of having access to places which were within easy reach of Shah Nawaz. Shah Nawaz was on friendly terms even with the deputy commissioner of the town, whereas Maula Dad had not gone beyond the four walls of the municipal corporation.

'We too have slaughtered five kafirs. Sons of...!'

Shah Nawaz pretended not to have heard what Maula Dad said and started the car.

Hardly had the car moved, when from a side-lane emerged a crowd of people heading towards the road. They were all walking silently, with their heads bowed, as they crossed the road. It was a funeral procession. At the head of it walked Hayat Baksh in his white shirt and salwar with a *kulla* (a skull cap worn under a turban) on his head. The soft patter of their feet appeared to be stroking the air. It must be the funeral of the Musalman who had been killed, thought Shah Nawaz. Behind the coffin walked two small boys, who, he guessed were the sons of the deceased. Passing through the gate, Shah Nawaz parked the car under a tree and swinging the key-ring in his hand, walked towards the bungalow. Raghu Nath's wife was the first to see him from behind a curtained window and was overjoyed.

Knocking at the door, Shah Nawaz shouted: 'O karar! do you hear? Open the door!'

Raghu Nath's wife ran towards the bathroom: 'Shah Nawaz is here! I shall attend to him. Don't take too long!' Shah Nawaz's voice was again heard: 'O *Yabu* (a jocular mode of address among friends), now that you have begun living in a bungalow, you don't even open the door!'

Raghu Nath's wife opened the door.

'Salaam bhabhi, where is my yaar?' he said and walked into the sitting room.

'He is in the bathroom,' she said and sat down in a chair near him.

'How do you find it here, bhabhi? Any problem? You did the right thing, getting out of that place.'

'It is all right here, but no place can be as good as one's home. We don't know if we shall ever be able to go back to our own house,' she said and her eyes filled with tears.

Shah Nawaz felt deeply touched.

'If I am alive, I shall see you safely back into your house. Rest assured.'

Raghu Nath's wife did not observe purdah from Shah Nawaz. And Raghu Nath felt proud of the fact that his closest friend was a Muslim.

'How is it that you always come alone and never bring Fatima with you?'

'There is trouble in the city, bhabhi. You think I have come out on an excursion?'

'She had only to sit in the car. If you can come, why can't she?'

Just then Raghu Nath appeared.

'Come, yabu, here too you must go to the toilet every five minutes. You have come away to a safe place, kafir, and are still shitting all the time.'

Both embraced each other. Shah Nawaz became sentimental. 'I would rather lay down my life than see any harm come to him. If anyone dare so much as touch him, I shall skin him alive.'

As bhabhi got up to go, Shah Nawaz stopped her. 'Where are you going, bhabhi? I am not going to eat here.'

'Janaki,' said Raghu Nath to his wife. 'This man will keep saying no. But you go and prepare the meal.'

'You want me to eat bhindi, I don't eat bhindi. Bhabhi, don't cook anything for me.'

But Janaki had left. Shah Nawaz shouted after her: 'I am in a hurry, bhabhi. I have come only for a couple of minutes.'

Janaki came back: 'You may not take your lunch with us, but you can have some tea with snacks.'

'I knew you were not very serious about lunch. But OK, let it be tea. I shall have tea.'

As the friends sat down, Raghu Nath said in a sombre tone: 'Things have taken a bad turn. One feels so bad. Brother killing brother.'

But after saying this, Raghu Nath suddenly felt that his utterance had created some sort of a distance between them. Their mutual relationship had been on a different plane whereas the Hindu-Muslim relationship was a different matter. He had, by this utterance, unwittingly linked the two kinds of relationships, their personal relationship with that existing between the two communities, about which both of them had their own individual perceptions.

'I am told the trouble is spreading to the villages too,' Raghu Nath said.

There was little scope for further conversation on this issue. Both felt awkward and embarrassed. It cast a pall over their informal, friendly dialogue.

'Come off it, yabu, talk about yourself,' said Shah Nawaz, changing the subject. 'Do you know whom I met yesterday? I met Bhim, of all the people.'

'Which Bhim are you talking about?' Raghu Nath asked and both of them burst out laughing. Bhim had been their classmate during school days, the son of a very junior postal official but who would always introduce himself by his father's designation. That was why all his friends used to make fun of him.

'The rascal has been living in this very town for the last two years and hasn't even bothered to meet us,' Shah Nawaz said and again started laughing, clapping his hands. 'I recognized him once from a distance and I shouted, "Deputy Assistant Postmaster Sahib!" The fellow stood stock-still! But when he recognized me he met me very warmly.'

Bhabhi had brought in tea.

'I have a favour to ask, Khanji,' she said, putting down the tray.

Both of them felt relieved on bhabhi's arrival. It was awkward for them to talk about the riots, yet in the kind of atmosphere that prevailed, to talk about childhood pranks and jokes also sounded hollow.

'Yes, bhabhi, what can I do for you?'

'If it is not inconvenient... if it is not going out of your way...'

'Why are you hesitating, bhabhi, tell me.'

'There is a box of jewellery lying in the house. It contains all our family ornaments. When we left the house, we couldn't bring anything except a few articles of use.'

'That is no problem. Where is the box lying?'

'It is in our small luggage room on the mezzanine floor.'

Shah Nawaz knew every nook and corner of their house.

'But the room must be locked.'

'I shall give you the keys and also explain to you where exactly the box is kept.'

'No problem. I can bring it to you even today.'

'Milkhi, our servant is there. He will open the lock for you.'

'Milkhi is very much there, I know. I went there this morning on my round. I keep pulling him up.'

'How is he?'

'He has the whole house to himself, bhabhi. He must be cooking for himself in the kitchen.'

'The provisions in the house are enough to last him a year,'

Raghu Nath's wife said. 'Then, shall I get you the keys?'

Shah Nawaz felt elated at the thought that so much trust was reposed in him, that bhabhi was handing over keys for jewellery worth thousands of rupees, that she regarded him as one of their own.

Janaki came in, the bunch of keys jingling in her hand.

'What if I decamp with all the jewellery, bhabhi?'

'Even if you throw away the box, Khanji, I shall say, "Forget it!"'

She picked out the right key and explained at length the exact location of the box.

A little while later, Shah Nawaz got up to leave. Both the friends stepped out of the house together and stood by the car.

'I have no words to thank you, Shah Nawaz. You have done for me what no one else would have done.'

This was a spontaneous expression of gratitude straight from the heart.

'Shut up, karar!' Shah Nawaz retorted. 'Go back in and sit on the shit-pot,' and opening the door of the car, got in.

Raghu Nath stood where he was, overwhelmed and somewhat nonplussed.

'Go in, go back to the house, don't bore me.'

Deeply moved, Raghu Nath put out his hand for a handshake.

'Go in, go in, I can't dirty my hand! Talk to someone who knows you! Why are you eating up my brain? I have seen many like you,' he said, speaking in the bantering language of their boyhood days, and started the car.

It was late in the afternoon when Shah Nawaz arrived at Raghu Nath's ancestral house to get the jewellery box.

Milkhi took time to open the door.

'Who is it, kind sir?'

'Open the door. It is Shah Nawaz.'

'Who?'

'Open the door. It is Shah Nawaz.'

'Yes, sir, yes, Khanji! Just a minute, Khanji! The door is locked from inside, I shall run and get the key, Khanji. It is lying on top of the fireplace.'

As Shah Nawaz turned round, he saw, across the road, Feroz Khan, the hide-seller, standing like a statue, on the projection of his godown, staring hard at him. Shah Nawaz looked away. But it seemed to him that Feroz was still looking at him with intense hatred in his eyes, which seemed to say: 'Even today you are kneeling at the door of the kafirs.'

A tonga passed by. Maula Dad in his queer costume of khaki breeches and a fluttering green scarf was making a round of Muslim localities in an open tonga. He laughed as his eyes fell on Shah Nawaz and waving his right arm longer than necessary, shouted: 'Salaam-e-leiqum!'

Shah Nawaz felt embarrassed. He felt angry at the servant who was taking so long to open the door.

From inside came the sound of the lock being opened. Milkhi opened the door slightly, and on seeing Shah Nawaz smiled broadly, showing all his teeth. Shah Nawaz kicked the door open and entered.

'Shut the door behind you.'

'Yes, Khanji.'

As he crossed the long dark corridor, Shah Nawaz felt the warm cosiness of the house. It was after a long time that he had come into the house through this entrance. He liked the familiar odour. Years earlier when he would enter the house through the dark corridor, Raghu Nath's young daughter would stare at him, her forefinger between her teeth, and would then raise both her arms wanting to be picked up. Every time he came, she would go running to the end of the corridor, raise both her arms and start giggling. In those early days the young women of the household would run inside on seeing him. It was only when they recognized who it was would they come back laughing.

'Oh, it's you, Khanji. We thought God knows who had come in,' they would say.

Shah Nawaz felt deeply moved. He had spent many lovely evenings with Raghu Nath and his family. As soon as he entered, the young wife of Raghu Nath's younger brother would go into the kitchen to prepare an omelette for him. Everyone knew that Shah Nawaz was fond of eating omelette. And gradually, one by one, all the members of the family would come and sit with him in the inner courtyard.

'I hope all is well at home, Khanji?' Milkhi said with folded hands.

It was then that Shah Nawaz became aware of Milkhi's presence. Milkhi stood there, with folded hands, a beseeching smile on his face. Shah Nawaz had never liked Milkhi for his beggarly way of talking, his muddy eyes and shrivelled body. Sometimes when a family member would poke fun at him, Milkhi would hide his face in his arm in embarrassment, which would set the whole family laughing. At such times Shah Nawaz did not dislike Milkhi. But generally, he always reminded him of a slimy lizard. No one knew from where he had descended on the household. He was neither a Punjabi nor a Garhwali. He would utter words of some hybrid dialect, squeezing them out, it seemed, from the stumps of his teeth.

Right in the middle of the inner courtyard stood an improvised choolha made from three bricks, the ashes from which lay scattered on the floor, as also butts of the bidis.

'Why don't you cook your meal inside the kitchen?' asked Shah Nawaz. Milkhi merely tilted his head to one side and grinned.

'I am all alone, Sahibji, I cook my dal here only.'

'You have enough provisions here. You don't need anything, do you?'

'There is plenty, Khanji. The nanbai outside also keeps asking me. You had spoken to him.'

'Which nanbai?'

'Khanji, the one who sits by the ditch. He also throws packets of bidis for me. He is a very good man.'

The staircase went up from the side of the kitchen. As he put his foot on the first step, Shah Nawaz looked around. The door of the living room was shut tight. Shah Nawaz knew every article that lay in that room—the big bedstead, the large portrait of

Raghu Nath's mother on the mantelpiece. The sight of the closed door gave him a sense of desolation. Lying against the closed door was Milkhi's hookah, with a dirty rag nearby.

'What do you keep doing here? You don't even sweep the floor.'

'They have gone away, Khanji. What's the use of sweeping the floor?' said Milkhi, grinning.

To Shah Nawaz it seemed as though their voices were like echoes coming from a vaulted dome, and when they ceased talking an eerie silence descended on the house.

'The store room is on the mezzanine, isn't it?'

'Yes, Khanji. Right opposite the staircase. All the big trunks are lying there,' said Milkhi as he followed Shah Nawaz up the staircase.

There were no fewer than fifteen keys, big and small, in the bunch. Bhabhi had singled out the key of the big lock hanging on the door outside and shown it to him and thereafter a small brass key to the cupboard in which the jewellery box lay, and had said, 'This is the key, Khanji. I hope you won't forget.'

But Shah Nawaz was finding it difficult to locate the right key.

'Which one is the key to the big lock? Do you know?'

'Yes, Sahibji, I shall show you.'

And Milkhi bent over the bunch, looking for the right key, like a clerk bending over his account book. The diminutive Milkhi barely came up to Shah Nawaz's waist, maybe a little higher. Shah Nawaz's eyes fell on the thin tuft of hair on Milkhi's head, his *chutia* falling over his left ear like a centipede, and it gave him a creepy feeling.

Milkhi opened the lock. It was dark and stuffy inside the small room. Milkhi stepped forward and unbolted one of the windows which opened towards the back of the house and overlooked the inner courtyard of a neighbouring mosque. Everything inside the room was now clearly visible.

It was stuffy inside but there was also the tantalizing odour of women's clothes. The wives of all the three brothers had hurriedly made bundles of their clothes and thrown them in. The room was chock-full of boxes and trunks.

Threading his way through the boxes, Shah Nawaz reached the cupboard which contained the jewellery box. As he looked casually out of the window he saw a large group of people sitting close to the water-tank where the devotees washed their hands and feet before offering the namaz. Then his eyes fell on a dead body, duly covered, in their midst. The scene of the funeral procession which he had seen that morning on his way to Raghu Nath's house also flitted across his mind. For a long time Shah Nawaz stood looking out of the window.

It did not take long to take out the jewellery box. Covered with blue velvet, it must have been given in dowry to one of the women of the house. He took it out carefully and locked the cupboard.

As they came down the staircase, Milkhi was in front holding the bunch of keys while Shah Nawaz followed with the jewellery box in both his hands, when suddenly something snapped in Shah Nawaz's mind. How and why this happened cannot be easily explained—whether it was the chutia on Milkhi's head, or the grieving crowd of people he had seen in the mosque or the funeral procession he had seen that morning on his way to Raghu Nath's house, or what he had been hearing during the last few days and—Shah Nawaz gave a sharp kick to Milkhi on his back. Milkhi stumbled and fell head downward. As he went tumbling down, his head struck against the wall at the turn in the staircase; his forehead split and his spine broke. When Shah Nawaz came down the staircase, Milkhi's head was hanging downward from one of the last steps in the staircase. Shah Nawaz was still in a rage, the spurt of anger had not subsided. Coming down the staircase, as he passed by Milkhi's body, he felt like lifting his foot and hitting Milkhi on the face so as to crush the centipede. But he desisted lest he should lose his own balance.

Coming down into the courtyard, he turned round to look at Milkhi. Milkhi's eyes were open and set on Shah Nawaz's face, as though wanting to know for which fault of his Khanji had done him to death. As Milkhi fell a muffled cry had escaped his lips out of sheer fright.

Shah Nawaz left him where he was, put the jewellery box under his arm and came out of the house. He put the lock which Milkhi used to put on the inside, on the door outside.

That very evening, handing the jewellery box to bhabhi, Shah Nawaz was not perturbed. As bhabhi took the box, her eyes filled with tears, she had no words to express her sense of gratitude, and Raghu Nath was overwhelmed by the nobility of his friend's character and the loftiness of his thoughts—even in such inflammatory times he could retain his balance of mind and remain loyal and steadfast.

'But there is one bad news, bhabhi.'

'What is it? Has there been a theft? Has our house been burgled?'

'No, bhabhi. Milkhi fell down from the staircase and has perhaps fractured a bone or two. At first I thought I should go for a doctor, but then, doctors are not so easily available these days. But don't worry, I shall attend to it tomorrow.'

'Poor Milkhi!'

'If you like I can bring him along and leave him here and put one of my own men to guard your house. The poor fellow is so utterly alone there.'

But both Bhabhi and Raghu Nath had their reservations. They were strangers in the locality and could not arrange for the injured man's treatment. If it was difficult for Shah Nawaz to get a doctor, it would be well-nigh impossible for them to get one.

'Don't worry. I shall look to it. There should be no problem.'

For this too, the Bhabhi felt beholden to Shah Nawaz and looking at his high forehead and beaming face she felt as though she was standing before a saint.

11

After taking his morning bath, Dev Datt came and stood outside his house, rubbing his hands. Every time he rubbed his hands, or put his hand to his nose or gently stroked his cheeks and again rubbed his hands, it meant that he was busy preparing his work-schedule for the day. There lay a diary in his brain. By rubbing his hands and stroking his nose he was making one entry after another into that diary, another item of work to be attended to. 'There is trouble in Ratta, the comrade there will not be able to send his report, we must send another comrade there.' 'To put a stop to the riots, it is imperative that we bring together leaders of the Congress and the Muslim League, to arrange a meeting between Hayat Baksh and Bakshiji.'

On the previous day too, Dev Datt had somehow managed to call on some people. Raja Ram had straightaway shut the door in his face. Ram Nath had said derogatory things about the communists. Hayat Baksh had agreed to attend the meeting even though he had turned red in the face and, with his eyes burning, had started raising slogans and shouting, 'We shall not rest till we have achieved Pakistan... Pakistan will become a reality!' He had not given Dev Datt even the chance to speak. 'It will be necessary to go to him again today.' Dev Datt again rubbed his hands and stroked his nose. 'Send Bakshiji to Hayat Baksh; take Atal along and go to Bakshiji, and take Amin along and go to Hayat Baksh.' But then he rejected the whole idea. 'Leave out the leaders. Let ten persons each from the Congress, the Muslim League and the Singh Sabha be brought together and have a joint meeting. No, this too will not work. This proposal will have to be discussed in the Party office with other comrades. Another problem. Every effort must be made to stop communal riots from spreading to the labourers' colony. To have only one comrade there is not enough. Ratta is a Muslim area. Comrade Jagdish is there, but he alone cannot be effective. Besides, two or three comrades must be sent to the villages; they must go from village to village, and try to stop the riots from spreading. We have so few comrades.' He again moved his hand over his face, then looked at his wrist-watch. 'There is a meeting in the commune at ten'clock, in which comrades will present reports about their respective areas. It is time to leave,' Dev Datt said to himself and quietly went back into the house to take out his bicycle from the veranda.

'Who is there? Is that you Dev Datt?'

Dev Datt left the cycle and went into the room.

'Are you going out again?' asked his father, a bulky, middle-aged man sitting on a cot. 'If you are bent upon getting killed, then first kill all of us, all your family members. Can't you see what is happening?'

Dev Datt stood in the doorway without uttering a word, rubbing his hands and stroking his nose. His mother came out of the kitchen, wiping her hands on her dupatta.

'Why must you torment us? Don't you know how we passed the night—that horrible fire raging and you not at home? Have you no thought for us? You were away the whole night.'

Dev Datt rubbed his hands and said, 'This entire area, right up to Murree Road on one side and the Company's Garden on the other side is inhabited by the Hindus, and well-to-do Hindus at that. There is no danger to you here.'

'Have you had a revelation that there is no danger to us?' growled the father.

'In this row of houses, ten families have licensed guns. The members of the Youth League of this area have already committed three murders.'

'You swine! Who is thinking of danger to us? It is you we are worried about.

'There is nothing to worry about,' Dev Datt said and came back into the veranda to take out his cycle.

His mother put the wrapper round her neck and tried to block his way. 'I passed the whole night tossing in bed. Don't you see the awful times we are living in?'

The problem was getting complicated, thought Dev Datt, his hand going back to his nose. He put his mouth close to his mother's ear and said, 'Don't worry, Ma. I shall come back soon.'

'You try to fool us all the time. Yesterday too you said the same thing. Put your hand on my body and swear that you will come back before nightfall.'

'I can't promise, Ma, but I shall come back.' And he began taking out his cycle.

From inside the house came the thundering voice of his father. 'Why are you breaking your head against a wall? The swine won't agree. He must disgrace us. He has no thought for his parents! He thinks he will stop the riots. Bastard!'

His father's fulminations continued: 'No one has a good word to say about him! Good-for-nothing fellow, goes about gathering petty labourers, load-carriers, coolies and lectures to them. Hasn't even started shaving and has become a leader, swine!'

Dev Datt had already reached the road-crossing.

The situation had further deteriorated. Practically every road was now deserted. Not even a tonga plied anywhere. Shops were closed. If the panels of any shop were open, it meant that the shop had been looted. If some people carrying lathis were standing in a group somewhere, it meant that they were standing close to the dividing line between the mohalla of their community and that of the hated 'adversary'. But all the mohallas had not been so divided. The houses by the roadside, invariably pucca double-storeyed houses, were of the Hindus, whereas the single-storeyed, mud-houses at the back were of the Muslims, or, to use Dev Datt's terminology, of the deprived classes.

'Dev Datt!' someone called.

The voice had come from the left side of the road-crossing.

Applying the brakes and putting his foot on the ground, Dev Datt stopped.

'Don't go further. A man is lying dead there!'

A short-statured man with a lathi came up to him.

'Where?'

'Beyond the crossing. On the slope.'

'Who was he?'

'A Musla, who else? Where are you off to at this time?'

'To the Party office. I have work to do.'

'A Hindu is lying dead in the graveyard on the other side,' said the dwarfish fellow, adding angrily, 'Go and tell your Muslim patrons since you are always fawning on them, to take away their kinsman's body from the slope and deliver our dead body to us.'

From a balcony on the right came a voice: 'Don't go that way. The fellows there may cut you to pieces.'

'No one will kill him. He is always hobnobbing with the Muslims.'

'But he is a Hindu all the same.'

Those who had earlier been working under cover, had by then, come into the open.

'Go and tell them, if one of our men is killed we shall kill three of theirs.'

The man on the slope was perhaps not yet dead, and was struggling for breath, since his body had moved a little down the slope. He had a greyish beard but it looked red now, drenched in his own blood. His khaki coat had cheap nickel buttons on it— one could get eight such buttons for one pice—the shoe-laces had been loosened, as though he had loosened them himself in preparation for his journey to the next world. He appeared to be a Kashmiri. Dev Datt looked back towards the road. A group of men stood there, staring hard at him. When he again looked at the dead body, he recognized the person. He was a Kashmiri load-carrier who worked at the nearby timber-stall belonging to Fateh Chand, and carried firewood and charcoal to the customers' houses.

Dev Datt thought for a while, his hand stroking his nose. Then he shook his head. 'No. This is not the time to attend to this man, alive or dead. Nor is this the time to go and see the Hindu's dead body. I must proceed straight to the Party office.'

The Party office had any number of flags, but only three persons were sitting there. The commune consisted of eight comrades; five of them were on duty at that time. There was one bad news, though. A Muslim comrade had lost faith and was leaving the commune.

'Mischief of the British! You call this mischief of the British! They throw a dead pig at the door of the mosque? Are there any British to be seen here?' the erstwhile comrade said, his lips trembling with rage. 'Three poor Muslims have been hacked to death before my very eyes and you call this British machination. To hell with it all!'

All Dev Datt could say to him to cool his temper was: 'Don't take any step in haste, comrade. The class to which we belong—the middle class—is easily affected by traditional influences. Had you come from the working class, the question of Hindu and Muslim would not have bothered you so much.'

But the comrade picked up his handbag and left.

'The comrade's ideological understanding is weak. To view things emotionally can be very misleading for a communist. It is necessary to understand the evolutionary process of society.'

The meeting began. The situation in the town, particularly with reference to the working-class areas, was the first item on the agenda.

'In no working-class area has there been any rioting so far. The information about Ratta is misleading. But tension remains. Comrade Jagdish's presence is effective— people still listen to him. There are twenty Sikh houses in the colony. Not a single incident has occurred so far. But Comrade Jagdish reports that the situation is worsening. There was a tiff between two workers yesterday. They abused each other. The rumours about what is happening elsewhere are affecting the morale of the workers. The decision is taken: Send Comrade Kurban Ali also to Ratta, so that Comrade Jagdish is not alone.' Dev Datt jotted down the decision.

'Dada has already left for the countryside. There has been no news from him so far. All traffic has come to a standstill—only one Buick car, of deep blue colour, has been seen going from village to village. Some people say that it is Shah Nawaz's car. Why is he going from village to village is not known.'

The meeting went on for a long time, with the three comrades deliberating over each item. And every item, on conclusion, was duly ticked on the notebook with a pencil by Dev Datt.

Then came the last item: to convene a joint meeting of the representatives of all parties.

'It will not be possible to hold such a meeting,' said one comrade. 'The Congress office is locked. If you talk to the members of the Muslim League, they start shouting slogans. Over every issue, their first demand is: Let the Congressmen first admit that the Congress is the party of the Hindus, then alone shall we sit with them. Besides, no one is stirring out of his mohalla. With whom will you hold the meeting?'

Dev Datt stroked his nose for some time and then dismissed the idea of having a joint meeting of ten representatives from each party. It wouldn't work. 'But we must bring together some select leaders. They may bring along some of their fellow-workers.'

'No one will come, Comrade,' said one comrade. 'If at all they do, there will only be accusations and counter- accusations. No positive result can be expected from such a meeting.'

'Comrades,' said Dev Datt, 'the very fact of their sitting together will exert a good influence on the people. We can then issue an appeal in their name asking the citizens to maintain peace. It can be put across through the loudspeakers in every mohalla.'

'What is the situation like at the moment? There is no large-scale killing but sniping continues.'

'It is of paramount importance to bring together leaders of political parties.'

A few other issues were also discussed. What should be the venue of this meeting? It was decided to hold it at Hayat Baksh's house.

'I shall bring Bakshiji there. As we enter the mohalla, Comrade Aziz will receive us at the entrance along with two or three other Muslim residents and we shall proceed to Hayat Baksh's house.'

'Have you spoken to Hayat Baksh?'

'I shall go now and talk to him.'

'Comrade, which dream-world are you living in? Who will let you reach his house?'

'You will accompany me,' Dev Datt said smilingly to Aziz.

'You are trying to put out a raging fire by merely sprinkling water on it. The fire will not be put out that way.'

But after the meeting, Dev Datt and Aziz went through lanes and by-lanes, hiding here and there, receiving threats and abuses and eventually succeeded in reaching Hayat Baksh's house.

And truly enough the meeting did take place that afternoon at Hayat Baksh's residence. Bakshiji was brought to the meeting by Dev Datt. Had he asked some other Congressman, he might have met with a refusal, but Dev Datt was sure that Bakshiji would not refuse. The man's thinking may not be very clear and he may not be good at solving political tangles, but he had spent a total of sixteen years of his life in jail and he abhorred bloodshed. During the last few days he had been speaking irritably with one and all because he felt both deeply disturbed and helpless. Even as he came with Dev Datt he kept talking ill of the communists all the way. But he did come, and also brought along two young Congress workers with him and the meeting did take place. At the meeting, there was angry exchange of words and accusations. For a full half hour Hayat Baksh kept insisting that Bakshiji must first declare that he had come as a representative of the Hindus and that the Congress was a party of the Hindus. At last Dev Datt had got up and said, 'Sahiban, this is not the time to go into such discussions. Outside, innocent people are being killed, houses are being burnt, and there is danger of the trouble spreading to the villages. Therefore it is our duty to stop this fire from spreading.'

Thereafter, Dev Datt read out the draft of the Appeal for Peace. Again a discussion started. 'The appeal cannot be issued in the name of the Congress and the Muslim League. It can only be issued in the personal names of Hayat Baksh and Bakshiji.' It was also suggested that some other persons too should be associated with it.

By then the people had grown tired. Hayat Baksh's son whispered into his father's ear that the appeal was an innocuous one since it was only an appeal for peace and that there was no harm in signing it. And so Hayat Baksh put his signature to it. Bakshiji too signed it. Thereafter slogans of Pakistan Zindabad were raised, and amidst these slogans, while Bakshiji was putting on his shoes, the news came that in the labour colony of Ratta too rioting had started and that two Sikh carpenters had been hacked to death.

Dev Datt refused to believe it. He thought it was a baseles rumour. Has anyone seen the rioting? With his own eyes? That was his first reaction. He kept repeating the question till the very end. Nevertheless, he was downcast, his head bowed and he felt that if the workers had started fighting one another, it meant that the poison had spread deep. Which also meant that the meeting had been a futile exercise.

Dev Datt decided that he would pick up his cycle from the Party office and forthwith proceed to Ratta. 'Come what may, I must reach Ratta. It will no longer be possible for Comrade Jagdish to face the situation alone. With my presence there the situation may improve and the workers may not lift their hands against one another.'

But when Dev Datt reached the Party office he found his father standing there, stick in hand. And when Dev Datt presented a Marxist analysis of the situation and said that every effort was being made to stop the riots, and began taking out his cycle, his father lost his temper. 'Swine, if you get killed, there will be no one even to pick up your dead body. Don't you see what is happening all around? You alone are going to stop the riots?'

and the father stepped forward and shut the door opening into the lane. He would have given his son a thrashing, he even lifted his stick, but then burst out crying: 'Why are you tormenting us? You are our only son. Be sensible. Don't you see how miserable your mother is? If you want, I shall put my turban at your feet. Come home.'

Dev Datt's hand went to his nose, he rubbed his hands. The situation was getting out of hand. It was necessary to seek someone's help. Someone will have to escort father home.

'I must go to Ratta. I cannot stay back here. But I shall make arrangements to see you home. Comrade Ram Nath will go with you.'

That very afternoon another death took place. The Jarnail was killed. Whimsical as he had always been, he set out to quell the riots, marching military style, with the cane tucked under his arm. No one was any the wiser for his thoughts, but his heart certainly surged with emotions and also perhaps a crazy whim, that what was happening in the town was deplorable and that all those Congressmen who were sitting at home were traitors.

He set out on his mission, and at numerous places, sometimes from the projection of a shop or at a street corner, he would stand and address the citizens:

'Sahiban, I wish to inform you that when Pandit Jawaharlal Nehru, on the bank of the Ravi took the pledge of full Independence, he danced round the national flag, and so had I. I too had danced with him. We had all taken the pledge on that day. Today all those who are sitting at home are traitors. Is this the day to sit at home? I say put on burkas and apply henna to your hands like women, if you have to sit at home.'

'Sahiban, Gandhiji has said that Hindus and Muslims are brothers, that they should not fight one another. I appeal to all of you, young and old, men and women, to stop fighting. It does great harm to the country. India's wealth is swallowed up by that fair-faced monkey who bosses over us...'

Through lanes and along streets he went making his appeal for peace till he entered the Committee Mohalla. The day was declining when, while he was delivering his speech quite a few bystanders gathered round him, and without knowing where he was, he went on in his usual vein:

'Sahiban, Hindus and Musalmans are brothers. There is rioting in the city; fires are raging and there is no one to stop it. The deputy commissioner is sitting in his bungalow, with his madam in his arms. I say, our real enemy is the Englishman. Gandhiji says that it is the Englishman who makes us fight one another. We should not be taken in by what the Englishman says. Gandhiji says, Pakistan shall be made over his dead body. I also say that Pakistan shall be made over my dead body. We are brothers, we shall live together, we shall live as one...'

'You, son of a...' shouted someone standing behind him, and with one swing of his lathi, hit the Jarnail on his head and broke his skull into two. Jarnail fell down in a heap, with his cane, his green 'military' uniform, his torn turban and his torn chappals, before he could finish his sentence.

12

'One of you will keep watch on the balcony,' Ranvir turned round and ordered. After passing the initiation test by slaughtering the hen, he had developed supreme self-confidence. There was now a ring of authority in his voice. And he was, without doubt, the smartest in his group of young 'warriors'.

The 'armoury', despite the sticks, the woodchopper, knives, daggers, bows and arrows, and the catapults, still looked rather bare. Outside the room, a little removed from the staircase stood an oven with a cauldron of oil on it, but the idea of boiling the oil had been given up due to shortage of firewood.

'Yes, Sardar!' Shambhu said and marched towards the balcony.

All the four 'warriors' were itching for action. Time had come to enter the battlefield and show one's feats of valour. Standing on the balcony they felt the same way as the Rajputs of yore did, who, taking cover behind rocks and dunes waited for the mleccha hordes to enter Haldi Ghati before they pounced upon them.

Ranvir was short of stature, that is why, he visualized himself in the role of Shivaji. With eyes screwed up he would survey the road below and the adjacent area. He had an intense longing to wear an *angarakha* and a yellow turban with a steel ring covering it, and carry a sword hanging from his broad waistband. A shapeless pair of pyjamas, an ordinary shirt and a worn-out pair of chappals was no dress for a 'warrior', and that too on the verge of a mighty conflict! But the impress of authority which his dress lacked was more than made up for by the tenor of his sharp commanding voice. He gave orders like a seasoned army commander, and enforced strict discipline on the members of the group. With his hands joined behind his back, and a slight stoop of his shoulders he would stroll up and down the 'armoury' in much the same way as Shivaji must have strolled, before taking on Aurangzeb.

'Sardar!'

Ranvir turned round. It was Manohar who had been putting small piles of pebbles beside the catapult on the window-sill.

'We have run short of firewood and therefore the oil cannot be boiled.'

'Don't we have charcoal?'

'No, Sardar!'

Ranvir strolled up and down the room for some time. War strategy demands that the commander assess the situation in all its aspects and take a quick decision. That was imperative for a leader.

'Get it from your house, coal or firewood, whichever is available, in whatever quantity. Without delay!'

But Manohar continued to stand, somewhat nonplussed.

'What is it?'

'What if mummy doesn't let me?'

Ranvir stared hard at Manohar's face and shouted fiercely: 'What are you looking at my face for? Get firewood from wherever you can.'

'Yes, Sardar!' and Manohar stepped back.

'But wait. I can't send you home at this time.'

The idea of boiling oil was given up for the time being.

The 'armoury' had been set up on the upper floor of a double-storeyed house which was lying vacant. The ground floor was occupied by Shambhu's grandparents. The balcony on the upper storey faced the road. A stately banyan tree stood in front of the house. Its thick foliage provided a safe cover to anyone standing on the balcony. The entrance to the house was, however, from the side-lane—a dark, narrow lane with many turns and twists in it. A person entering it from the roadside would get lost in it in no time. While describing the locale to Ranvir, Shambhu had likened the entrance of the lane to the entrance to the Chakra Vyuh of Mahabharata and therefore eminently suitable as their base of operations. The lane, after some distance, turned to the left. At the turn stood a dilapidated grave of some pir, and right opposite the grave lived an old Musalman who had two wives. A little farther down was the municipal water-tap to which no one came till four in the afternoon. The houses beyond the tap were all inhabited by Hindus. Only at the end of the lane were there two or three mud houses in which Muslim families lived. In one of them lived Mahmud the washerman and in the other, Rahman who ran a hamam. Besides, there were many by-lanes which branched off from this lane and went in different directions. If a mleccha had to be attacked in this lane, then it had to be done in the area between the water-tap and a little before the end of the lane. If anything went amiss, one could immediately get into the entrance of a Hindu's house.

'What do you know about the mlecchas who live in this lane?' Ranvir had asked Shambhu.

'I know them well enough, Sardar. Mahmud, the washerman washes our family's clothes; and the Mianji who lives opposite the gate is on very cordial terms with my grandfather.'

'We shall not operate in this lane,' said Ranvir decisively.

Shambhu felt greatly discouraged.

The day had come to launch their operations, when they would attack their first victim. So far the 'warriors' had been preoccupied with preparations. The day had come to prove their mettle. The line of a war-song: 'Go into the battlefield like a whirlwind and vanquish the foe!' had been ringing in Dharam Dev's ears since long. Manohar was a little nervous. He had come away without telling his mother and it was nearing two in the afternoon. Manohar was afraid that his mother, after winding up her kitchen work, might come out looking for him and trace him out in that house.

Ranvir summoned the three 'warriors' into the armoury and reflecting over the strategy declared:

'Time has not yet come for the use of boiling oil. It is when the enemy attacks your fortress and other weapons become ineffective that you pour boiling oil on the enemy.'

Then, after thinking for a while he added: 'Here only a dagger will serve the purpose, a dagger with a spring.'

Turning to Inder, the Sardar said, 'We want to see your footwork. Give us a demonstration of how you will turn on your feet while attacking the enemy. Pick up a knife from the window-sill.'

Inder promptly brought the knife and came and stood in the middle of the room, his legs apart. Holding the knife in his right hand, its blade directed inward, he lifted his left foot, took a sudden leap in the air and making a semi-circular movement, came down on the floor, with his knife aimed at Ranvir's back.

Ranvir shook his head.

'Never aim at the enemy's chest or back. Always plunge the knife into his waist or stomach. And when the blade is inside, give it a twist; this will pull out his intestines. If you attack the enemy in a crowd, do not pull out the knife. Leave it there and get lost in the crowd.'

Ranvir was only repeating what he had heard from Master Dev Vrat's mouth.

A little later, the group was divided into two sections. It was decided that Inder would be the first one to attack. Hence, while Manohar stood watch on the balcony, Inder, Shambhu and the Sardar came downstairs into the entrance. Whereas Manohar would keep his eyes on the road, the other three would watch the lane. And when Ranvir gave his signal, Inder would step out of the house and pounce upon the enemy. On opening the door slightly one could see a part of the road and the front part of the lane. Beyond the thick trunk of the banyan tree the road was bathed in the afternoon sunlight.

A tonga stopped at the entrance to the lane. Through a chink in the door, they all looked out. A man was alighting from the tonga.

'Who is he?' whispered Inder.

They all put their eyes to the chink.

'It is Jalal Khan, Nawabzada Jalal Khan,' whispered Shambhu. 'He lives across the road. A big landlord. Goes to meet the deputy commissioner twice a month.'

Through the chink the fluttering tuft of his white turban, his pointed moustaches and ruddy face could be seen. But he disappeared as quickly as he had become visible. As he passed through the lane, the rustling sound of his well-starched salwar and shoes was heard. But before any decision could be taken the man had already gone into some house. All the 'warriors' stood non-plussed. Otherwise too the man was tall and well-built, and on seeing him pass by, they felt overawed. He had given them so little time to think.

Masterji had said that one must never look closely at the enemy, because then, one begins to waver in one's resolve. Looking closely at any living being produces sympathy in one's heart, which must not be allowed to happen.

A door opened in the lane and was immediately shut with a bang. All the three 'warriors' pricked their ears. Ranvir adjusted the panels of the door in such a way that the chink between them revealed more of the lane.

'Who is there?' asked Inder in a low whisper.

'A mleccha,' replied Ranvir.

Both the warriors glued their eyes to the chink, one below the other. An elderly man with a beard was coming through the lane towards the road.

'It is Mianji,' Shambhu said, on recognizing him. 'He lives in the house opposite the pir's grave. He goes everyday at this time to the mosque to offer his namaz.

'Shut up!'

The man went out of the lane and, near the banyan tree, turned left. He was wearing a black waistcoat, a salwar and a loose pair of chappals. A small rosary dangled from his right hand. Being an old man he walked slowly with a stoop.

'Shall I go?' Inder asked the Sardar.

'No, he is already on the road.'

'So what?'

'It is forbidden to attack a person on the road.' Shambhu had felt shaken by Inder's insistence, but felt greatly relieved when Ranvir said 'no' to him.

Some more time passed. At four o'clock, women would start going with their pitchers to the water-tap. And therefore, with the afternoon declining, more and more people would start stepping out of their houses.

Two persons, one behind the other, entered the lane from the roadside. One of them, wearing spectacles, was plying along a cycle.

'That is Babu Chunni Lal. He works in some office. He has a dog.'

The patter of their shoes was heard as they went through the lane.

The sound of footsteps was again heard. The 'warriors' put their eyes to the chink.

'Who is it?'

'It is some pedlar,' Inder whispered.

'No,' said Shambhu. 'He sells oils and scents. He comes from far away everyday at this time. He is a mleccha.' A bulky person, his peaked beard and moustaches dyed in henna, with two or three bags hanging from his shoulders and one on his back, came in sight, entering the lane from the side of the banyan tree. Due to the heavy load he was carrying, drops of perspiration had gathered on his forehead. There were swabs of cotton in his ears and a couple of long needles stuck into his turban.

Ranvir felt as though something had moved behind his back. He turned round. Inder's hand had gone to his pocket in which lay the long knife with a spring.

Time was passing. The decisive moment had come. The man was a mleccha, loaded with bags so that he could neither run, nor defend himself, besides, he was tired—all these were favourable factors. Time was passing and the pedlar was moving farther and farther away into the lane. Ranvir made a sign, and the next moment, Inder had leapt into the lane. There was a flash of light as the door was opened, but Ranvir immediately shut the door.

Not a sound anywhere. Ranvir and Shambhu stood behind

the door with bated breath. Ranvir became extremely tense. He couldn't control himself. He softly opened the door and looked out. The scent-seller, his back bent was walking unsteadily, swaying from side to side. And the tiny Inder followed him at some distance, his hand in his shirt pocket.

Ranvir was in a fix. He was too curious to know what was happening and yet could not open the door, whereas Shambhu was scared stiff, his legs trembling. The last glimpse Ranvir had was of Inder walking alongside the bulky pedlar when both of them were turning the corner in the lane.

Shambhu bolted the door from inside.

Both of them stood facing each other in the dark, breathing hard. Ranvir was becoming increasingly impatient to go out and see what was happening; for Shambhu it was becoming impossible even to keep standing.

As they turned the corner, the scent-seller's eyes fell on the boy. Because of the sound made by his own shoes the pedlar had not heard him approaching.

The scent-seller smiled.

'Where are you going, son, at this time of the day?' and putting out his hand, patted him on his head.

Inder stopped short and stared hard at the man's face. His right hand was inside his pocket. Subconsciously he took note of the fact that the pedlar had bloated cheeks, and Masterji had once said that people with bloated cheeks were cowardly, that they had weak digestion and could not run, that they became breathless very soon. And the man was actually breathing hard.

Inder was balancing himself before pouncing upon his victim. His eyes were still riveted on the pedlar's face.

To the scent-seller the boy appeared to be young and tender, perhaps he was walking with him for protection. Perhaps the boy was frightened. Everyone in the city was frightened that day.

'Where do you live, child? Keep walking along with me. One should not stir out of the house on a day like this.'

But Inder was not shaken in his resolve. He still had his eyes on the pedlar's face.

'You can come with me up to Teli Mohalla. If you have to go farther, I shall ask someone to accompany you. There is trouble in the city.'

And without waiting for the boy's reply, continued walking.

For a brief moment, Inder paused and stood where he was, but then stepped forward and continued walking.

There was silence all round. The houses around stood in utter darkness.

'I too should not have come out on my round today.' He said to Inder. 'The town is stricken by drought, as it were. This is not a day for selling one's wares. But then I thought, if I can make even a few annas, it will not be bad. If a pedlar sits at home, how will he eat?' And the man laughed.

They were getting close to the water tap, which was as yet dry. The stone slab under it had become hollow with time; a few wasps were hovering over it. Inder used to catch wasps here.

'Even if only four cotton swabs are sold in a day, we make four annas, which is good enough,' the scent-seller was saying, as though talking to himself. It seemed he wanted to talk, either to while away the time, or because it helped him somehow to walk through deserted streets.

'I know who my potential buyers are in every street of the town,' he said. 'A man with two wives is my potential client. He must buy scent; he will also buy henna and collyrium. An ageing man with a young wife will also buy scent. Shall I tell you more?' He said wanting to entertain the boy.

The scent-seller's continuous monologue succeeded in steadying Inder and he was able to walk more confidently, his hand firmly on the handle of the knife. He was all concentration now, and his eyes were set on the scent-seller's waist, as intently as Arjun's must have been on the bird on the branch of the tree. The bag hanging from the left shoulder of the scent-seller swayed to and fro like the pendulum of a clock, exposing his thick cotton shirt covering his waist.

The water-tap was left behind. Inder's attention now centred on his right hand. He was aware of every step he took. It appeared as though the pattering of the pedlar's shoes was marking time with the swaying bag.

'In the bazaar, the cotton swabs sell more, whereas in the lanes, oil and scent are more in demand.' The scent-seller was saying.

Suddenly, Inder took a leap and made a quick movement. The pedlar felt as though something had moved with a flash on his left side. But before he could turn round to see what it was, he felt as though something had pricked him badly under the bag. Inder had struck accurately, and as instructed by the Sardar, had given a twist to the handle too, while the blade was still inside, and thus entangled it with the intestines.

The scent-seller had hardly turned round when he saw the boy running away, with his back towards him. Even then he did not understand what had happened. He wanted to call the boy back, but then he noticed drops of blood falling on his shoes and felt as though something was tearing his waist. As yet the sensation was not so sharp, but it was soon followed by searing pain. The man became extremely nervous. Stricken with fear he shouted:

'O, I have been killed!'

He was so terribly frightened that he could hardly shout. He was dying, not so much from the wound inflicted on him, as from sheer fright. He still couldn't believe that an innocent-looking boy could have attacked him. The load on his back and shoulders became unbearable, and it was under its weight that he fell face downward.

Only a few seconds earlier he had clearly seen the boy's running feet, but there was now no sign of the boy in the lane.

'O, I have been killed!' he whispered.

A hoarse cry escaped his lips and his eyes rested on a patch of the deep-blue sky over and above the narrow lane, in which two or three kites were flying. Soon enough the number of kites seemed to increase and the patch of blue got blurred.

13

Nathu was deeply disturbed. Sitting outside his house he was puffing at his hookah incessantly. His heart would sink every time he heard about the killings. He would try again and again to console himself: 'I am not a know-all. How could I know for what purpose I was being asked to kill a pig?' For some time he would overcome his uneasiness and feel reassured. But he would again lose his peace of mind when he would hear about some other incident. 'It is all the result of my doing.' Since morning, his fellow-skinners in the colony had been sitting and chatting outside one another's houses. Time and again, Nathu would go and sit with them. He would try to join in the conversation, but each time he tried, his throat would go dry and his legs would tremble, and he would go back into his house. 'Should I speak out? Tell my wife everything? She is a sensible woman, she will understand and I shall feel relieved.' Sometimes he wished he could gulp down a glassful of country wine so that he could lie unconscious. 'To tell my wife can be risky. Suppose, in an unguarded moment, in a casual conversation, she blurts out what really happened. What then? No one will spare me. I may be put behind bars. The police can put me under arrest and take me away. What will happen then? No one will believe me if I said that I had done the job on Murad Ali's instructions. And Murad Ali is a Musalman. Will a Musalman get a pig killed so that it can be thrown outside a mosque?' He would again become extremely restless. He would again try to divert his mind by arguing with himself: 'It couldn't have been the same pig that was thrown outside the mosque. I have not seen it, but any pig can be of black colour. Can't there be two pigs of the same colour? I am worrying about it without any rhyme or reason. It was certainly some other pig.' Reassured by such thoughts he would begin to chat and laugh with his wife. He would even go to his neighbour's house and begin talking about the fire in the grain market. But such a state of mind would not last long. He had only to remember what had happened during the previous night— from the moment the pig was pushed into the filthy hut to the arrival of the pushcart under cover of darkness in that desolate area—the whole episode would be like a nightmare and he would relapse into the same jittery state of mind. 'Will a veterinary surgeon procure a slaughtered pig in this way? "The pigs go roaming about there, get hold of one... a pushcart will come to take the carcass; don't move out of the hut; wait for me." Is this the way jobs are done?' Nathu had a mind to go straight to Kalu, the scavenger and ask him where he had delivered the pig. Go straight to Murad Ali... 'But what will Murad Ali say? If there is evil in his heart, he will push me out of his house, hold me guilty and get me arrested. He is quite capable of doing this.'

He again picked up his hookah. 'To hell with Murad Ali and his pig! I have done nothing on purpose. Whatever I did, was done in ignorance. What about those who are setting fire and killing innocent pedestrians and committing such heinous crimes? Why are they indulging in such foul acts with wide open eyes? I have killed one pig. Of what consequence is the killing of one pig? If I am a criminal, aren't they worse criminals? If I am guilty, aren't they guilty too? What about those who have set fire to the grain market? I have not done anything deliberately. Whatever had to happen, has happened; I have nothing to do with it all...'

Nathu thought of his father. He was a God-fearing man who always used to say, 'Son, keep your hands clean. A man whose hands are clean, will never do an evil deed. Earn your bread with dignity and self-respect.' As Nathu remembered his father's words, tears came into his eyes. And his heart became heavy once again.

Across the yard, a man walking along the road, had stopped
and was looking intently towards the skinners' colony. Nathu's
heart missed a beat. It seemed to him that the man was looking
for him; as though he had come to spot out the man who had
killed the pig.

Nathu's wife came out wiping her hands with a corner of her
dhoti. Nathu again felt uneasy. He felt like telling her everything.
'There should at least be someone to whom I can open my heart.'
Nathu's eyes again turned towards the man standing across the
yard.

'What are you looking at?' His wife said, then turning her
eyes towards the road, asked, 'Who is he? Do you know him?'

'No. How should I know him?' Nathu replied with a
bewildered look in his eyes. 'Why are you standing there? Go
inside,' he said brusquely.

She promptly went into the room.

Nathu again looked towards the road through the corner of
his eyes. The man was moving away. On reaching the end of the
yard, he lighted a cigarette and went away puffing at it.

'I was mistaken,' Nathu said to himself. 'On a working day so
many people come here on some business or the other.'

He felt relieved. 'It was wrong of me to have spoken so roughly
with her.'

'Listen,' he said to her. 'Make some tea for me.'

His wife came and stood in the doorway. There was something
about her which gave Nathu a sense of confidence. He felt more
secure if she was by his side. Her presence in the house imparted
a sense of stability. When she was not around, it was as though
things were going haywire. Today too he was inwardly very keen
that she sit close to him. She was never restless or tense or nervous;
nothing ever seemed to gnaw at her heart. It was so, he thought,
because she was physically buxom, not a dried-up stick as he
was, with hollow cheeks and a perpetually worried mind. She
was relaxed, with a steady, balanced mind and a warm presence.

She came and stood on the threshold, a soft smile on her lips.

'You generally don't ask for tea at this time of the day. You seem to be enjoying a holiday today. Is that why you want tea?'

'Am I enjoying a holiday? Do you think it is a holiday?' Nathu said peevishly, 'If you can't make it, I shall make it myself. Why are you making such a fuss about it?' So saying Nathu got up and went into the room.

'Why are you cross? I shall make it for you in a minute.'

'No, no, you needn't bother. I shall make it myself.'

'I would rather die than let you light the fire when I am around,' she said and pulled him by his arm.

Nathu stood up. He felt a stab of pain in his heart. For a second he stood undecided. Then, with all the eagerness of his heart, he clasped his wife to himself.

'What is the matter with you today?' His wife said, laughing. But in his ardent embraces she sensed his disquiet. There is something troubling him, otherwise he wouldn't behave in this queer manner.

'What has come over you? Since last night you have been behaving in a strange sort of way. Tell me what is on your mind. I feel frightened.'

'What have we to be afraid of? We have not set fire to anyone's house.' Nathu came out with this odd reply.

His wife's hand stopped stroking his back, but she did not disengage herself from him.

Nathu became all the more agitated. He was behaving like a crazy person.

Suddenly, the pig's carcass flitted across his mind. It lay, right in the middle of the floor, with its legs raised and a pool of blood under it. Nathu trembled and went limp and cold in every limb. His shoulders were covered with cold sweat. It appeared to his wife as though his mind had again wandered off to something else. Suddenly Nathu tried to suppress a sob, and disentangling himself from his wife's embrace, muttered, 'No, not today. I don't feel like it. See what is happening outside. People's houses are burning.'

And for a long time he stood where he was, as though in a daze. His wife grew anxious.

'What is on your mind? Why have you become so quiet? Swear by me that you will tell me the truth.'

Nathu stepped aside and quietly went and sat down on the cot.

'What is it?'

'Nothing.'

'There is something. You are hiding it from me.'

'There is nothing,' he said again.

Nathu's wife came over to him and stroking his hand said, 'Why don't you speak? Say something.'

'I would tell you if there was anything to tell.'

'Wait. I shall get you some tea.'

'I don't want tea.'

'A little while ago you were asking for it. You were going to make it yourself. And now you don't want it.'

'No, I don't want it.'

'All right then, come to bed,' she said laughing.

'No.'

'Are you angry with me? You are losing your temper over every little thing,' she said somewhat resentfully.

Nathu remained quiet. He was actually behaving like a sulky child.

'Where did you go last night? You have not told me anything,' Nathu's wife said, sitting down on the floor beside him.

Nathu looked at his wife, as though taken aback. 'She has sensed it. Soon enough, everyone will know about it,' Nathu trembled at the thought.

'If you won't tell me, I shall break my head against the wall. You have never concealed anything from me. Why are you doing so today?'

Nathu's eyes rested on his wife's face. 'If she suspects anything, then God knows what she must be thinking.' His wife's trusting and beseeching eyes were still looking at him.

'Do you know why the grain market is burning?'

'I know someone killed a pig and threw it outside a mosque. And then the Musalmans set fire to the grain market.'

'I killed that pig.'

Nathu's wife turned pale.

'Did you? Why did you commit such a loathsome act?'

All the blood drained out of her face and she stared at her husband.

'Did you throw the pig outside the mosque too?'

'No. Kalu the scavenger took it on his pushcart.'

'Kalu is a Musalman. How could he carry it?'

'Kalu is not a Musalman. He is a Christian. He goes to church on Sundays.'

Her eyes were still on Nathu's face.

'What a horrible thing you have done. But you are not to blame. You were tricked into doing it,' she muttered, as though to herself. But she had trembled while listening to Nathu's account, and felt as though the shadow of some dreadful omen had fallen on their home which could not be eliminated even by fasts and prayers.

His mind felt weighed down by the confession. Nathu was deeply troubled at heart. His wife raised her eyes and looked at him. On seeing him so unhappy, a surge of warm feeling rose in her heart. She got up and sat down by his side, and taking his hand into hers, said, 'Now I know. I would say to myself, why is he so upset? But how could I know? Why didn't you tell me earlier? It is wrong to keep your grief to yourself.'

'Had I known what it involved, I wouldn't have done it,' Nathu muttered. 'I was told that the veterinary surgeon had asked for a pig,' said Nathu, sinking deeper into despondency. 'I saw Murad Ali last night. But he wouldn't talk to me. I ran after him, but he wouldn't stop. He quickened his pace and went farther and farther away. He didn't even care to talk to me.' Nathu's voice was again lost in doubt and uncertainty. He had once again begun to doubt whether he had actually seen Murad Ali or not.

'How much did you get for killing the pig?'

'Five rupees. He paid the money in advance.'

'Five rupees? So much money? What did you do with it?'

'Four rupees are still left with me. They are lying on the shelf.'

'Why didn't you tell me?'

'I thought I would buy a couple of dhotis for you.'

'Shall I get dhotis with tainted money? Shall I not throw this money into the fire?' Nathu's wife said angrily. But then she restrained herself and making a vain attempt to smile, added, 'But this is your hard-earned money. I shall buy with it whatever you say.'

She got up, went to the shelf, lifted herself on her toes, saw the coins lying on the shelf and turned round. Nathu sat with his head bowed, as though sunk deeper into despair.

'Did you notice the man who was standing on the other side of the yard?' Nathu asked, raising his head.

'Yes, I did. But how does it concern us?'

'I think it was his pig that I pushed into the room. He must have come to know of it.'

'What nonsense! If he has come to know of it, let him come and demand it from you,' Nathu's wife said somewhat loudly, then, shaking her head, added, 'Listen. We are chamars. To kill animals and skin hides is our profession. You killed a pig. Now, how does it concern us whether they sell it in the market or throw it on the steps of a mosque?' Then added, chirpily, 'I shall certainly buy dhotis with this money. You have earned it with your hard labour.' Then, going back to the shelf she picked up the money, but the next moment put it back.

'You are perfectly right,' exclaimed Nathu. 'How does it concern me? To hell with Murad Ali and his pig! Yesterday too I thought the same way,' he said, with a ring of self-assurance in his voice.

'I have full fifteen rupees with me now. You too can buy something for yourself.'

'I don't need anything,' said Nathu feeling elated. 'When you are by my side, I feel I have everything.'

Nathu's wife went straight to the fireplace and sat down to make tea.

'God is never angry with a person whose heart is clean. Our hearts are clean. Why should we be afraid of anyone?' she said and then added, 'You have told me about it but don't tell anyone else in the colony.'

'You too don't tell anyone,' said Nathu.

Nathu's wife was pouring tea into glasses, when she heard the sound of running feet outside. Her hand shook. She raised her eyes and looked at Nathu, but did not say anything. Instead, she smiled.

A little later, they heard one skinner asking another, outside, in the colony. 'What's happened, uncle?'

'A riot has broken out in Ratta.'

'Where?'

'In Ratta. Two persons have been killed.'

'Who was the fellow running away?'

'I don't know. Must be some outsider.'

Silence fell again. The skinner had either gone into his house or towards the back of the colony.

Handing the glass of tea to Nathu, his wife said, 'You too should go and meet the fellow-skinners. It is not good to remain aloof from them. Let's go together; I too will come along.'

Nathu's wife got up, but then, without any explicable reason, picked up the broom and started sweeping the floor. She swept every nook and corner, picked up things and swept the floor under them. She herself did not know why she was doing it. It was as though, with the help of the broom she was trying to cast out some phantom or spectre from the room. After sweeping, she washed the floor clean, pouring as much water as she could. But when she sat down tired, on the cot, it seemed to her that the phantom was crawling back into the room through the chinks of the closed door and that the house was once again becoming dark with its presence.

14

Starting from Khanpur, the first bus would normally reach the village at eight o'clock in the morning. After every hour or two, buses would begin to arrive from the city or from Khanpur. It was already midday and as yet no bus had arrived. In the tea shop, the water in the kettle for tea had been boiling since morning. Both the benches in front of the tea shop lay vacant. Earlier, there used to be so many customers that the benches were always occupied. There was hardly a person who, passing by Harnam Singh's tea shop would not sit down for a glass of tea. At the bus stop too, only a couple of stray dogs were to be seen moving about. A pall of silence lay over everything.

A woman has a keener insight into things. Since the previous evening, Banto had been insisting, 'Let us get away from this village and go to Khanpur where some of our relatives are living. In this entire village we are the only Sikh couple, all the others are Muslims.' But Harnam Singh would not agree. 'How can we shut down a running shop and go away? Riots and disturbances keep taking place but that is no reason why one should close down one's business. And where shall we go? Shall we go to the city which is already in flames? If we go to Khanpur, who will feed us there? What if our shop is looted when we turn our back on it? How shall we live? Shall we go to our son? He is living twenty miles away in Mirpur. He is as much alone there as we are here. Let us leave ourselves in Guru Maharaj's hands and stick on where we are. If we go to our son, won't we be a liability on him? Will he try to protect us old people or try to save his own life? For how long can we be fed by others? And for how long can we live on our savings?' And sitting on his stool, Harnam Singh would fold his hands and recite a couplet: 'Blessed with your protecting hand, Lord, how can anyone suffer?'

Banto would listen and fall silent. But then, whenever she felt nervous and anxious she would say, 'Let us go to my sister's village, that is nearby. We shall not stay with her, we shall stay in the gurdwara. Besides, there is a fairly large community of Sikhs living there. They are our own people. We shall feel safe living among them.' But Harnam Singh would not agree to this either. He was somehow convinced that while other people might have difficulties to face, nothing untoward would happen to him.

'Listen, my good woman, we have never thought ill of anyone; we have never harmed anyone. People in the village too have been good to us. We do not owe anyone anything. Right in your presence, Karim Khan has assured me no less than ten times that we should continue to live here with an easy mind, that no one would dare cast an evil eye on us, and who in the village enjoys more respect than Karim Khan? We are the only family of Sikhs living in the village. Will they not feel ashamed of attacking two defenceless old people?'

Banto again fell silent. Argument can counter argument, but argument is helpless against faith. While Banto's heart would, time and again, sink with anxiety, Harnam Singh did not feel restless even once. His face glowed and God's name was ever on his lips, and this would impart courage to Banto too.

But on that day no bus had arrived and not a single customer had come to his shop. The road bore a deserted look. On the other hand, two or three persons whom he had never seen before, while going towards the village, had eyed him and his shop very closely.

When the afternoon sun was declining, he heard the sound of familiar footsteps coming from the side of the slope. Harnam Singh felt reassured on seeing Karim Khan coming towards his shop, pattering along with his stick. Karim Khan would give him the news besides good counsel. 'If it becomes unsafe, we can take shelter in Karim Khan's house,' thought Harnam Singh.

Karim Khan came over but did not stop at his shop. As he passed by, he merely turned his face once towards Harnam Singh, slowed down his pace, and muttered while pretending to cough: 'Things have taken a bad turn, Harnam Singh. Your welfare lies in leaving the place.'

Then after taking a couple of more steps added, 'Local people will not do you any harm but it is feared that marauders may come from outside. We will not be able to stop them.'

And coughing and pattering his stick, he moved on.

For the first time, his faith which had all along given him moral strength was badly shaken. Karim Khan did not stop at his shop, which meant that the danger was real. He must have come here at some risk to himself. The news did not scare him so much as it made him sad. He felt disenchanted, rather than angry or frightened.

About five minutes later Karim Khan was seen coming back. Climbing up the slope, his hand on his waist, coughing and breathing hard, he again slowed his pace and muttered: 'Don't delay, Harnam Singh. The situation is not good. There is fear of marauders attacking.'

And he continued climbing up, breathing hard, with his hand on his waist.

Where was Harnam Singh to go? For miles on end, on all sides, stretched roads and vast stretches of land. Karim Khan had of course advised him to leave, but leave for where? Where could he get shelter? At sixty and with a woman by his side, how far could he run for safety?

A voice again came from within him: 'Do not go anywhere, stay where you are. When the marauders come, offer them both your shop and your lives. It is better to die rather than to go knocking from pillar to post.' Harnam Singh still could not believe that anyone from the village would raise his hand against him or that the village folk would allow the outsiders to attack them.

Harnam Singh got up and went into the room at the back of the tea shop where Banto was sitting.

'Karim Khan was here a moment ago. He said that we should leave the village immediately, that there was danger of marauders coming from outside.'

Banto's blood froze. She sat petrified. Night was approaching and there was nowhere to go. And there, in the middle of the room, stood her husband, a picture of despondency.

There was no time to think, nor could they linger here any longer.

'We must get away from here as soon as it gets dark.'

'I still maintain that we should stick on here,' said Harnam Singh. 'We shouldn't go anywhere.' Then, pointing to his double-barrelled gun hanging on the wall, he added, 'If it comes to killing or getting killed, I shall shoot you down with this gun first and then kill myself.'

Banto listened in silence. What could she say? What counsel could she give? They were left with no choice.

Harnam Singh came back to the shop. He collected his earnings from under the coir-matting on which he used to sit, separated the currency notes from the coins, put back the coins, and put the wad of notes in the inner pocket of his waistcoat. Thereafter he took down the gun from the wall and hung it from his shoulder. He was unable to decide what else to take with him. 'Shall I take the papers concerning the registration of the shop?' But there was no time to look for them or to take them out. Banto too was in a fix. 'Should I take my jewellery along? Shall I cook something for the way? Make a couple of chapattis? Nothing may be available on the way. Shall I change my clothes? One should wear clean and tidy clothes when going out.' Banto too was unable to decide what she should pick up, and what leave behind.

'What should I do with my ornaments?' she asked. 'Should I put them on?'

'Put them on,' Harnam Singh said, but then thought for a moment and said, 'No, don't put them on. Anyone seeing you with ornaments will be tempted to kill you. Go and bury them at the back of the house.'

Banto decided to put on some ornaments under her shirt; of

some others she made a small bundle in a handkerchief and put
it in a trunk; the rest she took with her to the backyard behind
the shop and buried them in the ground near the vegetable-beds.

The living room behind the tea shop was full of boxes, beddings
and other household stuff. They had got so many things made at
the time of their daughter's wedding yet nothing could be taken
along.

'Shall I make a couple of chapattis? Who knows where we
may have to go knocking?'

'There is no time for making chapattis now, good woman.
Had we thought of leaving earlier, it could have been done.'

Just then came the sound of beating drums from far away.
Both stood staring at each other.

'The marauders are here. They seem to be coming from
Khanpur.'

The sound of drums was soon followed by another sound—of
slogans being raised from the other side of the mound in the
village.

'Ya Ali!'

'Allah-o-Akbar!'

'It must be Ashraf and Latif who are shouting these slogans,'
murmured Harnam Singh. 'They are members of the League in
the village and keep shouting Pakistani slogans.'

The atmosphere became tense.

Evening had fallen but it wasn't dark yet. The sound of the
marauders appeared to be coming from the other side of the
ravine.

Just then Harnam Singh's eyes fell on the small cage hanging
from the roof in which sat their little pet-bird myna.

'Banto, take the cage to the backyard, and let the myna fly
away.'

Only a little while earlier Banto had put water and bird-feed
in the two small cups lying in the cage. Now, as she took down
the cage and carried it to the backyard, the little myna repeated
by rote: 'God be with you, Banto! May God be with everyone.'

On hearing the words Banto's throat choked. In answer to

the bird, Banto too repeated the words: 'Myna, may God be with you! May God be with everyone!'

The myna had learnt these words from Harnam Singh, who, while sitting in the shop, would often talk to Banto sitting in the back room about the Gurbani and other religious matters, and every time he would stand up or sit down he would utter such words as 'God is the Protector! God is everyone's protector!' Gradually, the myna had begun to repeat the words.

But the utterance of the myna gave a lot of strength to Banto. She regained courage and her steadiness, as though the little bird had taught her a lesson.

In the small backyard Harnam Singh had planted a few vegetables besides a mango tree. On reaching the middle of the backyard, Banto opened the cage and said softly:

'Go, fly away my little myna!

'May God be with you! May God be with everyone!'

But the myna continued to sit inside the cage.

'Fly away, my little one!

'Fly away!'

And Banto's throat again choked. Leaving the cage on the ground, she came back into the room.

The sound of beating drums was again heard. This time it came from somewhere nearby. The hum of sounds from the village too had grown louder. A large number of people seemed to be advancing from somewhere. From within the village, the sound of slogans came intermittently.

Banto and Harnam Singh, locked the shop and came out. They left with a little cash, a gun and the clothes on their back. No sooner had they stepped out of the house that the entire place became alien to them. Which way were they to turn? To the left lay the sprawling village. In that very direction was the ravine, from the other side of which came the sound of beating drums. To their right was the pucca road that led towards Khanpur. To go in that direction was not without danger. Across the road, at some distance, flowed a streamlet with a wide bed and a high embankment. That was the only way of escape. They could cover a long distance without being noticed. To go along the road was risky. The streamlet had no water in it; its broad bed was dry and full of sand, pebbles and stones. Both of them crossed the road, and walking a few yards, went down the slope of the embankment. The marauders had already reached the outskirts of the village and seemed to be advancing in this very direction. The atmosphere resounded with the sound of drums and slogans.

Banto and Harnam Singh were going down the bed of the stream when they heard a thin, soft voice:

'Banto, May God be with you! May God be with everyone!'

The myna had come flying after them and had perched on a tree nearby.

The marauders had by then reached the top of the mound, at the foot of which, to the right side Harnam Singh had his tea shop. They came down the mound, shrieking and shouting and raising slogans, and beating their drums.

The moon had risen and its soft light spread all over. One felt as though an unknown enemy lurked behind every tree and rock. Under the light of the moon, the dry stream-bed looked like a white sheet of cloth. Both of them had come down the slope and, turning to the right, were walking slowly along the foot of the embankment. The edge of the stream-bed being strewn with stones and pebbles, they soon grew tired and breathless. Even as they walked they were all ears to every sound coming from the direction of the village.

The noise which had earlier risen to a high pitch had somewhat subsided. It appeared to Harnam Singh as though the marauders had stopped in front of his shop and were not able to decide their next move. Harnam Singh felt grateful to Karim Khan for his timely warning which had made it possible for them to escape. Suddenly they heard the sound of heavy blows falling on something. Harnam Singh understood that they were breaking down the door of his shop. Their legs trembled, making it difficult for them to continue walking. Holding each other's hand they slowly moved forward.

'Pray to God and walk on, Banto,' said Harnam Singh, pulling along his wife.

A dog suddenly barked somewhere. Both looked up. At the top of the embankment a fierce-looking black dog stood barking at them. Harnam Singh's face turned livid.

'For which sins of ours are we being punished so severely by Guru Maharaj? The marauders have only to hear the barking of the dog and they will come running after us.'

'Keep walking, don't stop!'

The dog was still barking. It was the same dog which Harnam Singh had often seen in front of his shop, sniffing at things. After walking some distance, Banto turned round. The dog was still barking but it had neither moved down towards them nor along the top of the embankment.

They continued walking at a snail's pace.

'Let us somehow get away from the village. The rest is in God's hands.'

'The dog is not coming after us.'

'But it is still barking.'

Both of them took cover behind a boulder, and with bated breath listened to the barking of the dog.

The door of the shop had fallen, and the marauders, with a loud 'Ya Ali!' had rushed into the shop.

'They are looting our shop! Our house!'

The barking of the dog had gone unnoticed by the marauders. The husband and wife felt somewhat relieved. Even if the dog had attracted their attention they might not have cared to pursue the old couple, since there was so much in the shop for them to lift.

'Whose shop and whose house? It is no longer our shop, they stopped being ours the moment we walked out of the house.'

With the bed of the stream gleaming in the moonlight, a cluster of trees here and there, and the dog still standing on the top of the embankment, the entire scene seemed like a dream. How quickly had everything changed! They had lived at that place for twenty long years, yet within the twinkling of an eye, had been turned into homeless outsiders. Harnam Singh's hands were cold and wet with perspiration. The only sentence which he was repeating to himself over and over again, was 'Get away from here, by whatever means you can! Just get away from here!'

The village was left behind. The dog still stood there at the top of the slope; it had not come after them; very likely it would go back after a while. The shop had been looted. The marauders were no longer shouting; the noise had subsided. Perhaps they were satiated with the loot. But who knows, they may come looking for them now. Now, only the sound of pebbles under their staggering feet could be heard, in the surrounding silence. They walked on and covered some more distance. It seemed to Banto as if some light had spread in the sky. As she turned round she noticed that behind the top of the slope the sky was turning crimson. Banto stood transfixed.

'What is that? Do you see?'

'It is our shop burning, Banto!' said Harnam Singh.

He too was looking in the same direction. For some time they continued looking at the flames, as though under a spell. The flames rising from one's own house must be in some way different from the flames rising from someone else's house, otherwise why should they have stood like statues, watching them?

'Everything reduced to dust!' Harnam Singh said in a low whisper.

'Before our very eyes.'

'Guru Maharaj must have willed it so.' He heaved a deep sigh and they both resumed their trudge.

Walls keep men concealed, but here there were no walls, only mounds and rocks here and there, behind which a person could hide. But for how long? Within a few hours the darkness of the night would be dispelled and they would be rendered 'naked' as it were, once again shelterless; there would be no place for them to hide their heads.

Banto's throat was dry and Harnam Singh's legs would falter again and again. But at that time, not only them, but innumerable villagers were knocking about in search of shelter; the sound of crashing doors was falling on many ears. But they had no time either to think or to make any plans for the future. They barely had time to run for their lives. 'Keep walking so long as the shades of night provide you cover. Soon enough the day will break and terrors of the day, like hungry wolves, will stare you in the face.'

Within a short time they found themselves utterly exhausted.

But feeling relieved at having come out alive, the faces of their son and daughter began to appear before their eyes again. Where must Iqbal Singh be at this time? What must he be going through? And Jasbir? They were not so worried about Jasbir because the Sikh community in her village was fairly large. It may be that the entire community has moved into the gurdwara and found some way of protecting itself. But Iqbal Singh in a small village, running a cloth shop, was all alone. He might have left the village in good time, or he too may be knocking about for shelter. Every thought was acutely disturbing.

Harnam Singh shut his eyes, folded his hands, and with the name of Guru Maharaj on his lips, repeated the words of his prayer:

'With your protecting hand over his head, My Lord, how can anyone suffer?'

When the day broke, they were sitting by the side of a brook. Harnam Singh was well familiar with the surrounding area. He knew that they were close to a small village, Dhok Muridpur by name. They had passed the whole night praying, brooding and dragging their feet. But as the day dawned, their minds were at peace, for no explicable reason. The sweet fragrance of the lukat trees, wafted from far away filled the air. The moon which was orange-red in colour a little while earlier had turned pale yellow. The colour of the sky too changed from muddy grey to pale yellow and soon to silvery white. Soon enough it would be limpid blue. Birds were chirping on all sides.

'We can have a wash in this brook, Banto, and then say our prayers and leave.'

'But where shall we go?' asked Banto anxiously.

'We shall go to this village and knock at someone's door. If he has mercy in his heart, he will open the door to us and let us in; if not, then whatever is God's will.'

'Don't you know anyone in Muridpur?'

Harnam Singh smiled. 'No one gave us shelter where I knew everyone, our shop was looted and our house set on fire. Many of the villagers had been my childhood playmates, we had grown up together.'

When the morning mist cleared, they set out for the village. They first came to a grove of mulberry and shisham trees, at the end of which was a graveyard with broken-down graves, big and small. Near it stood, what appeared to be the grave of some pir for an earthen lamp had been lighted on it and green pennets hung over it. Then they came to the fields—the wheat crop was ready for harvesting. Beyond the fields stood the cluster of flat-roofed, mud-houses. Cows and buffaloes, tied to their pegs, stood outside. Hens with their chicks ran about looking for their feed.

'Banto, if we find them hostile, then I shall first finish you off with my gun and then kill myself. I won't let you fall into their hands so long as I am living.'

They stopped in front of the very first house to which they came, standing at the edge of the village. The door was closed. It was a discoloured door, made of thick timber. God alone knew whose house it was and who lived behind the closed door, and what fate awaited them when the door would open.

Harnam Singh raised his hand, for a second or two, his hand remained suspended in the air, and then he knocked at the door.

15

The gurdwara was packed to capacity. The entire congregation was swaying in ecstasy. It was a rare moment. The singers sang with their eyes closed, in frenzied exaltation: 'Who is there, beside you my Lord...'

Everyone sat with hands folded, eyes closed and heads swaying to the right and left. Here and there a devotee kept time with the tune by clapping his hands. The ecstatic rhapsody expressing sentiments of supreme self-sacrifice was once again being heard after a lapse of centuries. Three hundred years earlier, a similar 'war song' used to be sung by the Khalsa before taking on the enemy. Oblivious of everything they sang, imbued with the spirit of sacrifice. In this unique moment, their souls had merged, as it were, with the souls of their ancestors. Time had again come to cross swords with the Turks. The Khalsa was again facing a crisis created by the Turks. Their minds had been transported to those earlier times. The Khalsa did not know from which direction the enemy would launch his offensive, whether they would be outsiders or local residents. There was no trusting the enemy, but every 'Singh' in the congregation was ready for sacrifice.

The light in the gurdwara came from two stained-glass windows in the back walls set with green, red and yellow panes. The stool on which the Guru Granth Sahib lay, stood within four wooden pillars covered with a silken piece of cloth of red colour fringed with a gold braid. One end of this cloth stretched right down to the floor where sheets of white long-cloth had been spread. Coins and currency notes lay scattered on one end of it while on the other was a pile of wheat flour.

As one entered the gurdwara, the women members of the congregation sat on the left, their heads covered with dupattas, their faces aglow and their eyes lit up with the light of devotion and the spirit of sacrifice. Here and there a woman had a kirpan hanging by her side. Everyone in the congregation, man or woman, intensely felt that he or she was a link in the long chain of Sikh history, an integral part of it and, at that moment of crisis, like the ancestors, was ready to lay down his or her life.

Weapons were being stored in the long corridor at the back of the stool and in the Granthi's room. Seven members of the congregation possessed double-barrelled guns, with five boxes of cartridges. Jathedar Kishen Singh was organizing the defence. Kishen Singh was a war-veteran; he had taken part in the Second World War on the Burmese front and he was now hell-bent on trying the tactics of the Burmese front on the Muslims of his village. On acquiring the command for defence, the first thing he did was to go home and put on his khaki shirt which had been a part of his military uniform and on which dangled three medals received from the British government and a number of coloured strips. The shirt was crumpled but there was no time to get it ironed. Two pickets were set up, one at each end of the lane in front of the gurdwara, each provided with two guns. Later, the picket to the right of the gurdwara proved ineffective, since Hari Singh, in whose house the picket had been set up had been reluctant to open fire on his Muslim neighbours. With the remaining three guns a picket was set up on the roof of the gurdwara under the command of Kishen Singh. Kishen Singh had got himself a chair in which he sat all the time. That is how the seven guns had been utilized. The other weapons such as lances, swords, lathis, etc. had been placed against the back wall of the gurdwara. Swords in velvet scabbards of different colours stood side by side in a neat arrangement as though in an exhibition. The light of the sun through the windows fell straight on them, making them look very impressive. The light also fell on the points of the lances making them glitter. There were a few shields too which had been provided by the Nihang Sikhs. Two Nihang Sikhs stood guard on the roof of the gurdwara, one at each end, facing the lane. Both were in their typical attire, a long, blue robe, blue turban covered with an iron disc and yellow waistband. Lance in hand, each stood to attention with his eyes gazing far into the distance. No one knew from which direction the enemy might come raising clouds of dust.

'Lower your lance, Nihang Singhji, its tip glitters in the light of the sun; the enemy can see it from far off,' said Kishen Singh to the Nihang on guard duty. This annoyed the Nihang.

'A Nihang's lance can never be lowered.' He shot back and continued standing lance in hand as before, with his eyes on the horizon. Before Nihang Singh's eyes still floated visions of old battles, of armies marching, naked swords blazing in the sun, horses neighing and the air resounding with the beat of drums. These visions would instil in him new vigour and valour worthy of the Sikhs.

Two Nihangs had been posted below, at the entrance to the gurdwara. Lances in their hands, both stood to attention, their moustaches duly twirled and yellow waistbands tied over their blue robes. In olden times it was customary for the Khalsa to go to battle in yellow robes, yellow being the colour of selfless sacrifice. In the existing situation, everyone had made the effort to wear something which was emblematic of the old tradition— a yellow handkerchief, a yellow scarf or a yellow dupatta, etc., which would link him or her emotionally with their heroic past. Thus, Bishen Singh, a haberdasher by profession, who had been made in-charge of the community kitchen, had stuck into his turban a yellow silk kerchief, which originally belonged to his son who had donned it at the Basant Panchami fair. Bishen Singh had practically snatched it out of his boy's hands to stick it into his turban. In the congregation some people had tied yellow waistbands. But most people were in their everyday dress of salwar-kameez; even Kishen Singh was wearing, below his crumpled, medal-studded shirt, a pair of striped pyjamas. For most of them this was no time to bother about dress, since the heart was afire with the spirit of do or die.

The atmosphere in the gurdwara was as solemn as water-laden clouds. Heads swayed in the congregational singing; the minds imbued with the past—engendered by the spirit of sacrifice, the presence of the Muslim foe, the Guru's 'prasad', the paraphernalia of past battles, the sword, the shield, the lance, and the bond that united them into one unbreakable entity. If anything was not there, it was the British presence. Hardly twenty-five miles away there was the sprawling British cantonment, the biggest in the country. But it was nowhere in their thoughts. Nor were the British officers, stationed in the city and in the entire province. They too did not exist in their consciousness. If anything did exist it was the Turk, the traditional enemy of the Khalsa, the advancing hordes of the Turks, the imminent combat which was to them like the great ritual into which they would plunge, ready to lay down their lives.

The danger of attack lay at the back of the gurdwara, where stood the house with the green balcony belonging to the Sheikhs. Inside that house, the Muslims of the village had been storing arms and ammunition. Inside the Sheikh's mansion too the atmosphere was very similar to the one prevailing in the gurdwara. Here too, all the Muslims of the village—farmers, oil-crushers, bakers, butchers—had assumed the role of *mujahids*, and preparations were going on to launch a Jihad against the kafirs. Here too, the eyes were bloodshot and hearts afire with the spirit of sacrifice.

Right in front of the gurdwara, across the lane, was a row of shops belonging to the Sikhs, behind which a slope went right down to the bank of a stream. Beyond the stream lay a big orchard of the lukat fruit. Therefore, there was little danger of an attack being mounted from the front. If anyone dared do so, the guns of Kishen Singh, stationed on the roof, would make mincemeat of them.

To the left of the gurdwara, some of the houses near the end of the lane belonged to the Muslims, behind which stood the Khalsa School. Beyond the Khalsa school, stretched the fields.

To the right of the gurdwara, where the lane ended, there was a mohalla of Muslim houses. There too, in the last house in the lane a picket had been set up.

The Sheikh's house with the green balcony, however, was located at the back of the gurdwara, beyond two narrow lanes. It was Sheikh Ghulam Rasul's double-storeyed house and, according to the information brought by the informers, it had been turned into a fortress by the Musalmans. All the doors opening on the green balcony were shut tight. The room on the top floor too, with the green windows was closed. Not a soul was to be seen standing anywhere. But everyone feared that the first shot would be fired from that house.

The village otherwise was a lovely one, nestled in idyllic surroundings. Anyone visiting it in normal times would be enthralled by its picturesque beauty. As the saying went: 'God had made it with His own hands.' Overlooking the small stream the village stood in the form of a horse-shoe built on a small hillock. Across the bluish water of the stream there was the thick orchard of lukat trees where numerous brooks flowed. The fruit was ripening in those days, and the orchard resounded with the incessant chirping of birds, notably parrots. The colour of the stream was as blue as the colour of the sky while that of the earth was reddish brown. Outside the town, the fields stretched far into the distance, right up to the foot of the low hill. After every few hours, the colour of the hill would change. Sometimes it would be covered with a blue haze, at another time its face would be flushed burnished copper. Fluffy white clouds played on its slopes almost all the time. Stretches of green foliage covered its lower parts. At the foot of the hill there were innumerable springs flowing under the shade of banyan and fig trees. It was in the lap of these idyllic surroundings that the inhabitants had been living from generation to generation.

Suddenly, something electrifying occurred in the gurdwara. All eyes turned towards the gate of the gurdwara through which Sardar Teja Singh, the chief of the congregation was entering. On stepping up to the raised projection of the gurdwara, Sardarji went down on his knees, and then bowing low touched the threshold with his eyes. The fingers of both his hands resting on the floor were trembling.

For a long time, Teja Singh kept his head bowed, his forehead touching the threshold. Teja Singhji was in an ecstatic state of mind. Tears streamed from his eyes. Every pore of his body throbbed with the spirit of sacrifice in defence of the Faith.

He stood up and with folded hands and bowed head, his flowing white beard covering his chest, he came and stood before the Guru Granth Sahib, the Holy Book. Here too, he stood with bowed head for a long time. His face was flushed and tears flowed from his eyes on to the white sheet of cloth spread on the floor.

The entire congregation watched with bated breath and rapt attention. They were deeply moved. When Teja Singhji stood up, a wave of emotion coursed through the entire congregation.

He slowly stepped up to a pillar against which stood an old sword in a red scabbard. With trembling hands he picked up the sword from its handle and came and stood in the middle of the hall. This was his maternal grandfather's sword, whose father had been a courtier in the royal court of Maharaja Ranjit Singh.

He had hardly raised the sword when a feeling of self-immolation surged through the entire congregation. Heads swayed. Young Pritam Singh, standing by the door, burst into a full-throated slogan:

'Jo Boley So Nihal!' (Redemption to the one who responds.)

To which the entire congregation answered with one voice:

'Sat Sri Akal!'

The walls of the gurdwara shook under the resounding response to the slogan. Even though it was forbidden to raise slogans, lest the enemy should know that the entire Sikh community of the village had gathered in the gurdwara, the surge of emotions was such that it could not be contained. The pent-up emotions could only be released through a full-throated response to the slogan.

Sardar Teja Singh, now holding his sword in both trembling hands raised it and kissed it with both his eyes, at which the entire congregation sobbed uncontrollably. The head of the Nihang standing at the gate swayed to the right and left. Hundreds of heads swayed.

'Once again, today, the Khalsa Panth needs the blood of the Guru's Sikhs,' he began in a voice trembling with intense emotion. 'Time has come when our faith will be put to test. Time has come of our trial. The Maharaj has only one behest for this time: "Sacrifice! Sacrifice! Sacrifice!"' (Die for the Panth! Die for the Panth! Die for the Panth!)

A kind of golden dust filled Teja Singh's mind. His ecstasy bordered on frenzy! All his emotions centred round the word 'Sacrifice!'

'Chant the *Ardas*, you Singhs of the Guru!'

The entire congregation stood up, and with heads bowed, hands folded began chanting the hymns of the Gurvani in full-throated voices. The gurdwara resounded. The entire prayer was recited, which took quite some time. At the concluding words the chant was at its loudest:

The Khalsa shall rule.
None shall remain in subjugation!

The chanting rose like waves, striking against the walls of the gurdwara.

No sooner had the prayer been chanted, than the Nihang standing at the gate raised his hand and with his eyes closed, shouted the slogan in a voice so piercing that the veins of his throat swelled:

'Jo Boley So Nihal!'

In answer to which the entire congregation, with hands raised responded with all the vocal strength at their command:

'Sat Sri Akal!'

There was a fresh upsurge of emotions. The raising of slogans added poignancy to the feelings of solidarity and sacrifice!

Just then, from a distance came a piercing sound: 'Nara-i-Takbir!' followed by the resounding answer:

'Allah-o-Akbar!'

The Nihang at the gate once again clenched his fist and, raising it above his shoulders, was about to raise a slogan when Teja Singh stopped him.

'Enough! The enemy has learnt about our presence!' But the answering slogan of the Muslims brought home to the congregation something relating to the prevailing situation.

'We do not want the enemy to know about our strength. We do not want them to know that the entire Sikh community has gathered in the gurdwara. It is a matter of strategy.' And giving an exposition of the prevailing situation, he said, 'We have tried to inform the highest authority of the district, the deputy commissioner sahib Bahadur about the nefarious activities the Muslims have lately been indulging in. I know Richard Sahib personally. He is a gentleman, sagacious and justice-loving. This is the best that we could do—inform the highest authority about our situation. All sorts of news is reaching us. We have come to know that weapons are being stored in the house of Rahim, the oil-crusher, that a motor-car of blue colour came in the afternoon from the direction of the city and stopped outside the house of Fazal Din the schoolmaster, that some articles were taken out of the car and delivered to Master Fazal Din. This car has been going in different directions and stopping at different places. It has also come to our knowledge that the local Muslims have sent word to the Muslims of Muridpur that they should send men and weapons to them. We have tried hard to talk to Sheikh Ghulam Rasul and other Muslims of the village, but the fellows cannot be trusted.'

'You have made no efforts. It is a lie.'

Suddenly a voice was heard in the congregation. Silence fell on all sides. Who was this intruder? People in the gurdwara were enraged.

A frail young man stood up.

'We should not forget that we are being incited against the Muslims, and the Muslims against us. Due to rumours of all kinds tension is mounting and tempers are running high. On our part we should try our best to maintain contact with the Muslims and continue to interact with them, and see that violence does not break out.'

'Sit down! Shut up!'

'Traitor! Who the hell is he?'

'I won't sit down. I must have my say. We must make every effort to meet Ghulam Rasul and other sober-minded Muslims of the village. If Ghulam Rasul is not amenable to reason there must be other peace-loving Muslims with whose cooperation we can maintain peace in the village. If they are getting weapons from Muridpur, aren't we trying to get weapons from Kahuta? No one wants bloodshed. The Sikhs and Muslims of the village should meet one another and maintain peace in the village. Only this morning I met Ghulam Rasul and some other Muslims...'

'What? What took you there? Is Ghulam Rasul your foster father?'

'Allow me to speak. It is the ruffians from another village who will do the mischief. We should try our best to see that no outsider comes into the village. That can be done only if the peace-loving Sikhs and Muslims jointly stop them from coming. They are collecting weapons out of fear of us and we are doing the same out of fear of them.'

'There is no trusting the Muslims. Sit down.'

'Those people say that Sikhs cannot be trusted.'

'Sit down!' an elderly man shouted, his lips trembling, 'Who are you to butt in? Your mother's milk has not yet dried on your lips and you have come to advise your elders?'

Three or four Sardars stood up at different places.

'Don't you know that they have set fire to the grain market in the city?'

'It is entirely the mischief of the British.' Sohan Singh's voice grew louder. 'It is in our interest that the riot does not break out. Listen, Brothers, roads are being blocked. No bus has come from the city today. The entire area is inhabited by Muslims. If people from outside attack the village, how will you defend yourselves? Just think. How much assistance can you expect from Kahuta?

What are you so confident about?'

For some time there was silence in the hall.

Then, Teja Singhji came and stood in the middle of the hall and said, his voice trembling: 'It breaks my heart to see our misguided young men talk like this, and raise their voice against their own faith. Do we want bloodshed? I told Sheikh Ghulam Rasul myself and he put his hand on his heart and assured me that nothing untoward would happen in the village. But hardly had I turned my back when the Khalsa School was attacked, the school peon, a Brahmin, put to death and his wife carried away. I did not give this information earlier because I did not want that you should get worked up.'

A wave of shock and indignation swept through the entire congregation.

'You have been misinformed,' said Sohan Singh. 'The Khalsa School was attacked but it was not the Muslims from this village but gangsters coming from Dhok Ilahi Baksh who attacked it. Mir Dad, our comrade, who has come from the city, got there in time and he, along with two or three local boys intervened and saved the situation. The peon was only injured; he is not dead. And his wife was not carried away. She is very much present in the school premises.'

'Who is this Mir Dad?' one Sardar asked.

'I saw this fellow sitting with Mir Dad in a tea shop. God knows what confabulations were going on between them. At a time when Muslims are molesting our women, our boys are socializing with them.' Then, turning to the same frail Sardar, he said, 'What are you trying to teach us? Why don't you go and teach the Muslims? Have the Sikhs, till now, killed anyone? Looted anyone's house? And here is a fellow teaching us what we should do.'

The atmosphere again became tense. The Nihang standing at the gate came over and gave the frail Sardar a blow on his neck.

'Enough, enough! Don't beat him.'

A few persons, sitting nearby stood up and intervened, pulling away the Nihang.

At the time when this flare-up was taking place in the gurdwara, in another part of the village, Mir Dad was being heckled by a few Muslims.

In the butchers' lane, though the shops were closed, three butchers sat on the projections of their shops, having a heated argument with Mir Dad.

'You shut up. The Englishman was nowhere around. In the city so many Musalmans have been done to death; their bodies are still lying in the lanes. Were they killed by the Englishman? A pig was thrown outside a mosque; was that too done by the Englishman?'

'Try to understand,' said Mir Dad, with a wave of his hand, 'If Hindus, Sikhs and Muslims are united, the position of the Englishman becomes weak. If we keep fighting among ourselves, he remains strong.'

It was the same hackneyed argument which these people had heard before. In the prevailing situation, it would cut no ice with them.

'Go and massage your head with almond oil,' the fat butcher said. 'How has the firanghi harmed us? The Hindus and Muslims have been at daggers drawn all along. A kafir is a kafir and until he accepts the "faith" he is an enemy. To kill a kafir is a virtuous act.'

'Listen, uncle,' Mir Dad said. 'Who is the ruler?'

'Of course it is the Englishman, who else?'

'And whose is the army?'

'Of the Englishman.'

'Then, can't he stop us from fighting?'

'He can, but he does not want to interfere in our religious matters. The Englishman is justice-loving.'

"Which means that we should kill one another while he would call it a religious matter and keep watching it as a spectator. What sort of ruler is he?'

The fat butcher grew angry.

'Listen, you chit of a fellow, Mir Dad. The fight is between the Hindu and the Muslim. The Englishman has nothing to do with it. You stop jabbering. If you are your father's real son, go to the gurdwara and tell them not to collect arms. If they agree let them leave all their weapons in the gurdwara and go to their houses. We too do not want bloodshed. We too shall go and sit in our homes. If you are the son of a real man, go and talk to them. Don't go on blabbering here.'

Ever since the communal trouble started, Mir Dad would go and sit wherever he would find four or five persons chatting—at the baker's shop, at Ganda Singh's tea shop, at the village well, or at the Sheikh's courtyard and converse with them. People would listen to him because he had received some education, had travelled to Bombay, Lahore, Madras, and so on, and had also come from the city. He had originally come with the intention of meeting his brother Allah Dad in the village, and in due course of time to open a school here which could serve as a meeting place for the villagers where they could sit and talk about their affairs, where someone could read a newspaper to them, which could develop their understanding and widen their outlook and sphere of interests. But he had not been able to cut much ice with the people. The reason being that he had neither a piece of land of his own nor a roof over his head. He would sleep at night on a cot outside the baker's shop. The village-folk thought that he had come to open a school in order to eke out a living for himself, whereas Mir Dad's objective was to provide and develop a community centre in the village.

At that particular juncture Dev Datt had sent him to the village to stay put there and try to prevent the riot from breaking out. Sohan Singh too had been sent for the same purpose. Both were activists of the same party, both had relatives living in that village. But with the tension mounting and all sorts of news pouring in, both of them were getting more and more isolated.

It was while Mir Dad stood talking to the butcher that a small incident occurred nearby. In the dark part of the lane close by, sitting behind a sack-cloth curtain a man was listening to their conversation. He had been sent from the gurdwara to gather information about the plans of the enemy. Gopal Singh was his

name. He had climbed over the back wall of an old widow's
house and posted himself there. The adjoining houses on both
sides were those of Muslims. While listening to the dialogue
between Mir Dad and the butcher, he lifted a corner of the sack-
cloth curtain and quietly stepped into the lane and sat down
behind the chabutra of the adjoining house. From there the words
of their dialogue were more clearly audible. Since the doors of
houses were shut and it was dark in the lane, Gopal Singh had
calculated that in the event of any sound coming from anywhere,
he would rush back into the widow's house and hide behind the
sack-cloth curtain. But he did not have the chance to do so. His
ears were glued to the conversation when suddenly he heard an
odd kind of sound behind him. He at once turned round. In the
murky light of the lane, a man from the adjoining house had
stepped out, and was advancing towards him. The man had
stepped down from the projection, and was putting both his hands
under his shirt-front, as though to pull out his dagger. Gopal
Singh stood up, nervous in the extreme and a loud cry escaped
his lips. Instead of turning to the sack-cloth curtain, he ran for
his life and, in the confusion, collided against the man who, he
thought, was taking out his dagger from under his shirt-front. In
reality, before the collision took place, the man had untied the
tape of his pyjamas and had almost sat down by the drain to
ease himself. In his nervousness Gopal Singh had not noticed
that the man was old, bald and toothless, and almost blind. After
the collision, the old man—Nur Din was his name—cried out
loudly:

'O, I am slain! O, I am killed!'

All that had happened in the twinkling of an eye. As old Nuru's
cries and the sound of running feet fell on the ears of the butchers,
two men picked up their lances and went after them. Ashraf, the
butcher, pursued the man who was running, and threw his stick
at him. The lance did not hit the informer, but as it fell close to
him, he lost his nerve and began shouting:

'O, save me! They are killing me!'

Those who stood inside the lane shouted to Ashraf: 'Come

back! Don't go farther! Come back!'

Mir Dad, who too stood in the lane, went over to the old man and helped him stand up. Seeing this, the fat butcher shouted angrily at Mir Dad, 'Haven't you seen with your own eyes, rascal! Has Nur Din been attacked by an Englishman? Get out of my sight, this minute, or you shall have it from me! Leave at once. Go away' and almost pushed Mir Dad out of the lane.

'Homeless beggar! Has come here to bring about peace! Has neither a roof over his head nor anyone to call his own. Who the hell are you? Fellows whom even their mothers do not recognize come to show us the way! Bloody beggar, living on crumbs thrown by others.'

At the end of the lane, Mir Dad again turned round to say something but the butcher again shouted fiercely at him, 'Go! Get away from here! Bloody eunuch! I will give you one on the jaw and all your teeth will fall out! Go and lecture your father!'

Mir Dad, his shoulders bent, moved away. Earlier, some people would listen to him and would even nod their heads to what he said, but now such people were nowhere to be seen. Even this man, the fat butcher used to talk to him in a friendly way, laugh and chat with him, but now his eyes were bloodshot.

Gopal Singh, the spy, kept running and shouting for help, right up to the gate of the gurdwara. On hearing his cries a wave of anger surged through the congregation. People came out in great agitation. All discipline went haywire. Both the Nihangs on gate-duty rushed out; and the Nihangs posted on the roof came running down the staircase.

'What's the matter? What's happened?'

Those inside the gurdwara stood up.

No fewer than ten persons examined Gopal Singh's body limb by limb. There was no sign of any injury anywhere. He was breathless and his throat was dry. He tried hard but could not comprehend what had actually happened.

'He was coming straight to attack me.'

'Who was he?' asked Teja Singhji.

'Baba Nura,' he blurted out the name unwittingly. A split-second before running away, he had recognized Baba Nura.

'What? The blind Baba Nura?'

'How could I know who it was? He had come out of Baba Nura's house...'

'What happened then?'

'People came after me from the Butchers' Lane. They threw sticks at me.'

People in large numbers had come out into the lane, while one Sardar was persuading them to go back into the gurdwara:

'There is nothing to worry. The Singh Khalsa has come back from the enemy-lines safe and sound. He has had a narrow escape, though. Go in, please!'

When Gopal Singh was able to breathe more freely, Teja Singhji asked him in a whisper: 'What did you find out? What are their plans?'

'Mir Dad was blabbering away. I couldn't listen clearly. The fat butcher was telling him, "Tell the folks in the gurdwara to go back to their houses, and we too will go back to ours"... he was saying something like this.' The congregation again gathered in the gurdwara. Gopal Singh, by his shouting, had added considerably to the excitement. The kirtan was resumed. The sound of cymbals, tablas and harmonium grew louder.

'What do you have to say now, Sardar?' A man, standing in the middle of the hall was shouting at Sohan Singh, 'He has barely managed to come back alive. The Muslims tried their best to kill him. And here you are, trying to teach us what we should do.'

Another angry member of the congregation shouted, 'This man should be thrown into a dungeon, kept in solitary confinement! We cannot trust him. Who knows he may be spying for them.'

At this Nihang Singh stepped forward and gave another blow to Sohan Singh on his jaw.

'Enough, enough!'

'Go and give your sermons to your blood-relatives, in whose lap you are sitting all the time. Get out of here!'

The kirtan was resumed.

Shades of evening had begun to fall. Two large lamps, which resembled chandeliers, hanging from the roof, one to the right and the other to the left of the raised platform on which lay the Holy Book, were lighted. Under the blue turban of Sardar Teja Singh, his white beard and the white shawl over his shoulders, became all the more pronounced. Light also fell on the excited faces of women. Their eyes reflected apprehension as also boundless devotion. Here and there a young girl looked at the unusual scene with curious eyes. Among these young women was Jasbir too—the daughter of Harnam Singh, the tea shop owner. She had been married in that very village. She had inherited from her father the intensely devotional frame of mind. At the time of the chanting of the Ardas, the only voice which did not harmonize with the voice of the rest of the congregation was that of Jasbir. A thin, somewhat shrill voice but she sang supremely unconscious of everything. A short kirpan tied with a black ribbon-band, hung from her waist. Everyone in the congregation was familiar with this voice and everyone called her 'the daughter of the Guru'. Her broad, beaming face was flushed most of all. Jasbir would wash the steps of the gurdwara with her own hands, she had embroidered the silken cloth-piece covering the Holy Book. It was from her effusive heart that all sorts of initiatives would spring. She would stand up on her own and start fanning the congregation, would serve cool water, keep watch over the shoes of the congregation. In moments of ecstatic elation, would even wipe their shoes with a part of the dupatta with which she covered her head, and put them before the members to wear, nay, even help them put them on with her own hands. Ever since the crisis began, her eyes were riveted on Teja Singhji's face, as though she expected a divine message from his lips; and her ears were all too eager to hear it. A sentiment, very similar, coursed through the hearts and minds of all the members of the congregation.

Just then, one of the Nihangs posted on the roof, noticed a cloud of dust, far on the horizon. He looked intently. Yes, it was a cloud of dust and it was growing bigger. He came and told

Kishen Singh about it, and Kishen Singh looked towards it through the peephole and kept his eyes on it for a long time. It was really a cloud of dust and it was surely advancing towards the village. At first he did not believe his eyes, but gradually as he looked, a deep, humming sound too became audible to him. He felt alarmed. Everyone had thought that the mischief would begin from within the village itself, that such people as Kalu, the loafer, Ashraf, the butcher and Nabi, the oil-crusher were dead set on creating trouble, but now, it was the marauders from outside, advancing towards the village. He was still watching when a deep muffled sound of drum-beat fell on his ears. What he saw and heard was alarming. The situation had taken a serious and dangerous turn. He decided to go down and inform Teja Singhji, but thinking that it was essential to keep constant watch on the movements of the enemy, he asked the Nihang to convey the information to Teja Singhji.

The Nihang went running down the staircase, and on reaching the last step, shouted at the top of his voice:

'Turks! The Turks are coming!'

The entire congregation was electrified. The drum-beat was now clearly audible.

For some time Teja Singhji stood bewildered. He had not expected that outsiders would attack them. As a matter of fact he had not thought that an attack would take place at all. He had thought that a stray incident or two might occur in the Teli Mohalla or on the outskirts of the village and if the Sikhs stood firm the Muslims of the village would not persist. The Sikhs were in larger numbers and most of the Muslims had dealings with them. Besides, the Sikhs were financially better off and were well provided with weapons. But the whole situation appeared to have changed radically.

The sound of drums drew nearer. The slogan 'Ya Ali!' was also heard close by. Just then, from behind the gurdwara came the slogan:

'Allah-o-Akbar!'

Eerie silence fell over the entire congregation in the hall. But it was soon followed by a powerful surge of excitement when, in answer to the slogans of the Muslims, the full-throated Sikh slogan 'Boley So Nihal—Sat Sri Akal' rent the air.

'No one shall leave the hall! Everyone to his or her post!'

Jasbir Kaur's hand immediately went to her kirpan. The Sardars, one after the other, picked up the swords. The entire congregation was on its feet.

'Turks! Turks have come! Turks are here!' was on the lips of everyone.

'Turks are coming!' repeated Jasbir Kaur, in a voice trembling with emotion. Taking the dupatta off her head she hung it round her neck, and clasped the woman standing next to her in a tight embrace exclaiming in a voice choking with emotion: 'The Turks are here!'

The women took off their dupattas, hung them round their necks, and embracing one another repeated in a frenzied voice: 'The Turks are here! The Turks have come!'

The men too, the 'Singhs of the Guru' were likewise doing the same.

Some of the 'Singhs' had taken off their turbans, loosened their hair, and taken the swords out of their scabbards.

'Everyone to his or her post!' reverberated the command.

Once again the slogan: 'Jo Bole So Nihal!' rose from the depths of their beings, as it were, and the gurdwara resounded with: 'Sat Sri Akal!'

All the three members of the War Council, Sardar Mangal Singh, goldsmith, Pritam Singh, cloth merchant, and Bhagat Singh, general merchant, went up to the roof to ponder over the changed situation in consultation with Sardar Teja Singh and Kishen Singh.

Beating their drums the Turks had arrived in the village. It was, very probably to give notice of their arrival that a gunshot was fired in the air.

The whole atmosphere reverberated with the shouting of slogans: 'Ya Ali!'

'Allah-o-Akbar!'

'Sat Sri Akal!'

Then someone said that the Turks were advancing from the side of the stream. This meant that climbing up the slope they would fall upon the houses of the Sikhs, loot and burn them.

At that time, besides some old people left behind by their sons in the excitement of protecting the Faith, there was no one to guard them.

It was not yet completely dark, and the water in the stream looked crimson under the light of the setting sun. The picket set up at the end of the lane, to the left of the gurdwara, was at considerable distance from the houses which were at that time exposed to the attack of the Turks.

Suddenly Baldev Singh was troubled by the thought of his mother. He had left her alone in the house and had not thought of her the whole day long. She must be in great danger. There were some other persons too in the congregation who became anxious about their aged relatives left behind.

In a state of frenzy, Baldev Singh loosened his hair, took off his pyjamas, took the sword out of its scabbard and with only a vest and underwear on his body, he, waved the naked sword over his head and ran towards his house.

'Blood for blood!' he shouted.

Some people shouted to him to come back but he wouldn't listen.

'Blood for blood!' he shouted as he went running through the lane.

Baldev Singh was neither hefty nor strong. As he ran, his thin legs looked like the legs of a goat. People were unable to make out why he had taken to the lane on the left. It would have been understandable if he had gone down the slope, indicating that he had gone to settle scores with the marauders. Had he taken the lane to the right it would have meant that he was going to the Butchers' Lane. What was the point in taking the lane to the left?

A little while later however, he was seen coming back towards the gurdwara. He still held the sword in his hand but he was not waving it over his head. In the darkening light of the evening, the blade of the sword too looked dark. As he drew near, people noticed that blood was dripping from the sword. There were drops of blood on his vest and underwear too. He was no longer shouting, nor was he running. On the other hand he looked ghastly pale and frightened.

Some people had correctly surmised that he was returning after killing someone. Convinced that his mother could no longer be saved, that the Turks must have made short shrift of her, he had plunged his sword into the bosom of the old blacksmith Karim Baksh, the only person to whom he had access, thereby avenging his mother's murder.

Shades of night were falling over the village. But the noises had grown louder and sharper. Sound of slogans resounded with sounds of yelling and shrieking, of doors being battered and windows being pulled down.

The excitement inside the gurdwara was turning into a frenzy.

16

When Harnam Singh knocked at the door a second time, a female voice answered from the other side: 'Menfolk are not at home; they have gone out.'

Harnam Singh stood undecided, looking to the right and left and wondering if anyone had seen them. Then turning to his wife, said, 'Banto, you ask. It is a woman speaking from behind the door' and stepped aside.

Banto knocked at the door and said in a loud voice: 'Kind ones, open the door. We are in distress.'

Listening to his wife's entreaty, Harnam Singh felt stricken with remorse. Fate had willed it so that a time would come when his wife would be begging for shelter.

There was a sound of footsteps on the other side of the door followed by someone lifting the latch. The door opened. A tall, elderly village woman stood before them, both her hands covered with cow-dung and her head uncovered. Behind her stood a young woman with dishevelled hair; she too had her sleeves rolled up from which one could conclude that she was preparing fodder for the cattle.

'Who are you? What do you want?'

The elderly woman asked, although at the very first glance she had understood their predicament.

'We are ill-fated ones, coming from Dhok Ilahi Baksh. The marauders came and looted our house and set fire to it. We have been walking the whole night.'

The woman paused. For a moment the woman stood

undecided. It was that fateful moment when a person has to make up his or her mind, goaded by lifelong influences and beliefs. The woman kept looking at them, then, throwing the door open, said, 'Come. Come inside.'

Banto and Harnam Singh looked up, and stepping over the threshold came into the inner courtyard. As they came in, the woman peeped out to right and left and quickly bolted the door.

The young woman kept staring hard at them. There was suspicion and doubt lurking in her eyes.

'Spread the cot, Akran,' the woman said and herself sat down on the ground and resumed making dung-cakes.

Akran came out of the inner room covering her shoulders with a dupatta and spread the cot which was standing against the wall.

'May God bless you, sister. We have been rendered homeless in one night' and Banto's eyes filled with tears.

'We have spent our whole life in Dhok Ilahi Baksh,' said Harnam Singh. 'There we had our shop and our own house. At first everyone said, "Stay here, nothing untoward will happen to you." But yesterday Karim Khan advised us to leave immediately. He said it would be dangerous for us to continue living in the village. He was right. Hardly had we turned our back when the marauders came. They looted the shop and then set fire to it.'

The woman remained quiet. Meanwhile Banto got down from the cot and sat down on the ground beside her.

Akran came and picking up the tray full of dung-cakes, went to one side and began sticking them on the wall one by one. The elderly woman went on making dung-cakes with her hands, from the heap of dung lying before her.

'Where have your menfolk gone?' asked Harnam Singh.

The woman turned round and looked at Harnam Singh but did not answer his question. Harnam Singh suddenly realized where the male members of the family must have gone and his whole body trembled.

'We came out in the clothes we were wearing,' Banto said, 'May God bless Karim Khan, he virtually saved our lives. And may God bless you, sister, for giving us shelter.'

An uncanny silence prevailed over the house, causing Harnam Singh to fall silent again and again. The younger woman had gone into the inner room and Harnam Singh felt that standing in the darkness of that room, she was staring at them.

The elderly woman got up, washed her hands with the water in the basin where the kitchen utensils lay. She then picked up an earthen bowl and filling it with butter-milk brought it over. Harnam Singh still had his gun hanging from his shoulder. The belt containing cartridges, drenched with his perspiration, clung to his shirt.

'Here, drink some buttermilk. You must be exhausted.'

Taking the bowl in his hand, Harnam Singh burst out crying. A whole night's fatigue, nervous agitation, and suppressed emotions, suddenly burst forth as it were, and he began to cry bitterly like a child. He had, after all, been a well-to-do shopkeeper, even now carried in his pocket a couple of hundred rupees, had never stretched his hand before anyone all his life, and now, hardly a day had passed when he was knocking from pillar to post.

'Don't cry so loudly, Sardarji, the neighbours will hear and come running. Sit quietly.'

Harnam Singh suppressed his sobs and became quiet, and wiped his tears with the tail-end of his turban.

'May God bless you, sister, what you have done for us we shall never be able to recompense.'

'God forbid that a person should become homeless. But with God's grace, everything will turn out all right for you.'

The bowl of buttermilk in her hand, the woman offered it to Banto, but Banto hesitated to take it, and looked towards her husband, who was himself looking at her. How could she take the bowl from the hand of a Muslim? At the same time she was dog-tired and her throat was dry. The woman understood her discomfiture.

'If you are carrying any of your own utensils, I can pour the buttermilk into it for you. We have a pundit's shop in the village.

I could go and get a couple of utensils for you, but how do I know if the pundit will be there? You may not take it from my hand but how will you pass the day on an empty stomach?'

At that, Harnam Singh put out his hand and took the bowl from her.

'From your hand, sister, it is like nectar for us. We shall never be able to repay what you have done for us.'

The sun had risen and voices began to be heard from neighbouring houses. Harnam Singh drank a few mouthfuls from the bowl and passed the bowl on to his wife.

'Listen, Sardarji, I won't hide anything from you,' the mistress of the house said. 'Both my husband and my son have gone out with some men from the village. They may be back any time now. My husband is a God-fearing man, he won't say anything to you. But my son is a member of the League and I cannot say how he will behave towards you. He has some other people with him too. It is for you to decide what you should do.'

Harnam Singh's heart missed a beat. Only a little while earlier the woman was offering to get utensils for them, and now she was playing a different tune.

Harnam Singh folded his hands. 'It is broad daylight now. Where can we go?'

'What can I say? Had it been some other time, it would have been different. But nowadays everyone wants to go his own way. Nobody listens to others. I have told you that our men have gone out and that they must be about to return. I do not know how they will treat you. Don't blame me if anything goes wrong.'

Harnam Singh was lost in deep thoughts. After some time he raised his head and said in a weak voice: 'As you say, sister. Whatever is God's will, will happen. There was compassion in your heart, so you opened your door to us. Now if you tell us to go away, we shall do your bidding. Let us go, Banto.'

Harnam Singh picked up his gun and both husband and wife moved towards the door. He knew that the jaws of hell would open wide for them, the moment they stepped out. But there was no choice.

The woman continued to stand in the middle of the courtyard looking at them.

When Harnam Singh raised his hand to open the door, the woman said, 'Wait. Don't go. Put the latch back. You knocked at my door with some hope and expectation in your heart. We shall see what happens. Come back.'

Young Akran, who stood watching from the inner room, stared hard at her mother-in-law and came forward: 'Let them go, Ma. We have not even asked our menfolk. They may not like it.'

'I shall answer them myself. Go and get the ladder from inside. Hurry up. Shall I push out a person who has come seeking shelter? Everyone has to go into God's presence one day. What are you staring at my face for? Go and get the ladder.'

Harnam Singh and his wife turned back from the door. Harnam Singh again folded his hands:

'May Wahe Guru's protecting hand be over your head, sister. We shall do whatever you tell us to do.'

By then it was broad daylight. Women from neighbouring houses had started stepping into one another's house. Everyone talked about the riots. In that village too, the previous evening, many men had been raising slogans, waving lathis and lances and beating drums. They had been going about in the village and later they had left the village and gone out, towards the East. No one knew where they went and what they did during the night. But now it was daylight and they were expected back any time.

Akran brought the ladder. Her mother-in-law took the ladder from her and put it against the wall, just below the loft.

'Come here, both of you,' she said. 'Go up the ladder into that loft and sit there. Don't make any sound. No one should know that you are here. For the rest, leave it to God.'

Harnam Singh, being of a bulky frame, found it difficult to go up the ladder. Besides, the gun hanging from his shoulder kept getting between his legs. Breathless, he somehow managed to go into the loft. Banto followed. The loft was a small one with a low roof. One had to double up in order to be able to sit in it, and there was barely room to sit. At the back of the loft, all sorts of household stuff was stacked. When Harnam Singh shut the small door, it became utterly dark inside. Both sat staring into darkness. They could neither speak nor think of anything. Their fate hung by a thread.

It was not only dark, it was also very stuffy inside, and for a long time Harnam Singh could not breathe normally. After sitting there for some time, Harnam Singh, out of sheer desperation opened the door a little so that they could have some light inside. Out of that thin opening, he could see the door that opened outside as also a small part of the inner courtyard. It was silent below. It seemed to him that the girl and her mother-in-law had left the courtyard.

'If anything untoward happens, Banto, and our life is in danger, I shall first press the trigger of the gun on you; I would rather kill you with my own hand,' Harnam Singh said in a hoarse whisper, for the third time.

Banto remained silent. She was living by the seconds. Her mind could not think of anything.

Below, in the back room, the two women were talking in low tones.

'You are doing something very wrong, giving shelter to kafirs. What are they to us? Abba Jan will be terribly offended. They are sitting up there at a vantage point; the Sikhra has a gun with him. What if he fires the gun when our menfolk are here? You just took them at their word and sent them up there.'

The mother-in-law looked at Akran's face. There was sense in what she was saying. 'If the men fell out with one another, and Ramzan had almost been in a frenzy these several days what if the fellow sitting up there fires his gun? It will certainly kill the man standing below. It is one thing to give shelter to someone, it is quite another to jeopardize the lives of your son and husband. Nothing could be more foolish. Why did this not occur to me?'

She came and stood under the loft.

'Listen, Sardarji, listen to what I say,' she said in a low tone. Harnam Singh opened the door a little wider.

'What is it, sister?'

'Give that gun to me. Hang it down, I shall take it.'

Harnam Singh was taken aback.

'How can I give away my gun, sister?'

'No, give me your gun. You cannot sit up there with a gun.'

Silence ensued between them. To surrender the gun meant surrendering one's life into their hands. If he declined, she would at once turn them out of the house, and once outside, even if he was carrying a gun, it would not be safe.

'Are you listening, Sardarji? Give over the gun. Why do you need a gun, sitting in my house?'

'I shall become totally unarmed, sister. With the gun I feel safe.'

'Hand over the gun. Hang it down. I shall give it back to you when you leave my house.'

Harnam Singh looked at his wife, and then quietly lowered the gun to her.

After handing over the gun, Harnam Singh suddenly realized that he had delivered a loaded gun to her, that he should have taken the cartridges out before giving it away. But then he shook his head. When life itself is hanging in uncertainty, what difference does it make whether one has taken out the cartridges or not. Had I taken them out, there would only be one chance less of death, and not taking them out meant one more chance added to the thousand other chances of likely death. Harnam Singh heaved a deep sigh, so deep that Banto thought the women standing below must have heard it.

It was once again dark inside the loft.

What a transformation! Only yesterday, at this time, Banto was tidying her box of clothes, whereas today, both she and her husband were like two rats shut in a hole! Yesterday, Harnam Singh and Karim Khan were condemning the riots, condemning those indulging in them as people who had lost all sense of decency, as though what was happening was something so remote that they could talk and comment on it in a detached way. And now, with one gust of the wind, as it were, they had been thrown overboard.

His heart sank within him as he suddenly realized that he was without a gun, that he might never get it back. 'What have I done? I have myself cut off my hands. The gun with me was like the blind man's staff. I shall never get it back now.' Harnam Singh felt as though he was drenched in cold sweat. By this act, his wife's situation had become all the more precarious. 'With what sense of confidence will I be able to take her along with me now? People can now stone us to death.' In one stroke of stark reality, Harnam Singh had lost all that he had earned through a lifetime of devotion, faith and love of humanity.

'I wish we had some news of Jasbir,' Banto muttered suddenly.

Harnam Singh did not say anything. Now and then, the mother in Banto would cry out. The previous night too, as they trudged along the dry bed of the stream, Banto had time and again thought of her children. Every time the shadow of danger lifted a little, her thoughts would turn to her children.

There was noise in the village outside and it was increasing. Men and women seemed to be talking animatedly. Then someone knocked at the door and a woman's voice was heard:

'Ai Akran, come out. Our menfolk are on their way.' It was one of Akran's girlfriends, shouting. Akran opened the door and ran out.

Harnam Singh's heart sank within him. Banto looked up at her husband's face. The face which had always looked radiant had turned pale, while his clothes were crumpled and dirty.

Through the slightly open window of the loft, Harnam Singh saw the mistress of the house. She was standing, both her hands on her waist in front of the open door of the courtyard. Looking at her tall figure and her graceful bearing, his faith returned, as it were. He once again felt like reposing all his confidence in her. So long as she is there, there is still hope; everything is not lost.

'Through Guru Maharaj's kindness, we shall come out unscathed. You are a devotee of God. Why should you be afraid?' said Banto trying to instil confidence in her husband. Harnam Singh remained silent.

Voices grew louder outside. Sounds of loud laughter, jovialities as also of advancing footsteps increased. Suddenly, Akran's voice was heard, talking and laughing loudly. Harnam Singh understood that the male members of the family had arrived after their night-long outing.

Akran and her father-in-law hauled in a big, black trunk into the courtyard. The turban on the man's head was sunk in indicating that he had carried the trunk on his head all the way through.

Harnam Singh put out his hand and touched his wife on her knee.

'Banto, it is our trunk, the big black trunk. They have been looting our shop.'

Banto made no effort to look out.

'It is still locked. The lock on it is still there,' Harnam Singh whispered.

Akran's father-in-law sat down on top of the trunk; he took off his turban and wiped the perspiration off his forehead with it. His wife stepped forward and shut the door.

'Why hasn't Ramzan come?'

'Ramzan has gone to participate in Tabligh.'

Harnam Singh again stretched out his hand and touched his wife's knee: 'It is Ehsan Ali. I know him. I have had dealings with him.'

'Abba, you have brought a locked trunk. Heaven knows if there is anything worthwhile in it.',

'Why, it was so heavy, my back bent double carrying it. It is bound to be full of many things.'

'And it is only one trunk you have brought. Hasn't Ramzan brought anything?'

'It was he who pulled it out. We have brought a full trunk. What more do you want?'

'Let's open it. Shall we break the lock?' Akran said and ran into the back room to bring a hammer.

In her eagerness to see what the trunk contained, she forgot to tell him about the kafirs sitting in the loft. Her mother-in-law still stood nearby without uttering a word.

'Get me some lassi, Rajo. I am dying of thirst,' said the father-in-law at which his wife went forthwith to fetch buttermilk.

Akran began hammering at the lock.

With the bowl in his hand Ehsan Ali drank buttermilk when Rajo, his wife, told him that she had given shelter to a Sardar and his wife in the house.

Just then, Harnam Singh opened the little door of the loft and putting out his head said, 'Child, why are you hammering at the lock? Here is the key. It is our trunk.' Then, turning to Ehsan Ali, said, 'Ehsan Ali, I am Harnam Singh. Your wife has been so kind as to give us shelter. May Guru Maharaj's blessings be on you both. This trunk is ours. But consider it your own. Good that it fell into your hands.'

Ehsan Ali looked up and felt embarrassed, as though he had been caught stealing.

Akran's hands too stopped moving, and she shouted, 'Ma has given them shelter. I told her that she should not let kafirs into the house but she wouldn't listen.'

Akran was saying all this to please her father-in-law, but Ehsan Ali still stood perplexed, feeling uneasy. Once upon a time they had had dealings with each other, and knew each other well enough. He had not anticipated such an encounter and therefore did not know how he should treat Harnam Singh. Besides, he was not so hot-headed either as to get enraged at the mere sight of a Hindu or a Sikh.

'Come down, Harnam Singh,' and as though covering his theft with the good turn done by his wife, said somewhat boldly, 'Thank your stars that you took shelter in my house. Had you gone elsewhere, you wouldn't have been alive by now.'

Akran was impatient to open the lock but Rajo had snatched the key from her hand and despite her repeated requests would not give it to her.

'I shall be considerate towards you, Harnam Singh, because you have come to my house, but you had better go away now. If my son comes to know that you are here, he will not treat you well. If the village folk come to know that we have given you shelter, they will be hard on us.'

'We shall do whatever you tell us, Ehsan Ali. We have no choice, no say. But who will leave us alive if we go out at this time, in broad daylight?'

Ehsan Ali fell silent and looked at his wife, so as to say, what a messy situation she had landed him in:

'People were looking for you last night,' Ehsan Ali said. 'If they come to know that you are hiding here, they won't spare us. It is as much in your interest as in ours that you leave this place.'

Akran brought the ladder of her own accord and put it below the loft. Both husband and wife quietly came down. Both looked like sacrificial goats.

Then the same drama was enacted as had been played in the morning. Both of them came down, resigned to their fate. Both of them were composed. Neither of them demeaned themselves by asking for consideration. As they stood in the yard, Harnam Singh was about to ask for his gun from Rajo, who stood in the middle of the yard, her hands on her waist, when Ehsan Ali suddenly said, 'Take them into the godown, Rajo, where we stack hay. Let them sit there and lock the door from outside. Here, take this very lock and put it on the door. Hurry up.' Then trying to show his magnanimity, he said to Harnam Singh, 'It is out of consideration for our past contacts, Harnam Singh, otherwise by God, what the kafirs have done in the city, makes one's blood boil.'

Rajo led the way and Harnam Singh and Banto followed her. They were taken to a godown at the back of the house. It smelled strongly of cow-dung, fodder and wet hay. It was stacked with hay, from top to bottom.

'Sit down here. My husband is a pious man. I did not know that you knew each other. Try to pass the time somehow.'

Here too, Harnam Singh and his wife accepted the situation as they had earlier when they had been asked to sit in the loft. Rajo shut the door and locked it from outside.

Time passed. Both felt that till nightfall they were assured of shelter. Some time during the day, Rajo came and gave them some chapattis and buttermilk. The food gave them much-needed respite. For a long time both sat staring into the darkness with wide open eyes. Banto again said to Harnam Singh: 'Where do you think Iqbal Singh must be at this time? I wonder if he is still in his village or has gone elsewhere.' 'Whatever is Wahe Guru's will. I hope some kindhearted person has come his way and saved his life. Thank God Jasbiro is not alone. Many of our people are there. I hope all of them have gathered in one place.'

At this Harnam Singh said, 'I hope these people give us back our gun. What do you think, Banto? I don't suppose they will.'

They talked in low whispers for a long time. Although the godown did not have a window or a ventilator, it was not so sultry as it had been in the loft. Sitting on a heap of sheaves, both felt sleepy. They had not had a wink of sleep during the previous night. A little later, both fell into deep slumber. They were suddenly woken up by someone battering the door with a pickaxe.

'Come out, bastards, come out, you...'

Harnam Singh and his wife woke up as though they had seen a nightmare.

'Where is the key? Give me the key. You kafirs, I'll show you...' and blow after blow fell on the door.

'Don't shout, Ramzan, don't shout.' A female voice was saying. Perhaps it was Akran, pressing her husband not to speak so loudly.

Blows from the pickaxe continued to fall and soon enough there was a crack in the upper part of the door. Through the crack some light entered the dark godown.

Thereupon the voice of another woman was heard, 'What has come over you, Ramzan? Stop shouting, and stop breaking the door. Where is this damned girl? Couldn't you keep your mouth shut? I shall pull out your tongue, haramzadi, I had told you not to tell Ramzan. Stop it, Ramzan. Will you kill those who have taken shelter in our house? This man is known to us. At one time we owed him money.'

'Stop chattering, Ma. In the city they have killed two hundred Musalmans.' And blows from the pickaxe began to fall on the door again. 'Come out, you kafirs, you bloody...'

Another two blows and the door fell open. The godown was suddenly filled with light. Pickaxe in hand, Ramzan stood outside, breathing hard. Close by him stood Akran, her face pale and frightened. On one side stood Rajo, her hands on her waist.

'Come out, you kafirs...' said Ramzan peeping in.

Harnam Singh and his wife sat close to each other, their eyes dazzled as they tried to look out. As the door was broken open, Harnam Singh stood up and slowly came out.

'Put me to death if you want to,' he said in a hoarse voice.

'You...' Ramzan shouted and putting out his left hand caught hold of Harnam Singh by the throat. The collar button on Harnam Singh's shirt broke and fell down on the floor, and the turban on his head became loose. With the swiftness with which he had caught hold of Harnam Singh's neck, he let go off it too. His fingers left reddish marks on Harnam Singh's neck.

He too had recognized Harnam Singh, for he had tea at his tea shop a couple of times. Harnam Singh's beard had turned grey and he looked thinner.

Twice Ramzan raised his pickaxe to strike, but both times he let it fall. It is one thing to kill a kafir, it is quite another to kill someone you know and who has sought shelter in your house. A thin line was still there which was difficult to cross, despite the fact that the atmosphere was charged with religious frenzy and hatred. Ramzan stood there for some time, breathing hard and then, uttering abuses, went out of the house.

It was nearing midnight, when the tall, stately figure of Rajo, walking in front, led Harnam Singh and Banto out of the house and in the direction of the grove of trees. A bright moon shone above and bathed in its light the view on all sides looked ethereal and dreamlike. Patches of light and shade appeared to be playing hide and seek. The grove of trees and the vast valley beyond looked mysterious and almost frightening. Rajo, carrying the double-barrelled gun in her hand, looked sedate and very graceful.

They were again going towards the dry bed of the stream. Towards the left the sky was turning crimson. Harnam Singh softly pressed his wife's hand and said, 'Look towards the left, Banto! What do you see?'

'Yes, I have seen. Some village is burning.'

'Wahe Guru!'

They walked on. Harnam Singh again paused. Far into the distance, on the other side too, the horizon was turning red.

'Which village is that? That too is burning!'

Banto remained silent.

Harnam Singh turned round and looked towards the village that they had left behind. The flat-roofed mud- houses were bathed in the moonlight. Here and there, in some houses was the glimmer of light from the earthen lamps. Outside the houses, in the yards, stood haystacks, a bullock-cart here and there.

As they passed by the grove, their eyes fell on the pir's grave. No light was burning there. People had forgotten to light the earthen lamp on it that day.

Rajo walked along the edge of the grove. As they reached the end of the grove, they climbed up a small mound. It was from the top of this mound that Harnam Singh and Banto had gone down to the village that morning.

Rajo stopped. Handing the gun to Harnam Singh she said, 'Now go. May God be with you. Go along the edge of the stream. May Fate be kind to you.'

There was a slight tremor in her voice.

'We are deeply indebted to you, Rajo sister. We shall never be able to repay you for what you have done for us.'

'If we survive, we shall, one day...' and Harnam Singh's voice shook and he could not complete the sentence.

Rajo said, 'Everyone to his or her fate. I do not know whether I am saving your life or pushing you into the jaws of death. Fires are raging on all sides,' and so saying she put her hand into her shirt-pocket and took out a small bundle wrapped in a piece of cloth.

'Here, take this. It is yours.'

'What is it, Rajo sister?'

'I found this in your trunk and took it out. It is your jewellery. It will stand by you in difficulty.'

'We must have done some good deeds in our past life to have met you,' Banto said and burst into tears.

'It is getting late. Move on. May God be with you,' Rajo said. She could not tell them in which direction they should go, or towards which village or at whose door they should knock.

Husband and wife went down the slope. Rajo kept standing at the top of the mound. Once again it was the same stream-bed, strewn with pebbles and sand. Under the light of the moon the entire valley was divided into dark and bright patches.

After having covered some distance, they looked back. Rajo was still standing on top of the mound, as though watching their footsteps leading them towards the unknown. Then, as they looked, she turned and went back towards the village.

As she went out of sight a frightful desolation descended on all sides.

17

In the meantime, another drama was being enacted in the rugged countryside of this rural district. Ramzan and his fellow freebooters were returning from their exploits in Dhok Elahi Baksh and Muradpur. Chatting and laughing, and carrying their booty they suddenly noticed a young Sikh, at some distance running for his life, near a small mound. It is difficult to say whether he had started running on seeing the marauders, or had already been running frantically in search of shelter. When they set their eyes on him, they were greatly excited as though they had found a sport. 'Ya Ali!' Ramzan shouted and all the fellows—there must have been twenty or thirty of them—ran after him. The ground was uneven, with many small mounds, ravines, and hollows and deep recesses like tunnels inside the mounds. The young Sardar was heading towards some village but had left the road and chosen to go through the fields and the rugged area, thinking that in doing so he would escape the notice of those going by the main cart road.

The Sardar was soon lost from view.

'The Sikhra has gone into hiding,' said Ramzan and quickened his pace. When the pursuers had covered some distance—the Sardar must be about fifty yards away from them—they got another glimpse of him. He was running across a ravine towards a mound. But when they reached that spot he had again disappeared.

'He has gone into some hole,' Nur Din said. 'Let us get him out. Son of a...'

They went and stood on top of a mound. A little while earlier, these religious enthusiasts had picked up stones and clay-balls and hurled them at the Sardar, but now they began pelting stones into the holes and deep recesses inside the mounds, thinking that when a few stones would hit him, he would come out crying and whimpering. Had the Sardar continued running, he would certainly have been stoned to death like a rat under a volley of stones during the monsoons. But instead of running any farther, he had entered a deep, dark recess in one of the mounds, which looked deep enough and sat down in it, crouching to one side. All around were innumerable recesses or tunnels, so it was difficult for his pursuers to know in which particular recess the fellow was hiding.

'O Sikha! Vadi Trikha!' shouted Nur Din at which there was a guffaw of laughter. Nur Din belonged to the same village as Ramzan. His occupation was to carry donkey-loads of bricks and earth from place to place. He was conspicuous by his very red gums. Each time he laughed his red gums would be visible from a long distance.

Some persons ran down the mound.

'He must be hiding in this hole,' someone said. 'Come out, you son of a...'

No sound came. It was dark inside and the cave was deep.

Then many of them picked up stones and hurled them into the cave. But to no effect.

'We won't find him this way. Let someone go in and see,' Ramzan said.

'Be careful, Ramzan, the fellow must be carrying a kirpan.'

Ramzan laughed but to be on the safe side he took out his knife and flicked it open. As Ramzan went in, two others followed suit.

'Come out, you karar!'

They searched the hole thoroughly. The Sardar was not there.

'The bastard must be hiding in some other hole.'

Then another member of the gang who was standing on top of the mound, shouted: 'There he is! There he goes,' and pointing towards a mound which was located behind two or three mounds, said, 'He has gone in that direction.' He had caught a glimpse of the Sardar's white clothes.

All of them ran in that direction. Stones began to be hurled into two or three caves simultaneously. In one of the caves, a stone hit the Sardar on his right knee but he did not cry out; and crouched closer to the wall of the cave. This was followed by a volley of stones. Some stones hit the wall of the cave while others hit his knees or shoulders or forehead. The Sardar was in great pain but suppressed his sobs. Stones continued to be pelted in all the three caves. After some time the sound of low moaning and sobbing was heard from one of the caves. Detecting the exact cave in which the Sardar was hiding, the marauders increased instantly the volley of stones.

Then someone in the gang shouted: 'Stop! Stop pelting stones!' At this, the volley abated, but a stray stone now and then continued to be hurled.

The one who had shouted came and stood at the mouth of the cave and said: 'Sardar, we shall spare your life, if you accept the Faith.'

No answer came from the other side. Only the sound of low moaning continued to be heard.

'Speak Sardar, what do you say? Will you accept Islam or not? If you agree, then come out on your own. We shall not harm you. Otherwise we shall stone you to death.'

There was still no answer from inside. An occasional stone continued to be hurled to intimidate the Sardar into taking a decision quickly.

'Come out, you son of a...., otherwise only your dead body will be left there.'

No sound came from inside. The pelting of stones was resumed. Ramzan Ali picked up a big stone and went and stood at the mouth of the cave.

'Come out at once, otherwise with this stone I shall make mince-meat of you.'

Some fellows laughed. Pelting of stones continued.

Then, crawling on all fours, the Sardar came to the mouth of the cave. His turban was untied and hung loose round his head, his clothes torn in many places were smeared with mud and dust, his forehead and knees were bruised and swollen and blood oozed out of them.

The Sardar was still on all fours, gazing into vacancy. Because of pain his face was contorted.

'Tell us. Will you recite the Kalma or not?' Ramzan said. He was still holding the big stone in his hands.

The frightened Sardar stared wide-eyed into vacancy and then nodded his head.

A man standing behind Nur Din recognized the Sardar. He was none other than Iqbal Singh, who ran a cloth-shop in Mirpur; his father Harnam Singh owned a tea shop in Dhok Elahi Baksh. Very likely he was going towards Dhok Elahi Baksh to join his parents when he was waylaid. The moment he recognized him, the man stepped back a few steps so that their eyes did not meet. As a matter of fact, after this, he remained in the background, he neither spoke nor threw stones, but at the same time he did not stop others from tormenting the Sardar. He knew well enough that no one would listen to him, even if he tried to do so.

'Speak, you son of a—! Speak or this stone will crush your skull.'

'I shall recite the Kalma,' Iqbal Singh muttered between his sobs.

At this, a resounding slogan reverberated the air:

'Allah-o-Akbar!'

'*Nara-e-Taqbir*—Allah-o-Akbar!'

All joined in the full-throated response to the slogan.

Ramzan threw away the stone to one side. Everyone threw away the stones that he held in his hands. Ramzan put out his hand and said,

'Get up! You are now our brother!'

Iqbal Singh's body pained in every limb; he was still moaning piteously. Still fear-stricken and in great pain, he could not stand.

'Come, let's embrace each other!' Ramzan said and put his

arms round Iqbal Singh.

Thereafter, everyone by turns, embraced Iqbal Singh. The man embracing him would put his head on Iqbal's right shoulder, and then, by turn, on his left shoulder and back again on his right shoulder. This was the cordial Muslim embrace. Iqbal Singh's throat was parched and his legs shook under him, but after practising the embrace three or four times, he got the hang of it.

Iqbal Singh had not expected that the situation would change so radically and so soon for him, that people who were thirsting for his blood would begin to embrace him like a blood relation.

They came out into the open, leaving the area of the mounds behind. They were soon walking through green fields where the wheat-crop was ripening, driving Iqbal Singh along, as they would, a beast. They still did not know how they should look upon him, as a trophy of their victory, or as a hated foe who had tried to escape but had been caught, or as a fellow-Muslim whom they had clasped to their bosom. Iqbal Singh was unable to walk steadily. No fewer than five stones had hit his left knee, besides, his forehead was still bleeding. At one place, as they crossed one field and went into another, he staggered, Nur Din gave him a push and Iqbal Singh fell on his face.

'See Ramzanji, they are still pushing me,' he moaned, as he tried to stand up, like a boy who despite his assurance that he would behave better, was still being pushed around.

'Don't push, oi!' shouted Ramzan, and looking at his associates, smiled and winked.

'Don't push, oi!' someone else too repeated, imitating Ramzan and gave a shove to Iqbal Singh.

Hostility and hatred cannot turn into sympathy and love so suddenly, they can only turn into crude banter. Since they could not physically hit him, they could at least make him the butt of their vulgar jokes.

'See Ramzanji, someone has again pushed me.'

Iqbal Singh had, by then, touched the lowest level of demoralization. A person clinging to life can only grovel and cringe. If you tell him to laugh, he will laugh, if you tell him to cry, he will begin to cry.

Then Nur Din thought of a practical joke.

'Stop oi!' shouted Nur Din to Iqbal Singh.

Iqbal Singh, with a frightened look in his eyes turned to Nur Din.

'Take off his salwar. The bastard was trying to hoodwink us.'

And he put his hand into Iqbal Singh's salwar. Some fellows began to laugh.

'Do you see, Ramzanji?' wailed Iqbal Singh, looking at Ramzan.

'Don't! No one will take off his salwar.' Ramzan shouted.

'He has not yet recited the Kalma. Therefore he is still a kafir, not a Musalman. Take off his salwar.'

Iqbal Singh felt encouraged when he saw that Ramzan was sympathetic to him; so he too shouted, 'I won't let anyone take off my salwar. Come what may.'

Some people laughed at this.

Thus, bullying and humiliating him, they arrived in the village.

It was in the house of Imam Din the oil-crusher that the conversion ceremony took place. The village barber too arrived on the scene, so did the mullah from the mosque. A whole crowd gathered in the courtyard.

The barber's fingers began to ache as he cut off Iqbal Singh's hair. Surrounded by a big crowd Iqbal Singh's bewilderment intensified. In the beginning, the barber used only his scissors, but later, he tied his hair into tufts with the help of horse-dung and urine, and cut it tuft by tuft. In the end he brought along a pair of shears to help him out. As the shears worked, furrows appeared on Iqbal Singh's head. Thereafter, his head was shaved with a razor. It was only then that Iqbal Singh could lift his head. When the time came to cut his beard, many voices rose simultaneously:

'Give his beard a Muslim cut.'

'Trim the beard. Make it angular. Make the moustache thin.'

Iqbal Singh's shrivelled face, despite his frightened eyes,

actually began to look like that of a Muslim.

Then came Nur Din, making his way through the crowd. When Iqbal Singh's hair was being cut, he had slipped out, unnoticed. But now, he was pushing people aside, in order to get in.

'Get out of the way. Let me go in.'

On entering, he went straight to Iqbal Singh, and sat down by his side. With his right hand he forced open Iqbal Singh's mouth and with his left hand, in which he held a big piece of raw meat, dripping with blood, forced it into his mouth. Iqbal Singh's eyes popped out; he was unable to breathe.

'Open your mouth wide, you son of a.... Suck it now. Bloody...'

And Nur Din, turning towards the crowd laughed, showing his red gums.

Just then the mullah of the mosque arrived, along with an elderly man of the village. The elderly man snubbed Nur Din for being flippant on a pious occasion:

'Get up. You are pestering someone who will soon be our co-religionist, one who is going to accept our faith.'

With the arrival of the elderly man the entire scene changed. People stepped back and became quiet. Iqbal Singh was given support to stand up. One man brought in a cot and Iqbal Singh was seated on it. The rest of the ceremony was conducted with care and attention. Rosary in hand the mullah made Iqbal Singh recite the Kalma: 'La Ilah Illallah! Muhammad ar Rasulallah!'

The Kalma was recited three times. People standing around touched their eyes with the tips of their fingers and then kissed them. Thereafter nearly everyone in the crowd embraced Iqbal Singh one by one.

He was then taken to the village well in a procession. After the bath he was given new clothes to wear. As he emerged after the bath in his new clothes, Iqbal Singh actually looked like a Muslim. Once again the slogan went up: 'Nara-e-Takbir, Allah-o-Akbar!'

The procession again proceeded towards the house of Imam Din the oil-crusher. The atmosphere now was more solemn, full of religious ardour. Before the shades of evening fell, the circumcision ceremony had been performed. The pain involved had not been so unbearable for Iqbal Singh. The elderly man all the time beguiling his mind with temptations, whispering into his ears:

'We shall get you a buxom wife, the widow of Kalu, a peach of a woman... Now you are one of our own; you are now Iqbal Ahmed.'

By the time evening fell, all the marks of Sikhism on Iqbal Singh's person had been replaced by the marks of the Muslim faith. A mere change of marks had brought about the transformation. Now he was no longer an enemy but a friend, not a kafir but a believer; to whom the doors of all Muslim houses were open.

Lying on his cot, Iqbal Ahmed kept tossing and turning the whole night.

18

The Turks had come, but they had come only from one of the neighbouring villages. The Turks too mentally viewed their attack as an assault on the citadel of their age-old enemy, the Sikhs. In the minds of the Sikhs too they were the Turks of the bygone medieval times whom the Khalsa used to confront in battle. This confrontation too was looked upon as a link in the chain of earlier confrontations in history. The 'warriors' had their feet in the twentieth century while their minds were in medieval times.

A bitter fight took place. It went on for two days and two nights. Then the ammunition was exhausted and it became impossible to go on. At the back of the low platform on which the Sacred Book was placed, seven dead bodies covered with white sheets of cloth lay in a row. Five women sat with the heads of their husbands in their laps. For some time they would leave, when repeatedly persuaded to do so, but again, Sardar Teja Singh had only to turn his back and they would come back. Two dead bodies had no claimants. One of these was of a Nihang, who even under the hail of bullets stood on duty on the roof, with his moustaches twirled and his chest sticking out. The other one was that of Sohan Singh, who had come all the way from the city to prevent the riot from breaking out. His dead body was found lying at the end of the lane near the gurdwara. On the second day of the 'battle' he had been sent with a proposal for the 'cessation of hostilities' to Ghulam Rasul's house. His dead body was the adversary's answer to that proposal. His dead body would have continued to lie near the wall where he had been killed, had it not been picked up late in the night by some Muslims and left near the gurdwara to inform the Sikhs about the fate of their peace-proposal. His dead body lay to one side and no one put his head in his or her lap. Even otherwise, the status of both Sohan Singh and Mir Dad had been reduced from peace-makers to that of couriers.

Besides these, quite a few dead bodies lay scattered here and there in the village. The question of attending to them did not as yet arise. The dead body of the peon of Khalsa School lay in the courtyard of the school itself. On the day the attack took place, while the 'community' was gathering in the gurdwara, the peon was exhorted to stick to his duty of guarding the school. The peon's wife was alive and said to be safe and sound because she had been forcibly taken by the *numbardar* of the village to his house. Mai Bhagan's dead body was found lying in the inner yard of her own house. One stinging slap had been enough to finish her. Her jewellery, however, was saved because it lay concealed inside a wall, and her house escaped being set on fire because it stood adjacent to the house of Rahima teli. Saudagar Singh was another old man who lay dead and whose body due to oversight was not carried to the gurdwara.

There were some more dead bodies too that lay here and there. One of them lay face downward near a well. The man had been killed by mistake. He was the water-carrier, Allah Rakha, who, despite the raging riot, had been sent to fetch water since they had run short of water in the Sheikh's house and children were howling for water. As he reached the well, under the light of the moon, a bullet accurately aimed from the roof of the Sheikh's house itself had made short shrift of him. Another dead body of a Sardar who had come from the city lay on the road. Two small children, working as shop-boys in Fateh Din the baker's shop were also found dead. The baker's shop was located at the end of the lane that led to the gurdwara. There was no stopping these boys from playing in the lane. Time and again they would rush out chasing each other.

Flames of fire still rose from the building of the Khalsa School.

All the houses belonging to the Sikhs on the slope overlooking the stream had been gutted. Besides, all the three shops of the butchers, and the houses of three or four Muslims in the Teli Mohalla, had been set on fire.

The ammunition inside the gurdwara was almost exhausted. Kishen Singh, stationed on the roof, had begun to fire his gun sparingly. He would fire a shot after every few minutes, so that the enemy might know that the front was holding out. Inside the gurdwara however, the morale was pretty low. A sense of fatigue and helplessness had set in. Eyes would meet but lips would not open. No one knew who it was who had first uttered the words: 'Ammunition is finishing.' But it had left the listeners petrified. The ammunition was finishing even in the Sheikh's fortress. But to cover the reality, slogan-shouting on both sides had become all the more vociferous. 'Allah-o-Akbar!' had begun to be heard, not from one but from three directions. The slogan in reply, from the gurdwara was even louder. But the slogan-shouting too had begun to sound hollow.

The intelligence men had brought the news that the Muslims were getting succour from outside. The contact of Sikhs with the outside areas had virtually been cut off. Two men had been secretly sent to Kahuta for assistance, but they had not returned until then. The War Council was of the view that with the help of money peace might be bought; and so they had started negotiations through emissaries.

Inside the gurdwara, near the main door, members of the War Council sat discussing with Teja Singhji the possible terms and conditions for bringing about a truce.

'They are demanding two lakhs of rupees. This is an impossible amount,' Teja Singh said irritably.

'What offer did you make to them through the younger Granthi who was sent by you to them?'

After the death of Sohan Singh, Teja Singhji had tried to seek the help of Mir Dad for purposes of mediation, since before the riots, Mir Dad had been trying to bring about an understanding between the two communities, but when Mir Dad learnt that cessation of hostilities was being bargained for with money, he turned his back on it. Not knowing what to do, Teja Singhji had sent the younger brother of the Granthi, who was generally addressed as the 'younger Granthi', as an emissary.

'I told him to quote anything between twenty and thirty thousand rupees,' said Teja Singhji, 'but they are demanding two lakhs.'

'They must have come to know that our position is no longer strong.'

'How could they?' retorted Hira Singh, the general merchant. 'Our killings have in no way been fewer than theirs. It is our bad luck that we have run short of ammunition.'

From a distance was heard the slogan:

'Allah-o-Akbar!'

'How much of jewellery and ornaments have we been able to collect?'

Teja Singhji got up and went towards the box lying in front of the chowki of the Sacred Book and opening it, took the ornaments into his hand and tried to assess their value from their approximate weight.

'They can't fetch more than twenty to twenty-five thousand rupees. But they are demanding two lakhs!' Teja Singh repeated, like the refrain of a song.

'You alone can pay two lakhs, Teja Singhji, if you so desire. You have amassed quite a fortune.'

But Teja Singhji thought it fit to ignore the comment.

'Offer them a sum of fifty thousand.'

'Fifty thousand is too little. I don't think they will agree.'

'To begin with, we must quote a low figure. If you will start from a low figure, it will be possible to strike a bargain at a lakh of rupees.'

Teja Singh sent for the younger Granthi: 'Try to strike a bargain for any amount up to one lakh rupees, starting from a low figure. We shall make the payment only after the outsiders have gone to the other side of the stream. Make it clear to them. Thereafter, they can send three of their men for money, our representatives will be standing with the money bags.'

The younger Granthi folded his hands and said, 'Truth resides on your tongue, Good Sir, but what if they insist that money must be paid first and then alone will the outsiders go across the stream?'

At this the general merchant flared up: 'Why? Are we Lahorias or Amritsarias that our word cannot be trusted? We are citizens of Sayedpur, and our word is carved on stone.'

The Sikhs were as proud of being the inhabitants of Sayedpur as were the Muslims. Both took equal pride in the red soil of Sayedpur, its top-quality wheat, its orchards of lukat fruit, even in its severe winters and razor-sharp cold winds. Both took pride in the hospitality and liberality of the Sayedpur citizens, their sunny, hail-fellow-well-met temperaments. And ironically enough, while jumping into the fray against one another, both had boasted of their valour too, in the same vein, proudly striking their chests.

The moon had risen, presenting, a frightful view to those on guard. If there was firing again, anything could happen—arson, loot, murder. All earlier moves had proved disastrous. It was a big blunder to have gathered in the gurdwara; it was a big blunder to have snapped contact with Sheikh Ghulam Rasul. There was no end to such blunders. Had these moves brought success, they would have been viewed as examples of excellent strategy.

Some people sat chatting on the terrace of Sheikh Ghulam Rasul's house. They too had not had the time to attend to their dead. But whereas the position of the gurdwara was like that of a house under siege, the house of the Sheikh had no such duress; it could maintain contact even with far-flung villages.

The mujahids sitting on the Sheikh's terrace had come from outside. They were narrating their exploits and experiences to one another.

'When we got into the lane, the karars began to run this way and that way. A Hindu girl went up to the roof of her house. As soon as we saw her, we ran after her. There were nearly ten of us. She was trying to jump over the low wall on the roof to go over to the adjoining house when she fell into our hands. Nabi, Lalu, Mira, Murtaza all had a go at her one by one.'

'Is that true? Swear by your faith.'

'By God it is true, every word of it. When my turn came there was no sound from her; she wouldn't move. I looked at her; she was dead. I had been doing it to a dead body,' he laughed a hollow kind of laughter, and turning his face to one side, spat on the floor.

'I swear that it is true. Ask Jalal, he was also there.'

Another mujahid had his own story to tell.

'It is all a matter of chance,' he was saying. 'We caught hold of a bagri woman in a lane. My hand was working so well, I would chop off a head at one go. The woman began crying and begging: "Don't kill me," she said, "All seven of you can have me as your keep."'

'Then?'

'Then what? Aziza plunged his dagger into her bosom and she was finished there and then.'

In the moonlit night, the younger Granthi was slowly going down the slope. The group of deputies from the Muslim side sent to negotiate peace-terms stood at the edge of the stream. Through one of the windows of the gurdwara the slope was clearly visible, and many had their eyes on it, watching the young Granthi with bated breath. In the moonlight only a figure in silhouette could be seen moving down the slope. Suddenly from the roof above came the sound of running feet and a Nihang shouting:

'Turks are coming from the western direction. The enemy has received succour from outside.'

And soon enough the familiar war-cries along with the beating of drums were heard.

'Allah-o-Akbar!'

Teja Singh's face fell. The elder Granthi who stood at the window watching his brother, suddenly called out to his brother: 'Don't go further, Mehar Singh! Come back!'

But the younger Granthi did not hear. He continued going

down, walking unsteadily over the pebbles and stones which lay scattered by the side of the stream.

'Come back, Mehar Singh! Come back!' shouted the elder Granthi. Thereupon others too joined in. The younger Granthi looked back once but then continued going down. The drum-beat and war-cries of the advancing marauders grew louder every minute. The mujahids standing at the edge of the stream responded to their compatriots with full-throated 'Allah-o-Akbar!'

Under the light of the moon the figure of the younger Granthi would again and again be lost from view because of the patches of light and shade.

The view from the window was not so clear now. It appeared that some people had stepped forward to meet the younger Granthi; it also appeared as though the younger Granthi had been surrounded on all sides. It seemed to some as though a few lathis had been raised. Something glittered too in the light of the moon which was either a pick-axe or the naked sword of the younger Granthi.

'Allah-o-Akbar!' the slogan was again raised.

Blood drained from Teja Singh's face, and his heart sank within him. The elder Granthi, standing at the window, suddenly cried out:

'Killed! They have killed my brother!' and without a second thought rushed out of the gurdwara, and crossing the lane, ran barefoot down the slope.

'Stop! Somebody stop him!' someone shouted at the top of his voice at which the Nihang posted at the gate ran after the Granthi and by the time the latter had reached the middle of the slope, overtook him and putting his arm round his waist, lifted him up with both his arms and turned back.

The drum-beat of the marauders was now heard from inside the village. Slogans were being raised from all sides. Once again bullets began to be showered and people were seen running in all directions.

'Jo Boley So Nihal!

'Sat Sri Akal!'

The slogan pierced through the air.

A group of Sikhs—the elder Granthi was among them—brandishing their swords, and challenging the enemy, their hair loosened, ran down the slope, as though determined to do or die!

Inside the gurdwara, a large number of women and children sat huddled against the wall to the left. In the rising crescendo of shouting and shrieking, all the women had gathered in one place. The face of Jasbir Kaur was flushed as though she was in a state of frenzy. Her hand was on the handle of the kirpan, holding it tightly.

Women had started chanting the Japji Sahib; their murmuring voice gradually grew louder.

Flames of fire were seen rising from behind the houses standing at the end of the lane to the left, and the sky was turning crimson, even a deeper crimson than before.

'Fire is rising from the lane near the school...It is Kishen Singh's house burning!'

The words fell on Jasbir's ears too, but it seemed as though she had not heard them. A surge, a wave rose and fell within her, again and again. But she saw nothing clearly before her eyes, as though everything was floating, everything in a sort of twilight, everything going round and round, revolving round her. She was standing right under the light in the middle of the hall, and her face glowed as though with celestial light.

The picket on the left collapsed. Under the light of the moon, some men were seen crawling up the slope. The Nihang Singh posted on the roof was the first one to see them. He promptly informed Kishen Singh, but Kishen Singh was so despondent, he merely shook his head. The number of dark figures crawling up the slope was increasing every minute. They became clearly visible now because of the fire in the lane. But where was the ammunition to stop them, or even to arrest their advance? Kishen Singh pressed the trigger once or twice but then sat down, in despair.

The picket to the left having collapsed, another band of Sikhs,

standing sword in hand outside the gurdwara, their hair hanging
loose, rushed towards the end of the lane on the left. The Turks
could attack the gurdwara only from that side, through that
opening. A volley of fire followed by the shouts of 'Allah-o-
Akbar!' rent the air.

The band of Sardars brandishing their swords were soon
swallowed up by the darkness at the end of the lane. Just at that
time a group of women, emerged in a row from the gurdwara.
At their head was Jasbir Kaur, her eyes half-open, her face flushed.
Almost all the women had taken their dupattas off their heads
and tied them round their waists. They were all bare-footed,
their faces too were flushed. As though under a spell, they came
out of the gurdwara.

'The Turks are here! The Turks have come!' Some of the
women shouted, while some others chanted the verses of the
Gurbani and still some others, shouted in frenzied voices: 'I too
shall go where my lion-brother has gone!'

Some of them had their children with them. Two or three
women had little babies in their arms, while some, holding their
children by their hands, were pulling them along.

Coming out of the gurdwara, the women turned to the right
and after covering some distance, took to a narrow path from
between two houses which went its zigzag way, down the slope
right up to a well, at the bottom of the slope.

The atmosphere resounded with cries and wailing. Tongues
of flame now rose from two places, their shadows danced on the
walls of houses, on the slope, on the cobbled street, and were
reflected in the water of the stream, turning the water red, as it
were.

To the deafening noise was added the noise of doors being
battered, and the shouts of plunderers. In front of the gurdwara,
a Nihang Singh stood right in the middle of the lane, waving his
lance and shouting: 'Come, Turks, come if you dare! I challenge
you, come!'

The throng of women headed towards the well located at the
foot of the slope. This was the well to which the women used to

come every day to bathe, to wash their clothes, to gossip. They were now running fast towards it, as though under a spell. None knew why and wherefore they were heading towards it. Under the translucent light of the moon it appeared as though fairies were flying down to the well.

Jasbir Kaur was the first one to jump into the well. She raised no slogan, nor did she call anyone's name, she only uttered Wahe Guru and took the jump. After her, one by one, many women climbed up to the low wall of the well. Hari Singh's wife climbed up stood there for a moment, then pulled up her four-year-old son on to the wall and holding him by the hand, jumped too. Deva Singh's wife held the breast-fed child in her arms when she took the plunge. Prem Singh's wife jumped down, but her son was left standing on the wall. The child was pushed into the well by Gyan Singh's wife, and thus sent back into the arms of his mother. Within a matter of minutes tens of women had gone into their watery grave, some of them along with their children.

By the time the Turks actually entered the lane which led to the gurdwara, after walking over a heap of dead bodies at the entrance to the lane, there was not a single woman left in the gurdwara. The air was filled with the heart-rending cries of women and children coming from inside the well and were mingled with the loud shouts of 'Allah-o-Akbar' and 'Sat Sri Akal.'

The light of the moon turned pale. Slowly the day broke. The nightmarish atmosphere of the night began to be dispelled. Despite the smoke from the smouldering fires, a cool fresh breeze was blowing as it did every morning. The fields outside the village in which the wheat-crop had ripened softly waved in the breeze. The air was laden with the scent of the bursting lukat fruit. It also carried the soft fragrance of the wild rose which grew on bushes in this weather. Now and then parrots sitting on the branches would flutter their wings and chirping noisily fly off towards another tree or grove of trees. The colour of the water in the stream had already turned blue. Every gust of breeze would produce ripples on the surface of the water.

It was difficult to say when, during the night, looting and arson had ceased. Not many houses had been set on fire, since in most localities Muslims and Sikhs lived in adjacent houses. The fire was still smouldering in the Khalsa School building and the flat-roofed houses located at the turn in the lane leading to the gurdwara, but the flames had largely subsided, and the colour of the dying flames had already turned pale.

Within the gurdwara, one light was still burning. The War Council was still in session, its four members waiting, as it were, for the final fall of the curtain. Teja Singhji, tired and exhausted, with his head bowed sat disconsolate on a bag of wheat-grains in the store-room of the gurdwara. Kishen Singh still sat in his chair on the roof. A Nihang Singh, lance in hand, still stood guard at the entrance to the gurdwara.

When it was broad daylight, kites, vultures and crows arrived in large numbers and hovered over the village, and particularly in the vicinity of the villagewell. Many a vulture was already perched on the surrounding trees; some vultures with their sharp yellow beaks had landed on the wall of the well, where the bloated corpses were slowly rising towards the surface, or the mouth of the well. The lanes bore a deserted look. Dead bodies lying here and there, added to the gloom and sense of desolation all round. Footsteps of a man walking in a lane would produce a deafening sound. The marauders had left the village, carrying all the booty they could. On the path leading to the 'well of death', lay scattered hair-clips, ribbons, dupattas, broken pieces of bangles and the like, while the lanes in the village were littered with empty boxes, trunks, canisters and cots. telling the story of the scourge that had befallen the village. The doors of houses were either open or battered.

But the rioting had not completely ceased. The young son of the fat butcher had stealthily gone to the backside of the gurdwara, carrying a can in his hand and was sprinkling kerosene oil on its windows.

Suddenly a strange deep and buzzing sound was heard. What was that? It was heard by Teja Singh, sitting in the store room;

by Kishen Singh, on duty on the roof of the gurdwara; it fell on the ears of everyone in the Sheikh's house. They were all taken aback! The son of the fat butcher who was about to light the fire, stopped short not knowing what to do. What sort of sound was this? The low drone was getting louder. Some persons sitting inside houses, stepped out to find out what sound it was. Kishen Singh stood up from his chair and rushed to the parapet wall.

It was an aeroplane. Flying over hills and valleys, with its wings outspread, it was coming towards the village, making its hoarse, buzzing sound. Sometimes, its wings would turn black, at others, they would glitter like silver. Sometimes its right wing would bend downward, at others its left wing. The aeroplane was, it would seem, out on a joy-flight.

As it approached the village, people came out; they stood on raised platforms on roofs of houses and stared hard at the aeroplane with breathless curiosity. While flying over the village, it dropped height so that one could see the pilot sitting in the cockpit—he was a white man, waving his hand to the people standing below. Some people could even see the smile on his lips. He was wearing big goggles over his eyes.

'He smiled. I swear, I saw it with my own eyes,' one boy said to another, standing in a yard outside their house.

'He has white gloves on. He was waving his hand like this. Didn't you see?'

There would be no more disturbances. The news of the riots had reached the right ears, the ears of the firanghi; no shot would be fired now, nor a house set on fire. The fat butcher's son, who had already sprinkled oil on the windows of the gurdwara, and had only to light a match-stick, hastily withdrew his hand and stood standing wide-eyed at the aeroplane.

As he flew over the gurdwara, the white man sitting in the cockpit waved his hand. To Kishen Singh, standing on the roof, it appeared as though the white man had specially waved to him; that one soldier had saluted another fellow-soldier. Kishen Singh who till then had been feeling depressed, stood up to attention and clicking his heels gave a salute in return, and his heart leapt with joy. A soldier after all, was a soldier. During the war-days on the Burmese front, Kishen Singh would go every evening to meet Captain Jackson, his superior officer. And Captain Jackson would always lend an attentive ear to whatever he had to say. Not only that, he would always acknowledge his salute with a salute in return.

Excited beyond words, Kishen Singh waved his hand and shouted: 'God save the King, Sahib, God save the King!'

The aeroplane had by then moved ahead and was flying over the Sheikh's house. Kishen Singh stared wide-eyed towards it. People had run up to the roof of the Sheikh's house too and were waving excitedly at the white man. Kishen Singh was keen to know if the white man, the British soldier, acknowledged the salutations too; and it actually appeared to him as though the pilot had withdrawn his gloved hand into the cockpit. Kishen Singh was thrilled at this and shouted: 'Had you come a couple of days earlier, we would not have suffered so. But it is still OK Sahib!'

Thereupon, excited in the extreme, Kishen Singh clenched his fist towards the house of the Sheikh and shouted at the top of his voice: 'Why don't you fire your guns now? Here, fire at me, I am standing before you! You thought you were hellishly brave! Now fire! Why don't you?'

And the stocky, pot-bellied Kishen Singh, like a man in a frenzy, waving his hand and showing his clenched fist, danced behind the parapet wall.

At the back of the gurdwara, the fat butcher's son, emptied the can of kerosene oil in the drain and hid the empty can under a projection, threw the dry rags into the gurdwara through a window and lighting a cigarette with the match-stick in his hand, went merrily puffing back home.

The aeroplane circled twice over the village. Quite a crowd of people had by then come out and were waving to the white sahib! After the third round, the aeroplane flew away towards other villages.

The atmosphere in the village changed radically. People started coming out into the open. There was little apprehension of any trouble erupting. Corpses began to be removed. People went back to their houses to check on their jewellery and household goods. The *sevadars* and the Nihangs began to wash the floors and to tidy up the gurdwara. On the other side under Sheikh Ghulam Rasul's orders, the floors of the mosque were being washed. People of both communities were washing clean their respective holy places.

Over whichever village the aeroplane flew, hostilities ceased, drums stopped beating, slogan-shouting ceased, looting and burning stopped.

19

As you walked along the roads of the city, you sensed a change in the atmosphere. In front of the mosque in Qutab Din street, four soldiers in uniform sat in chairs. At every important crossing in the city, two or three armed soldiers were seen either sitting on terraces or standing by the roadside. Army pickets had been set up in the city. On the fourth day of the riots, an eighteen-hour curfew had been clamped on the city; on the fifth day, however, the curfew had been relaxed to twelve hours from 6 p.m. to 6 a.m. The news had gone round that the deputy commissioner was doing the rounds of the city in an armoured car. Here and there a shopkeeper had begun sitting in his shop, with only one panel of the shop door open. Mounted constabulary patrolled the streets led by two officers with pistols hanging by their sides. Offices, schools and colleges were still closed. In the dark corners of lanes or at street turnings, small groups of men sat with lances and lathis in their hands and their faces half-covered, but after the imposition of the curfew and the setting up of pickets, the situation was no longer that of a disturbed city. People had begun to stir out, they would go from one locality to another, although still looking apprehensively to the right and left. The tenor of the news too had changed. It was strongly rumoured that two refugee camps would soon be set up, each having the capacity of accommodating refugees from twenty villages. Two government hospitals—one in the city and the other in the cantonment—were already attending to the treatment of the wounded and the disposal of dead bodies. In every piece of news, the name of the deputy commissioner figured prominently. His pipe between his teeth, he was seen everywhere. It was said about him that once, on one of his rounds during curfew hours, when he found a young fellow standing outside a hospital, he gave him two warnings and then shot him dead. By this single act, the whole city had been alerted. People understood that rioting would not longer be tolerated. The National Congress had set up a Relief Office inside a school building which was crowded all the time since refugees were pouring in from the villages. The deputy commissioner had visited even this Relief Office no less than three times. The impression gaining ground was that the government was keen to resolve the situation with the cooperation of the public bodies. And so, leaders of public bodies had begun to work with alacrity. So much so that even in Congress circles, the opinion about the deputy commissioner had begun to be revised. 'A deputy commissioner may be only a cog in a machine but this particular deputy commissioner is different, he is sympathetic and capable.' It was said that the day he shot down the young man outside a hospital, he could not sleep the whole night. Prof. Raghu Nath was of the view that the man was not cut for administrative service, that the man was too sensitive, gifted with too warm a heart, that the British government had done grave injustice by appointing him to that administrative post. Some political activists sharply condemned him, though, and held him directly responsible for all the mischief that had taken place.

On one of his rounds, the deputy commissioner's jeep stopped outside the health officer's residence. The health officer had been duly informed on the telephone that the deputy commissioner was on his way. Greatly excited, the health officer got ready, put on, instead of the usual workday clothes of coat, tie and trousers, his native Punjabi dress—a long silken kurta, a well-starched salwar and a pair of Peshawari chappals on his feet. His wife forthwith made arrangements for tea and coffee. The deputy commissioner came into the courtyard bringing with him the aroma of pipe tobacco. He did not take either tea or coffee. He merely stood in the courtyard and that too for a few minutes, and talked of business. As he shook hands with the health officer, he remarked, smilingly: 'Even in these days you can be so particular about the clothes you wear, Mr Kapur. Nice. Very nice. The Indian dress suits you.'

Then, shaking hands with the health officer's wife, who was in her dressing gown, he remarked, 'The day doesn't seem to have begun for you yet, Mrs Kapur.' and turning to the Health Officer began talking about the business at hand.

'It will be necessary to check up on the arrangements for the water-supply to the refugee camps,' he said, in a manner as though talking to himself. 'The drains have still not been dug for the outflow of the water.' He smiled, shaking his head.

The smile was meant as a reminder to the Health Officer that a task assigned two days earlier had not so far been attended to.

'All arrangements have been made, Sir, work will commence today.'

'Good,' said the deputy commissioner and smiled again.

'I would like you to visit the village where women jumped into the well. Some disinfectant must be sprayed over the well, otherwise there is great danger of a contagion spreading.'

'Yes, sir,' said the health officer, but he felt somewhat shaken. People were running away from that village, seeking shelter in the city. It would be unsafe going there, he thought.

But the deputy commissioner was well aware of the situation.

'It is the third day going,' he went on. 'The swollen dead bodies must have begun to decompose. A disinfectant must be sprayed. Do go there tomorrow morning.' And then, to allay his discomfiture, added, 'An armed police guard will go with you. There is nothing to fear.'

The deputy commissioner had his finger on the pulse, not only of the city but of the entire district.

The health officer's wife, in the meanwhile, had changed her clothes and tied her hair into a knot, and was pressing for tea and coffee.

'There will be time for tea, Mrs Kapur, but not now. Thank

you,' said the deputy commissioner smiling. Then, in his typical persuasive manner, added, 'You too must lend a hand, Mrs Kapur. Two thousand cots will be delivered at the refugee camp today. We need to have beddings and clothes for them. I believe a small committee comprising of women can do a lot of good work. Do think it over, Mrs Kapur,' and Richard again smiled and nodded his head.

Richard had this great quality in his character. He would give instructions in a manner as though he was suggesting a proposal to the other person, and seeking his opinion. The health officer's wife felt flattered. The deputy commissioner was offering her the opportunity of her life. She would be working in close association with the deputy commissioner's wife, what more did she want? But before she could give a reply, the deputy commissioner, taking the health officer along, had already crossed the yard and was going out of the gate.

'What do you think about the disposal of dead bodies, Mr Kapur? I think the municipal committee can handle this work very well—the bodies can be disposed of quietly. To let all and sundry know about it might create unnecessary tension. What do you think?'

The health officer was a hundred per cent in agreement.

'That's the only way, Sir, throw the bodies into pits and bury them. There can't be a funeral for each deceased,' the health officer said, then warming up, added, 'At first they go and kill one another, and then expect the government to dispose of their dead too with proper ceremony.'

The deputy commissioner looked at the Health Officer through a corner of his eyes, paused for a moment, and then, smiling said, 'Well, let's get going. There's a lot to do,' and nodding his head got into his jeep.

Ten minutes later he was at the Relief Committee Office, giving a resume of the government plans concerning relief work, before a gathering of prominent citizens: 'The markets have opened. Four wagons containing charcoal are already in the railway yard. Ten more wagons will have arrived by Tuesday. Twelve-hour night curfew will have to continue for some more time, the army pickets and police patrolling will also continue. Dead bodies have been removed and the administration is attending to them. The post offices will reopen this afternoon. A lot of mail has accumulated and cannot be taken in hand. Those heaps of letters have been put outside the General Post Office. But so far as registered letters and parcels are concerned, every effort will be made to sort out and distribute them.'

Sometimes, while speaking, Richard's face would get flushed and he would appear to be struggling for words like one who is not adept at speech-making, but no word or phrase would be superfluous or out of place.

'We would like public bodies to assist the administration in running the refugee camps. Arrangements have been made for the supply of rations, tents have been pitched as you know. We shall need some doctors, and quite a number of volunteers who can assist us in looking after the refugees.'

As he spoke, Richard's penetrating eye recognized quite a few faces in the audience, and also sensed their likely reactions to what he was saying. Near the threshold stood the dark and fat Manohar Lal, his arms folded on his chest and a derisive, cynical smile on his lips. He was the very person who, before the commencement of the riots, had come with the delegation of citizens and had shouted all sorts of vituperative things against the government outside his office. He might again give vent to his spleen. There was also Dev Datt, the communist. Richard had twice sent him to jail for his inflammatory speeches among workers against the government, but of late, he had been working for peace in the town and had been trying to get the leaders of political parties together. He would not rake up any other issue. There was also Mr Bakshi, the elderly Congress leader and several others whom he knew, several lawyers whom he recognized. There was also one of 'our own' intelligence men, who was both a Congress activist and a functionary of the Socialist Party. This man might be vociferous in raising slogans, swear at the government and even use abusive language.

But Richard saw to it that he confined himself to simple statements and proposals and after giving his resume, promptly sat sown.

Hardly had Richard sat down, when Lala Lakshmi Narain stood up: 'We assure the deputy commissioner sahib Bahadur that the citizens and all the institutions shall wholeheartedly cooperate with the government. It is our great good fortune that so capable and sympathetic an officer is the head of the administration in the district and is present in our midst.'

Richard got up, took leave of the members of the Relief Committee and left. Lala Lakshmi Narain and some lawyers went running to escort him to his jeep. Thereafter the meeting was over in fifteen minutes.

Suddenly someone was heard shouting near the door:

'All the toadies have gathered here. Flatterers, sycophants, all! I am not in the habit of mincing matters. I tell a fellow to his face what I think of him. Where was the government when the tension in the city was mounting? Couldn't the curfew be clamped at that time? Where was the sahib Bahadur then and what was he doing? We talk straight, to a fellow's face...' It was Manohar Lal, letting off steam.

But by then the jeep had left.

'Enough, enough, what do we get by raking up such issues now?'

The members of the Relief Committee were getting up when one of them said to Manohar Lal as he passed by him: 'What's the point in abusing the government all the time? What do you gain by it?'

'O Bakshiji, I am amazed at you, that you too should talk like this. Go home and ply the charkha, or sweep the lanes. You are not cut out for politics.'

'Why do you shout? Don't I know that riots are manoeuvred by the British? Hasn't Gandhiji said so umpteen times?'

'What were you doing then?'

'Why, what have we not done? Didn't we approach the Muslim League to work jointly with us to preserve peace in the city?

Didn't we go to the deputy commissioner and ask him urgently to take preventive measures, to station troops and so on, so as to prevent the riot from breaking out? And now when homeless refugees are pouring into the town, what should we do? Should we help them or should we go on abusing the government? Tell us what we should do, the big revolutionary that you are!'

'I have seen many like you, Bakshiji, don't force me to speak. Members of the Congress are seeking contracts from the government for supplies to the refugee camps.'

'What am I to do if they are taking contracts?'

'You have made them honored members of your organization. That's what you have done. Put them on a pedestal.'

Just then, an activist went over to Manohar Lal and putting his hand round his waist took him out of the room.

'Let go of me, yaar, I have seen many such fellows. They are all Gandhi's parrots. Gandhi, sitting in Wardha makes statements, and they go on repeating them. They have no mind of their own. Why was the deputy commissioner invited? What business had he to come here?'

But his friend pulled him along right up to the gate. As they reached the gate, Manohar Lal stopped grumbling.

'Out with a cigarette,' Manohar Lal said to his friend. 'Let me have a puff at least.'

Both the friends sat down on a projection near the gate.

Inwardly, Bakshi too had been feeling uneasy.

'This is the role the British have all along played—they first bring about a riot and then quell it; they starve the people first and then give them bread; they render them homeless and then begin to provide shelter to them.'

Ever since the riots had broken out, Bakshi's mind had been in a sort of mist. He kept saying to himself again and again that the British had again had the last word, had again had the better of them while his own hold on the situation had been feeble all along.

While Richard was out on his rounds, Liza was in the throes of acute boredom. She left her bedroom and came into the big living room. The rows upon rows of books looked as oppressive as ever before. It appeared to her as though time had stopped and everything was in a state of paralysis. If there was anything alive, it was the wily eyes of the Buddhas and the Bodhisattvas, who, from the dark corners in which they stood, kept looking at her and laying traps for her. She was now scared of even entering the room in the evening. The heads of the statuettes, standing at numerous places, looked to her like so many heads of cobras!

She went into the dining room. The atmosphere here was less oppressive. Here, there were flowers and the light was soft, and the room was free from statuettes and the unbearable burden of books. It had some warmth too because of the soft light; in which a person could relax, and forget a lot, as also remember a lot, as he pleased. Soft light was meant for relaxing, for making love, for sweet hugs and kisses. Liza felt as though her throat was parched and there was a prickly sensation in her eyes. Something was welling up in her again. Her restlessness increased. The cosiness of the room soon gave her an appalling sense of desolation, which made her feel all the more restless. She got up, suppressing her sobs and went to the veranda that led to the kitchen, and once there, shouted at the top of her voice: 'Waiter!'

From somewhere far away, making its way through innumerable doors, came the answer: 'Memsaab!'

And soon enough, the waiter came running into the memsahib's presence, a duster on his shoulder. It was nearing four o'clock in the afternoon and he could anticipate what the memsahib's order would be. Memsahib gradually lost her patience and self-control any time between three and four-thirty in the afternoon and would shout for him, from wherever she happened to be, at the top of her voice: 'Get me some beer! Chilled beer!'

Liza, sighing deeply returned to the dining room. She was wearing her housecoat of which the belt had not been tied. In the wilderness in which she lived, beer was her only solace.

When Richard returned home by eight o'clock in the evening,

he found Liza dead drunk, and asleep, sprawling on the sofa. There was still some beer left in the bottle standing on the tea-poy. Liza's head was hanging from the arm of the sofa, her hair covering half her face. The flaps of her housecoat having slipped, her knees lay bare.

'Damn this country! Damn this life!' muttered Richard, as he stood in front of the sofa.

On reaching home, Richard would find himself in a different world. It was his private world, his little England, with problems all its own, which were not even remotely related to the outside world. Within the home was his real life. In the outside world he pursued his profession, which was so extraneous to his 'real' life. Of course he had his books, his statuettes which belonged neither to one nor to the other world. He would bury himself in his books to forget both the worlds.

He sat down at the edge of the sofa and bending forward, kissed Liza on the cheek, as though performing a duty. Her body which he, at times, would clasp to himself with such intense ardour, felt coarse and fleshy and unalluring. Liza was again putting on weight, he thought, and crow's feet had appeared under her eyes. Boredom was making her obese. On coming home, whenever he saw Liza in that state, his mind would be filled with revulsion.

'Liza!' he almost shouted into her ear, and, putting out his hand, brushed aside the tuft of hair on her forehead.

Liza was too drowsy to open her eyes. Seeing that Liza was in no position to go to the dining table to have dinner with him, he thought it would be better to put her to bed; Richard put his right hand under her head and the left one under her knees, and lifted her up. As he did so, Richard felt that Liza's housecoat was wet under her, and his eyes fell on a roundish patch on the sofa. As he stood, his mind filled with repugnance, Richard shook his head. 'The story is beginning to repeat itself,' he muttered.

Liza had only recently returned from home after spending nearly a year in London. Earlier, she had virtually run away from India out of boredom. 'She may again run away,' he was thinking, 'or I shall have to get myself transferred to some other station.'

Looking at the patch on the sofa, Richard was reminded of a strange coincidence that had occurred, and a smile flickered on his lips. He had got the sofa from Mr Lawrence, the commissioner when the latter was leaving for Lucknow under transfer orders. When he had removed the cover from the sofa he had noticed an ugly patch on it; the kind of patch that he was seeing then. And he had learnt that the commissioner's wife too was a victim of boredom who would, when in her cups, wet the sofa either in a fit of laughter or of crying. The commissioner too kept getting himself transferred to different stations, till at last his wife had left him and married a young army captain. Richard looked at his wife and again at the sofa. 'A similar fate awaits this marriage too, it seems,' he muttered to himself and lifting up Liza, carried her to the bedroom.

By the time they reached the bedroom, Liza had woken up, she had also sobered a little.

'What is it, Richard? Where are you taking me?'

'Your gown is wet under you, Liza, I am taking you to your room.'

But Liza did not catch the import of what Richard had said.

He put Liza down into an armchair by the bedside.

'Shall we have dinner, Liza? Would you like to eat something?'

'Eat? Eat what?'

Richard felt like holding her by her shoulders and giving her a big shake. That would wake her up at once. But he desisted from doing so. Instead, he kept looking at her, his hands on his waist.

Liza lifted her face, over which her hair had again tumbled.

'Richard, are you a Hindu or a Musalman?' she asked and laughed softly. 'I didn't know when you came. Have you come home to take lunch or dinner?'

For a moment Richard thought that Liza was being ironical, that she was not as drunk as she was pretending to be. He sat down on the bed in front of her and putting his hand on her arm, said, 'I have too much work on hand these days, Liza, you must understand. The grain market in the city has been burnt down, and no fewer than a hundred and three villages razed to the ground.'

'One hundred and three villages, and I know nothing about it? Did I sleep that long? Richard, you should have woken me up and told me. Such big events occurred and you did not tell me about them.'

'Go to sleep, Liza. Change your clothes and go to sleep.'

'Sit by me. I can't sleep alone.'

'Go to sleep, Liza. I have a lot of work to do.'

'So many villages burnt down, Richard, and you still have work to do? What more is there for you to do?'

Richard stopped short. Is Liza being ironical? Has she developed an aversion for me that she is talking in this vein?

Like any drunk person, Liza too was babbling away, saying whatever came into her head. She got up from the chair and staggered to the bed and sat down close to Richard. She put her arm round Richard's neck and her head on his chest. No, it cannot be aversion, he thought, she must have uttered these words unconsciously.

'You don't love me. I know you don't love me. I know everything.'

Then, stroking Richard's hair, she said, 'How many Hindus died, Richard, and how many Muslims? You must be knowing everything. What is Anaj Mandi, Richard?'

Richard kept looking at her. 'The more she drinks, the more unattractive she is becoming,' he thought to himself. 'A relationship of this kind cannot last long.' Richard's eyes rested on Liza's face. His feelings towards her were rather indefinable. 'Why not put an end to this relationship? Snap the marital tie. But this question needs to be viewed in the context of my career, my future prospects. This is a decisive moment in my career. So far I have done extremely well in implementing policies. But at this juncture, a delicate balance has to be maintained; it is extremely necessary to see that the discontent among the people does not explode against the government. People are impressed with my sincerity. They think I am a sagacious and efficient officer. At this time, therefore, it is extremely necessary to keep Liza by my side.'

He bent forward and kissed Liza on her cheek.

'Listen, Liza,' he said enthusiastically. 'I have to go to Sayedpur tomorrow, to get a disinfectant sprayed into a well in which many women and children jumped to their death. Why don't you come along too? It is a lovely drive. From there we can proceed to Taxila. We can have a look at the museum there—it is a unique museum. What do you say? The entire area is very lovely.'

Liza looked at Richard with drowsy eyes. 'Where do you want to take me for a drive, Richard? Will you take me for a drive through burning villages? I don't want to see anything. I don't want to go anywhere.'

'No, no, what's the point in sticking on at home? The situation is different now. No one can move about freely,' he said, trying to keep up the pretence of enthusiasm. 'Now we can go out together. You have not seen the rural area; in these parts, it is lovely. The other day, in Sayedpur itself, while on my rounds I saw a lark. I heard it singing in an orchard. It is true. I never thought a lark was to be found in India. There are several other kinds of birds too, which you couldn't have seen before.'

'Is it the same place where women had drowned themselves?'

'Yes, yes, the same. A stream flows near the well. It is a lovely stream. And across the stream is the fruit orchard.'

A fleeting smile appeared on Liza's lips; and she kept looking at Richard's face.

'What sort of a person are you Richard, that in such places too you can see new kinds of birds and listen to the warbling of the lark?'

'What is so strange about it, Liza? A person in the Civil Service develops the quality of mental detachment. If we were to get emotionally involved over every incident, administration would not go on for a single day.'

'Not even when a hundred and three villages are burnt down?'

Richard paused a little and then said, 'Not even then. This is not my country, Liza, nor are these people my countrymen.'

Liza kept looking at Richard's face.

'But you were planning to write a book about these people, Richard, about their racial origin. Isn't that so?'

'To write a book is something different, Liza. What has that to do with administration?'

Finding Liza unresponsive, Richard said, 'Two camps are being set up for the refugees. I told the wife of the health officer this morning to take up relief work with other women. I believe you too could lend a hand in that work, collect clothes and things for the refugees, toys, etc. for their children and so on. It will give you a chance to move about...'

Liza still remained silent. Richard again bent forward and kissed her on the cheek, and stroking her hair with his right hand, added, 'I must be going, Liza. There's a lot of work waiting for me. At this time I should have been in my office.'

And he got up.

'Shall see you later, Liza. Don't wait for me. And be ready to go to the villages tomorrow morning. We shall start at eight o'clock.' He left the room.

For a long time Liza sat looking towards the door. A shiver ran through her, and an oppressive silence again descended over the house.

20

'I want figures, only figures, nothing but figures. Why don't you understand? You start narrating an endless tale of woe and suffering. I am not here to listen to the whole "Ramayana". Give me figures—how many dead, how many wounded, how much loss of property and goods. That is all.'

The functionary of the Relief Committee (or the 'Statistics Babu' as he was called) with the register lying open before him, would get impatient with the refugees, would even shout irritably at them, but the refugees were such that they wouldn't understand. One might keep sitting the whole day long, scribbling in one's register, yet, at the end of the day, when the figures were summed up and the list finalized, not even two villages might have been covered. Who could make them understand—the Statistics Babu would say—one couldn't speak roughly to them, or turn them out of one's office—they would keep barging in, even if you did—nor did they observe any order; instead of one, three refugees would start speaking at the same time—sometimes it would appear to the Statistics Babu as if hundreds of refugees were speaking at the same time, dinning their tales of woe into his ears. But what could one tell them? They had been rendered homeless, ruined and helpless, and had nowhere to go. They all kept bending over his table. If they didn't start narrating their experiences, it would not take more than a few minutes to collect figures for the entire village. 'Don't tell me all this, give me just figures, only numbers,' but Kartar Singh, the man sitting in front of him with his hands folded, would go on speaking.

'I told him again; I said, "Imdad Khan, we were once playmates, you seem to have forgotten me." It is morning time, babuji, I wouldn't tell an untruth. The fact is, Imdad Khan did not first raise his hand against me.'

The babu was at his wits' end. He asked for figures, whereas the refugees showed him their wounds.

'The sickle hit me on my forehead and tore this eye of mine. What do you say, babuji, will my eye be cured? My grandfather said, "Ganda Singh, don't remove the bandage from your eye." And I have not removed it since.'

These were not figures, these were lamentations.

Another fellow had come and was sitting in the chair in front of him.

The babu, without lifting his eyes from his register, went on asking questions and putting down answers:

'Name?'

'Harnam Singh.'

'Father's name?'

'Sardar Gurdial Singh.'

'Village?'

'Dhok Elahi Baksh.'

'Tehsil?'

'Nurpur.'

'How many houses belonging to the Sikhs and Hindus?'

'Only one house. That was ours.'

The babu lifted his eyes. An elderly Sardar was answering his questions:

'How have you come out alive?'

'We had very good relations with Karim Khan. In the evening when...'

The babu raised his forefinger, asking him to keep quiet.

'Any life lost?'

'No, babuji, my wife and I have come out alive. But our son Iqbal Singh was in Nurpur; we have no news of him. And our daughter, Jasbir Kaur was in Sayedpur. She jumped into the well and is no more.'

The babu again raised his forefinger and the Sardar fell silent.

'Come straight to the point. Any life lost?'

'Our daughter died by drowning herself.'

'But she did not die in your village?'

'No, babuji.'

'Her death occurred in a different village. Talk only about your own village. Any material loss?'

'Our shop and house were looted and burnt down. There was one big trunk, it was taken away. There were two gold bracelets lying in it. But I gave away the trunk myself to Ehsan Ali. Rajo, his wife, a very God-fearing woman...'

The babu had again raised his forefinger, and Harnam Singh had become silent.

'The value of your shop?'

'Let me ask my wife,' and turning round he said, 'Banto, what must be the value of our shop?'

'Give me total value, including the goods. Hurry up. I have other work to do too.'

'About seven or eight thousand. There was a piece of land at the back, besides some...'

'Shall I put down ten thousand?'

'Yes, I think you may.'

'Do you want any goods to be recovered?'

'Yes. There is a gun, babuji, a double-barrelled gun, left with Jalal Din Subedar in Adhiro.'

'But you are not from Adhiro... You are from Dhok Elahi Baksh.'

'We had run away from Dhok Elahi Baksh. We walked the whole night. The whole of next day we were in Ehsan Ali's house. During the next night we again kept walking. In the morning, we were given shelter by Subedar Jalal Din at Adhiro. He is a noble soul. He gave us utensils to cook our own food...'

'Enough, enough... What is the name of the Subedar and his address.'

Harnam Singh wanted to narrate the whole story of what had transpired at Adhiro. He also wanted that enquiries should be made about the whereabouts of his son, Iqbal Singh. But the babu would have none of it. He kept putting his forefinger to his lips and then dismissed him.

'You can go now.'

The babu dealing with figures had got what he wanted. He had picked out the grains, the rest was all chaff. Just chaff. But sometimes, the babu could not help lending an ear to what the refugee was saying, the account would be so compelling that it would entice his mind and heart.

'Why, babuji, it may be that my Sukhwant did not jump into the well. Who knows, she may be still hiding in the village, along with her son. You see, Asa Singh was wounded and I had gone to fetch a charpai from my house. It was then that I saw a large number of women coming out of the gurdwara. Sukhwant was also among them. How could I know where they were going? Her hands were raised high and her wrapper was hanging round her neck. When I came back with the charpai, Sukhwant was standing in the middle of the lane. She had stayed back, she had not gone with the other women; our son, Gurmeet, was standing on the raised platform of the gurdwara. At that time the light in the lane would sometimes become dim. It was because of the flames from the school building which was on fire, which would sometimes flare up and sometimes subside. I noticed that Sukhwant was nervous. She had never been nervous before. She came back, came back to her son. Again when the flames of fire rose, I noticed that she was again standing in the middle of the lane, trembling all over. "Sukho, what are you doing?" I shouted. But then, where was the time to think or say anything. If at that time, Sukhwant's eyes had fallen on me, she wouldn't have taken Gurmeet with her. She went towards her son and again stopped short. How could I know what was on her mind? Just then, a loud noise was heard from the outskirts of the village. Slogans of "Ya Ali! Ya Ali!" were heard. And Sukhwant leapt back, picked up Gurmeet in her arms and began running towards the group of women. The last I saw of her, her green wrapper was fluttering in the air and she was turning the corner at the end of the lane. Then she vanished from sight. That is why I say, babuji, it may be my Sukhwant did not jump into the well. It may be she did not take little Gurmeet with her. Who knows, he may be loitering about near the well, babuji, can't you find out?'

But in the entire episode there were no statistics, no figures. The recovery of living beings was not his job. That was being looked after by Dev Raj—all the work relating to recovery, whether it was jewellery or household goods or living persons.

'Sardarji,' the babu said. 'It is the third time you have come to me, and you repeat the same story every time you come. It is not my job to listen to all this.'

But the Sardar continued sitting and looking hard at the babu's face. 'Clinging to what hope does he come running to me? How can I make him understand that I can do nothing for him in this regard?'

'Sardarji,' the babu said in low tones, 'Next Monday a bus will go to your village. I shall ask Dev Rajji to take you along too. But don't tell anyone about it; otherwise any number of people would want to go there.'

But to no effect. The Sardar was still going on with his story.

'If my son is hiding somewhere, on seeing me he will come running to me. Or will shout to me from wherever he is: "Search me out, papa, search me out!" as he used to do at home. Every time I came home, he would hide behind a door and shout, "Search me out! Search me out, papa!"...'

The babu quietly got up from the chair and went out of the office.

It was when one came out and stood on the balcony that one realized what a vast concourse of refugees had gathered in the compound of the Relief Office. The compound was teeming with refugees. They were sitting in groups everywhere, on the raised projection at the back from where the vanaprasthi used to deliver his sermons and expatiate on the grandeur of Vedic religion; refugees were sitting even on the steps.

'Don't cry, Ganda Singh,' the babu heard someone say. An elderly man was trying to console someone, 'Those that have gone are now in God's care, dear to the Lord. They have made supreme sacrifice for the Panth. They have become immortal.'

'Wahe Guru! Wahe Guru!

'*Sat Naam, Sache Padshah*!' three or four Sardars sitting on the steps prayed.

The Statistics Babu was still standing on the balcony when another Sardar, with large eyes and a bulky frame, came over to him. He too had been 'pestering' him a good deal. He came and, as was his habit, put his mouth close to the babu's ear, and said, 'You said that a bus would leave. When will it leave? I hope it will surely go.'

'I shall let you know when it leaves, even though it is not part of my job...'

'I hope my work will be done.' Thereupon putting his mouth close to the babu's ear, said, 'You will have your share, I assure you.'

At this the babu said somewhat peevishly, 'Talk sense, Sardarji. No fewer than twenty-seven women jumped to their death in the well. How will you be able to make out who among them was your wife?'

'Leave that to me, Virji. I shall recognize her from her bracelets. She was wearing a gold chain round her neck. Of course, I am not the only sufferer, what happened to many others, happened to me also. But how can I give up my claim to the gold chain and the bracelets? What do you say, Virji?'

Then again putting his mouth to the babu's ear, said, 'I shall not be ungrateful if you will get me my ornaments, I shall duly repay you. The good woman should have at least thought of it and left the ornaments with someone before jumping to her death. Isn't that so, Virji? What do you say? I shall not be ungrateful. You get this work done for me.' Then, stepping aside, looked at the babu's face, 'No one else need know about it. Let it remain between you and me.'

'O, Sardarji, the corpses are swollen and have come up to the surface. Can you take a bracelet off the wrist of a swollen body? Talk sense. Will the authorities permit you to do that?'

'Why, it is my wife, it is my jewellery that I am claiming. I got the bracelets made with my own money. I have not stolen them. We have only to take along a hammer and chisel and the work will be done in a matter of minutes. If you like, we can take some goldsmith's boy with us. Where there is a will, there is a way.'

'Talk sense, Sardarji. The government will demand proper identification. Witnesses.'

'But, Virji, that is your job. If I have to give you your share, you will at least do this much. Won't you?'

'Sardar, understand once for all, this is not my job. I only collect statistics. In the Lost Property list, I have included your wife's bracelets and chain. Recovery is not part of my job.'

'Don't be annoyed, Virji. The affairs of the world do not come to a stop,' and taking the babu's right hand into his, separated his three fingers one by one, and whispered into the babu's ears 'Do you agree?' (To hold three fingers means three times twenty, i.e. sixty rupees.)

'Why are you wasting your time, Sardar? I cannot help you.' The Sardar let go of the babu's hand but kept staring at the babu's face for a long time. Then, adjusting the sheet of cloth over his shoulders turned towards the staircase. Getting close to the staircase he turned round again.

'O babu, what do you say?' and putting up his hand, showed four of his fingers. 'Do you agree?'

The babu turned his face away.

A little while later, the Sardar was heard saying, 'Have some pity on us. We have been ruined.'

When the babu turned round, he was going down the staircase.

After some time the babu himself felt tired and went down into the yard. To keep sitting at the table for long was impossible. By the time it was evening a resume would be prepared by adding up the figures collected during the day, one copy of which would be sent to the press, another to the Congress office, while the third one would go into the file. He had by then concluded that in the matter of deaths, the number of Hindus and Sikhs killed equalled more or less the number of Muslims killed. The material losses of Hindus and Sikhs were much higher.

Dev Datt had come the previous evening.

'What have been your figures for today?'

'Today I got the figures for Tehsil Nurpur. There is not much difference in the number of deaths. Almost the same number of deaths among Muslims as among Hindus and Sikhs.'

Dev Datt picked up the register, and kept turning its pages for some time, then, putting it down said, 'Add another column to your tabulations indicating the number of poor people killed as against well-to-do people.'

'What is the sense in that? You bring in the rich and the poor into everything.'

'It is an important aspect which will reveal to you quite a few things.'

As he went through the yard, the babu could recognize a good number of faces. At the foot of the staircase, a little to the right, the girl whose fiance's whereabouts were not known, still stood bewildered as on previous days, a vague look in her eyes. She had been to all the hospitals, but to no avail. A little farther down, sat Harnam Singh with his wife, the man who only talked about the recovery of his double-barrelled gun. The babu looked away. He knew that if their eyes met, the Sardar would again start bothering him about his gun.

On one side of the platform sat a few Congress workers, having a heated argument. Kashmiri Lal was saying: 'Give a straight answer. What should I do, if I am physically attacked by someone? Being a believer in non-violence should I fold my hands before the fellow who has come to kill me and say, "I shall not resist since I am a believer in non-violence. You can chop off my head?"'

'Who will care to kill a puny, little fellow like you?' Shankar said, in his usual bantering tone.

'Why, are only wrestlers attacked? It is always a weak person that is attacked.'

'It is not a trivial matter. I am not joking. I want to know

what guidance non-violence has to give me at such a juncture,'
he said to Bakshiji, but Bakshiji had not been very attentive to
what was being said.

'Tell me, Bakshiji. Don't be evasive.'

'What is it? What do you want to know?'

'Bapu has advised us not to use violence. If, in the event of a
riot, a man were to attack me, what should I do? Should I fold
my hands and say, "Come, brother, kill me. Here is my neck?"'

Shankar, intervening, said, 'Gandhiji has said that a person
himself should not indulge in violence. Nowhere has he said that
if a person is subjected to violence he should not resist.'

'What should I do?'

'If anyone attacks you, Kashmiri,' said Jit Singh, 'You tell
him, "Just wait brother, let me run up to the Congress office and
ask them what my line of action should be. Whether I should
defend myself or not."'

'Bapu has advised us not to use violence. If such an eventuality
arises, my first duty is to tell the fellow patiently that what he is
doing, is something very wrong, that he should desist from doing
it.'

'I would say, fight the fellow tooth and nail,' said Master Ram
Das.

'Fight him with what? All I have in my house is my charkha.'

'You are yourself a charkha that has taken up this issue after
the riots, after all the killing has been done.'

'You fellows are making light of it, but the matter is serious,'
said Jit Singh.

'Listen, son,' said Bakshiji, with a tremor of emotion in his
voice. 'The Jarnail did not suffer from any such mental conflict.
He was never bothered about his personal safety. Jarnail was
eccentric, unlettered, crazy, but he was never worried as to what
he should do in the event of his being attacked...'

All fell silent. Everyone had been deeply pained over Jarnail's
death.

'But this is being oversentimental,' Kashmiri said, after some
time.

'Listen,' Bakshiji said. 'You yourself should not indulge in violence. That is number one. You should persuade the fellow to desist from using violence. That is number two. And if he does not listen, fight him tooth and nail. That is number three.'

'That's it. That's what I call an answer. Are you satisfied, Kashmiri? Now keep your mouth shut.'

But Kashmiri Lal was still arguing: 'But with what weapons? With the charkha?'

'Why with the charkha? Fight him with a sword,' said Jit Singh.

'Then, am I allowed to keep a sword, Bakshiji? What do you say?'

Bakshiji made no answer.

'Or a pistol?'

'Pistol is too violent a weapon.'

'Is a sword any the less?'

'Yes. You have to use your own energy to wield a sword, whereas with a pistol you have only to press the trigger.'

'Then I should buy myself a sword. What do you say, Bakshiji?'

Bakshiji did not answer. Had he spoken, he would again have cited Jarnail's example.

The Statistics Babu moved away, shaking his head. To him a discussion of this nature, after the riots, sounded so pointless.

Like the receding tide of the sea, the tide of the riots had subsided, leaving behind all kinds of litter and junk and garbage.

By the side of the door that led to the veranda a group of refugees seemed to be having a good laugh over something. As the babu drew near, he saw an elderly, short-statured Sardar with a thick, greying beard, lying on the floor in their midst. The man, his eyes twinkling, was shaking his legs and striking the floor with his heels and laughing like a child, while those sitting around him appeared to be enjoying a dialogue with him.

'Will you go to your village, Natha Singh?'

At this, Natha Singh, who was lying on the floor, folded up his legs, turned on one side and joined both his hands between his thighs.

'No, I won't.'

'Why won't you go?'

'No, I won't,' he repeated, shaking his head from side to side like a child, and clasped his hands still more tightly between his thighs, and joined his knees together. It appeared to the babu that the question had so often been put to the man that the whole exercise had turned into a prank.

'Why won't you?'

'No, I won't,' he said and folded up his legs even tighter and again shook his head from side to side.

'But why won't you go?'

'There they will circumcise me.' And he began laughing as he folded his legs even more tightly and shook his head. All the Sardars burst out laughing.

At the other end of the veranda stood the room of the school peon. Outside the room, as on previous days, sat a Brahmin pundit and his wife, a picture of despondency with their heads bowed. On the first day of their arrival, the school peon had brought them to the babu. Their daughter was missing, and both husband and wife had cried bitterly and had beseeched the babu with folded hands to recover the girl. The Brahmin had also said that a tonga-driver of the village had kidnapped the girl. But thereafter they had not come to him.

The Statistics Babu walked over to them.

'A bus will leave for Nurpur tomorrow morning, with an armed police guard and a government officer. They will help you trace your daughter.'

The pundit looked at the babu with his rheumy eyes and shaking his head in despair, said, 'She can't be traced now, babuji; our Parkasho can't be traced now. She is lost for ever.'

'But you told me that a tonga-driver of the village had kidnapped her, and was keeping her in his house.'

The pundit again shook his head and said, 'God alone knows what has been her fate.'

'There will be other people too going in the bus. What does your wife say?'

The pundit's wife raised her head and, as though looking into vacancy, said, 'What should I say, babuji? May our Parkasho live happily wherever she is.'

The babu was taken aback by the answer. He thought the parents of the girl were scared of going to the village.

'You explain to me the location and the address and I shall make enquiries through the police.'

'Of what use is her coming back to us?' said the woman peremptorily. 'They must have already put the forbidden thing into her mouth.'

To which the pundit added: 'It is hard for us to make both ends meet, babuji. There is not a pie in our pockets. How are we going to feed her as well?'

The Statistics Babu, well familiar with such experiences, stood there for a while and then moved on.

Parkasho had really been kidnapped by Allah Rakha and brought into his house. When the riot broke out mother and daughter were collecting faggots from the slope of the hill. Allah Rakha, along with two or three of his friends, was already on the prowl, waiting for an opportunity. They came running, Allah Rakha picked up Parkasho, who shouted and cried but to no avail, and brought her home, while her mother, dumbfounded, looked on and then came whimpering home. During the first night, Parkasho was left alone in a dark room. On the second day, Allah Rakha got some sort of nikah rites performed and married her, and brought a new pair of clothes for her to wear. For two days Parkasho lay crying without a morsel of food or a drop of water going into her, and kept staring at the walls of his house. But on the third day she accepted a glassful of lassi from his hand and also washed her face. The faces of her father and mother were constantly before her eyes but Parkasho was painfully conscious of the fact that as against Allah Rakha, they were too feeble to rescue her. Gradually her eyes began to turn towards the objects that lay around her in Allah Rakha's house. Outside his mud-house, stood a horse tied to a peg. Every time it flicked its tail, the flesh on its back rippled. Outside the house under a tree stood Allah Rakha's tonga. Earlier too Parkasho had seen the tonga several times. As a matter of fact, Allah Rakha had had his eyes on Parkasho for quite some time. Parkasho too had, time and again sensed it, while going about in the village drawing water from the spring or washing clothes. Allah Rakha would tease her, pass all sorts of remarks and, on the sly, throw pebbles at her. She knew it was him who threw them, but would not complain to her father because she knew that he would not be able to do anything. She was afraid of both Allah Rakha and her father.

And then, during the riots, Allah Rakha had succeeded in carrying away the hapless girl, crying and shouting, and brought her home. At the time when, in the Relief Office, Parkasho's mother was crying her eyes out remembering her daughter and could not muster enough courage to try to get her back, at that very time, Parkasho was sitting on a cot in Allah Rakha's house, having put on, under duress, the new suit of clothes brought for her by Allah Rakha. Then, Allah Rakha had come, opened a small box and holding it out to her had sat down on the cot beside her, saying: 'Eat! Here, Eat!'

Parkasho had her downcast eyes fixed on the strings of the cot. She did not lift her eyes either to look at Allah Rakha or at the packet, nor did she utter a word.

'Eat! It is mithai, haramzadi, eat! I have brought it for you.'

This time Parkasho cast a glance at the sweetmeats, but she still did not have the nerve to look at Allah Rakha.

'Eat!' Allah Rakha suddenly shouted at which Parkasho trembled from head to foot.

'It is mithai, not poison. Eat!'

Allah Rakha picked up a piece of milk-cake and bending forward pressed her cheeks with his left hand, and with his right hand thrust the sweetmeat into her mouth.

Parkasho sensed a certain eagerness in Allah Rakha's brusque manner but she still sat frightened and subdued. How could she eat a sweetmeat from the hand of a Musalman?

'It is from a Hindu sweet-shop, haramzadi, eat!'

Slowly, the frightened Parkasho began chewing the piece in

her mouth. Allah Rakha laughed, 'Is it a sweetmeat or poison?'

Parkasho would, from time to time, move her jaws and then would stop masticating and shut her mouth tight.

'Eat!' Allah Rakha would shout and Parkasho's jaws would start working again.

The odour from Parkasho's body had begun to work as an intoxicant on Allah Rakha, making him increasingly restless.

'Now eat with your own hand.'

This time there was a touch of softness in Allah Rakha's voice.

'If you don't, I shall lay you down and force all the mithai down your throat. Eat.'

Parkasho raised her eyes and looked at him. She had seen Allah Rakha several times earlier too but never from such close quarters. She noticed his thin, black moustache. Allah Rakha had put collyrium in his eyes, combed his hair and was wearing clean clothes.

Parkasho's fear grew less somewhat, but she continued to look frightened and subdued.

'Will you eat or shall I force it down your throat?' and his left hand again rose to catch hold of Parkasho's chin.

Slowly Parkasho began to feel as though the fear of Allah Rakha was subsiding within her. Chewing the piece of milk-cake she again looked at him. This time her eyes fell on the black thread round his neck to which an amulet was tied. The collar button was open. Her eyes also fell on his striped shirt. Allah Rakha looked very clean and tidy.

Allah Rakha was holding another piece of sweetmeat in his hand waiting for Parkasho to finish chewing so that he could force another piece into her mouth. Parkasho's eyes also rested on his hand. Suddenly, Parkasho said in a low voice: 'You eat!'

The words had an electrifying effect on Allah Rakha.

'At last you spoke! Now, eat!'

'No.'

'Eat!'

Parkasho shook her head. It appeared to Allah Rakha as though a flicker of a smile had crossed Parkasho's lips. Parkasho raised her eyes to look at Allah Rakha.

'I shall eat if you will put it into my mouth,' he said.

For a few seconds Parkasho's eyes rested on Allah Rakha's face. Then she slowly picked up a piece. Even after picking it up, she was unable to lift her hand towards him. Parkasho's face had turned pale and her hand trembled as though with the sudden realization of how her parents would react were they to know what she was about to do. But just then she saw Allah Rakha's eyes full of eager desire and Parkasho's hand went up to Allah Rakha's mouth.

Both were opening up to each other. Allah Rakha moved closer to her and enveloped her in his arms. Even though frightened and subdued, she became receptive to his embraces. It seemed to her as though the past had drifted far away, while the present was waiting to receive her with open arms. The situation had so radically altered that Parkasho's parents had begun to appear irrelevant to it.

They remained wrapped up in each other's arms for a long time. For a long time too Parkasho did not speak. But when her back was turned towards Allah Rakha and her eyes rested on the wall opposite, she said softly: 'Why did you throw pebbles at me when I went to fetch water?'

In answer to this, Allah Rakha raised his hand and put it on Parkasho's waist.

'I would throw pebbles because you wouldn't speak to me.'

'Why should I have spoken to you?'

'Aren't you speaking to me now?'

Parkasho remained quiet for some time, then said softly: 'Where is my mother?'

'How should I know where your mother is. She is not in her house.'

A sigh rose from the inner depths of her being and her eyes brimmed with tears. She felt as though her parents had been left far behind and that she would never see them again.

'Did you set fire to our tenement?'

'No. People wanted to burn it down, but I stopped them. I put a lock there.'

His answer comforted her. She slowly lifted her hand and put it on Allah Rakha's hand which rested on her waist.

Every person coming to the Relief Office had, as it were, brought with him, his bag of experiences. But no one had the ability to assess these experiences or to draw inferences from them. They all stared into vacancy and listened, with their ears pricked to whatever anyone said. A rumour would spread and people in the yard would stand up on their toes, or gather into knots in order to listen to what was being said. No one knew in which direction to turn, or what lay in store for him or her, or the kind of future it would be. It appeared as though a remorseless whirl of events would occur into the vortex of which they would all be sucked, none having either the capacity or the option to stay out, that no one would be able to take into his own hands the reins of his life. They moved about like puppets, when hungry they would put into their mouths whatever they would get, they could cry when tormented by the memory of what had happened to them, and from morning till night would listen to whatever anyone would say.

21

People were gathering in the college hall for a meeting of the Peace Committee. The place chosen for the meeting was, for once, non-controversial—the college was neither of the Hindus, nor of Muslims, it was run by a Christian Mission. The Principal too was not an Indian, he was an American missionary, a very sociable, peace-loving man. There was still time before the meeting commenced; all the prominent citizens, of all shades of opinion and party affiliations had been invited. Quite a few had already arrived and strolled up and down the long veranda exchanging views or stood inside the hall, lost in discussions.

The short-statured property dealer was saying to Sheikh Nur Elahi: 'This is the right time to strike a bargain. Property prices are low. But soon they will begin to rise. I am the one who should know. If you have any intention of buying property, this is the time.'

'The prices may fall further,' the Sheikh commented.

'They have already touched rock-bottom. How much more can they fall?' the property dealer said. 'Earlier I had myself sold land at Rs 1500 per *ahata*. The same ahata, in the same locality is now available at Rs 750.' Then, putting his hand on the Sheikh's elbow, and standing on his toes, added, 'When conditions become peaceful, will the land-prices go up or come down?'

'I shall think it over.'

'Do. But do not keep thinking indefinitely. Earlier too you missed good bargains.'

After the riots a strong trend had set in—Muslims were keen

to move out of Hindu localities, and likewise, Hindus and Sikhs from predominantly Muslim localities.

'I shall try to bring down the price by another hundred rupees. This is a good bargain. You were keen to buy a house on the main road in a Muslim locality. Weren't you?'

'Yes, yes. I shall let you know soon.'

Had Sheikh Nur Elahi continued to stand there for another two minutes, there was every danger that the deal might have been struck; but he had succeeded in shaking off Munshi Ram, the property dealer and gone and joined the group of Municipal Councillors. For a while Munshi Ram continued to stand where he was, then he moved slowly over to Babu Prithmi Chand.

'The house adjoining yours is on sale, Babuji.'

'You call that pigsty a house?'

'Even if it is a pigsty I would advise you to buy it. It is going darned cheap. You can pull it down and rebuild it as part of your house.'

'What if Pakistan is formed?'

'Oh, go on, Babuji, these are only gimmicks of the politicians.' Then lowering his voice, added, 'Even if it is formed, people are not going to run away from their homes.'

Munshi Ram did not want the day to pass without a bargain. It was not always that so many well-to-do people got together at one place.

Babu Prithmi Chand's reaction was different: 'When conditions become normal, no one would like to leave the locality he has been living in.'

'Get such thoughts out of your mind, Babuji,' said Munshi Ram.

'No Muslim wants to live in a Hindu mohalla any longer. This is as sure as daylight. Whether Pakistan comes into being or not, this is sure as daylight.'

As he saw Lakshmi Narain approaching from a distance, Sheikh Nur Elahi remarked jokingly: 'So you too have come, karar.'

As he drew closer, Sheikh Nur Elahi said more loudly, 'So,

you saw to it that the riot broke out. You couldn't rest content otherwise.'

People standing around, laughed. Sheikh Nur Elahi and Lala Lakshmi Narain were on informal terms, both had studied together in the local Mission School, both were cloth merchants.

'There is no trusting a karar, I tell you.'

On seeing them talking so cordially to one another, Sardar Mohan Singh who was standing on one side, said to the person standing close to him: 'Come what may, ultimately we all have to live here. There may be ups and downs and fits of frenzy, but the reality is that all of us have to live here. Small tensions are of little consequence; even the utensils in a kitchen keep striking against one another. Neighbours too have quarrels, but the fact remains that all of us have to live here. To think of it, a neighbour is like one's right hand.'

Both embraced each other. Deep inside, both were fanatics, but since they had been playmates in their younger days they had retained an air of friendly relations with each other. In times of need they would be helpful to each other too. But it was difficult nonetheless to fathom whether Sheikh Nur Elahi's words were spoken in jest or were an expression of sheer hatred for the Hindus.

And then, he added softly: 'I got your bales shifted from the godown.'

Lakshmi Narain smiled. Thereupon Nur Elahi added jocularly: 'At first, I said to myself, let the karar's bales be put to flames, but then, something within me said, "No, a friend is a friend after all."'

To people standing around such encounters among friends made a very pleasant and favourable impression.

Nur Elahi was saying, 'It was not easy to get coolies that night. My son did not know what to do. But I said to him, "By whatever means you can, get the bales shifted, otherwise the Lala will make life hell for me." Eventually, he managed to get two coolies from somewhere.'

Both of them laughed.

The jocularity, coupled with a measure of consideration for each other, was all very well, only it lacked sincerity. Within their hearts lurked aversion, even hatred. But both were elderly, worldly-wise businessmen, who knew well enough that they needed each other.

Standing on the steps facing a lawn, Hayat Baksh was describing the locality of some town to a Sardar: 'In the evening when the lights went up, the whole town would be lit up; the seaside, the roads, all looked so resplendent like a newly-wed bride.'

'Whose panegyric are you singing, Hayat Baksh?'

'It is Rangoon I am talking about. What a city! I was there during the war days. How can I describe it to you?'

Men from different communities were purposely avoiding any reference to the riots in their conversation. Otherwise who would talk about a town as pretty as a bride in the context of burning villages and the grain market in flames?

At some distance from them, standing in the midst of a group, Babu Prithmi Chand was saying in his sharp, squeaky voice: 'I said to them, "Fools that you are, do you think, by putting up an iron gate at the entrance to your lane, you will become any the safer? Talk sense," I said to them, "if an outsider is prevented from coming in, a resident of the locality too, out on an errand, will find it difficult to come in. By getting the iron-gate fixed, you will be putting up a prison wall for yourselves. Talk sense," I said.'

In another part of the veranda, Lala Shyam Lal had caught hold of the Statistics Babu and was taking him to one side: 'You have to listen attentively to what I tell you. Let us sit down on this bench and talk.'

Both sat down. The Lala put his mouth close to the babu's ear and said, 'Who will be the Congress candidate for the municipal elections from our ward?'

'I don't know, Lalaji, at present everyone is engaged in relief work.'

'Not everyone. Only you are engaged in relief work. But you

must have heard something.'

'No, Lalaji, I have not heard anything so far. But I doubt very much if under the prevailing conditions the municipal elections will at all take place.'

'Affairs of the world do not come to a stop. I have already met the deputy commissioner. Elections will be held after two months. June 15 is the date fixed for filing in nominations. Therefore there is not much time left.'

'I plead ignorance, Lalaji, I am sorry.'

'One should go about in the world with eyes and ears open, son. Men of my generation will not be here for long now; it is you who have to take over.' Then putting his mouth close to the babu's ear, added, 'I am standing for elections.'

The babu turned round and looked at the Lala's face.

'My information is that Mangal Sen will get the Congress ticket from our ward.'

'But Lalaji, what for should you need the Congress ticket?'

But hardly had he put the question, when the babu, as in a flash, understood the change that had occurred in the situation. If a Hindu stood for elections now, he would need the support of the Congress, likewise if a Muslim stood for elections, he would need the support of the Muslim League. Such a polarization had taken place. Lala Shyam Lal was not an activist of the Congress. He was close to the Congress only to the extent of wearing clothes made from material resembling khadi.

'What will be left of the Congress image if it gives tickets to such fellows?' and again putting his mouth close to the babu's ear he said, 'He runs a gambling den. He runs two such dens. He is hand in glove with the police in running those dens. He dances attendance on Gandhiji and Pandit Nehru when they visit the town, but that does not make him a genuine Congress worker. He does not even wear khadi.'

'He does,' said the Statistics Babu.

'It is only recently that he has started wearing khadi. He never wore it earlier. Nobody wears khadi in his house.'

Finding in the babu a patient listener, Lalaji went on: 'He

drinks beer. If you don't believe me, go to the club in the Company's Garden any evening and see for yourself. His father too was an addict.' Thereupon, the Lala, twisting his facial muscles into a scowl, said venomously, 'His father had a carbuncle, and he died of that carbuncle. This fellow too will one day die of carbuncle.'

The Statistics Babu did not know what exactly a carbuncle was, but he was surprised why Lalaji felt so bitter about Mangal Sen.

'If I were to expose him, the fellow would be stark naked before the public in one day, but I say what's the point, it is his own business how he lives. But then, he should not cheat people, throw dust into their eyes.'

'But Lalaji, Mangal Sen is a member of the District Congress Committee, whereas you are not even a four-anna member of the Congress. How can you claim a ticket from the Congress?'

'Who is asking for a ticket? All that I want is that the Congress should not put up its own candidate from this ward. If anyone wants to stand for election, let him stand in his individual capacity.'

Close to where they sat, Lala Lakshmi Narain was enquiring about some herbal medicine from Hayat Baksh. Hayat Baksh knew about some medicinal herbs, as for instance, about the herb that cured stone in the bladder; he would prepare the medicine himself and give it free of charge but would not disclose the prescription to anyone, since he was of the firm belief that a medicine lost its efficacy if the prescription was given out or if the person made money out of it.

Ranvir, Lala Lakshmi Narain's son had sprained his foot. While running, his foot had fallen into a gutter, his knees too had been badly bruised. Hayat Baksh listened patiently about the boy's ailment and then said, 'No, no, no oil massage. This oil has a cooling effect. I have got some oil which Ashraf had brought from Lahore. That will relax the boy's nerves. I shall send it on to you. Don't worry; the boy will get well soon.'

Then, lowering his voice, he said confidentially, 'How did the boy sprain his foot?' Then, lowering his voice still further, added, 'I hear he has been taking part in some Youth Organization.' Then, without waiting for Lakshmi Narain's answer, said, 'Do as I tell you. Send him away for a few days. There is a danger of arrests being made.'

Lala Lakshmi Narain pricked his ears but did not betray any nervousness.

'He is only a child, barely fifteen years of age. What can a child do?...' he said, but he made a mental note of the suggestion that the boy should be whisked away somewhere for a few days.

Close to the college gate, two college peons sat on a bench talking to one another. One said to the other: 'We poor people are such ignorant fools, we go breaking one another's head. These well-to-do people are so wise and sensible. They are all here, Hindus, Muslims, Sikhs. See how cordially they are meeting one another.'

The representatives of almost all the political parties had arrived, except Bakshi who was being awaited. Dev Datt was happy at heart that at last, going from house to house, he had succeeded in getting all the leaders under one roof. His organizational skill was again manifest, in the way, at the very commencement of the meeting, he had proposed the name of Mr Herbert, the Principal of the Christian College, as the chairperson for the meeting. Mr Herbert, an elderly person, an American, had taught three generations of local students; he was not an Englishman, nor was he a Hindu, Sikh or Musalman. In the midst of loud applause, he came and sat down in the president's chair. People from the veranda sauntered into the hall one by one and took their seats. Just then a heated argument started between a young Muslim League member and a Congress activist.

The Muslim League member sprang up on his feet and shouted: 'No one can stop us from achieving the goal of Pakistan. Bakshiji, (who had in the meanwhile arrived) had better give up this farce, once and for all and admit that the Congress is the organization of the Hindus, and I shall hug him to my heart. The Congress cannot speak for the Muslims; the Congress does not represent the Muslims.'

Such an utterance used to be heard frequently enough even before the riots. Just then another raised the slogan: 'Pakistan Zindabad!' This was followed by many voices shouting: 'Silence! Silence!'

Mr Herbert stood up:

'Gentlemen, at this delicate juncture, we should all strive together to improve the atmosphere in the town. Eminent personalities of the town are present here. Their voices will be heard with respect by the people. I am of the view that a Peace Committee should be set up here and now and that the members of the Peace Committee should go into every mohalla, into every locality of the town and spread the message of peace. The Peace Committee should comprise representatives of all the political parties. I believe a bus could be arranged, fitted with a microphone and loudspeaker, in which representatives of all political parties could go from place to place making a fervent appeal for peace. This will have a salutary effect.'

The proposal was greeted with loud applause.

Suddenly a person stood up. It was Shah Nawaz: 'I shall make the necessary arrangement for the bus.'

There was again a loud applause. Dev Datt came forward and said, 'We learn that the arrangement for the bus will be made by the government.'

Again, there was loud applause. Shah Nawaz was still standing: 'I shall pay for petrol,' he said.

'O Fine! Bravo! Wonderful!'

At this another person got up and said, 'Gentlemen, before drawing up the programme, won't it be better to set up a regular committee, elect the office bearers and proceed in a systematic manner?'

That was a danger signal—the question of elections was being raised. Dev Datt immediately stepped forward and said, 'I propose there should be three vice presidents of this Peace Committee. I propose the names of Janab Hayat Baksh...'

'Please wait!' someone shouted. 'Let us first decide about the number of vice presidents we should have, whether three or more or less. I would propose that there should be five vice presidents. The more vice presidents we have, the more representative will the Peace Committee be.'

A Sardarji raised his hand: 'Let the number of vice presidents remain three: one Hindu, one Muslim and one Sikh. The Executive Committee may be expanded to accommodate as many persons as you like.'

'The question of Hindu and Muslim should not be raised here. This is a Peace Committee.' Dev Datt was again on his feet. 'Eminent leaders from all political parties should be included. My proposal is: Janab Hayat Baksh from Muslim League, Bakshiji from the Congress and Bhai Jodh Singhji from the Gurdwara Prabandhak Committee should be elected as vice presidents.

One person got up:

'If representation on the Peace Committee has to be on the basis of political parties, then I would propose that presidents of all the three political parties should ipso facto be on the Committee in their capacity as presidents. Their names should not be mentioned.'

Lala Lakshmi Narain was on his feet.

'I am deeply pained to see that you have named three political parties but forgotten the Hindu Sabha. Isn't it a political party too?'

'No. Hindu Sabha is not a political party.'

'If it is not a political party, then the Gurdwara Prabandhak Committee is also not a political party.'

Five or six persons got up, all together.

'It is an insult to the Sikh community. The Gurdwara Prabandhak Committee alone represents the Sikhs.'

Dev Datt leapt forward again:

'Gentlemen, this will not lead us anywhere; and we shall not be able to do any work. We have to fight against communal elements. It is not important who gets the representation. What is important is that the Peace Committee becomes the joint forum of all communities, so that all of us, Hindus, Muslims, Sikhs, Christians, can issue an appeal for peace from a joint platform. Keeping this in view I propose that Janab Hayat Baksh, Bakshiji and Bhai Jodh Singhji be elected as vice presidents of the Peace Committee.'

'Agreed! It is right. Now move to the next item.'

A voice was heard. Someone clapped. And then there was more clapping and thus no chance was given to anyone opposed to the proposal to raise his voice. The proposal was adopted unanimously.

Master Ram Das got up:

'For the post of general secretary I propose the name of Comrade Dev Datt. He is a tireless worker; it is thanks to his efforts that we have all assembled here today. The next few days are going to be rather challenging. The Peace Committee will have to be very alert and persevering. Comrade Dev Datt is eminently suited for this post.'

'Are all other young men dead in the town?' It was Manohar Lal, standing near the door with his arms folded on his chest.

'I want to know if this work can only be done by lackeys of the British government and traitors of the nation, the communists? Are there no suitable young men left in the town? As a mark of protest, I refuse to participate in the deliberations of the meeting.'

And he turned round to walk out of the hall.

'Wait, Manohar Lal. Don't behave like a child. Allow some work to be done.'

But Manohar Lal, still in his tantrums, shouted back: 'Let me be. I have seen many like him. Manohar Lal is not afraid of anyone. We talk straight to a fellow's face.'

But some young Congress members held him back. One of them put his arm around Manohar Lal's waist, lifted him up and lugged him back into the hall.

'All toadies of the government have gathered here. I know each one of them.'

'Silence! Silence!'

'I second the name of Comrade Dev Datt.'

'I support him.'

Loud applause. Once again the meeting appeared to proceed smoothly.

But when it came to the election of the Working Committee members all sorts of names began to be thrown up—Lakshmi Narain, Mayyadas, Shah Nawaz. Suddenly some Muslim members got up all together and went towards the door. At their head was Maula Dad.

'Hindus are in a majority in this committee. We cannot work in such a committee. This meeting is nothing but a trickery of the Hindus.'

Ten persons, including Dev Datt ran after them to dissuade them from walking out of the meeting. There was quite a scene near the door for some time. Eventually, a formula was evolved for the election of the members to the Working Committee, viz, that the Committee, consisting of a total of fifteen members will have on it, seven Muslims, five Hindus and three Sikhs. A discussion ensued which went on for a long time, so much so that people began to grow tired. In the end, the formula was accepted and Lala Lakshmi Narain, was also included, as also Mangal Sen, Shah Nawaz and quite a few others. Poor Lala Shyam Lal's name was not proposed by anyone. He kept pulling at the Statistics Babu's coat for a long time but the latter continued to waver and vacillate. At last Lala Shyam stood up:

'I would request that I too should be permitted to serve on this Committee.'

'All the seats have been filled. Please sit down,' said Mangal Sen.

Another gentleman got up.

'I see no harm if one more Hindu, one Sikh and one Muslim are added to the Committee.'

'This cannot be done.' Mangal Sen said again, 'How can you go on adding more and more names?'

The matter was still under discussion when the blaring sound of a loudspeaker was heard and Comrade Dev Datt went over to where the president sat, and addressing the audience, said, 'Gentlemen, the bus for Peace is here. We shall set out on our mission right from here and now. I would request that besides the president and the vice presidents all those who wish to come along are most welcome. Please get into the bus. As you know, a loudspeaker has been fitted into the bus. The bus will keep stopping at regular intervals on the way, and our eminent leaders, by turns, will address the citizens and appeal to them to maintain peace in the city.'

The meeting dispersed, people began stepping out.

The bus for Peace stood there in all its glory, pink and white stripes painted on it. On the roof of the bus, at both ends, facing the road, fluttered the flags of the Congress and the Muslim League. Two amplifiers, one in front and the other at the back of the bus, had been fitted. 'Put up a Union Jack too on the bus,' shouted Manohar Lal sarcastically. As the members came out, the air resounded with slogans: 'Long Live Hindu Muslim Unity!'

'Peace Committee Zindabad!'

'Hindus and Muslims are one!'

The bystanders peered into the bus to see who it was that was raising the slogans. On the seat next to that of the driver sat a man, holding a microphone in his hand. Many did not recognize him, but some did. Nathu was dead, or he would have recognized him at once. It was Murad Ali, the dark-complexioned Murad Ali, with bristling moustaches, his thin cane lying between his legs, peering to the right and left with his small ferretty eyes and raising slogans with all the passion at his command.

There was a brief discussion before they set out on their Peace Mission—who should sit in which seat and who should be the first speaker, and which slogans were to be raised.

The presidents of the Congress and the Muslim League sat, not one behind the other, but side by side, on the seats behind the driver.

For some time there was confusion. The bus had got heavily crowded partly because some people intended to get down on the way near their houses. Manohar Lal was still throwing tantrums.

'I refuse to sit in a bus in which a communist, a traitor to the country, is sitting.'

Dev Datt, who was standing on the footboard of the bus, said: 'Manohar Lal, we don't mince matters. We are not the tail of the Congress. We are professional revolutionaries. We are working to bring about peaceful conditions in the town and to that end it is necessary to bring together the leaders of all the parties, including your party of which you are the sole follower. We too know who is what; but the need of the hour is to bring all parties on one platform.'

'The peace you are talking about,' said Manohar Lal sardonically, 'has already been brought about by your British master. It was he who instigated the riots, now it is he who is working for peace.'

Standing in the veranda Lala Shyam Lal had begun canvassing for support for the forthcoming municipal elections for which he was standing from such and such a ward. In the meanwhile Mangal Sen had jumped into the bus and had gone and sat down in one of the front seats. On seeing him, Lala Shyam Lal, piqued in the extreme, whimpered. 'No one tells me to get into the bus, no one asks me,' and lunged forward, and pushing his way through the bystanders climbed into the bus, breathing hard.

Sitting beside the president of the Muslim League, Bakshiji was looking towards the road, but was feeling extremely sad.

'Kites shall hover, kites and vultures shall continue to hover for long...'

Just then, Murad Ali, sitting next to the driver, began raising slogans and in the midst of the resounding slogans the Peace Bus set out on its Peace Mission.

Sitting opposite each other in the soft, mellow light of the dining room, Richard and Liza sat ruminating over their future plans. Liza had regained her composure. Richard too had little work to do that day. Life in the town had begun to move, more or less, on an even keel. Junior officers had assumed control of their departments.

'I had very much wanted to continue living here, do a bit of work in the Taxila museum; study the genealogy of the local inhabitants, but it doesn't seem likely that I shall live here for long.'

Liza was inwardly pleased to hear the tidings.

'Will you be transferred? Will you be promoted, Richard?'

Richard smiled. He did not say anything.

'Why don't you tell me? Are you really going to be promoted?'

'It is not a question of promotion, Liza. If there are disturbances in a place, the government usually effects a change of personnel at the higher level, senior officers are transferred and new officers sent in.'

'Shall we have to leave soon?'

'Perhaps. I do not know for certain.'

'But you said you wanted to live here, to work in the Taxila museum, didn't you? To write your book...'

Richard shrugged his shoulders. He then lighted his pipe and, stretching his legs under the table, said, 'Wherefrom should I begin?'

'Begin what, Richard?' said Liza, raising her eyebrows.

'You wanted to know about the developments that had taken place here, didn't you?'

This time it was Liza who shrugged her shoulders, as though to say, 'You may or may not, Richard. It makes little difference.'

STORIES

SAADAT HASAN MANTO

Translated from the Urdu by
Khalid Hasan

Mishtake

Ripping the belly cleanly, the knife moved in a straight line down the midriff, in the process slashing the cord which held the man's pyjamas in place.

The man with the knife took one look and exclaimed regretfully, 'Oh no! . . . Mishtake.'

Colder than Ice

As Ishwar Singh entered the room, Kalwant Kaur rose from the bed and locked the door from the inside. It was past midnight. A strange and ominous silence seemed to have descended on the city.

Kalwant Kaur returned to the bed, crossed her legs and sat down in the middle. Ishwar Singh stood quietly in a corner, holding his kirpan absent-mindedly. Anxiety and confusion were writ large on his handsome face.

Kalwant Kaur, apparently dissatisfied with her defiant posture, moved to the edge and sat down, swinging her legs suggestively. Ishwar Singh still had not spoken.

Kalwant Kaur was a big woman with generous hips, fleshy thighs and unusually high breasts. Her eyes were sharp and bright and over her upper lip, there was a faint bluish down. Her chin suggested great strength and resolution.

Ishwar Singh had not moved from his corner. His turban, which he always kept smartly in place, was loose and his hands trembled from time to time. However, from his strapping manly figure, it was apparent that he had just what it took to be Kalwant Kaur's lover.

More time passed. Kalwant Kaur was getting restive. 'Ishr Sian,' she said in a sharp voice.

Ishwar Singh raised his head, then turned it away, unable to deal with Kalwant Kaur's fiery gaze.

This time she screamed: 'Ishr Sian', then she lowered her voice and added: 'Where have you been all this time?'

Ishwar Singh moistened his parched lips and said: 'I don't know.'

Kalwant Kaur lost her temper: 'What sort of a motherfucking answer is that!'

Ishwar Singh threw his kirpan aside and slumped on the bed. He looked unwell. She stared at him and her anger seemed to have left her. Putting her hand on his forehead, she asked gently: '*Jani*, what's wrong?'

'Kalwant.' He turned his gaze from the ceiling and looked at her. There was pain in his voice and it melted all of Kalwant Kaur. She bit her lower lip: 'Yes, jani.'

Ishwar Singh took off his turban. He slapped her thigh and said, more to himself than to her: 'I feel strange.'

His long hair came undone and Kalwant Kaur began to run her fingers through it playfully. 'Ishr Sian, where have you been all this time?'

'In the bed of my enemy's mother,' he said jocularly. Then he pulled Kalwant Kaur towards him and began to knead her breasts with both hands. 'I swear by the Guru, there's no other woman like you.'

Flirtatiously, she pushed him aside: 'Swear over my head. Did you go to the city?'

He gathered his hair in a bun and replied: 'No.'

Kalwant Kaur was irritated. 'Yes, you did go to the city and you looted a lot more money and you don't want to tell me about it.'

'May I not be my father's son if I lie to you,' he said.

She was silent for a while, then she exploded: 'Tell me what happened to you the last night you were here. You were lying next to me and you had made me wear all those gold ornaments you had looted from the houses of the Muslims in the city and you were kissing me all over and then, suddenly, God only knows what came over you, you put on your clothes and walked out.'

Ishwar Singh went pale. 'See how your face has fallen,' Kalwant Kaur snapped. 'Ishr Sian,' she said, emphasizing every word, 'you're not the man you were eight days ago. Something has happened.'

Ishwar Singh did not answer, but he was stung. He suddenly took Kalwant Kaur in his arms and began to hug and kiss her ferociously. 'Jani, I'm what I always was. Squeeze me tighter so that the heat in your bones cools off.'

Kalwant Kaur did not resist him, but she kept asking: 'What went wrong that night?'

'Nothing.'

'Why don't you tell me?'

'There's nothing to tell.'

'Ishr Sian, may you cremate my body with your own hands if you lie to me!'

Ishwar Singh did not reply. He dug his lips into hers. His moustache tickled her nostrils and she sneezed. They burst out laughing.

Ishwar Singh began to take off his clothes, ogling Kalwant Kaur lasciviously. 'It's time for a game of cards.'

Beads of perspiration appeared over her upper lip. She rolled her eyes coquettishly and said: 'Get lost.'

Ishwar Singh pinched her lip and she leapt aside. 'Ishr Sian, don't do that. It hurts.'

Ishwar Singh began to suck her lower lip and Kalwant Kaur melted. He took off the rest of his clothes. 'Time for a round of trumps,' he said.

Kalwant Kaur's upper lip began to quiver. He peeled her shirt off, as if he was skinning a banana. He fondled her naked body and pinched her arm. 'Kalwant, I swear by the Guru, you're not a woman, you're a delicacy,' he said between kisses.

Kalwant Kaur examined the skin he had pinched. It was red. 'Ishr Sian, you're a brute.'

Ishwar Singh smiled through his thick moustache. 'Then let there be a lot of brutality tonight.' And he began to prove what he had said.

He bit her lower lip, nibbled at her earlobes, kneaded her breasts, slapped her glowing hip resoundingly and planted big wet kisses on her cheeks.

Kalwant Kaur began to boil with passion like a kettle on high fire.

But there was something wrong.

Ishwar Singh, despite his vigorous efforts at foreplay, could not feel the fire which leads to the final and inevitable act of love. Like a wrestler who is being had the better of, he employed every trick he knew to ignite the fire in his loins, but it eluded him. He felt cold.

Kalwant Kaur was now like an overtuned instrument. 'Ishr Sian,' she whispered languidly, 'you have shuffled me enough, it is time to produce your trump.'

Ishwar Singh felt as if the entire deck of cards had slipped from his hands on to the floor.

He laid himself against her, breathing irregularly. Drops of cold perspiration appeared on his brow. Kalwant Kaur made frantic efforts to arouse him, but in the end she gave up.

In a fury, she sprang out of bed and covered herself with a sheet. 'Ishr Sian, tell me the name of the bitch you have been with who has squeezed you dry.'

Ishwar Singh just lay there panting.

'Who was that bitch?' she screamed.

'No one, Kalwant, no one,' he replied in a barely audible voice.

Kalwant Kaur placed her hands on her hips, 'Ishr Sian, I'm going to get to the bottom of this. Swear to me on the Guru's sacred name, is there a woman?'

She did not let him speak. 'Before you swear by the Guru, don't forget who I am. I am Sardar Nihal Singh's daughter. I will cut you to pieces. Is there a woman in this?'

He nodded his head in assent, his pain obvious from his face.

Like a wild and demented creature, Kalwant Kaur picked up Ishwar Singh's kirpan, unsheathed it and plunged it in his neck. Blood spluttered out of the deep gash like water out of a fountain. Then she began to pull at his hair and scratch his face, cursing her unknown rival as she continued tearing at him.

'Let go, Kalwant, let go now,' Ishwar Singh begged.

She paused. His beard and chest were drenched in blood. 'You acted impetuously,' he said, 'but what you did I deserved.'

'Tell me the name of that woman of yours,' she screamed.

A thin line of blood ran into his mouth. He shivered as he felt its taste.

'Kalwant, with this kirpan I have killed six men . . . with this kirpan with which you . . .'

'Who was the bitch, I ask you?' she repeated.

Ishwar Singh's dimming eyes sparked into momentary life. 'Don't call her a bitch,' he implored.

'Who was she?' she screamed.

Ishwar Singh's voice was failing. 'I'll tell you.' He ran his hand over his throat, then looked at it, smiling wanly. 'What a motherfucking creature man is!'

'Ishr Sian, answer my question,' Kalwant Kaur said.

He began to speak, very slowly, his face coated with cold sweat.

'Kalwant, jani, you can have no idea what happened to me. When they began to loot Muslim shops and houses in the city, I joined one of the gangs. All the cash and ornaments that fell to my share, I brought back to you. There was only one thing I hid from you.'

He began to groan. His pain was becoming unbearable, but she was unconcerned. 'Go on,' she said in a merciless voice.

'There was this house I broke into . . . there were seven people in there, six of them men . . . whom I killed with my kirpan one by one . . . and there was one girl . . . she was so beautiful . . . I didn't kill her . . . I took her away.'

She sat on the edge of the bed, listening to him.

'Kalwant jani, I can't even begin to describe to you how beautiful she was . . . I could have slashed her throat but I didn't . . . I said to myself . . . Ishr Sian, you gorge yourself on Kalwant Kaur every day . . . how about a mouthful of this luscious fruit!

'I thought she had gone into a faint, so I carried her over my shoulder all the way to the canal which runs outside the city . . . then I laid her down on the grass, behind some bushes and . . .

first I thought I would shuffle her a bit . . . but then I decided to trump her right away . . . '

'What happened?' she asked.

'I threw the trump . . . but, but . . .'

His voice sank.

Kalwant Kaur shook him violently: 'What happened?'

Ishwar Singh opened his eyes. 'She was dead . . . I had carried a dead body . . . a heap of cold flesh . . . jani, give me your hand.'

Kalwant Kaur placed her hand on his. It was colder than ice.

The Return

The special train left Amritsar at two in the afternoon, arriving at Mughalpura, Lahore, eight hours later. Many had been killed on the way, a lot more injured and countless lost.

It was at ten o'clock the next morning that Sirajuddin regained consciousness. He was lying on bare ground, surrounded by screaming men, women and children. It did not make sense.

He lay very still, gazing at the dusty sky. He appeared not to notice the confusion or the noise. To a stranger, he might have looked like an old man in deep thought, though this was not the case. He was in shock, suspended, as it were, over a bottomless pit.

Then his eyes moved and, suddenly, caught the sun. The shock brought him back to the world of living men and women. A succession of images raced through his mind. Attack . . . fire . . . escape . . . railway station . . . night . . . Sakina. He rose abruptly and began searching through the milling crowd in the refugee camp.

He spent hours looking, all the time shouting his daughter's name . . . Sakina, Sakina . . . but she was nowhere to be found.

Total confusion prevailed, with people looking for lost sons, daughters, mothers, wives. In the end Sirajuddin gave up. He sat down, away from the crowd, and tried to think clearly. Where did he part from Sakina and her mother? Then it came to him in a flash—the dead body of his wife, her stomach ripped open. It was an image that wouldn't go away.

Sakina's mother was dead. That much was certain. She had

died in front of his eyes. He could hear her voice: 'Leave me where I am. Take the girl away.'

The two of them had begun to run. Sakina's dupatta had slipped to the ground and he had stopped to pick it up and she had said: 'Father, leave it.'

He could feel a bulge in his pocket. It was a length of cloth. Yes, he recognized it. It was Sakina's dupatta, but where was she?

Other details were missing. Had he brought her as far as the railway station? Had she got into the carriage with him? When the rioters had stopped the train, had they taken her with them?

All questions. There were no answers. He wished he could weep, but tears would not come. He knew then that he needed help.

A few days later, he had a break. There were eight of them, young men armed with guns. They also had a truck. They said they brought back women and children left behind on the other side.

He gave them a description of his daughter. 'She is fair, very pretty. No, she doesn't look like me, but her mother. About seventeen. Big eyes, black hair, a mole on the left cheek. Find my daughter. May God bless you.'

The young men had said to Sirajuddin: 'If your daughter is alive, we will find her.'

And they had tried. At the risk of their lives, they had driven to Amritsar, recovered many women and children and brought them back to the camp, but they had not found Sakina.

On their next trip out, they had found a girl on the roadside. They seemed to have scared her and she had started running. They had stopped the truck, jumped out and run after her. Finally, they had caught up with her in a field. She was very pretty and she had a mole on her left cheek. One of the men had said to her: 'Don't be frightened. Is your name Sakina?' Her face had gone pale, but when they had told her who they where, she had confessed that she was Sakina, daughter of Sirajuddin.

The young men were very kind to her. They had fed her, given her milk to drink and put her in their truck. One of them had given her his jacket so that she could cover herself. It was obvious that she was ill-at-ease without her dupatta, trying nervously to cover her breasts with her arms.

Many days had gone by and Sirajuddin had still not had any news of his daughter. All his time was spent running from camp to camp, looking for her. At night, he would pray for the success of the young men who were looking for his daughter. Their words would ring in his ear: 'If your daughter is alive, we will find her.'

Then one day he saw them in the camp. They were about to drive away. 'Son,' he shouted after one of them, 'have you found Sakina, my daughter?'

'We will, we will,' they replied all together.

The old man again prayed for them. It made him feel better.

That evening there was sudden activity in the camp. He saw four men carrying the body of a young girl found unconscious near the railway tracks. They were taking her to the camp hospital. He began to follow them.

He stood outside the hospital for some time, then went in. In one of the rooms, he found a stretcher with someone lying on it.

A light was switched on. It was a young woman with a mole on her left cheek. 'Sakina,' Sirajuddin screamed.

The doctor, who had switched on the light, stared at Sirajuddin. 'I am her father,' he stammered.

The doctor looked at the prostrate body and felt for the pulse. Then he said to the old man: 'Open the window.'

The young woman on the stretcher moved slightly. Her hands groped for the cord which kept her shalwar tied round her waist. With painful slowness, she unfastened it, pulled the garment down and opened her thighs.

'She is alive. My daughter is alive,' Sirajuddin shouted with joy.

The doctor broke into a cold sweat.

A Tale of 1947

Mumtaz was speaking with great passion: 'Don't tell me a hundred thousand Hindus and the same number of Muslims have been massacred. The great tragedy is not that two hundred thousand people have been killed, but that this enormous loss of life has been futile. The Muslims who killed a hundred thousand Hindus must have believed that they had exterminated the Hindu religion. But the Hindu religion is alive and well and will remain alive and well. And after putting away a hundred thousand Muslims, the Hindus must have celebrated the liquidation of Islam; but the fact is that Islam has not been affected in the least. Only the naive can believe that religion can be eliminated with a gun. Why can't they understand that faith, belief, devotion, call it what you will, is a thing of the spirit; it is not physical. Guns and knives are powerless to destroy it.'

Mumtaz was very emotional that day. The three of us had come to see him off. He was sailing for Pakistan, a country we knew nothing about. All three of us were Hindus. We had relatives in West Punjab, now Pakistan, some of whom had lost their lives in anti-Hindu riots. Was this why Mumtaz was leaving us?

One day Jugal had received a letter which said that his uncle who lived in Lahore had been killed. He just couldn't believe it. He had said to Mumtaz, 'If Hindu-Muslim killings start here, I don't know what I'll do.'

'What'll you do?' Mumtaz had asked.

'I don't know. Maybe I'll kill you,' he had replied darkly.

Mumtaz kept quiet and for the next eight days he didn't speak to anyone; on the ninth day he had said he was sailing for Karachi that afternoon.

We had said nothing to him nor spoken about it. Jugal was intensely conscious of the fact that Mumtaz was leaving because of what he had said, 'Maybe I will kill you.' He wasn't even sure if the heat of religious frenzy could actually bring him to kill Mumtaz, his best friend. That afternoon Jugal was very quiet; it was only Mumtaz who didn't seem to want to stop talking, especially as the hour of departure drew close.

Mumtaz had started drinking almost from the moment he climbed out of bed. He was packing his things as if it was a picnic he was going on, telling jokes then laughing at them himself. Had a stranger seen him that morning, he would have come to the conclusion that his departure from Bombay was the best thing that had ever happened to him. However, none of us were fooled by his boisterousness; we knew he was trying to hide his feelings, even deceive himself.

I tried a couple of times of talk about his sudden decision to leave Bombay but he didn't give me an opportunity.

Jugal fell into an even deeper silence after three or four drinks and, in fact, left us to lie down in the next room. Brij Mohan and I stayed with Mumtaz. There was much to do. Mumtaz wanted to pay his doctor's bill; his clothes were still at the laundry, etc. He went through all these chores with the utmost aplomb. However, when we went to buy cigarettes from our regular shop in the corner, he put his hand on Brij Mohan's shoulder and said, 'Do you remember, Brij . . . ten years ago when we were all starving, this shopkeeper, Gobind, lent us money?' His eyes were moist.

He didn't speak again till we got home—and then it was another marathon, an unending monologue on everything under the sun. Not much of what he was saying made a great deal of sense, but he was talking with such utter sincerity that both Brij Mohan and I had no option but to let him go on, getting in a word edgeways when we could. When it was time to leave, Jugal came in, but as we got into the taxi to go to the port everyone became very quiet.

Mumtaz was looking out of the window, silently saying goodbye to Bombay, its wide avenues, its magnificent buildings. The port was crowded with refugees, mostly poor, trying to leave for Pakistan. But as far as I was concerned, only one man was leaving today, going to a country where no matter how long he lived he would always be a stranger.

After his baggage was checked in, Mumtaz asked us to come to the deck. Taking Jugal's hand, he said, 'Can you see where sea and sky meet? It is only an illusion because they can't really meet but isn't it beautiful, this union which isn't really there?'

Jugal kept quiet. Perhaps he was thinking, 'If it came to that, I may really kill you.'

Mumtaz ordered cognac from the bar because that was what he had been drinking since morning. We stood there, all four of us, our glasses in our hands. The refugees had started to board. Jugal suddenly drank his glass down and said to Mumtaz, 'Forgive me. I think I hurt you very deeply that day.'

After a long pause, Mumtaz asked, 'That day when you had said, "It is possible I may kill you," did you really mean that? I want to know.'

Jugal nodded, 'Yes, I am sorry.'

'If you had killed me, you would have been even sorrier,' Mumtaz said philosophically. 'You would have realized that it wasn't Mumtaz, a Muslim, a friend of yours, but a human being you had killed. I mean, if he was a bastard, by killing him you wouldn't have killed the bastard in him; similarly, assuming that he was a Muslim, you wouldn't have killed his Muslimness, but him. If his dead body had fallen into the hands of Muslims, another grave would have sprung up in the graveyard, but the world would have been diminished by one human being.'

He paused for breath, then continued, 'It is possible that after you had killed me, my fellow Muslims may have called me a martyr. But had that happened, I swear to God, I would have leapt out of my grave and begun to scream, "I do not want this degree you are conferring on me because I never even took the examination." In Lahore, a Muslim murdered your uncle. You heard the news in Bombay and killed me. Tell me, what medals would that have entitled you to? And what about your uncle and his killer in Lahore? What honour would be conferred on them? I would say those who died were killed like dogs and those who killed, killed in vain.'

'You are right,' I said.

'No, not at all,' he said in a tense voice. 'I am probably right but what I really wanted to say, I have not expressed very well. When I say religion or faith I do not mean this infection which afflicts ninety-nine per cent of us. To me, faith is what makes a human being special, distinguishes him from the herd, proves his humanity.'

Then a strange light came into his eyes. 'Let me tell you about this man. He was a diehard Hindu of the most disreputable profession, but he had a resplendent soul.'

'Who are you talking about?' I asked.

'A pimp,' Mumtaz said.

We were startled. 'Did you say a pimp?' I asked. He nodded. 'Yes, but what a man, though to the world he was a pimp, a procurer of women!' Then Mumtaz began his story.

'I don't remember his full name. It was something Sehai. He came from Madras and was a man of extremely fastidious habits. Although his flat was very small, everything was in its right place, neatly arranged. There were no beds, but lots of floor cushions, all spotlessly clean. A servant was around but Sehai did most things himself, especially cleaning and dusting. He was very straight, never cheated and never told you anything which was not entirely true. For instance, if it was very late and the liquor had run out, he would say, "Sahib, don't waste your money because in this neighbourhood they will only sell you rubbish at this hour." If he had any doubts about a particular girl, he would tell you about them. He told me once that he had already saved up twenty thousand rupees. It had taken him three years, operating at twenty-five per cent. "I need to make only another ten thousand and then I'll return to Benaras and start my own retail cloth business." Why he wanted to earn no more than that I didn't know nor did I have any idea what he found so attractive about the retail cloth trade.'

'A strange man,' I said.

Mumtaz continued: 'First I thought he cannot really be what he appears to be. Maybe he is nothing but a big fraud. After all, it was hard to believe that he considered and treated all the girls that he supplied to his customers as he would his own daughters. I also found it strange that he had opened a postal savings account for each of them and insisted that they should put their earnings there. There were some whose personal expenses he subsidized. All this was unreal to me because in the real world these things do not happen. One day when I went to see him, he said to me, "Both Ameena and Sakeena have their weekly day off. You see, being Muslims, they like to eat meat once in a while but none is cooked in this house because the rest of us are all strictly vegetarian." One day he told me that the Hindu girl from Ahmedabad, whose marriage he had arranged with a Muslim client of his, had written from Lahore, "I went to the shrine of the great saint Data Sahib and made a wish which has come true. I am going again to make another wish, which is that you should quickly make thirty thousand so that you can go to Benaras and start that retail cloth business of yours." I had laughed, thinking that he was telling me this story about the popular Muslim only because I was Muslim.'

'Were you wrong?' I asked Mumtaz.

'Yes—he really was what he appeared to be. I am sure he had his faults but he was a wonderful man.'

'How did you find out that he wasn't a fraud?' Jugal, who hadn't spoken until now, asked.

'Through his death,' Mumtaz replied. 'The Hindu-Muslim killings had started. Early one morning, I was hurriedly walking through Bhindi Bazaar, which was still deserted because of the night curfew. There were no trams running and taxis were out of the question. In front of the J.J. Hospital I saw a man lying in a heap on the footpath. I first thought it was a *patiwala*, who was still sleeping, but then I saw blood and I stopped. I detected slight movement and bent down to look at the man's face. It was Sehai, I realized with a shock. I sat down on the bare footpath. The starched and spotless twill shirt that he habitually wore was drenched with blood. He was moaning. I shook him gently by the shoulder and called his name a couple of times. At first, there was no response but then he opened his eyes; they were expressionless. Suddenly his whole body shook and I knew he had recognized me. "It's you." he whispered.

'I showered him with questions. What had brought him to this preponderantly Muslim locality at a time when people preferred to stay in their own neighbourhoods? Who had stabbed him? How long had he been lying here? But all he said was, "My day is done; this was Bhagwan's will."

'I do not know what Bhagwan's will was but I knew mine. I was a Muslim. This was a Muslim neighbourhood. I simply could not bear the thought that I, a Muslim, should stand here and watch a man, whom I knew to be a Hindu, lie there dying at the hands of an assassin who must have been a Muslim. I, who was watching Sehai die, was a Muslim like his killer. The thought did cross my mind that if the police arrived on the scene I'd be picked up, if not on a murder charge, certainly for questioning. And what if I took him to the hospital? Would he, by way of revenge against the Muslims, name me as his killer? He was dying anyway. I had an irresistible urge to run, to save my own skin, and I might have done that except he called me by my name. With an almost superhuman effort, he unbuttoned his shirt, slipped his hand in but did not have the strength to pull it out. Then he said in a voice so faint I could hardly hear it, 'There's a packet in there . . . it contains Sultana's ornaments and her twelve hundred rupees . . . they were with a friend for safe custody . . . I picked them up today and was going to return them to her . . . these are bad times you know . . . I wanted her to have her money and the ornaments . . . Would you please give them to her . . . tell her she should leave for a safe place . . . but . . . please . . . look after yourself first!"

Mumtaz fell silent but I had the strange feeling that his voice had become one with the dying voice of Sehai, lying on the footpath in front of the J.J. Hospital; and together the two voices had travelled to that distant blue point where sea and sky met.

Mumtaz said, 'I took the money and ornaments to Sultana, who was one of Sehai's girls, and she started crying.'

We stepped down the gang-plank. Mumtaz was waving.

'Don't you have the feeling he is waving to Sehai?' I asked Jugal.

'I wish I were Sehai,' he said.

MOZAIL

Tarlochan stepped out on the balcony and looked up at the pre-dawn sky. It occurred to him that he hadn't done something like that for years. He felt tired and listless and in need of fresh air.

It was clear, with not a cloud in the sky under whose vast, spotless tent lay the city of Bombay. He could see the lights, twinkling like little stars which had somehow fallen to earth and got lodged in thousands of residential high-rise buildings.

Like most residents of Bombay, Tarlochan was a flat-dweller who hardly ever came outdoors, but standing there under the open sky, he felt good. It was almost like a new experience. He felt as if he had kept himself imprisoned in his flat for four years.

It was well past midnight. The breeze which blew from the sea was light and pleasant after the heavy, mechanically stirred air of the fan under which he always slept. His agitation was gone. All alone, in the open air, he felt calm. He could think clearly.

Karpal Kaur and her entire family lived in a mohalla which was predominantly and ferociously Muslim. Many non-Muslim houses had been set on fire since the start of the city's communal riots. Many people had died. Tarlochan would have brought Karpal Kaur and her family to his flat—which was safer—except that a 48-hour curfew had been imposed by the authorities.

The Muslims of the area were greatly agitated. Reports were pouring in from Punjab about atrocities committed on the Muslims by the Sikhs. He shuddered to think what an enraged Muslim could do to Karpal Kaur to avenge Muslim massacres in Punjab.

Karpal Kaur's mother was blind and her father was a cripple. There was a brother, Naranjan, who lived in another suburb because of a construction contract he had recently been given.

Tarlochan had been trying to persuade Naranjan for weeks to move with his family to his flat. He had told him: 'Forget about your business for the time being. We are passing through difficult times. You should stay with your family, or better, move to my flat. I know there isn't enough space, but these are not normal times. We'll manage somehow.'

Naranjan had smiled through his thick beard and said: 'This is not Amritsar or Lahore. I have seen many communal riots in Bombay. They always pass. And remember, you have only known the city for four years. I've been around for twelve. I know what I'm talking about.'

Tarlochan wasn't convinced. He knew it in his bones. He had reached a point where were he to read in the morning papers that Karpal Kaur and her parents had been massacred the night before, he would not have been in the least surprised.

He did not care much for Karpal Kaur's blind mother and her crippled father. If they were killed and Karpal survived, it would make things even easier for him. He couldn't give a damn what happened to her stupid brother either. He was only worried about Karpal Kaur. The others didn't matter.

The breeze felt good on his face. Tarlochan thought of Karpal Kaur again. She had grown up in the village, but she was delicate, completely unlike normal village girls who have to do hard labour in the fields and become masculine. Karpal Kaur was all woman.

She had very fine features and her breasts were small, still growing. She was fairer than most Sikh girls are, and compared with most of them, she was shy and withdrawn.

Tarlochan originally came from the same village, but he had left it years ago to go to school in the city. And though he had gone back several times in between, he had never met Karpal Kaur, though he knew the family. He had got to know her only in Bombay.

The building he lived in was called Advani Chambers and as

he stood on the balcony looking at the pre-morning sky, he thought of Mozail, the Jewish girl who had a flat here. He used to be in love with her 'up to his knees' as he liked to say. Never in his thirty-five years had he felt that way about a woman.

He had run into her the very day he had moved into Advani Chambers. His first impression was that she was slightly mad. Her brown hair was cut short and always looked dishevelled. She wore thick lipstick and a loose white dress, cut so low at the neck that you could see three-quarters of her big, bouncing breasts, tinged with faint blue veins.

Her lips were not as thick as they appeared, but it was the liberal quantities of lipstick she plastered on them that gave them the appearance of beefsteaks.

Her flat faced Tarlochan's, divided by a narrow corridor.

He remembered their first encounter. He was trying to slip the key into his front door when she had appeared, wearing wooden sandals which made a big racket when she walked. She had looked at him unabashedly and laughed. Suddenly she had slipped and fallen over him. It was very funny, with her legs pinning him to the ground in a scissor like grip and her gown trussed up to reveal her generous thighs.

He had tried to get up and, in so doing, brushed against every revealed and unrevealed part of her body. He had apologized profusely and Mozail had straightened her dress and smiled: 'These wooden slippers are always slipping.' Then she had carefully re-threaded her big toes in them and walked away.

Tarlochan was afraid it might not be easy to get to know her, but he was wrong. In a few days they had become great friends. She was both headstrong and unpredictable. She would make him take her out to dinner, the cinema or the beach, but whenever he tried to go beyond holding her hand, she would tell him to lay off.

Tarlochan had never before been in love—or was it infatuation? In Lahore, Burma, Singapore—where he had lived for the last ten years—he had found it convenient to pick up a girl and pay for the service. It would never have occurred to him that one day he would fall 'up to the knees' in love with a Jewish girl from Bombay.

Mozail was totally unpredictable. They would be in a cinema and she would suddenly spot a friend in the back row and, without saying a word, go and sit next to him for the duration of the show.

The same sort of thing had happened in restaurants. He would order a nice meal for her and then watch in agonized silence as she abruptly rose to join an acquaintance at the next table. When he protested she would stop meeting him for days and when he insisted she would pretend that she had a headache or her stomach was upset.

Or she would say: 'You are a Sikh. You are incapable of understanding anything subtle.'

'Such as your lovers?' he would taunt her.

She would put her hands on her hips, spread out her legs and say: 'Yes, my lovers, but why does it burn you up?'

'We cannot carry on like this,' Tarlochan would say.

And Mozail would laugh. 'You're not only a real Sikh, you're also an idiot. In any case, who asked you to carry on with me? I have a suggestion. Go back to your Punjab and marry a Sikhni.' In the end Tarlochan would always give in because Mozail had become his weakness and he wanted to be around her all the time. Often she would humiliate him in front of some young 'Kristan' lout she had picked up that day from somewhere. He would get angry, but not for long.

This cat-and-mouse thing with Mozail continued for two years, but he was steadfast. One day when she was in one of her high and happy moods, he took her in his arms and asked: 'Mozail, don't you love me?'

Mozail freed herself, sat down in a chair, gazed intently at her dress, then raised her big Jewish eyes, batted her thick eyelashes and said: 'I cannot love a Sikh.'

'You always make fun of me. You make fun of my love,' he said in an angry voice.

She got up, swung her brown head of hair from side to side

and said coquettishly: 'If you shave off your beard and let down your long hair which you keep under your turban, I promise you many men will wink at you suggestively, because you are very dishy.'

Tarlochan felt as if his hair was on fire. He dragged Mozail towards him, squeezed her in his arms and put his bearded lips on hers.

She pushed him away. 'Phew!' she said, 'I brushed my teeth this morning. You don't have to bother.'

'Mozail!' Tarlochan screamed.

She paid no attention, but took out her lipstick from the bag she always carried and began to touch up her lips which looked havoc-stricken after contact with Tarlochan's beard and moustache.

'Let me tell you something,' she said without looking up. 'You have no idea how to use your hirsute assets properly. They would be perfect for brushing dust off my navy-blue skirt.'

She came and sat next to him and began to unpin his beard. It was true he was very good-looking, but being a practising Sikh he had never shaved a single hair off his body and, consequently, he had come to assume a look which was not natural. He respected his religion and its customs and he did not wish to change any of its ritual formalities.

'What are you doing?' he asked Mozail. By now his beard, freed of its shackles, was hanging over his chest in waves.

'You have such soft hair, so I don't think I would use it to brush my navy-blue skirt. Perhaps a nice, soft woven hand-bag,' she said, smiling flirtatiously.

'I have never made fun of your religion. Why do you always mock mine? It's not fair. But I have suffered these insults silently because I love you. Did you know I love you?'

'I know,' she said, letting go of his beard.

'I want to marry you,' he declared, while trying to repin his beard.

'I know,' she said with a slight shake of her head. 'In fact, I have nearly decided to marry you.'

'You don't say,' Tarlochan nearly jumped.

'I do,' she said.

He forgot his half-folded beard and embraced her passionately. 'When . . . when?'

She pushed him aside. 'When you get rid of your hair.'

'It will be gone tomorrow,' he said without thinking.

She began to do a tap dance around the room. 'You're talking rubbish, Tarloch. I don't think you have the courage.'

'You will see,' he said defiantly.

'So I will,' she said, kissing him on the lips, followed by her usual 'Phew!'

He could hardly sleep that night. It was not a small decision. However, next day he went to a barber in the Fort area and had him cut his hair and shave off his beard. While this operation was in progress, he kept his eyes closed. When it was finished, he looked at his new face in the mirror. It looked good. Any girl in Bombay would have found it difficult not to take a long, second look at him.

He did not leave the flat on his first hairless day, but sent word to Mozail that he was not well and if she would mind dropping in for a minute. She stopped dead in her tracks when she saw him. 'My darling Tarloch,' she cried and fell into his arms. She ran her hands over his smooth cheeks and combed his short hair with her fingers. She laughed so much that her nose began to run. She had no handkerchief and calmly she lifted her skirt and wiped it. Tarlochan blushed: 'You should wear something underneath.'

'Gives me a funny feeling. That's how it is,' she replied.

'Let's get married tomorrow,' he said.

'Of course,' she replied, rubbing his chin.

They decided to get married in Poona, where Tarlochan had many friends.

Mozail worked as a salesgirl in one of the big department stores in the Fort area. She told Tarlochan to wait for her at a taxi stand in front of the store the next day, but she never turned up. He learnt later that she had gone off with an old lover of hers who had recently bought a new car. They had moved to Deolali and were not expected to return to Bombay 'for some time'.

Tarlochan was shattered, but in a few weeks he had got over it.

And it was at this point that he had met Karpal Kaur and fallen in love with her.

He now realized what a vulgar girl Mozail was and how totally heartless. He thanked his stars that he hadn't married her.

But there were days when he missed her. He remembered that once he had decided to buy her some gold earrings and had taken her to a jeweller's, but all she wanted was some cheap baubles. That was the way she was.

She used to lie in bed with him for hours and let him kiss and fondle her as much as he wanted, but she would never let him make love. 'You're a Sikh,' she would laugh, 'and I hate Sikhs.'

One argument they always had was over her habit of not wearing any underclothes. Once she said to him: 'You're a Sikh and I know that you wear some ridiculous shorts under your trousers because that is the Sikh religious requirement, but I think it's rubbish that religion should be kept tucked under one's trousers.'

Tarlochan looked at the gradually brightening sky.

'The hell with her,' he said loudly and decided not to think about her at all. He was worried about Karpal Kaur and the danger which loomed over her.

A number of communal incidents had already taken place in the locality. The place was full of orthodox Muslims and, curfew or no curfew, they could easily enter her house and massacre everyone.

Since Mozail had left him, he had decided to grow his hair. His beard had flourished again, but he had come to a compromise. He would not let it grow too long. He knew a barber who could trim it so skilfully that it would not appear trimmed.

The curfew was still in force, but you could walk about in the street, as long as you did not stray too far. He decided to do so. There was a public tap in front of the building. He sat down under it and began to wash his hair and freshen up his face.

Suddenly, he heard the sound of wooden sandals on the cobblestones. There were other Jewish women in that building, all of whom for some reason wore the same kind of sandals. He thought it was one of them.

But it was Mozail. She was wearing her usual loose gown under which he could see her breasts dancing. It disturbed him. He coughed to attract her attention, because he had a feeling she might just pass him by. She came towards him, examined his beard and said: 'What do we have here, a twice-born Sikh?'

She touched his beard: 'Still good enough to brush my navy-blue skirt with, except that I left it in that other place in Deolali.'

Tarlochan said nothing. She pinched his arm: 'Why don't you say something, Sardar Sahib?'

He looked at her. She had lost weight. 'Have you been ill?' he asked.

'No.'

'But you look run down.'

'I am dieting. So you are once again a Sikh?' She sat down next to him, squatting on the ground.

'Yes,' he replied.

'Congratulations. Are you in love with some other girl?'

'Yes.'

'Congratulations. Does she live here, I mean, in our building?'

'No.'

'Isn't that awful?'

She pulled at his beard. 'Is this grown on her advice?'

'No.'

'Well, I promise you that if you get this beard of yours shaved off, I'll marry you. I swear.'

'Mozail,' he said, 'I have decided to marry this simple girl from my village. She is a good observing Sikh, which is why I am growing my hair again.'

Mozail got up, swung herself in a semi-circle on her heel and said: 'If she's a good Sikh, why should she marry you? Doesn't she know that you once broke all the rules and shaved your hair off?'

'No, she doesn't. I started growing a beard the very day you left me—as a gesture of revenge, if you like. I met her some time later, but the way I tie my turban, you can hardly tell that I don't have a full head of hair.'

She lifted her dress to scratch her thigh. 'Damn these mosquitoes,' she said. Then she added: 'When are you getting married?'

'I don't know.' The anxiety in his voice showed.

'What are you thinking, Tarlochan?' she asked. He told her.

'You are a first-class idiot. What's the problem? Just go and get her here where she would be safe.'

'Mozail, you can't understand these things. It's not that simple. You don't really give a damn and that is why we broke up. I'm sorry,' he said.

'Sorry? Come off it, you silly idiot. What you should be thinking of now is how we can get . . . whatever her name is . . . to your flat. And here you go talking about your sorrow at losing me. It could never have worked. Your problem is that you are both stupid and cautious. I like my men to be reckless. OK, forget about that, let's go and get your whatever Kaur from wherever she is.'

Tarlochan looked at her nervously. 'But there's a curfew in the area,' he said.

'There's no curfew for Mozail. Let's go,' she said, almost dragging him.

She looked at him and paused. 'What's the matter?' he asked.

'Your beard, but it's not that long. However, take that turban off, then nobody will take you for a Sikh.'

'I won't go bareheaded,' he said.

'Why not?'

'You don't understand? It is not proper for me to go to their house without my turban.'

'And why not?'

'Why don't you understand? She has never seen me except in a turban. She thinks I am a proper Sikh. I daren't let her think otherwise.'

Mozail rattled her wooden sandals on the floor. 'You are not only a first-class idiot, you are also an ass. It is a question of saving her life, whatever that Kaur of yours is called.'

Tarlochan was not going to give up. 'Mozail, you've no idea how religious she is. Once she sees me bareheaded, she'll start hating me.'

'Your love be damned. Tell me, are all Sikhs as stupid as you? On the one hand, you want to save her life and at the same time you insist on wearing your turban, and perhaps even those funny knickers you are never supposed to be without.'

'I do wear my knickers—as you call them—all the time,' he said.

'Good for you,' she said. 'But think, you're going to go in that awful area full of those bloodthirsty Muslims and their big Maulanas. If you go in a turban, I promise you they will take one look at you and run a big, sharp knife across your throat.'

'I don't care, but I must wear my turban. I can risk my life, but not my love.'

'You're an ass,' she said exasperatedly. 'Tell me, if you're bumped off, what use will that Kaur be to you? I swear, you're not only a Sikh, you are an idiot of a Sikh.'

'Don't talk rot,' Tarlochan snapped.

She laughed, then she put her arms around his neck and swung her body slightly. 'Darling,' she said, 'then it will be the way you want it. Go put on your turban. I will be waiting for you in the street.'

'You should put on some clothes,' Tarlochan said.

'I'm fine the way I am,' she replied.

When he joined her, she was standing in the middle of the street, her legs apart like a man, and smoking. When he came close, she blew the smoke in his face. 'You're the most terrible human being I've ever met in my life,' Tarlochan said. 'You know we Sikhs are not allowed to smoke.'

'Let's go,' she said.

The bazaar was deserted. The curfew seemed to have affected

even the usually brisk Bombay breeze. It was hardly noticeable. Some lights were on but their glow was sickly. Normally at this hour the trains would start running and shops begin to open. There was absolutely no sign of life anywhere.

Mozail walked in front of him. The only sound came from the impact of her wooden sandals on the road. He almost asked her to take the stupid things off and go barefoot, but he didn't. She wouldn't have agreed.

Tarlochan felt scared, but Mozail was walking ahead of him nonchalantly, puffing merrily at her cigarette. They came to a square and were challenged by a policeman: 'Where are you going?' Tarlochan fell back, but Mozail moved towards the policeman, gave her head a playful shake and said: 'It's you! Don't you know me? I'm Mozail. I'm going to my sister's in the next street because she's sick. That man there is a doctor.'

While the policeman was still trying to make up his mind, she pulled out a packet of cigarettes from her bag and offered him one. 'Have a smoke,' she said.

The policeman took the cigarette. Mozail helped him light it with hers. He inhaled deeply. Mozail winked at him with her left eye and at Tarlochan with her right and they moved on.

Tarlochan was still very scared. He looked left and right as he walked behind her, expecting to be stabbed any moment. Suddenly she stopped. 'Tarloch dear, it is not good to be afraid. If you're afraid, then something awful always happens. That's my experience.'

He didn't reply.

They came to the street which led to the mohalla where Karpal Kaur lived. A shop was being looted. 'Nothing to worry about,' she told him. One of the rioters who was carrying something on his head ran into Tarlochan and the object fell to the ground. The man stared at Tarlochan and knew he was a Sikh. He slipped his hand under his shirt to pull out his knife.

Mozail pushed him away as if she was drunk. 'Are you mad, trying to kill your own brother? This is the man I'm going to marry.' Then she said to Tarlochan: 'Karim, pick this thing up and help put it back on his head.'

The man gave Mozail a lecherous look and touched her breasts with his elbow. 'Have a good time, sali,' he said.

They kept walking and were soon in Karpal Kaur's mohalla. 'Which street?' she asked.

'The third on the left. That building in the corner,' he whispered.

When they came to the building, they saw a man run out of it into another across the street. After a few minutes, three men emerged from that building and rushed into the one where Karpal Kaur lived. Mozail stopped. 'Tarloch dear, take off your turban,' she said.

'That I'll never do,' he replied.

'Just as you please, but I hope you do notice what's going on.'

Something terrible was going on. The three men had re-emerged, carrying gunny-bags with blood dripping from them. Mozail had an idea. 'Look, I'm going to run across the street and go into that building. You should pretend that you're trying to catch me. But don't think. Just do it.'

Without waiting for his response, she rushed across the street and ran into Karpal Kaur's building, with Tarlochan in hot pursuit. He was panting when he found her in the front courtyard.

'Which floor?' she asked.

'Second.'

'Let's go,' and she began to climb the stairs, her wooden sandals clattering on each step. There were large bloodstains everywhere.

They came to the second floor, walked down a narrow corridor, and Tarlochan stopped in front of a door. He knocked. Then he called in a low voice, 'Mehnga Singhji, Mehnga Singhji.'

A girl's voice answered. 'Who is it?'

'Tarlochan.'

The door opened slightly. Tarlochan asked Mozail to follow him in. Mozail saw a very young and very pretty girl standing behind the door trembling. She also seemed to have a cold. Mozail said to her: 'Don't be afraid. Tarlochan has come to take you away.'

Tarlochan said: 'Ask Sardar sahib to get ready, but quickly.'

There was a shriek from the flat upstairs. 'They must have got him,' Karpal Kaur said, her voice hoarse with terror.

'Whom?' Tarlochan asked.

Karpal Kaur was about to say something, when Mozail pushed her in a corner and said: 'Just as well they got him. Now take off your clothes.'

Karpal Kaur was taken aback, but Mozail gave her no time to think. In one movement, she divested her of her loose shirt. The young girl frantically put her arms in front of her breasts. She was terrified. Tarlochan turned his face. Then Mozail took off the kaftan-like gown she always wore and asked Karpal Kaur to put it on. She was now stark naked herself.

'Take her away,' she told Tarlochan. She untied the girl's hair so that it hung over her shoulders. 'Go.'

Tarlochan pushed the girl towards the door, then turned back. Mozail stood there, shivering slightly because of the cold.

'Why don't you go?' she asked.

'What about her parents?' he said.

'They can go to hell. You take her.'

'And you?'

'Don't worry about me.'

They heard men running down the stairs. Soon they were banging at the door with their fists. Karpal Kaur's parents were moaning in the other room. 'There's only one thing to do now. I'm going to open the door,' Mozail said.

She addressed Tarlochan: 'When I open the door, I'll rush out and run upstairs. You follow me. These men will be so flabbergasted that they will forget everything and come after us.'

'And then?' Tarlochan asked.

'Then, this one here, whatever her name is, can slip out. The way she's dressed, she'll be safe. They'll take her for a Jew.'

Mozail threw the door open and rushed out. The men had no time to react. Involuntarily, they made way for her. Tarlochan ran after her. She was storming up the stairs in her wooden sandals with Tarlochan behind her.

She slipped and came crashing down, head first. Tarlochan stopped and turned. Blood was pouring out of her mouth and nose and ears. The men who were trying to break into the flat had also gathered round her in a circle, forgetting temporarily what they were there for. They were staring at her naked, bruised body.

Tarlochan bent over her. 'Mozail, Mozail.'

She opened her eyes and smiled. Tarlochan undid his turban and covered her with it.

'This is my lover. He's a bloody Muslim, but he's so crazy that I always call him a Sikh,' she said to the men.

More blood poured out of her mouth. 'Damn it!' she said.

Then she looked at Tarlochan and pushed aside the turban with which he had tried to cover her nakedness.

'Take away this rag of your religion. I don't need it.'

Her arm fell limply on her bare breasts and she said no more.

Bitter Harvest

When Qasim walked through the door, all he was conscious of was a burning pain in his thigh because of the embedded bullet. But when he saw the blood-soaked body of his wife lying in the courtyard, he forgot his pain. He wanted to grab his axe and rush out of the house, killing everyone who came in his path, smashing everything that caught his eye. Then he thought of his daughter, Sharifan.

'Sharifan! Sharifan!' he shouted.

The doors of the two rooms in the house were shut. Was she hiding behind one of them, he wondered. 'Sharifan! Sharifan!' he screamed. 'This is me, your father.' There was no answer. He pushed open the first door with both hands. What he saw was so horrifying that he almost fainted.

On the floor was the nearly naked body of a young girl, her small, upturned breasts pointing at the ceiling as she lay on her back. He wanted to scream but he couldn't. He turned his face away and said in a soft, grief-stricken voice, 'Sharifan.' Then he picked up some clothes from the floor and threw them over her. He did not notice that they had missed their target by several feet.

As he ran out of the house, axe in hand, he was no longer conscious of the bullet in his thigh or the blood-soaked body of his wife, but only of Sharifan, the naked Sharifan lying dead in a heap on the floor of her room.

Axe in hand, he began to move like molten lava through the deserted streets of the city. He saw a Sikh in the main square, a big hulk of a man, but so ferocious and sudden was Qasim's attack, that the man fell to the ground like an uprooted tree, blood gushing out of his severed head.

Qasim could feel his own blood surging through his body, like boiling oil over which cold water is being sprinkled. He saw a group of five or six men at the far end of the road and moved towards them like an arrow. 'Har Har Mahadev,' they shouted, obviously taking him for a brother Hindu. 'Motherfuckers,' he screamed and rushed at them, swinging his axe wildly.

In a few seconds, three of them had fallen to the ground in a blood-smeared pile; the others had run away. Like a man demented, he kept hitting them, till he fell on top of one of the dead bodies himself. He wasn't sure if he had fallen or been overpowered. He lay there waiting for the blow to come, but nothing happened. After a few minutes, he slowly opened his eyes. There was no one on the road, just three dead men among whom he lay himself.

He almost felt disappointed that he had not been killed, but then he remembered Sharifan's naked body, an image which seared his eyes like molten lead. He picked up his axe and was soon running in the streets, shouting obscenities.

The city was deserted. He turned randomly into a small, side street, but was soon out of there when he realized that it was a Muslim neighbourhood. So far he had been hurling abuse at the mothers and sisters of his enemies; now he began to abuse their daughters.

He came to a stop in front of a small house. On the wooden door was a sign in Hindi. Qasim began to swing his axe at it and in a few minutes he had smashed the wood into a pulp. 'Come out, you bastards, come out!' he screamed as he went in.

One of the doors in the house creaked on its hinges and opened slowly to reveal a young girl. 'Who are you?' he asked. 'I am a Hindu,' she replied, running her tongue over her dry lips. She could not have been more than fourteen or fifteen.

Qasim threw away the axe and pounced on her like a wild beast, throwing her to the ground. Then he began to tear at her clothes and for half-an-hour he ravaged her like an animal gone berserk. There was no resistance; she had fainted.

When he finished, he realized that he was clutching her throat with both hands, his nails embedded into her soft skin. He released her with a violent jerk.

He closed his eyes and saw an image of his daughter, lying dead on the floor, her small breasts pointing upwards. He broke into an icy sweat.

Through the smashed street door, a man ran into the house, a sword in his hand. He found Qasim squatting on the floor, trying to spread a blanket over someone lying there.

'Who are you?' the stranger roared.

Qasim turned his face towards him.

'Qasim!' the man screamed in disbelief.

Qasim blinked his eyes; his face wore a blank expression. He couldn't even see properly.

'What are you doing in my house?' the man shouted.

With a trembling finger, Qasim pointed to the blanket-covered heap on the floor, 'Sharifan,' he said in a hollow voice.

The other man pulled off the blanket. The sword fell from his hand; then he staggered out of the house wailing, 'Bimla, my daughter, Bimla.'

A Believer's Version

I swear by Allah . . . recite the Kalima . . . There is no God but Allah and Mohammad is His Prophet. You are all believers. You must believe what I tell you . . . I speak nothing but the truth . . . This has nothing to do with Pakistan . . . I can lay down my life for my beloved Quaid-e-Azam, the great leader, Mohammad Ali Jinnah, but this has nothing to do with Pakistan . . . I swear by God.

Please let's not be in a hurry . . . I know there are riots on the streets and you have little time for me but in the name of God, I beseech you to hear me out . . . You've got to listen to my story . . . I have never denied murdering Tuka Ram. Yes, I ripped him open with a knife but I didn't kill him because he was a Hindu. Why did I kill him then? You have got a right to know . . . but you must let me tell you the entire story.

I'll speak the truth and nothing but the truth . . . recite the Kalima . . . there is no God but Allah and Mohammad is His Prophet. May I die in sin, an infidel, if I did what I did knowing it would lead to this. The last time we had Hindu–Muslim trouble, I killed three Hindus but that was different. This Tuka Ram business was something else.

You are men of learning . . . You know all about women . . . The wise have said . . . beware of their wiles and by God they are right . . . If you don't hang me, I promise you I'll never go near a woman as long as I live . . . Oh God! What a fool I've been! Show me a woman and I get all worked up. Yes, yes, I know we all have to go one day to the Maker and he is going to be asking questions . . . well, well Inspector sahib, I'll be straight with you . . . The moment I set eyes on Rukma, I knew I was in for it. What a woman!

You'd be perfectly right to tell me that someone who earns thirty-five rupees a month has absolutely no business running after women. I suppose I should have been doing my job, collecting rent, and keeping my nose clean. You see, I am a rent collector. But you should know how it all began. Flat 16 was where she lived. I had merely gone to collect the rent—all part of my monthly round. So I knock at the door and who opens it but Rukma Bai herself. I had seen her several times before but that day she looked ravishing. She had something flimsy on and her body shimmered. I think she had rubbed herself all over with oil. Oh God! I went crazy! I wanted to whip off that silly piece of cloth she had around her middle and start massaging her body— furiously. That was how it all began and before I knew it, I was her slave.

What a woman! Her body was solid as a rock . . . I used to bruise myself making love to her . . . And she! Ah! She would say, 'A little harder, a little harder!'

Married? Yes, Inspector, the bitch was married. She even had another lover on the side, or so she claimed. Khan, the night watchman. Oh! I am going to spill the beans on her.

I was crazy about her . . . and she knew it because she would sometimes look at me sideways and smile . . . and when she did that, I swear to God, a chill ran down my spine . . . Oh! How I pined for her! Let me start at the beginning, shall I?

I was obsessed with her. All I wanted was that woman. I couldn't think of anything else. I was snookered and I knew it. My problem was that blasted toy-maker husband of hers. He was always in that one-room flat of theirs with those silly wooden toys of his. I just couldn't find the opportunity to sneak in with her.

And then I got a break. I was bumming around in the bazaar when I saw that man . . . what was he called? Yes, Girdhari. He was sitting on the pavement selling those wooden toys of his. And before you could blink your eyes, I was standing in front of

Flat 16, my heart beating in my mouth. I knocked and she opened the door. I didn't know what to say. I almost turned and walked off but she smiled and called me in.

She closed the door, then asked me to sit down. 'I know what you are after but as long as Girdhari, my husband, is alive you can forget about it,' she said, the witch!

I stood up. She was so close to me, wearing the same flimsy excuse for a dress, her body glistening. Oh! I couldn't resist it any longer. I threw my arms around her. I was wild with excitement. 'I don't know what you are talking about,' I said. She embraced me right back. God, what a body that woman had, Inspector! But let me tell you my story.

'Girdhari can go burn in hell,' I whispered, 'I want you.'

Rukma pushed me away. 'You don't want your nice clothes soiled by the oil on my body, do you?'

'I don't care what I soil,' I said as I grabbed her once again.

Inspector sahib, if you had lashed my back with a whip, I wouldn't have let go of her. 'Sit down,' she purred. 'Don't stand there. Come, I want to talk to you,' she told me. I was like putty in her hands. So there I was sitting, not saying a word. What was she planning? That *sala*, Girdhari, was in the bazaar selling toys so what was she afraid of?

'Rukma,' I said breathlessly, 'There never will be an opportunity as good as this.'

She ran her fingers through my hair. 'There'll be better ones but you'll have to do something for me. Will you?'

Inspector Sahib, I was not myself at the time. I didn't know what I was doing. Oh, the devil had taken hold of me. I told her, 'I'll kill fifteen men if you want me to.'

She smiled, the witch, and said, 'I believe you.'

I spent some more time with her. She fed me something she had cooked. We talked of this, that and the other, you know. Finally, she asked me to leave.

Ten days passed. On the eleventh, at two in the morning, someone woke me up gently. I sleep on the landing; yes, in the same building where Rukma lives. It was she. My heart leapt with excitement. 'Come with me,' she said softly. I followed her on tiptoe. She pushed her door open and I slipped in after her. I lunged for her; I just couldn't wait. 'Not yet,' she said, as she switched on the light. Someone was asleep on the floor, face covered. 'Who's that?' I asked in sign language. 'Sit down,' she answered. She ran her fingers lovingly through my hair but what she said next so casually made me break out in a cold sweat. And you know what she said?

Recite the Kalima . . . There is no God but Allah and Mohammad is His Prophet . . . I speak the truth and nothing but the truth . . . a woman like Rukma, I've never met in my entire life. You know what she told me with a smirk? 'I've killed Girdhari.' Just like that! With her bare hands she had killed a strong, well-built man like her husband. Some woman she was! As God is my witness, Inspector sahib, when I think of that night, I break out in goose bumps. She had garrotted him to death with wire rope. She had squeezed the last breath out of his body by twisting the wire rope around his neck with the aid of a small stick. The poor man's tongue was hanging out and his eyes had nearly popped out of their sockets. She said it hadn't taken long.

She insisted that I should see Girdhari's face. My blood froze when I looked at him but Rukma, she didn't bat an eye. Then she lay down only a few feet from the body and told me to lie next to her. I felt dead myself but then she did something to me, something very unexpected, and I was suddenly on fire. I'll never forget that night! There lay Girdhari and there lay the two of us, one on top of the other.

What a night that was!

In the morning, quite methodically, Rukma and I cut Girdhari into three pieces with his very own tools. We must have made a bit of noise but the neighbours were used to Girdhari making his usual racket every morning as he got down to work. You may well ask, Inspector Sahib, why I went along with this grisly business, why I didn't rush to the police and rat on her? I'll tell you why. That one night with her had me eating out of her hand. If she had asked me to go kill fifteen men, I would have gone right out and done that.

There was the question of getting rid of the body. All said and done, she was a woman and needed a hand there. 'Not to worry, darling,' I told her. 'We'll put Girdhari in a trunk and as night falls, I'll take it out and dump it somewhere.' But God moves in strange ways. That day, Hindu-Muslim killings erupted in the city and a thirty-six-hour curfew was clamped on the worst-affected neighbourhoods. 'Abdul Karim,' I said to myself, 'You've got to do it tonight.' At two in the morning, I heaved that trunk down. God, it was heavy, but I didn't let that worry me. There I was, that dead weight on my back, taking rapid steps, praying all the time. Please, God, no police, not tonight. And God heard me. I crossed the street and was walking past a mosque when I had an inspiration. I put the trunk down, took Girdhari out, I mean all three pieces of him, and chucked them over the low protective wall right inside the mosque.

Truly God is great and moves in strange ways. Next morning I heard that the Hindus had burnt the mosque down. 'There goes poor Girdhari,' I said to myself, 'cremated like a good Hindu.' I advised Rukma to spread word that Girdhari had gone on a trip and hadn't come back as he should have. 'And, sweetheart, I'll be with you nights doing what I like best,' I added. 'Not so soon,' Rukma said. 'We must not see each other for at least fifteen days.'

Seventeen days passed and nothing happened. I had nightmares about Girdhari but I told him, 'You are dead Girdhari, so don't try to scare me. There is nothing you can do to me because you are no longer around. Ha, ha!'

A day later, I was sleeping in my usual place when Rukma woke me up around midnight. She asked me to follow her to her room. Then she lay down on that mattress of hers, naked as on the day she was born. 'I ache all over, darling, rub some oil on my body to soothe the pain,' she whispered in a husky voice. Quite happily I began to massage her all over. In an hour I was exhausted, with sweat dripping out of every pore in my body on to hers, but she did not say, 'That was nice, Abdul Karim, but you must be worn out yourself. That's enough.'

'I am done for, Rukma darling,' I finally said. She gave me one of those smiles. Then she pulled me down next to her and before I knew it I was sound asleep, one of my hands on her breasts.

I woke up with a start because there was something sharp and metallic around my throat but before I could do anything, Rukma had jumped on my chest and was tightening the noose. That was how she had killed Girdhari. I couldn't scream, though I tried to. Then everything went black.

When I came to, it was about four in the morning and I ached all over. Suddenly, there were voices. I lay without daring to breathe, so scared was I. I couldn't see anything but then I realized what was going on only a few feet from me. A man and a woman, locked in each other's arms, breathing heavily and making love. I heard Rukma's voice. 'Tuka Ram, switch on the light.' And his frightened voice, 'No, no, Rukma, please!' 'You big coward!' Rukma replied angrily. 'How are you going to chop him up in three pieces and carry him out for disposal?'

I must have fainted briefly for the next thing I remember is the light coming on. That made me sit up. Tuka Ram shrieked with fright and ran out of the room. Rukma bolted the door calmly. This Tuka Ram character I knew. He was a mango seller, the kind who went from house to house.

Rukma was looking at me as if she did not believe her eyes. She was sure she had killed me but there I was, sitting bolt upright. I didn't know what she was going to do to me because there was a knock at the door and I heard several voices. Rukma pushed me into the bathroom, telling me to stay there.

It was the neighbours wanting to know if everything was all right because they had heard strange noises. 'I must have been walking in my sleep,' she told them and they left. Then she bolted the door. I was very frightened. I knew she was going to kill me but, strangely, this conviction brought back my physical strength. I stepped out of the bathroom. She didn't hear me. She was leaning out of the window. I rushed forward, put my hands on her buttocks

and with all my strength, heaved her up and pushed her out.
There was a loud thud and that was that. I stalked out of her
room unobserved.

I lay low for the better part of the morning. My throat was
marked because the wire had cut into it. I put a handkerchief
around it after massaging it with oil. I was sure that when Rukma
was discovered in the morning, everyone would think she had
fallen out of the window because had she not told the neighbours
she walked in her sleep. By midday nothing had happened. Had
they found Rukma? She must have fallen into the dead-end street
at the back of two buildings, mostly used as a huge refuse bin by
the residents, but it was swept every morning. So why hadn't
they found Rukma? Maybe it hadn't been cleaned today.

Even by the afternoon nothing had happened. There was only
one thing to do. Check out that back street myself. I steeled myself
for the shock of discovering her broken body lying on flat stone
but there was nothing, no sign of her at all. What could have
happened? I swear on the Holy Book if I escape from this mess I
have got myself into, Inspector sahib, I'll not be half as surprised
as I am about the disappearance of that woman's body. After all,
she fell from the third floor and it is logical that the impact
should have killed her. That being so, why didn't I find her?
Perhaps she is alive, the witch. The neighbours think she has
either been abducted by a Muslim or she has been killed in the
riots. If she is dead, well that is the best which could have
happened and if she has been abducted, then God help the man
who took her. I know what lies in store for him.

Yes, sir, I must tell you about Tuka Ram. About three weeks
after that night I ran into him in the street. 'Where is she?' he
demanded. 'I don't know where she is,' I replied. 'You know
bloody well where she is,' he snarled. 'I swear by the Holy Book
I do not know,' I said sincerely but he didn't seem to believe me.
'You liar! You killed her! I am going to the police! You first
killed Girdhari, then you killed her!' he hissed.

After he left, I reviewed my situation. There were no two ways
about it. I had to kill him. So, Inspector Sahib, what was I to do?

I put my knife into my pocket and went out looking for Tuka Ram. I finally found him in the evening at, of all places, the public urinal. He was about to answer the call of nature when I got him. 'Tuka Ram,' I said, 'this is curtains for you.' And I plunged my knife into him. He put both hands on his stomach and fell forward. What a fool I am, Inspector sahib! I should have run but what did I do? I waited around, the knife still in my hand. I even bent down to feel his pulse, just to be sure he was dead. And you know, I have no idea where the pulse is— somewhere about the wrist but where exactly, well, I wasn't quite sure.

And just then, as I was fooling around with his wrist, in walks this burly policeman, looking rather keen to do something which nobody else could do for him and he sees me, knife in hand and the rest of it and I am nabbed, what else!

Read out the Kalima, the word of God, in a loud voice. There is no God but Allah and Mohammad is His Prophet . . . and what I have told you was the truth, nothing but the truth.

The Assignment

Beginning with isolated incidents of stabbing, it had now developed into full-scale communal violence, with no holds barred. Even home-made bombs were being used.

The general view in Amritsar was that the riots could not last long. They were seen as no more than a manifestation of temporarily inflamed political passions which were bound to cool down before long. After all, these were not the first communal riots the city had known. There had been so many of them in the past. They never lasted long. The pattern was familiar. Two weeks or so of unrest and then business as usual. On the basis of experience, therefore, the people were quite justified in believing that the current troubles would also run their course in a few days. But this did not happen. They not only continued, but grew in intensity.

Muslims living in Hindu localities began to leave for safer places, and Hindus in Muslim majority areas followed suit. However, everyone saw these adjustments as strictly temporary. The atmosphere would soon be clear of this communal madness, they told themselves.

Retired judge Mian Abdul Hai was absolutely confident that things would return to normal soon, which was why he wasn't worried. He had two children, a boy of eleven and a girl of seventeen. In addition, there was an old servant who was now pushing seventy. It was a small family. When the troubles started, Mian sahib, being an extra cautious man, stocked up on food . . . just in case. So on one count, at least, there were no worries.

His daughter Sughra was less sure of things. They lived in a three-storey house with a view over almost the entire city. Sughra could not help noticing that whenever she went on the roof, there were fires raging everywhere. In the beginning, she could hear fire engines rushing past, their bells ringing, but this had now stopped. There were too many fires in too many places.

The nights had become particularly frightening. The sky was always lit by conflagrations like giants spitting out flames. Then there were the slogans which rent the air with terrifying frequency—Allah o Akbar, *Har Har Mahadev*.

Sughra never expressed her fears to her father, because he had declared confidently that there was no cause for anxiety. Everything was going to be fine. Since he was generally always right, she had initially felt reassured.

However, when the power and water supplies were suddenly cut off, she expressed her unease to her father and suggested apologetically that, for a few days at least, they should move to Sharifpura, a Muslim locality, to where many of the old residents had already moved. Mian sahib was adamant: 'You're imagining things. Everything is going to be normal very soon.'

He was wrong. Things went from bad to worse. Before long there was not a single Muslim family to be found in Mian Abdul Hai's locality. Then one day Mian sahib suffered a stroke and was laid up. His son Basharat, who used to spend most of his time playing self-devised games, now stayed glued to his father's bed.

All the shops in the area had been permanently boarded up. Dr Ghulam Hussian's dispensary had been shut for weeks and Sughra had noticed from the rooftop one day that the adjoining clinic of Dr Goranditta Mall was also closed. Mian sahib's condition was getting worse day by day. Sughra was almost at the end of her wits. One day she took Basharat aside and said to him, 'You've got to do something. I know it's not safe to go out, but we must get some help. Our father is very ill.'

The boy went, but came back almost immediately. His face was pale with fear. He had seen a blood-drenched body lying in the street and a group of wild-looking men looting shops. Sughra took the terrified boy in her arms and said a silent prayer, thanking God for his safe return. However, she could not bear her father's suffering. His left side was now completely lifeless. His speech had been impaired and he mostly communicated through gestures, all designed to reassure Sughra that soon all would be well.

It was the month of Ramadan and only two days to Id. Mian sahib was quite confident that the troubles would be over by then. He was again wrong. A canopy of smoke hung over the city, with fires burning everywhere. At night the silence was shattered by deafening explosions. Sughra and Basharat hadn't slept for days.

Sughra, in any case, couldn't because of her father's deteriorating condition. Helplessly, she would look at him, then at her young frightened brother and the seventy-year-old servant Akbar, who was useless for all practical purposes. He mostly kept to his bed, coughing and fighting for breath. One day Sughra told him angrily, 'What good are you? Do you realize how ill Mian sahib is? Perhaps you are too lazy to want to help, pretending that you are suffering from acute asthma. There was a time when servants used to sacrifice their lives for their masters.'

Sughra felt very bad afterwards. She had been unnecessarily harsh on the old man. In the evening when she took his food to him in his small room, he was not there. Basharat looked for him all over the house, but he was nowhere to be found. The front door was unlatched. He was gone, perhaps to get some help for Mian sahib. Sughra prayed for his return, but two days passed and he hadn't come back.

It was evening and the festival of Id was now only a day away. She remembered the excitement which used to grip the family on this occasion. She remembered standing on the rooftop, peering into the sky, looking for the Id moon and praying for the clouds to clear. But how different everything was today. The sky was covered in smoke and on distant roofs one could see people looking upwards. Were they trying to catch sight of the new moon or were they watching the fires, she wondered?

She looked up and saw the thin sliver of the moon peeping through a small patch in the sky. She raised her hands in prayer, begging God to make her father well. Basharat, however, was upset that there would be no Id this year.

The night hadn't yet fallen. Sughra had moved her father's bed out of the room onto the veranda. She was sprinkling water on the floor to make it cool. Mian sahib was lying there quietly looking with vacant eyes at the sky where she had seen the moon. Sughra came and sat next to him. He motioned her to get closer. Then he raised his right arm slowly and put it on her head. Tears began to run from Sughra's eyes. Even Mian sahib looked moved. Then with great difficulty he said to her, 'God is merciful. All will be well.'

Suddenly there was a knock on the door. Sughra's heart began to beat violently. She looked at Basharat, whose face had turned white like a sheet of paper. There was another knock. Mian sahib gestured to Sughra to answer it. It must be old Akbar who had come back, she thought. She said to Basharat, 'Answer the door. I'm sure it's Akbar.' Her father shook his head, as if to signal disagreement.

'Then who can it be?' Sughra asked him.

Mian Abdul Hai tried to speak, but before he could do so, Basharat came running in. He was breathless. Taking Sughra aside, he whispered, 'It's a Sikh.'

Sughra screamed, 'A Sikh! What does he want?'

'He wants me to open the door.'

Sughra took Basharat in her arms and went and sat on her father's bed, looking at him desolately.

On Mian Abdul Hai's thin, lifeless lips, a faint smile appeared. 'Go and open the door. It is Gurmukh Singh.'

'No, it's someone else,' Basharat said.

Mian sahib turned to Sughra. 'Open the door. It's him.'

Sughra rose. She knew Gurmukh Singh. Her father had once done him a favour. He had been involved in a false legal suit and Mian sahib had acquitted him. That was a long time ago, but every year on the occasion of Id, he would come all the way from his village with a bag of homemade noodles. Mian sahib had told him several times, 'Sardar sahib, you really are too kind. You shouldn't inconvenience yourself every year.' But Gurmukh Singh would always reply, 'Mian sahib, God has given you everything. This is only a small gift which I bring every year in humble acknowledgement of the kindness you did me once. Even a hundred generations of mine would not be able to repay your favour. May God keep you happy.'

Sughra was reassured. Why hadn't she thought of it in the first place? But why had Basharat said it was someone else? After all, he knew Gurmukh Singh's face from his annual visit.

Sughra went to the front door. There was another knock. Her heart missed a beat. 'Who is it?' she asked in a faint voice.

Basharat whispered to her to look through a small hole in the door.

It wasn't Gurmukh Singh, who was a very old man. This was a young fellow. He knocked again. He was holding a bag in his hand, of the same kind Gurmukh Singh used to bring.

'Who are you?' she asked, a little more confident now.

'I am Sardar Gurmukh Singh's son Santokh.'

Sughra's fear had suddenly gone. 'What brings you here today?' she asked politely.

'Where is Judge sahib?' he asked.

'He is not well,' Sughra answered.

'Oh, I'm sorry,' Santokh Singh said. Then he shifted his bag from one hand to the other. 'These are homemade noodles.' Then after a pause, 'Sardarji is dead.'

'Dead!'

'Yes, a month ago, but one of the last things he said to me was, 'For the last ten years, on the occasion of Id, I have always taken my small gift to Judge sahib. After I am gone, it will become your duty.' I gave him my word that I would not fail him. I am here today to honour the promise made to my father on his death-bed.'

Sughra was so moved that tears came to her eyes. She opened the door a little. The young man pushed the bag towards her.

'May God rest his soul,' she said.

'Is Judge sahib not well?' he asked.

'No.'

'What's wrong?'

'He had a stroke.'

'Had my father been alive, it would have grieved him deeply. He never forgot Judge sahib's kindness until his last breath. He used to say, "He is not a man, but a god." May God keep him under his care. Please convey my respects to him.'

He left before Sughra could make up her mind whether or not to ask him to get a doctor.

As Santokh Singh turned the corner, four men, their faces covered with their turbans, moved towards him. Two of them held burning oil torches, the others carried cans of kerosene oil and explosives. One of them asked Santokh, 'Sardarji, have you completed your assignment?'

The young man nodded.

'Should we then proceed with ours?' he asked.

'If you like,' he replied and walked away.

Wages

There was looting and rioting everywhere and to them had now been added widespread arson.

Quite unmindful of it all, a man was waltzing down the street, a harmonium strung around his neck, and a popular song on his lips:

She went away to a far land
Breaking my heart
Never again will I love another,
Never again . . .

A young boy went running by, cradling dozens of packets of papads in his arms. He tripped slightly and dropped one packet. As he stooped to try and pick it up, an older man with an obviously stolen sewing machine on his head, said, 'Why bother to do that son? The surface of the road is so hot that your papads will soon turn to a crisp.'

A gunnybag landed on the street with a thud. A man stepped forward and slashed it open with his big hunting knife, expecting perhaps to find a bleeding fugitive inside, but what came cascading out was sugar; white, fine-grained sugar. Soon a crowd gathered and people began to help themselves to the unexpected prize. One man in the crowd was only wearing a length of cloth loosely wrapped around his middle. As if it was the most normal thing to do, he freed himself of it, and standing stark naked, began to throw fistfuls of sugar into what was now a makeshift carrier-bag.

'Make way, make way, look out, look out.' It was a tonga, loaded with gleaming furniture made of fine wood.

From the top-floor window of a house overlooking the street, someone threw down a rolled length of muslin, but on its way down, it was licked by flames leaping out of a lower-storey window and by the time it hit the ground, it was nothing but a handful of ash.

They finally managed to haul the big steel safe out of the house and although there were many of them, all armed with sticks, they just could not get it to open.

One man stepped out of a shop carrying several tins of Cow & Gate dry milk. No one paid any attention to him as he disappeared down the street, taking slow, careful steps.

'Come on boys, treat yourself to cool lemonade. It is summertime,' came the loud invitation. One man with a car tyre around his neck, picked up two bottles and walked off without even saying thank you.

Someone screamed, 'Send for the fire brigade otherwise all these precious goods will be lost to the flames.' However, no attention whatever was paid to this eminently sensible suggestion.

And so it went on all day with the heat from the sun and the many fires blazing in all directions becoming almost unbearable. Suddenly, there was the sound of gunfire. By the time the police appeared, the street was quite deserted . . . except for a receding human figure at the other end moving very fast. The policemen, furiously blowing their whistles, ran towards what looked like an apparition appearing and disappearing through the haze and the smoke. And then he was in the clear, a Kashmiri seasonal labourer, one of thousands who came to the plains in search of daily work. There was a big gunnybag on his back. The policemen began to blow their whistles even more furiously but he did not stop. He was running as if what he was carrying on his back was no heavier than a feather.

The policemen began to tire. Even their whistles seemed to have gone hoarse. In exasperation, one of them pulled out his revolver and fired, hitting the Kashmiri labourer in the leg. The gunnybag fell off his back. He stopped, saw blood gushing out of the wound, but paid no attention to it. Picking up the gunnybag with one mighty heave, he broke into a sprint.

'Let him go to hell,' the policemen said, but just then, he staggered and fell to the ground in a heap, with the gunnybag resting on top of him.

The policemen took both the man and the gunnybag to the station. On the way, several times, he tried to soften the hearts of his captors but to no avail. 'Exalted sirs, why you catch this poor fellow? All he take is one little bag of rice. Brave ones, why you shoot down this poor man when all he done . . .'

At the station also, he made many efforts to present his case. 'Exalted sirs, other people steal big things. All poor me take is one bag of rice. Me very poor man, just eat rice . . .'

Ultimately, he gave up. Wiping his brow with his dirty skullcap, he looked at the bag of rice longingly and spreading both his hands in supplication before the police inspector, said, 'All right, exalted sir, you keep the rice, all poor me ask is my wages for carrying this bag . . . just four annas.'

The Last Salute

This Kashmir war was a very odd affair. Subedar Rab Nawaz often felt as if his brain had turned into a rifle with a faulty safety catch.

He had fought with distinction on many major fronts in the Second World War. He was respected by both his seniors and juniors because of his intelligence and valour. He was always given the most difficult and dangerous assignments and he had never failed the trust placed in him.

But he had never been in a war like this one. He had come to it full of enthusiasm and with the itch to fight and liquidate the enemy. However, the first encounter had shown that the men arrayed against them on the other side were mostly old friends and comrades with whom he had fought in the old British Indian army against the Germans and the Italians. The friends of yesterday had been transformed into the enemies of today.

At times, the whole thing felt like a dream to Subedar Rab Nawaz. He could remember the day the Second World War was declared. He had enlisted immediately. They had been given some basic training and then packed off to the front. He had been moved from one theatre of war to another and, one day, the war had ended. Then had come Pakistan and the new war he was now fighting. So much had happened in these last few years at such breakneck speed. Often it made no sense at all. Those who had planned and executed these great events had perhaps deliberately maintained a dizzying pace so that the participants should get no time to think. How else could one explain one revolution followed by another and then another?

One thing Subedar Rab Nawaz could understand. They were fighting this war to win Kashmir. Why did they want to win Kashmir? Because it was crucial to Pakistan's security and survival. However, sometimes when he sat behind a gun emplacement and caught sight of a familiar face on the other side, for a moment he forgot why they were fighting. He forgot why he was carrying a gun and killing people. At such times, he would remind himself that he was not fighting to win medals or earn a salary, but to secure the survival of his country.

This was his country even before it became Pakistan. This was his land. But now he was fighting against men who were his countrymen until only the other day. Men who had grown up in the same village, whose families had been known to his family for generations. These men had now been turned into citizens of a country to which they were complete strangers. They had been told: We are placing a gun in your hands so that you can go and fight for a country which you have yet to know, where you do not even have a roof over your head, where even the air and water are strange to you; go and fight for it against Pakistan, the land where you were born and grew up.

Rab Nawaz would think of those Muslim soldiers who had moved to Pakistan, leaving their ancestral homes behind, and come to this new country with empty hands. They had been given nothing, except the guns that had been put in their hands. The same guns they had always used, the same make, the same bore, guns to fight their new enemy with.

Before the partition of the country, they used to fight one common enemy who was not really their enemy perhaps but whom they had accepted as their enemy for the sake of employment and rewards and medals. Formerly, all of them were Indian soldiers, but now some were Indian and others were Pakistani soldiers. Rab Nawaz could not unravel this puzzle. And when he thought about Kashmir, he became even more confused. Were the Pakistani soldiers fighting for Kashmir or for the Muslims of Kashmir? If they were being asked to fight in defence of the Muslims of Kashmir, why had they not been asked to fight for the Muslims of the princely states of Junagarh and Hyderabad? And if this was an Islamic war, then why were other Muslim countries of the world not fighting shoulder to shoulder with them?

Rab Nawaz had finally come to the conclusion that such intricate and subtle matters were beyond the comprehension of a simple soldier. A soldier should be thick in the head. Only the thick-headed made good soldiers, but despite this resolution, he couldn't help wondering sometimes about the war he was now in.

The fighting in what was called the Titwal sector was spread across the Kishan Ganga river and along the road which led from Muzaffarabad to Kiran. It was a strange war. Often at night, instead of gunfire, one heard abuse being exchanged in loud voices.

One late evening, while Subedar Rab Nawaz was preparing his platoon for a foray into enemy territory, he heard loud voices from across the hill the enemy was supposed to be on. He could not believe his ears. There was loud laughter followed by abuse. 'Pig's trotters,' he murmured, 'what on earth is going on?'

One of his men returned the abuse in as loud a voice as he could muster, then complained to him, 'Subedar Sahib, they are abusing us again, the motherfuckers.'

Rab Nawaz's first instinct was to join the slanging match, but he thought better of it. The men fell silent also, following his example. However, after a while, the torrent of abuse from the other side became so intolerable that his men lost control and began to match abuse with abuse. He ordered them a couple of times to keep quiet, but did not insist because, frankly, it was difficult for a human being not to react violently.

They couldn't of course, see the enemy at night, and hardly did so during the day because of the hilly country which provided perfect cover. All they heard was abuse which echoed across the hills and valleys and then evaporated in the air.

Some of the hills were barren, while others were covered with tall pine trees. It was a very difficult terrain. Subedar Rab Nawaz's platoon was on a bare, treeless hill which provided no cover. His men were itching to go into attack to avenge the abuse which had been hurled at them without respite for several weeks. An attack was planned and executed with success, though they lost two men and suffered four injuries. The enemy lost three and abandoned the position, leaving behind food and provisions.

Subedar Rab Nawaz and his men were sorry they had not been able to capture an enemy soldier. They could then have avenged the abuse face to face. However, they had captured an important and difficult feature. Rab Nawaz relayed the news of the victory to his commander, Major Aslam, and was commended for gallantry.

On top of most of the hills, one found ponds. There was a large one on the hill they had captured. The water was clear and sweet, and although it was cold, they took off their clothes and jumped in. Suddenly, they heard firing. They jumped out of the pond and hit the ground—naked. Subedar Rab Nawaz crawled towards his binoculars, picked them up and surveyed the area carefully. He could see no one. There was more firing. This time he was able to determine its origin. It was coming from a small hill, lying a few hundred feet below their perch. He ordered his men to open up.

The enemy troops did not have very good cover and Rab Nawaz was confident they could not stay there much longer. The moment they decided to move, they would come in direct range of their guns. Sporadic firing kept getting exchanged. Finally, Rab Nawaz ordered that no more ammunition should be wasted. They should just wait for the enemy to break cover. Then he looked at his still naked body and murmured, 'Pig's trotters. Man does look silly without clothes.'

For two whole days, this game continued. Occasional fire was exchanged, but the enemy had obviously decided to lie low. Then suddenly the temperature dropped several degrees. To keep his men warm, Subedar Rab Nawaz ordered that the tea-kettle should be kept on the boil all the time. It was like an unending tea party.

On the third day—it was unbearably cold—the soldier on the lookout reported that some movement could be detected around the enemy position. Subedar Rab Nawaz looked through his binoculars. Yes, something was going on. Rab Nawaz raised his rifle and fired. Someone called his name, or so he thought. It echoed through the valley. 'Pig's trotters,' Rab Nawaz shouted, 'what do you want?'

The distance that separated their two positions was not great, the voice came back, 'Don't hurl abuse, brother.'

Rab Nawaz looked at his men. The word brother seemed to hang in the air. He raised his hands to his mouth and shouted, 'Brother! There are no brothers here, only your mother's lovers.'

'Rab Nawaz,' the voice shouted.

He trembled. The words reverberated around the hills and then faded into the atmosphere.

'Pig's trotters,' he whispered, 'who was that?'

He knew that the troops in the Titwal sector were mostly from the old 6/9 Jat Regiment, his own regiment. But who was this joker shouting his name? He had many friends in the regiment, and some enemies too. But who was this man who had called him brother?

Rab Nawaz looked through his binoculars again, but could see nothing. He shouted, 'Who was that? This is Rab Nawaz. Rab Nawaz. Rab Nawaz,'

'It is me . . . Ram Singh,' the same voice answered.

Rab Nawaz nearly jumped. 'Ram Singh, oh, Ram Singha, Ram Singha, you pig's trotters.'

'Shut your trap, you potter's ass,' came the reply.

Rab Nawaz looked at his men, who appeared startled at this strange exchange in the middle of battle. 'He's talking rot, pig's trotters.' Then he shouted, 'You slaughtered swine, watch your tongue.'

Ram Singh began to laugh. Rab Nawaz could not contain himself either. His men watched him in silence.

'Look, my friend, we want to drink tea,' Ram Singh said.

'Go ahead then. Have a good time,' Rab Nawaz replied.

'We can't. The tea things are lying elsewhere.'

'Where's elsewhere?'

'Let me put it this way. If we tried to get them, you could blow us to bits. We'd have to break cover.'

'So what do you want, pig's trotters?' Rab Nawaz laughed.

'That you hold your fire until we get our things.'

'Go ahead,' Rab Nawaz said.

'You will blow us up, you potter's ass,' Ram Singh shouted.

'Shut your mouth, you crawly Sikh tortoise,' Rab Nawaz said.

'Take an oath on something that you won't open fire.'

'On what?'

'Anything you like.'

Rab Nawaz laughed, 'You have my word. Now go get your things.'

Nothing happened for a few minutes. One of the men was watching the small hill through his binoculars. He pointed at his gun and asked Rab Nawaz in gestures if he should open fire. 'No, no, no shooting,' Rab Nawaz said.

Suddenly, a man darted forward, running low towards some bushes. A few minutes later he ran back, carrying an armful of things. Then he disappeared. Rab Nawaz picked up his rifle and fired. 'Thank you,' Ram Singh's voice came.

'No mention,' Rab Nawaz answered. 'OK, boys, let's give the buggers one round.'

More by way of entertainment than war, this exchange of fire continued for some time. Rab Nawaz could see smoke going up in a thin blue spiral where the enemy was. 'Is your tea ready, Ram Singha?' he shouted.

'Not yet, you potter's ass.'

Rab Nawaz was a potter by caste and any reference to his origins always enraged him. Ram Singh was the one person who could get away with calling him a potter's ass. They had grown up together in the same village in the Punjab. They were the same age, had gone to the same primary school, and their fathers had been childhood friends. They had joined the army the same day. In the last war, they had fought together on the same fronts.

'Pig's trotters,' Rab Nawaz said to his men, 'he never gives up, that one. Shut up, lice-infested donkey Ram Singha,' he shouted.

He saw a man stand up. Rab Nawaz raised his rifle and fired in his direction. He heard a scream. He looked through his binoculars. It was Ram Singh. He was doubled up, holding his stomach. Then he fell to the ground.

Rab Nawaz shouted, 'Ram Singh' and stood up. There was rapid gunfire from the other side. One bullet brushed past his left arm. He fell to the ground. Some enemy soldiers, taking advantage of this confusion, began to run across open ground to securer positions. Rab Nawaz ordered his platoon to attack the hill. Three were killed, but the others managed to capture the position with Rab Nawaz in the lead.

He found Ram Singh lying on the bare ground. He had been shot in the stomach. His eyes lit up when he saw Rab Nawaz. 'You potter's ass, whatever did you do that for?' he asked.

Rab Nawaz felt as if it was he who had been shot. But he smiled, bent over Ram Singh and began to undo his belt. 'Pig's trotters, who told you to stand up?'

'I was only trying to show myself to you, but you shot me,' Ram Singh said with difficulty. Rab Nawaz unfastened his belt. It was a very bad wound and bleeding profusely.

Rab Nawaz voice choked, 'I swear upon God, I only fired out of fun. How could I know it was you? You were always an ass, Ram Singha.'

Ram Singh was rapidly losing blood. Rab Nawaz was surprised he was still alive. He did not want to move him. He spoke to his platoon commander Major Aslam on the wireless, requesting urgent medical help.

He was sure it would take a long time to arrive. He had a feeling Ram Singh wouldn't last that long. But he laughed. 'Don't you worry. The doctor is on his way.'

Ram Singh said in a weak voice, 'I am not worried, but tell me, how many of my men did you kill?'

'Just one,' Rab Nawaz said.

'And how many did you lose?'

'Six,' Rab Nawaz lied.

'Six,' Ram Singh said. 'When I fell, they were disheartened, but I told them to fight on, give it everything they'd got. Six, yes.' Then his mind began to wander.

He began to talk of their village, their childhood, stories from school, the 6/9 Jat Regiment, its commanding officers, affairs with strange women in strange cities. He was in excruciating pain, but he carried on. 'Do you remember that madam, you pig?'

'Which one?' Rab Nawaz asked.

'That one in Italy. You remember what we used to call her? Maneater.'

Rab Nawaz remembered her. 'Yes, yes. She was called Madam Minitafanto or some such thing. And she used to say: no money, no action. But she had a soft spot for you, that daughter of Mussolini.'

Ram Singh laughed loudly, causing blood to gush out of his wound. Rab Nawaz dressed it with a makeshift bandage. 'Now keep quiet,' he admonished him gently.

Ram Singh's body was burning. He did not have the strength to speak, but he was talking nineteen to the dozen. At times, he would stop, as if to see how much petrol was still left in his tank.

After some time, he went into a sort of delirium. Briefly he would come out of it, only to sink again. During one brief moment of clarity, he said to Rab Nawaz, 'Tell me truthfully, do you people really want Kashmir?'

'Yes, Ram Singha,' Rab Nawaz said passionately.

'I don't believe that. You have been misled,' Ram Singh said.

'No, you have been misled, I swear by the Holy Prophet and his family,' Rab Nawaz said.

'Don't take that oath . . . you must be right.' But there was a strange look on his face, as if he didn't really believe Rab Nawaz.

A little before sunset, Major Aslam arrived with some soldiers. There was no doctor. Ram Singh was hovering between consciousness and delirium. He was muttering, but his voice was so weak that it was difficult to follow him.

Major Aslam was an old 6/9 Jat Regiment officer. Ram Singh had served under him for years. He bent over the dying soldier and called his name, 'Ram Singh, Ram Singh.'

Ram Singh opened his eyes and stiffened his body as if he was coming to attention. With one great effort, he raised his arm and saluted. A strange look of incomprehension suddenly suffused his face. His arm fell limply to his side and he murmured, 'Ram Singha, you ass, you forgot this was a war, a war . . .' He could not complete the sentence. With half-open eyes, he looked at Rab Nawaz, took one last breath and died.

Toba Tek Singh

A couple of years after the Partition of the country, it occurred to the respective governments of India and Pakistan that inmates of lunatic asylums, like prisoners, should also be exchanged. Muslim lunatics in India should be transferred to Pakistan and Hindu and Sikh lunatics in Pakistani asylums should be sent to India.

Whether this was reasonable or an unreasonable idea is difficult to say. One thing, however, is clear. It took many conferences of important officials from the two sides to come to this decision. Final details, like the date of actual exchange, were carefully worked out. Muslim lunatics whose families were still residing in India were to be left undisturbed, the rest moved to the border for the exchange. The situation in Pakistan was slightly different, since almost the entire population of Hindus and Sikhs had already migrated to India. The question of keeping non-Muslim lunatics in Pakistan did not, therefore, arise.

While it is not known what the reaction in India was, when the news reached the Lahore lunatic asylum, it immediately became the subject of heated discussion. One Muslim lunatic, a regular reader of the fire-eating daily newspaper *Zamindar*, when asked what Pakistan was, replied after deep reflection: 'The name of a place in India where cut-throat razors are manufactured.'

This profound observation was received with visible satisfaction.

A Sikh lunatic asked another Sikh: 'Sardarji, why are we being sent to India? We don't even know the language they speak in that country.'

The man smiled: 'I know the language of the *Hindostoras*.

These devils always strut about as if they were the lords of the earth.'

One day a Muslim lunatic, while taking his bath, raised the slogan 'Pakistan Zindabad' with such enthusiasm that he lost his balance and was later found lying on the floor unconscious.

Not all inmates were mad. Some were perfectly normal, except that they were murderers. To spare them the hangman's noose, their families had managed to get them committed after bribing officials down the line. They probably had a vague idea why India was being divided and what Pakistan was, but, as for the present situation, they were equally clueless.

Newspapers were no help either, and the asylum guards were ignorant, if not illiterate. Nor was there anything to be learnt by eavesdropping on their conversations. Some said there was this man by the name Mohammad Ali Jinnah, or the *Quaid-e-Azam*, who had set up a separate country for Muslims, called Pakistan.

As to where Pakistan was located, the inmates knew nothing. That was why both the mad and the partially mad were unable to decide whether they were now in India or in Pakistan. If they were in India, where on earth was Pakistan? And if they were in Pakistan, then how come that until only the other day it was India?

One inmate had got so badly caught up in this India-Pakistan-Pakistan-India rigmarole that one day, while sweeping the floor, he dropped everything, climbed the nearest tree and installed himself on a branch, from which vantage point he spoke for two hours on the delicate problem of India and Pakistan. The guards asked him to get down; instead he went a branch higher, and when threatened with punishment, declared: 'I wish to live neither in India nor in Pakistan. I wish to live in this tree.'

When he was finally persuaded to come down, he began embracing his Sikh and Hindu friends, tears running down his cheeks, fully convinced that they were about to leave him and go to India.

A Muslim radio engineer, who had an M.Sc. degree, and never mixed with anyone, given as he was to taking long walks by himself all day, was so affected by the current debate that one day he took all his clothes off, gave the bundle to one of the attendants and ran into the garden stark naked.

A Muslim lunatic from Chaniot, who used to be one of the most devoted workers of the All India Muslim League, and obsessed with bathing himself fifteen or sixteen times a day, had suddenly stopped doing that and announced—his name was Mohammad Ali—that he was Quaid-e-Azam Mohammad Ali Jinnah. This had led a Sikh inmate to declare himself Master Tara Singh, the leader of the Sikhs. Apprehending serious communal trouble, the authorities declared them dangerous, and shut them up in separate cells.

There was a young Hindu lawyer from Lahore who had gone off his head after an unhappy love affair. When told that Amritsar was to become a part of India, he went into a depression because his beloved lived in Amritsar, something he had not forgotten even in his madness. That day he abused every major and minor Hindu and Muslim leader who had cut India into two, turning his beloved into an Indian and him into a Pakistani.

When news of the exchange reached the asylum, his friends offered him congratulations, because he was now to be sent to India, the country of his beloved. However, he declared that he had no intention of leaving Lahore, because his practice would not flourish in Amritsar.

There were two Anglo-Indian lunatics in the European ward. When told that the British had decided to go home after granting independence to India, they went into a state of deep shock and were seen conferring with each other in whispers the entire afternoon. They were worried about their changed status after Independence. Would there be a European ward or would it be abolished? Would breakfast continue to be served or would they have to subsist on bloody Indian chapati?

There was another inmate, a Sikh, who had been confined for the last fifteen years. Whenever he spoke, it was the same mysterious gibberish: *Uper the gur gur the annexe the bay dhayana the mung the dal of the laltain.* Guards said he had not slept a wink in fifteen years. Occasionally, he could be observed leaning against a wall, but the rest of the time, he was always to be found standing. Because of this, his legs were permanently swollen, something that did not appear to bother him. Recently, he had started to listen carefully to discussions about the forthcoming exchange of Indian and Pakistani lunatics. When asked his opinion, he observed solemnly: '*Uper the gur gur the annexe the bay dhayana the mung the dal of the government of Pakistan.*'

Of late, however, the government of Pakistan had been replaced by the government of Toba Tek Singh, a small town in the Punjab which was his home. He had also begun enquiring where Toba Tek Singh was to go. However, nobody was quite sure whether it was in India or Pakistan.

Those who had tried to solve this mystery had become utterly confused when told that Sialkot, which used to be in India, was now in Pakistan. It was anybody's guess what was going to happen to Lahore, which was currently in Pakistan, but could slide into India any moment. It was also possible that the entire subcontinent of India might become Pakistan. And who could say if both India and Pakistan might not entirely vanish from the map of the world one day?

The old man's hair was almost gone and what little was left had become a part of the beard, giving him a strange, even frightening, appearance. However, he was a harmless fellow and had never been known to get into fights. Older attendants at the asylum said that he was a fairly prosperous landlord from Toba Tek Singh, who had quite suddenly gone mad. His family had brought him in, bound and fettered. That was fifteen years ago.

Once a month, he used to have visitors, but since the start of communal troubles in the Punjab, they had stopped coming. His real name was Bishan Singh, but everybody called him Toba Tek Singh. He lived in a kind of limbo, having no idea what day of the week it was, or month, or how many years had passed since his confinement. However, he had developed a sixth sense about the day of the visit, when he used to bathe himself, soap his body, oil and comb his hair and put on clean clothes. He never said a word during these meetings, except for occasional outbursts of *Uper the gur gur the annexe the bay dhayana the mung the dal of the laltain.*

When he was first confined, he had left an infant daughter behind, now a pretty young girl of fifteen. She would come occasionally, and sit in front of him with tears rolling down her cheeks. In the strange world that he inhabited, hers was just another face.

Since the start of this India-Pakistan caboodle, he had got into the habit of asking fellow inmates where exactly Toba Tek Singh was, without receiving a satisfactory answer, because nobody knew. The visits had also suddenly stopped. He was increasingly restless, but, more than that, curious. The sixth sense, which used to alert him to the day of the visit, had also atrophied.

He missed his family, the gifts they used to bring and the concern with which they used to speak to him. He was sure they would have told him whether Toba Tek Singh was in India or Pakistan. He also had a feeling that they came from Toba Tek Singh, where he used to have his home.

One of the inmates had declared himself God. Bishan Singh asked him one day if Toba Tek Singh was in India or Pakistan. The man chuckled: 'Neither in India nor in Pakistan, because, so far, we have issued no orders in this respect.'

Bishan Singh begged 'God' to issue the necessary orders, so that his problem could be solved, but he was disappointed, as 'God' appeared to be preoccupied with more pressing matters. Finally, he told him angrily: '*Uper the gur gur the annexe the mung the dal of Guruji da Khalsa and Guruji ki fateh . . . jo boley so nihal sat sri akal.*'

What he wanted to say was: 'You don't answer my prayers because you are a Muslim God. Had you been a Sikh God, you would have been more of a sport.'

A few days before the exchange was to take place, one of Bishan Singh's Muslim friends from Toba Tek Singh came to see him—the first time in fifteen years. Bishan Singh looked at him once and turned away, until a guard said to him: 'This is your old friend Fazal Din. He has come all the way to meet you.'

Bishan Singh looked at Fazal Din and began to mumble something. Fazal Din placed his hand on his friend's shoulder and said: 'I have been meaning to come for some time to bring you news. All your family is well and has gone to India safely. I did what I could to help. Your daughter Roop Kaur . . .'—he hesitated— 'She is safe too . . . in India.'

Bishan Singh kept quiet, Fazal Din continued: 'Your family wanted me to make sure you were well. Soon you will be moving to India. What can I say, except that you should remember me to bhai Balbir Singh, bhai Vadhawa Singh and bahain Amrit Kaur. Tell bhai Bibir Singh that Fazal Din is well by the grace of God. The two brown buffaloes he left behind are well too. Both of them gave birth to calves, but, unfortunately, one of them died after six days. Say I think of them often and to write to me if there is anything I can do.'

Then he added; 'Here, I brought you some rice crispies from home.'

Bishan Singh took the gift and handed it to one of the guards. 'Where is Toba Tek Singh?' he asked.

'Where? Why, it is where it has always been.'

'In India or in Pakistan?'

'In India . . . no, in Pakistan.'

Without saying another word, Bishan Singh walked away, murmuring: '*Uper the gur gur the annexe the bay dhayana the mung the dal of the Pakistan and Hindustan dur fittey moun*.'

Meanwhile, the exchange arrangements were rapidly being finalized. Lists of lunatics from the two sides had been exchanged between the governments, and the date of transfer fixed.

On a cold winter evening, buses full of Hindu and Sikh lunatics, accompanied by armed police and officials, began moving out of the Lahore asylum towards Wagha, the dividing line between India and Pakistan. Senior officials from the two sides in charge of exchange arrangements met, signed documents and the transfer got under way.

It was quite a job getting the men out of the buses and handing them over to officials. Some just refused to leave. Those who were persuaded to do so began to run pell-mell in every direction. Some were stark naked. All efforts to get them to cover themselves had failed because they couldn't be kept from tearing off their garments. Some were shouting abuse or singing. Others were weeping bitterly. Many fights broke out.

In short, complete confusion prevailed. Female lunatics were also being exchanged and they were even noisier. It was bitterly cold.

Most of the inmates appeared to be dead set against the entire operation. They simply could not understand why they were being forcibly removed, thrown into buses and driven to this strange place. There were slogans of '*Pakistan Zindabad*' and '*Pakistan Murdabad*', followed by fights.

When Bishan Singh was brought out and asked to give his name so that it could be recorded in a register, he asked the official behind the desk: 'Where is Toba Tek Singh? In India or Pakistan?'

'Pakistan,' he answered with a vulgar laugh.

Bishan Singh tried to run, but was overpowered by the Pakistani guards who tried to push him across the dividing line towards India. However, he wouldn't move. 'This is Toba Tek Singh,' he announced. '*Uper the gur gur the annexe the bay dhyana mung the dal of Toba Tek Singh and Pakistan.*'

Many efforts were made to explain to him that Toba Tek Singh had already been moved to India, or would be moved immediately, but it had no effect on Bishan Singh. The guards even tried force, but soon gave up.

There he stood in no man's land on his swollen legs like a colossus.

Since he was a harmless old man, no further attempt was made to push him into India. He was allowed to stand where he wanted, while the exchange continued. The night wore on.

Just before sunrise, Bishan Singh, the man who had stood on his legs for fifteen years, screamed and as officials from the two sides rushed towards him, he collapsed to the ground.

There, behind barbed wire, on one side, lay India and behind more barbed wire, on the other side, lay Pakistan. In between, on a bit of earth which had no name, lay Toba Tek Singh.